tinsel

LARK COVE SERIES

USA TODAY BESTSELLING AUTHOR

DEVNEY PERRY

Editing & Proofreading:
Elizabeth Nover, Razor Sharp Editing
www.razorsharpediting.com
Elaine York, Allusion Graphics
www.allusiongraphics.com
Julie Deaton, Deaton Author Services
www.facebook.com/jdproofs
Karen Lawson, The Proof is in the Reading
Kaitlyn Moodie, Moodie Editing Services
www.facebook.com/KaitlynMoodieEditing

Cover:
Sarah Hansen © Okay Creations
www.okaycreations.com

Formatting:
Champagne Book Design
www.champagnebookdesign.com

dedication

To my father-in-law, Richard.
Thank you for all of your input and knowledge
about the Blackfeet culture and living in Browning. I
continue to be awed by your life experiences and am so
grateful to be a part of your family.

prologue

SOFIA

Kindergarten

"Pop! Look it!" With a smile stretched across my face, I slid my drawing down the table toward Grandpa's seat.

His black-rimmed glasses were perched on the tip of his nose as he bent over my brother's homework. "So when you're changing a percentage to a whole number, all you have to do is move the decimal two places."

"Like this?" Logan asked, drawing a dot on his paper between some numbers.

"Exactly." Pop clapped him on the shoulder. "And then to change a whole number into a percentage, just—"

"Pop!" I shuffled my drawing, the paper swishing on the wooden table. "Look what I did."

That got his attention. He looked away from Logan's homework and picked up the drawing I'd done of our family, adjusting his glasses higher on his nose as he took it in. "Now what's this?"

"It's our family." I beamed with pride at the picture I'd drawn. "My teacher said we could draw our families on this paper, and then we get to hang them on the big board in my classroom tomorrow."

"Very nice."

"That's me." I pointed to the smallest person on the page. I'd used everyone's favorite color to draw them, so mine was in pink. "And there's Mommy in green. And that's Daddy in blu—"

"Pop, can you help me with my math too?" Aubrey shoved her way in between me and Pop.

"Sure, sweetheart."

I frowned when he slid my drawing away and shifted his seat to make room for my sister's homework.

"I did you in red, Pop. See?" I pushed the drawing back.

"Looks beautiful, princess," he said, though his eyes were locked on Aubrey's textbook.

I pouted. "You didn't look."

He sighed and met my gaze. "It's wonderful. Now you keep coloring while I help Logan and Aubrey with their important homework. Okay?"

"Okay," I muttered, taking *my* homework back. Then I slipped off my chair, which was quickly filled by Aubrey, and left the dining room.

Third Grade

"Daddy, are you coming to my recital?" I asked, standing in the doorway to his office.

He glanced at me then looked back at the mirror as he adjusted his tie. "I can't tonight. I have a meeting."

"You always have meetings," I muttered.

"Enough of that pouting, Sofia." The line between his eyebrows deepened as he scowled. "Adults have to work. Someday you'll understand."

I might only be eight, but I understood already. Daddy worked all the time. If we wanted to spend time with him, we had to come into his office.

I *hated* this room.

I hated the dark bookshelves that bordered the walls. I hated the leather couch that faced the gas fireplace. I hated the smell of his cigars that would stick to my hair. I really hated the desk in the middle of the room that sat on an ugly, expensive rug Mommy had picked out special last year.

I hated it all because Daddy spent more time in here than anywhere else in this house, including his own bedroom. If he was even home.

His fancy office in the city was even more hated than this one.

Because when he wasn't here, he was there. Or at dinner meetings, missing my important things. He didn't miss Aubrey's or Logan's things. Last week he'd gone to one of Aubrey's school debates. And he'd been at Logan's last soccer game.

I dropped my chin so he wouldn't see it quiver. "You miss all my recitals."

I'd been practicing my dance routine *so* hard for this recital because I got to be the leader of the chorus in front of all the other girls. My teacher had picked *me* to be first, and Daddy was going to miss it. But dance wasn't important to Daddy, not like the stuff Aubrey and Logan did at school. Ballet wasn't *practical*.

Daddy sighed, something he did a lot with me, and finished with his tie. Then he crossed the room to bend down in front of me. "I wish I could go to all of your recitals. But I have

VIII | DEVNEY PERRY

an important job."

"I never want to have an important job."

He chuckled and tipped my chin up. "Then you never have to. You can do whatever you want, my darling. Now give me a hug and then I've got to go."

I looped my little arms around his neck and squeezed him hard. Then I watched as he went out one door to work, and I went out the other to my recital.

One that he missed, along with all the others.

Sixth Grade

"But, Mom!" My voice echoed through the limousine.

"No, Sofia. You're not going."

I crossed my arms over my chest and scowled at the back of the driver's head. "This isn't fair."

"If you want to go to fashion week, I'll take you in a few years. But right now, I don't have the time to plan a trip to Paris."

I rolled my eyes. She didn't have time? *Yeah, right.*

She just didn't want me to go with Regan because her mom—an interior decorator—had called our house *out of touch*. Which was why Mom had acted on a sudden "whim" to redecorate. We'd been dealing with her own interior decorator coming in and out of our house for the last two months with painters and flooring specialists and construction people in tow.

"Logan gets to go to Washington, D.C. later this year," I reminded her. "And you let Aubrey fly across the country to Seattle, like, a month ago."

"Logan is almost eighteen and going to DC for his

senior-class trip. Aubrey went to Seattle for a Future Business Leaders of America national conference. Fashion week for an eleven-year-old is a bit different, don't you think?"

"Whatever," I mumbled. "Maybe fashion is what I want to do when I grow up."

Logan and Aubrey were already poised to take over the Kendrick family empire. Dad had plans for them both. And me? I could do whatever I wanted, just like he'd always told me.

What I wanted was to go to fashion week in Paris with my friend so we could come back home and brag about it at school.

"You're not going."

I hunched my shoulders forward, casting my eyes down to my lap. Then I let out a deep breath and lowered my voice. This pout was something I'd been practicing lately. It worked on Daddy like a charm, but so far, my luck with Mom had been hit or miss.

"Okay, fine. But would you take me shopping?" I asked. "Regan told me that she overheard Louisa Harty in the bathroom call my clothes old lady. I was hoping to pick up some tips from fashion week so she wouldn't make fun of me anymore."

"What?" Mom gaped, turning in her seat next to me.

I held back a smile that my fib had worked.

"Your clothes are not old lady," she said. "Everything you wear is this season and on trend."

I shrugged. "I thought so too, but . . ."

"We'll go together." Mom dug into her purse for her phone. "Besides, you're right. If this is what you want to do for your career, then you might as well get started early."

Before we made it home, she'd planned a trip for the two of us to Paris and gotten front-row seats along one of the most exclusive runways at the event, something Regan's mom would never have been able to secure.

As we pulled into the courtyard in front of our estate, a pang of regret poked my side for tricking Mom. Fashion wasn't all that interesting and certainly not something I wanted to do as a *job*.

Logan was the smart Kendrick child, the golden boy who would become a business tycoon like our father, Thomas. Daddy was always taking time to mentor him. Aubrey too. She constantly earned praise for how *bright* she was. She'd be right behind Logan, going to work with Daddy in the city every day.

My role in the Kendrick family was different. I wasn't going to get a job and miss out on the fun stuff. I wasn't going to spend more time in my office than exploring the world. I wasn't going to just let my money pile up in the bank when I could use it for an adventure.

Logan could be the future leader of the Kendrick family and Dad's right-hand man. Aubrey could be the gifted daughter Mom bragged about in her weekly society club meetings.

I had my own path in mind.

I was going to be the princess.

one

SOFIA

"**S**OFIA, YOU'RE GORGEOUS." MALCOM KEPT THE CAMERA pressed to his face as he moved behind me to shoot at a different angle.

I held my pose, keeping the pensive look frozen on my face, though I was smiling on the inside. Malcom didn't need to tell me how beautiful I looked today. I felt it.

My hair was pinned up in a billowing crown of espresso curls that had taken my stylist nearly two hours to perfect. My makeup had been applied by two artists who'd contoured and highlighted me so expertly I wouldn't need Photoshop touch-ups. And the outfit the magazine had chosen for me was straight off the runway.

My dress was a white strapless piece that fit snuggly to my chest. The sweetheart neckline plunged deep, giving me the illusion of cleavage. The A-line, tulle skirt poofed wide at my hips, making my waist look impossibly tiny.

It was freezing now that the sun was setting on this deserted corner of Central Park. We'd gotten an early snowfall this November, and the trees around us glittered with ice crystals and tufts of snow.

But I was surprisingly warm thanks to the white fur wrap

looped over my arms and strung across the middle of my back. My bare shoulders were still exposed to the cold, but excitement and anticipation kept the chill from soaking in.

I was going to be in a magazine. Me. Sofia Kendrick.

I'd made the society columns countless times. My name graced their pages whenever my family made a sizeable donation to a local charity or whenever one of my relationships failed. The press had spent weeks speculating why both of my marriages had ended. But this magazine article wasn't about my family or my failures. It was a feature about me and four other New York socialites, showcasing our unique lifestyle.

The reporter had already interviewed me for the piece, and after the photo shoot was complete, I'd only have to wait six short weeks until I could show off my magazine.

"Tilt your head down and to the left just slightly."

I did as Malcom ordered, the clicks from his camera telling me I'd gotten it right.

"Damn." He came to my side, showing me the display screen on the back of his camera.

This time my smile couldn't be contained.

He'd nailed it.

Malcom had captured me in profile, finding just the right angle so my face was in shadow compared to the bare skin on my shoulders. The late-afternoon light cast a golden glow on my already flawless complexion, accentuating the long lines of my neck. My Harry Winston earrings dangled from my ears and matched the ring on my right hand, which Malcom had delicately positioned in front of my chin.

Malcom's assistant nosed in next to him to see the camera. "That's your cover."

"The cover?" My mouth fell open.

"Ultimately the magazine has final say," Malcom said. "But this is the best picture I've shot for this project. Once I do some minor edits, it'll be the clear choice."

A feature in the magazine's interior was definitely worth boasting about. But the cover? That was on par with my sister's accolades.

Aubrey was always being mentioned and discussed in Fortune 500 magazines or in periodicals like *The Wall Street Journal*. This feature would be in *NY Scene* magazine, and though it was a lesser-known publication, it had been gaining a lot of popularity lately. People were calling *NY Scene* the next *New Yorker*.

And I was going to be on the cover for their New Year's edition.

Maybe the lifestyle I'd chosen wasn't such a mockery after all.

Maybe I'd finally be seen as something more than the *other* Kendrick child, the pretty one who hadn't amounted to much.

"Sofia, how could you not tell me about the article? You know we have to be careful around the press."

"I wanted it to be a surprise. And I didn't say anything bad. She took everything I said and twisted it around!" I wailed into the phone as I sat in a crumpled heap on my living room floor.

Tears coated my cheeks. Snot dripped from my nostrils. My normally tan and bright skin was a blotchy mess, and my eyes were too puffy. I was the definition of an ugly cry.

All because of that miserable magazine.

I'd been so excited an hour ago when my doorman had

brought up ten copies of *NY Scene*. I'd ordered extra so I'd have some to give to my parents and some to get framed.

But that was an hour ago, before I'd read the article.

Now I was dealing with the aftermath of another classic Sofia mistake. It never got easier to hear that I'd let down my father. It always hurt to read one of my sister's condemning texts.

Seriously? Could you at least try not to embarrass us?

It stung, though the pain was just a dull ache compared to my own agonizing humiliation. The words the reporter had used to describe me were cruel. Reading them had been like taking a lash to my skin.

Instead of stylish, she'd called me superficial and gaudy.

Instead of charming, she'd called me naïve and phony.

Instead of witty, she'd called me flighty.

Clearly, the woman had mixed up notes between interviews. That, or my self-image was off a touch.

"Sofia." Daddy sighed, his disappointment seeping through the phone. "I'll see if there is anything we can do, but since you didn't run this by me first, I doubt we'll be able to pull a retraction."

"O-okay." I hiccupped. "I'm s-sorry."

"I know you are. But next time you're asked to give an interview, I think you'd better have one of our lawyers come along too."

So basically, Daddy thought I needed a babysitter to speak. My sobs returned full force, and I barely heard him say his goodbye before hanging up.

I tossed my phone onto the carpet next to me and my ten magazines, then buried my face in my hands.

Everything was ruined. The reporter had been thorough in her portrayal of my life. She had found every unflattering detail and put them front and center in the article.

She'd written about both of my failed marriages and how I'd rushed into each, only dating my former husbands briefly before walking down the aisle in multimillion-dollar ceremonies.

She'd made sure to tell the world that I'd never had a job, and rather than dedicating my time to my family's charitable foundation, I spent my days shopping for new clothes and handbags.

She'd even interviewed my ex-boyfriend Jay to exploit the nasty details of our breakup. We'd been together for almost five years but had never married. I'd thought I was being smart, not hurrying into another marriage. Turns out, matrimony would have been better.

My ex-husbands had both signed confidentiality agreements as a condition of our divorce settlements. If the reporter had called them, they'd been forced to stay tight-lipped. But not Jay.

He'd told her I threw tantrums worse than a two-year-old when I didn't get my way and that I hadn't been supportive of his career.

Lies.

Jay hadn't loved me, he'd loved my trust fund. He'd been determined to win the World Series of Poker—except he wasn't good at poker. When I'd stopped covering his tournament fees, he'd picked a fight with me.

My *tantrum* had been me shouting at him in one of the dressing rooms at Bloomingdale's. He'd barged in on me, demanding I give him money. When I'd refused, he'd threatened to tell the tabloids I'd cheated on him with his scumbag manager. Again, another lie. But I'd lost it all the same and se-curity had been called to escort us both out of the store.

The reporter had zeroed in on the fight and security escort.

Her feature read more like an exposé, and her words had tainted Malcom's beautiful photograph on the cover.

But at least I wasn't alone. The reporter had ripped the other four socialites in her feature to shreds too. The five of us were a joke. A drain on society. We weren't princesses in five royal American families. We were silly women parading around a city of intellect and culture, infecting it with our shal-low existences.

A part of me wished my father were more vindictive. Or at least more protective of his baby girl. He could easily buy *NY Scene* and ruin that reporter's career.

Except he wouldn't do that. Because she hadn't really told a lie, had she?

That reporter had sat across from me on my cream couch in this very room, smiling and sipping a cappuccino while ask-ing me her questions and taking notes.

I'd told her how I'd gotten an interior design degree from an art institute in Manhattan, but by the time I'd graduated, I'd hated interior design. I'd told her I'd been unlucky in love, sparing her the details that were none of her or anyone else's business. I'd told her my preference for Fendi over Gucci. When she'd asked what accomplishment I was most proud of, I'd told her it was finding Carrie, my personal chef.

I'd told her about *me*.

And she'd turned me into a hideous fool.

"Oh my god." I sobbed harder into my hands.

Was I the person she'd portrayed? Was that how everyone saw me?

If it was, I couldn't stay here in the city. I couldn't stomach walking past people, wondering if they'd read the article.

I dried my eyes and picked up my phone then pulled up my older brother's number. He lived in Montana with his wife, Thea, and their three kids. They didn't sell *NY Scene* in Lark Cove, but there was no doubt he would have heard about the article by now.

News traveled fast across the country when the topic was my epic failures. I was sure Logan would be just as disappointed as Daddy. He'd told me on more than one occasion to grow up.

Whatever. I dialed his number anyway. I didn't expect or need his sympathy. What I needed right now was an escape, and Montana was the first place that came to mind.

"Hi, Sofia." He sounded annoyed. Aubrey had probably called him after sending me that text.

"Hi." I sniffled, wiping my nose with the back of my hand. "Look, before you lecture me, I know I screwed up. I trusted that reporter when the smart thing to do would have been to keep my mouth shut."

"Probably."

"I didn't mean to disparage our family. I just . . ." *Wanted to make you all proud.* "I just made a mistake."

"It happens." His voice softened. "Dealing with the press can be tricky."

"Yeah. It sucks."

"What can I do?"

"I was actually wondering if your boathouse was empty for New Year's."

"Sure. We'd love to have you. Just let me know when you'll be here, and I'll pick you up from the airport."

"Thank you." I pushed myself up off the floor, stepping on

one of the magazines as I walked out of the living room. "I'll be there tonight."

"Good morning," I said on a yawn, walking into the kitchen.

"Morning." Thea, my sister-in-law, was standing by the coffee pot. "You're up early."

I shrugged. "I'm used to meeting my trainer at seven, which is five Montana time."

"Coffee?" She took another mug from a cupboard.

"Yes, please." I slid onto a barstool at the island in their kitchen. "Thank you for letting me come out here on short notice."

She delivered my mug, then brought over her own and sat two barstools away. "You're welcome here anytime."

Was I? Her tone wasn't convincing.

Thea and I hadn't gotten off to a good start, which was my fault entirely. She'd come to New York with Logan about five years ago, just after they'd started seeing one another. Well, they'd actually met years before in the hotel bar where Thea had been working. They'd hooked up and gone their separate ways, but not before Thea had gotten pregnant with no way of tracking Logan down.

Lucky for them, fate had intervened and delivered Logan here to Lark Cove and back into Thea's life. And he'd met five-year-old Charlie—his daughter.

But fate wasn't something I believed in, so when he'd brought her home to meet our family, I'd been skeptical, to say the least. Actually, I'd been a total bitch, certain that Thea's story was full of holes and that all she really wanted was to steal our family's fortune.

I'd thrown one of Logan's ex-girlfriends in Thea's face. I'd treated her like trash and dismissed Charlie completely. I'd judged her solely on her occupation as a bartender.

Ugh, I'm the worst.

I'd been trying ever since to get into Thea's good graces. But since I only saw them two or three times a year, my progress had been slow. Especially because Thea and I had nothing in common except our last name.

Most would call us both beautiful. Thea certainly was with her long dark hair, sparkling eyes and blinding smile. But she had an inner beauty that catapulted her to a different level. She worked hard, running her own business. She was an artist, creating sculptures and paintings that spoke to the soul. She didn't care about material things or social status. Her goal in life was to raise happy children.

She probably agreed with everything that reporter had written.

Silence loomed in the kitchen as we drank our coffee. "It's, um, quiet this morning."

"The kids were up late last night. I'm sure they'll sleep in."

"Sorry." They'd stayed up late because my flight hadn't gotten in until nine. With the thirty-minute drive from the airport to Lark Cove added on top, they hadn't gotten tucked into bed until almost ten.

"Don't worry about it. A late night isn't going to hurt them."

"I can't believe it's already been six months since you guys came to the city. The kids sure have grown since this summer."

Charlie, Collin and Camila were eleven, four and two, respectively. While Charlie was still the same tomboy she'd always been, Collin and Camila were developing their own per-sonalities. Collin was a bundle of energy, never stopping as he explored the world. And Camila wasn't the baby she'd been last summer. Now she was talking and doing her best to keep pace with her older siblings.

Maybe she'd have better luck than I had.

Did they think their aunt was a complete failure too?

With talk about the kids out of the way, there wasn't much else to discuss at five in the morning. So we sat there, listening to the refrigerator hum. Halfway into my coffee, I wished I'd stayed in bed. There was an elephant in the room, and it was named *NY Scene*.

"You think it's true."

"Huh?" Thea asked.

"The magazine. You think what she wrote was true."

"The truth?" She sighed. "Yes and no. Yes, I think they cap-tured the facts. No, I don't think you're all of the things she called you."

"Thank you." My chin quivered. That was maybe the nic-est thing she'd ever said to me. "I, um . . . I feel kind of lost. I don't want to be that person." Useless. Spoiled. Petty.

Thea was quiet for a few moments then reached across the granite counter and covered my wrist with her hand. "I have an idea."

"What's that?" I looked up, my hopes skyrocketing that she'd help me out.

"You're going to have to trust me."

"I do." I nodded. "I trust you."

"Good." Thea smiled and went back to her coffee. I waited for her to tell me her idea, but she didn't say a word. She just kept sipping from her mug for a few minutes and then got up and went to the fridge for eggs.

"Uh, are you going to tell me your idea?"

She grinned over her shoulder then cracked the first egg on the edge of a bowl. "Just trust me."

I frowned at the dingy building outside the car window. A few hours after breakfast, Thea had loaded us all up in their SUV and ordered Logan to drive to the Lark Cove Bar.

"Are we getting lunch here or something?"

"No, I've got to get a few things organized before we can go."

"Where are we going?" Logan asked.

"Paris. We're leaving this afternoon."

"What? Paris?" I looked between them both in the front seat of their SUV. "Why didn't you say anything at breakfast? Or when I called you yesterday?"

"Um, because I didn't know," Logan told me then turned to his wife. "We're going to Paris?"

She nodded. "Isn't that what you gave me for my Christmas present?"

"Well, yeah. But we can go whenever you want."

"And I've decided I want to go for New Year's Eve. You can kiss me underneath the Eiffel Tower."

"Gross, Mom." Charlie groaned in her seat next to me. Collin and Camila just giggled from their car seats.

"I've already arranged for the kids to stay with Hazel and Xavier," Thea told Logan, earning a cheer from the kids that they'd be staying with their gran. "The jet is already here since Sofia flew over last night. We just have to pack and go."

"But what about the bar?" he asked. "Your New Year's Eve party is in two days. You really want to miss it?"

She shrugged. "They can party without us this year."

"But—"

"I rarely do anything spontaneous, gorgeous. I'm stepping way outside my comfort zone here. Just go with it."

His entire frame relaxed, and he reached across the car to take her hand. "Paris is what you want?"

"Paris is what I want." She nodded. "Ten days. Just the two of us."

"Okay. Then we'll go to Paris." He leaned across the car and planted a firm kiss on her lips, getting more groans and giggles from the kids.

"Is this your idea?" I asked. "For me to house-sit while you're gone?"

Thea gave Logan a grin that could only be described as diabolical. "Sort of."

"Wait. What do you mean—"

Before I finished my question, she opened the door and started unbuckling the kids.

I rushed to get out of the middle seat and follow, hurrying to catch up as she crossed the snow-covered parking lot. "Thea, what do you mean sort of?"

"Trust me."

"I'm starting to fear those two words."

She laughed and kept walking, Camila perched on her hip while Charlie and Collin raced around in the snow, kicking and throwing it at one another.

"Inside, guys!" Logan hollered, getting to the door first and holding it open for us.

Stepping inside and out of the cold, I took a few seconds to let my eyes adjust to the dark interior of the bar. Even with the blinds on the front windows open and the winter sun streaming inside, the bar was dim.

The kids rushed past me, bringing clumps of snow with them.

This was only the third time I'd been to Thea's bar and restaurant. All of my previous trips to Montana had been for family gatherings, so my time in Lark Cove had been confined to Logan and Thea's house on Flathead Lake. I didn't know this bar well, but it didn't take much of an inspection to know that it hadn't changed a bit since I'd been here last.

The ceilings were high with iron beams running the length of the open room. The bar ran in an L along the back walls. Behind it were mirrored shelves crowded with liquor bottles. The wooden plank floors matched the wooden plank walls, except while the dark floors were battered and covered in peanut shells, the dark walls were battered and covered in framed photos and the occasional neon sign.

Nothing else matched. Not the chairs or the stools or the tables. It was a mishmash of collectibles and went against every single one of the design principles I'd learned in college.

A strange twinge ran up my neck. It was the same feeling I'd had the other three times I'd been here, the same prickle I'd gotten when I'd ridden the subway once in high school for "fun." I was convinced that the next black plague would originate from those tunnels.

Maybe that twinge was my body's way of warning me of danger. Like it knew my immune system wouldn't be able to ward off the germs in places like this.

Not that the bar was dirty or grimy. It was actually quite clean and dust-free. The bar was just . . . old. And battered.

Some might call it rustic. But the only kind of rustic I enjoyed was the brand-new kind you found in Aspen estates.

I'd give Thea one thing: her bar was unique. The jukebox in the corner was ancient, filled with old country music I'd never heard of. There was a set of antlers hanging on one wall with a bra draped from the horns.

As the kids chased each other around a cocktail table in the middle of the room, Logan and Thea took turns grabbing them one by one to help them out of their winter coats.

The twinge in my neck was gone. The clean and refreshing smell in the room had chased it away. I guess this place wasn't like the subway—not even a little.

Bleach lingered in the air, hinting that someone had scrubbed the bar top not too long ago. They must not have gotten to the floors yet.

Beneath the cleaner, the air was infused with citrus. I spotted a cutting board and a knife on the bar next to the slotted tray of bar fruits. It was overflowing with lemon, lime and orange wedges.

"Hey." A smooth, deep voice echoed in the empty room as a man emerged from the hallway behind the bar. His long, tanned fingers were wrapped around a white dish towel as he dried his hands. "What are you guys doing here?"

"We're going on a vacation." Thea smiled and walked behind the bar. "So I need to grab a couple of things before we leave."

"Vacation? Like, today? That wasn't on the calendar."

She laughed. "I know. I'm being spontaneous."

"Something you are not." The man chuckled and a shiver rolled down my spine.

This bar might not have changed since I'd been here last,

but this man was definitely new. And definitely sexy.

His onyx hair was short on the sides and longer on top with wide swoops through the silky strands like he'd combed it out with his fingers. His face had this beautiful, odd symmetry that I felt the urge to sketch. His eyes were narrow and set in a harsh line above the wide bridge of his nose. His jaw was made entirely of hard, unforgiving angles. His cheekbones were so sharp they could cut glass. The only thing soft about this man's face were his full lips.

Apart, the features were all too strong and too bold, but mixed together, he was magnificent.

"Have you met Dakota before?" Logan caught my attention and nodded to the man I'd been blatantly studying.

"Pardon?"

"I'll take that as a no," he muttered. "Dakota Magee, this is my sister Sofia Kendrick."

Dakota jerked up his chin.

"Hi." I swallowed hard, finding it difficult to breathe when he was looking my way.

Those black eyes scrutinized me from head to toe, giving nothing away about what he found. He didn't blink. He didn't move.

I'd had my first boyfriend at thirteen and plenty of others since. I'd been married—and divorced—twice. I'd been on the receiving end of more pick-up lines and catcalls than a stripper headlining a Vegas show.

I knew when a man found me attractive. I knew when I stirred a man's blood.

But Dakota's stare gave nothing away. It was empty and cool. He looked right to my core, making my heart boom louder and louder with every passing second that I failed his inspection.

"So since I'm leaving on this last-minute vacation, I had an idea." Thea's voice came to my rescue, forcing Dakota to break his stare. "Sofia can help you out while I'm gone."

"I don't need help."

"I don't think that's such a good idea."

Dakota and Logan both spoke at the same time my stomach dropped. She wanted me to help? Here?

"With New Year's Eve, it'll be busy," Thea said.

"Then I'll call Jackson if I can't keep up," Dakota shot back.

Thea shook her head. "He and Willa made plans to go to Kalispell for New Year's."

"Fine." His jaw clenched, the angles getting angry. "Then I'll handle it. Alone."

"Listen. I feel awful leaving you here alone on one of the biggest days of the year when I'd planned to help out. But this will be perfect. You can teach Sofia the ropes for a couple of days, and then she can help during the party. It's a win-win."

He grumbled and crossed his arms over his chest. But he didn't argue with his boss.

"Thank you." Thea smiled, knowing she'd won. "Thank you both for doing this. It'll be great."

How could she think *me* working in her bar would ever be *great*? I had no experience, let alone desire, to mix other people's drinks.

Dakota's stern expression turned arctic as he leveled his gaze on me again. It was no secret he didn't want me here as much as I didn't wish to stay.

I inched backward, hoping to make an escape while I had the chance, but my foot caught on the edge of a chair. My feet slipped in the puddle of melted snow that had collected underneath my boots. My arms flailed as I tried to keep my footing, but when one heel went skidding sideways, I was doomed.

A cluster of peanut shells broke my fall as my ass collided with the floor.

"Ouch." My face burned with embarrassment as Logan rushed to my side.

"Are you okay?"

"Fine." I nodded, letting him take my elbow to help me back up. When my feet were steady, I rubbed the spot on my butt that was sure to bruise.

"Those peanut shells can be slippery," Thea told me. "My first two weeks here, I slipped constantly. But you'll get used to walking on them. And I guess you might as well start work by sweeping them all up."

"Sweep?" My mouth fell open. "I don't know how to sweep."

Dakota scoffed and turned on a heel, striding out of the room.

"Broom's in that closet over there." Thea pointed to a door next to the restroom then followed Dakota down the hallway.

Logan's mouth was hanging open like mine as he stared at the spot where Thea and Dakota had disappeared. He shook it off, blinked twice, then unglued his feet and hustled after them both.

Which left me in a *rustic* bar, surrounded by peanut shells, while my nieces and nephews played like this was just another normal day in paradise.

What kind of fresh hell was this?

two

DAKOTA

"**D**ID I DO SOMETHING TO PISS YOU OFF?" I CROSSED MY arms over my chest as Thea walked into her office behind me.

"I know you're not happy." She held up her hands. "I wouldn't be either, and I'm sorry. But just . . . go with me here. Okay?"

"I don't need help doing my job."

"You've worked here for five years, Dakota. I know you don't need help doing your job."

"Just checking."

We hadn't worked a shift together in ages. I didn't want her thinking I couldn't handle this place on my own, even for an event.

While her business partner, Jackson Page, and I worked the bar, Thea was in charge of managing the business. She still bartended a weeknight here and there, and she covered every third weekend. But mostly, she spent her days in this office.

Jackson had cut back on night and weekend shifts too these past couple of years. He and Thea both had young families. They didn't need to be working until two in the morning when I had nothing else to do and wanted the money. So I'd spent a lot of hours in this bar alone, and I'd learned quickly how to handle a large crowd.

In the summers, we'd often get a rush of people who'd just come off the lake looking for beer and pizza. Even with every table full, I had no problem making sure the bar was packed with only happy customers. The same was true in the fall when we'd get a crush of hunters looking to unwind after a long day in the mountains.

In five years, not once had someone complained to me or my bosses that I took too long to pour them a drink. I worked my ass off for each and every quarter in my tip jar. And I might not be the smartest guy in the room, but I sure as hell knew how to hustle.

New Year's Eve did get crazy. People would pack themselves inside the bar like sardines in an aluminum can. But it was nothing I couldn't handle. *Alone.* Something Thea knew.

So since that speech she'd just given in the other room was complete and utter bullshit, I was curious why she'd made me her sister-in-law's babysitter.

"Do you want to tell me what this is really about?" I asked.

"Her."

My eyes narrowed. "What about her?"

"She needs to find some purpose."

"And she's going to find it at the Lark Cove Bar?"

Thea shrugged. "Maybe. It's worth a try. It worked for me."

Logan walked into the office, shaking his head as he closed the door behind him and turned to his wife. "Well, that was interesting. You know I try and stay out of things at the bar unless you ask for my input, but do you think this is a good idea?"

"It's a great idea," she said.

Logan frowned. "She's never worked a day in her life."

"I know that. But she's smart and can learn. More importantly, she's *trying*. These last few years, she's been trying. Remember she helped your mom with that charity auction last Christmas? And she volunteered for the committee to put together the foundation's donor gift bags. This could give her another experience and show her we trust her. And even though I know you don't need it," she looked my way, "Sofia can help while we're gone."

"I don't have time to babysit her." I scowled. "If she's never done this before, it'll take me longer to teach her than to just do it myself."

We'd be busy on New Year's Eve, and I couldn't afford to spend the night mopping up her fuck-ups.

"Think of it as a promotion then. You're now the official trainer of new employees. She's your first student."

"Do I get a raise?"

She grinned. "Only if she can make a decent margarita by the time I get back."

"Then I'm fucked," I grumbled.

Logan gave me a sympathetic look.

At least he was on my side. I didn't want to get into an argument with my boss, but maybe he'd be able to convince Thea that having Sofia underfoot was a giant clusterfuck waiting to happen.

"Baby, she's no bartender." He placed his hand on her shoulder. "If you are trying to teach her some kind of life lesson, let's not put your business at risk. She'll flake out."

Thea rolled her eyes as she walked behind her desk and unplugged her laptop. "Give her some credit. It's not like she's going to burn the place down. She'll probably mess up on some drinks. Maybe she'll break a bottle or a couple glasses. My budget can withstand a few mistakes."

"But—"

"Logan, she's your sister."

"That's my point."

"I need you to trust me here." Thea rolled up the power cord to her laptop, then with both items tucked inside her purse, she came and stood in front of her husband. "Sofia just got a very public, very harsh reality check. This could be good for her. I know your sister and I got off on the wrong foot, but she's family. I really do want the best for her."

"I want that too. She's my sister, and I love her. But none of what was written in that magazine article should have been a surprise. We've all tried to talk to her, but she chose not to do anything with her life."

"I hear you." Thea nodded. "But maybe she's done more than we've all recognized. Maybe that's the reason she's taking this article so hard. Whatever it is, that magazine hit hard."

I had no idea what magazine article they were talking about, but I didn't need to read it to get the gist. Sofia had probably gotten slaughtered by some reporter and she was here in Montana to hide and lick her wounds.

"She's questioning everything about her lifestyle right now," Thea said. "And personally, I think it would be good for her. Maybe she'll get a tiny dose of reality."

"And you expect me to deliver it," I huffed. "Gee, thanks. I don't think this is going to work, Thea. I just met the woman."

"It's not you but the setting. This is as far out of her comfort zone as it gets. Maybe hard work in a new environment will give her some perspective. It could motivate her to make more significant changes in her life."

"All while you and Jackson are gone," I muttered. I was

going to be the unlucky bastard to teach Sofia this life lesson Thea was so hell-bent on delivering simply because I was here and not on vacation. "Where are you going anyway?"

"Paris."

"Paris, France?"

She nodded. "I've always dreamed of going. When I was in third or fourth grade, my teacher taught us all about countries in Europe. She gave us all these postcards of the Eiffel Tower. It seemed so magical and far away that I kept it. Logan found it in my art workshop a few months ago and promised me a trip to Paris for my Christmas present."

Well, shit. I had my own desires to see the far-off places in the world. I didn't want to deal with Sofia, but I wouldn't object and keep Thea from her dream trip.

One afternoon after I'd been working here for about two years, Thea told me how she'd grown up. She hadn't lived like the Kendricks, who had money coming out of their ears. As a kid, she'd known more hungry days than full. She'd worn more secondhand clothes than new. And she'd lived through most of her childhood alone in a New York City orphanage without any family to rely upon.

That was, until a woman had started working as a cook at the orphanage. Her name was Hazel.

Hazel had claimed Thea as her own all those years ago. And when she'd come across Jackson attempting to shoplift a candy bar, Hazel had done the same for him.

Eventually, all three had migrated to Lark Cove, Hazel leading the way back to her childhood hometown. She took over this bar after her parents had passed, and when she was ready to retire, Thea and Jackson took over for her.

The three of them had their own makeshift kind of family.

When Hazel had married my uncle Xavier, it'd brought me into the mix too.

They'd all supported me through a lot these last five years.

Whenever I went home to visit the reservation and came back angry that my family members still held a grudge over me leaving, Xavier would have me over for dinner and let me unload my frustrations over beer and Hazel's famous goulash.

When I'd told Thea and Jackson I was starting my own side business buying and managing rental properties in Kalispell, Thea had spent hours teaching me some accounting basics for my new company.

And when I'd bought my first place, a complete dump with the right price tag, Jackson and Logan had spent a weekend with me and my uncle cleaning the place out.

I owed them.

If dealing with Logan's younger sister for a few days would help them out, I'd put up with the princess.

"So what exactly am I supposed to do with her while you're gone?"

Thea grinned. "Start with the basics. Fill the cooler with ice. Empty the dishwasher. Whatever you want. And then give her more responsibility from there. I have faith in her, and I bet she'll surprise you. In ten days, she might even have graduated to mixing drinks."

"Okay—wait. Ten days?"

"Well, we're closed New Year's Day, so it's technically only nine. And Jackson will be back to help cover while I'm gone, unless you want the extra hours."

"You know I do."

I never turned down extra hours. Not once in the years I'd worked here. I'd work every single day if they'd let me because

I needed the money.

My paychecks and tips went straight into the three properties I'd bought over the last five years. And if those were breaking even, I put everything else into savings for a down payment on the next opportunity.

If Thea wanted to take a ten-day vacation with her husband, I'd be more than happy to take on her hours. There was a property I'd had my eye on for a couple of weeks, and I was worried that someone might come in and buy it if I didn't get an offer in soon. But I was still two thousand dollars short.

"Do I have to split my tips with her?" I asked.

Logan chuckled. "She's not an employee. She's more of an unpaid intern."

"But don't let her quit." Thea shoved her finger in my face. "I mean it. Make her come to work. She, um, doesn't have a car either so you'll have to pick her up and drop her off."

"Christ," I grumbled. "Fine." Babysitter. Chauffeur. Was I going to be her chef too?

"I owe you for this," Thea said.

"It's all good. Have a fun vacation. Send me a postcard of the Eiffel Tower."

"You got it."

I'd never been to Paris—I'd never been out of the country. But one day, I was going to travel the world. Maybe I'd start keeping postcards myself of the places I wanted to see.

"I think I have everything I need from here," Thea told Logan, taking one last glance around the office.

"Happy New Year." Logan shook my hand.

"You too." I followed him and Thea out of the office and down the hallway back into the bar.

To my surprise, Sofia hadn't run away and wasn't still

hovering by the door. She'd gone to get the broom out of the supply closet and was attempting to sweep up the peanut shells around one of the tables. She'd created a decent pile of them in the time we'd been talking in the back.

Maybe she wasn't hopeless.

Charlie, Collin and Camila raced around her legs as she stood guard over her pile. The look on her face was sheer terror as she shuffled around, trying to protect the peanut shells from the kids.

Her outfit was ridiculous for the freezing Montana winter. We'd gotten five inches of fresh snow over the last few weeks, but Sofia was dressed for a warm autumn afternoon of boutique shopping.

Her shiny, leather pants hugged her long, fit thighs all the way to her calves like a second skin. There was no way those were warm. Her olive sweater wasn't much better. It was loose, draping over one shoulder to show off her smooth, tanned skin. The material was no doubt cashmere or something else expensive, but it was too flimsy and completely impractical for below-zero temperatures. One tug at the collar and I could split the thing in half.

Fuck my life.

My brain might have categorized her as a hassle for the next ten days, but my body saw her without any filters. She was sexy, head to toe.

I schooled my features, making sure the flash of attraction was hidden. I didn't need Thea and Logan concerned I was going to make a move on my new charge.

In all the years I'd worked here, I'd never seen Sofia before. I'd met her older sister, Aubrey, a couple of times when she'd been out to visit. But Sofia hadn't come into the bar while I'd been working.

Sofia was different than her older siblings. They were all good looking, with the same straight nose and deep-brown eyes, but Sofia's hair was a shade darker than everyone else's in the family. She must have dyed it nearly black. But as she shifted underneath one of the overhead lights, a shimmer of Logan's brown snuck through.

But more than just some minor physical differences set her apart from her brother and sister. Sofia had a different kind of presence.

She was missing the power and command that shrouded both Logan and Aubrey. She didn't have the confident air that typically preceded them into a room.

They all screamed *money*. But she took it to the extreme.

Enormous diamond studs decorated her delicate earlobes. Her perfume permeated the bleach I'd used on the bar earlier. The floral tones were strong but not overpowering, which meant it was damn expensive. Add to that her clothes, and she was the odd one out with the rest of us in jeans.

Just like her snow boots.

Though, *snow boots* was a loose term for the things on her feet. The leather only came up past her ankles, and the wedge heels were at least four inches. Who wore high-heeled snow boots?

High-maintenance women. *Rich* women.

Even Logan, with all his millions, was dressed similarly to me in jeans and a thermal. Though, he probably hadn't bought his clothes at Boot Barn.

For the most part, Logan had become just another guy around Lark Cove. If you didn't know him, you wouldn't suspect he could buy the whole town with one swipe of his credit card. He coached Charlie's soccer team with Jackson. He worked here at the bar with Thea on her weekends. He actually made one hell of a good old-fashioned.

I bet his sister only let the finest champagne touch her supple red lips.

In a different time and place, I'd be up for the challenge of chasing her around this bar to try and steal a taste of my own.

Except in this situation, thoughts of winning Sofia's attention were ridiculous.

"Okay. We'd better get going." Thea had pulled on her winter jacket while I'd been watching her sister-in-law guard a pile of peanut shells. "I've got everything I need on my laptop to place this week's supply order, but I won't do it until after New Year's, so just email me if you run out of anything."

I nodded. "'Kay."

"Let's go, guys!" Logan announced and the kids scrambled toward the pile of coats and hats and gloves they'd left by the door.

Thea went over to Sofia and hugged her good-bye. "Thanks again. And have fun."

"Fun?" Sofia gaped. "I, um . . . this is not what I had in mind."

"Trust me. Working here isn't so bad."

"Best job ever," I muttered. Normally it was.

"Dakota will pick you up and drive you home," Thea told Sofia. "Spare key to the side door is under the mat. And you can always call Hazel if you need anything."

Sofia nodded, her eyes wide and unblinking.

"Thanks." Thea waved at me and joined her family by the door. "Call me if you need anything."

"I won't." I waved back. "Enjoy your trip."

"I will." The excitement she had for her Paris vacation filled the bar. "Bye!"

Logan came over to give a stunned Sofia a hug and kiss on the cheek, then he walked his family to the door.

With every one of his steps, Sofia's face went a shade whiter. The light from outside flashed bright as Logan opened the door and ushered the kids outside. When it slammed shut behind them, Sofia's entire body flinched.

Her eyes stayed fixed on the door. Her hands clutched the handle of the broom like it was a security blanket.

Sympathy and annoyance swirled in my gut. I was irritated to be stuck with her for ten days. But I had the overwhelming urge to pull her into my arms and promise this wouldn't be the worst experience of her life.

I shoved those feelings away, keeping my face impassive. The best thing for both of us was to get back to work. The quicker we did that, the sooner this would all be over.

"You can finish up there."

Sofia's head whipped around at my voice.

My chest tightened at the tears welling in her eyes. If she was going to cry through the next ten days, I was fucked. Crying women were a weakness of mine, along with beautiful women with dark hair and full lips.

So yeah, *fuck my life*.

I strode down the length of the bar to the cutting board I'd left out earlier. I had a couple more limes to slice up before we opened, so I placed the fruit on the board and picked up my knife.

Sofia was still standing with the damn broomstick in her white-knuckled grip. She didn't move an inch in the time it took me to finish one lime.

"Get to work." It came out harsher than I'd meant, and she flinched again. I glanced up, narrowing my gaze at the peanut-shell heap by her feet.

"O-okay." She propped the broom against a stool. Two seconds later, it slid off the rounded edge and smacked into the floor.

Christ. Maybe she hadn't been the one to sweep earlier. Maybe one of the kids had done it for her.

"Sorry," Sofia muttered, dropping down to her knees. Then with both hands, she scooped up some shells.

My chin dropped as she stood and carefully walked them to a garbage can at the end of the bar, losing a couple as she went. She tossed the pile in and then scurried back to the pile, bending to pick up more.

I don't know how to sweep.

That's what she'd told Thea, and it hadn't been a lie.

I put down my knife, wiping the lime juice on my jeans as I walked over to the supply closet. I opened the door and grabbed the dustpan and small brush, then took them over to Sofia.

She was still kneeling on the floor, picking up shells one by one and putting them into her palm.

"Here." I bent down, setting the edge of the dustpan next to the remaining pile. Then I used the brush to demonstrate what to do.

She dropped the shells in her hand in the pan and hung her head. "I'm such an idiot."

"Don't say that," I snapped, again harsher than I'd meant. Hearing her run herself down was worse than seeing her cry.

"Sorry."

"Forget it," I muttered, sweeping the shells into the pan.

"I've never done this before. Any of this. Unless it involves shopping or makeup or my hair, I'm basically useless."

I huffed and positioned the dustpan. Sofia's eyes were on the floor, her chin dropped to her chest, so I hooked my finger under it and tipped her head back.

The minute her doe eyes met mine, my heart squeezed.

Those crying eyes.

They were going to ruin me.

Sofia's eyes were a kaleidoscope. Every piece of happiness or shred of pain, she spun for the world to see in those choc-olate pools. She didn't keep anything for herself, no secrets or hidden agendas.

Her eyes were so full of hopelessness at the moment, I'd do anything to make that look go away.

Letting go of her chin, I slid my palm up her face. Her breath hitched as a firestorm ran up my arm.

Why was I touching her?

I didn't drop my hand.

The heat from my touch colored her cheeks, and her chest heaved underneath that flimsy sweater. Her pink tongue darted out between her lips, wetting the bottom one as her eyes held mine.

The hopelessness was gone—I'd accomplished one thing at least. Except the lust in her gaze was exponentially more dangerous.

She was attracted to me. I knew it just like I knew how to mentally tally up three beers, a vodka soda and a shot of Jack. She was attracted to me, and I was attracted to her.

Panic sent my hand flying away from her face. I stood in a flash, staggering back a few steps and crunching a peanut shell under my boot. Then I turned and put the bar, my cutting board and knife between us.

"When you finish with the floors, you can take a bar rag and wipe off all the tables."

"All right." Sofia nodded and went back to work.

It took her three times as long as it would have taken me to finish sweeping the floors. I used up every shred of patience by not ripping the broom out of her hand and finishing the job myself. We hadn't even opened yet, but my mood was shot by the time she walked over to the rag, pinching it between her thumb and index finger.

Her nose scrunched up at the scent of bleach on the white terry cloth. Holding it as far away from her clothing as possible, she walked over to a booth against the far wall and started wiping.

What the hell was taking her so long? Couldn't she hustle it up? The last thing I needed was her taking an hour to clean the tables, not only because we were opening in ten minutes, but because as she bent over, the hem of her sweater rose up, giving me the perfect view of her ass encased in those hot-as-fuck leather pants.

I concentrated on the neon sign in the window as she cleaned, but my eyes kept drifting down to her backside.

When she left that booth for the next, she'd missed all four corners of the booth's table and left a puddle in its center.

I frowned. I'd have to either redo it myself or teach her the right way to clean a damn table. My cock, which was begging to become Sofia's babysitter, loved the idea of bending over her, covering my hand with hers and using long, sure strokes to clean that table.

"Shit," I muttered, making an adjustment to my dick as I went around the bar. I walked to the booth, swiped the rag from Sofia's hand and nudged her out of the way with my hip. "Like this."

After cleaning the booth's table and another one, I handed back the rag.

"Sorry." Her eyes were full of tears again.

I didn't comfort her this time. Instead, I strode out of the bar, down the hallway and straight into Thea's office, where I took a red marker and circled January eighth.

Ten days.

It might as well have been a year.

three

SOFIA

TODAY HAD BEEN THE MOST HUMILIATING DAY OF MY LIFE. No contest.

Reading the magazine article had brought me to an all-time low. But after spending the day in the Lark Cove Bar with a gorgeous man who loathed everything about my existence, I'd found a new rock bottom.

It was here, on the floor by the dishwasher, where I was hunched over to pick up shards of broken glass.

"I'm sorry," I told Dakota for the fifth time.

He threw a cracked glass in the large garbage can. It shattered against the glasses he'd already tossed in there. "Glass comes out of the dishwasher hot."

"I know that." *Now.*

"Open the door. Let it cool. Then take stuff out," he snapped.

I stayed quiet but nodded so he'd know I'd heard him.

Dakota had ordered me to unload the dishwasher about five minutes ago. I'd opened the door and been immediately engulfed in a billow of steam. My makeup was probably running and the fine hairs at my temples were no doubt in frizzy kinks.

I'd batted the steam away then pulled out the top rack.

Obviously, I knew the inside was hot because of the steam. But I didn't realize the glasses would be scorching, not just warm.

I'd never unloaded a dishwasher before.

The instant my hand touched one of the pint glasses, my fingertips melted. I yelped and jerked my hand away, but as I was retreating from the dishwasher, my heel caught on one of the rubber floor mats.

I stumbled sideways and right into a neatly organized grid of clean glasses. My elbow caught four of them and sent them crashing onto the floor. Of course, they landed on one of the non-rubber-matted places and shattered instantly.

Dakota had cursed and then stomped over to help me clean them up. Correcting my mistakes was pretty much all he'd done today.

First it was the peanut shells. Then he'd taught me how to clean a table.

After that I'd learned that my way of dusting liquor bottles was wrong. My way of delivering the beer bottles he opened was wrong. My way of clearing the empty beer bottles was wrong too.

Everything I'd done today was wrong.

"Why don't you take a break." Dakota sighed. "I'll finish this." He walked away, leaving me still hovering over the floor.

I swiped my eyes dry so he wouldn't see the tears gathering.

I'd been on the verge of a full-on meltdown all day, but somehow I'd managed to keep it in. I think the shock had made me numb to a degree.

I was the crier in our family. I cried even more than Mom had during menopause.

And my crying annoyed *everyone*.

Aubrey would purse her lips whenever I started to tear up.

She'd tap her foot on the floor, like she was counting how many taps it would take me to pull myself together. That tapping always made it worse, knowing that my own sister didn't care about my bruised feelings.

Logan would just clench his jaw or shake his head. Dad would look up from his phone or computer then narrow his eyes, silently telling me to stop so he could concentrate on whatever email or message was more important than his daughter's silly emotions.

Mom was the only one who didn't make me feel awful for the tears, though she encouraged me to cry in private.

My family didn't understand me. They didn't realize I was softer than they were. I didn't have an edge or a protective shell that made me tough. I was just . . . me. And when things got difficult, I cried.

It made me feel better.

But crying wasn't allowed in this modern age when women were empowered to rule the world, when we were supposed to be made of steel and iron, stronger than the men who would hold us down if we showed a moment of vulnerability. In today's society, a crying woman was just pathetic. I was weak. My tears were pitiful.

But could I stop them from springing up? No. Even as I willed myself to stay strong, the tears came of their own volition.

At least I was able to choke back the sob that wanted to work its way free.

I dried my eyes, taking a few deep breaths, then stood.

The man sitting on the other side of the bar a few seats down was staring. He looked to be in his late fifties, his brown hair streaked with gray at the temples. He'd sat witness to the entire dishwasher, glass-breaking fiasco.

And he knew I was about to lose it.

But instead of a frown or a roll of his eyes, he gave me a reassuring smile. "It's just a couple of glasses."

"Today's not my day." This year wasn't my year.

"I'm Wayne." He extended his hand. "I come in here about every day to say hello and drink a beer. I guess some would call me a regular."

I shook his hand. "I'm Sofia. Sofia Kendrick."

From an early age, I'd gotten in the habit of using both my first and last name with introductions. People in New York heard the name Kendrick and paid attention. Except . . . was it pretentious to add it when Wayne hadn't offered his own?

"Kendrick. As in Logan and Thea Kendrick?" he asked.

I nodded. "Logan is my brother. I came out to visit them for New Year's, but they actually just left on vacation. I'm here trying to, um . . . *help* at the bar while they're gone."

Behind the bar, Dakota walked by with the dustpan and brush. He made short work of the remaining glass bits on the floor then tossed them into the garbage. With another one of my messes corrected, he scanned the bar to see if anyone needed anything. Seeing as our few customers were happy, he turned without a word and walked down the back hallway again.

My gaze lingered on his long legs, the way his jeans molded to his thighs and the globes of his really, *really* nice ass. It was grossly unfair that I had to share my lowest of low days with a man who was so devastatingly handsome.

Dakota's wide shoulders and towering frame filled doorways. His arms were so long he could reach the tallest liquor shelf, nearly to the ceiling, without a stretch. They reminded me more of wings than arms because he moved with such grace and silence. Even his thick-soled boots landed gently on the floor.

"So how long are you here?" Wayne asked.

"Ten days." I tore my eyes away from the hallway where Dakota had disappeared. "I came out here for a last-minute vacation, so I don't have a set schedule. But I'll probably go home once Logan and Thea get back from Paris."

"Good for you. I'm on vacation myself. I work as the chief maintenance officer at the school here in town. That's a title I gave myself a few years ago, by the way. Thought it sounded fancy. Anyway, the kids are all on break so I'm enjoying some downtime. Gotta love vacation."

"It's the best." I forced cheer into my voice, not wanting to tell him that I now considered *vacation* an evil word.

Taking one of the surviving pint glasses, I filled it with some ice. Then I went for the soda gun. I'd been studying Dakota today, not just because I found him so appealing, but so I could try and avoid embarrassing mistakes. Carefully, just as he'd done at least ten times today, I pointed the spout on the gun and pressed the white button for water.

It was stupid to feel relieved that I'd successfully filled a water glass. But today, I was taking whatever I could get. I stole three lime slices from the tray along the bar, plopped them in my water, then walked around the corner to sit on the stool next to Wayne.

My feet were killing me in these new snow boots. I was used to wearing heels every day but not actually walking around in them for hours on end. My driver, Glen, and my town car were never far away. When I shopped, I always had a nice place to sit and sip champagne whenever I needed to rest.

But today I hadn't had a single minute to sit. I'd been following Dakota around and taking his orders ever since Logan and Thea had abandoned me here.

Five years ago, I would have sent a string of nasty texts to my brother, using shouty caps to tell him how this was ridiculous and unfair. I would have called one of my girlfriends and bitched about my sister-in-law tricking me into manual labor. Then I would have called Mom and cried, begging her to get me out of this situation.

Even a week ago, I would have called and grumbled to anyone who would have listened.

But a week ago, the magazine article hadn't been published. I hadn't become a tornado of self-doubt.

A week ago, I was still pretending that my life was perfect.

So instead of resorting to my old tactics, I was sticking it out. Thea had asked me to trust her, and I was trying my best. Besides, where else did I have to go? I was useless. I was a mockery. As miserable as I was, helping at this bar was better than going back to New York and listening to people snicker behind my back.

Montana was my sanctuary for the next ten days until the gossip storm blew over.

"Cheers." Wayne lifted his glass full of Coors Light and Clamato, something I'd never heard of before.

I clinked his glass with my own and sipped my water, enjoying a quiet moment off my feet.

There were only two other people in the bar at the moment, a couple in one of the booths. Both were looking at their phones as the beers I'd brought them sat untouched, growing warm.

"How are you liking working here?" Wayne asked just as

Dakota emerged from the hallway.

It was like he had a sixth sense that I'd been about to tell Wayne the truth. His eyes narrowed at my lips as he walked our way and the answer I was going to give Wayne—that I needed a Xanax—disappeared off my tongue.

"It's been interesting. I've never worked in a bar before." *Or anywhere.* "So I'm learning a lot."

Like how to properly throw away a beer bottle. Even that simple job I'd failed.

Dakota had told me that instead of just tossing them into the garbage can, I had to empty out whatever was left, even if it was just backwash. Otherwise the garbage bag would get full of liquid and be a mess to toss in the Dumpster.

I'd also learned that when I delivered beer bottles, I was to use the stack of cardboard coasters, not the cocktail napkins. The coasters were free since some beer distributors had brought them in for promotion. The bar had to pay for the napkins.

I'd also learned that when you dusted liquor bottles, they had to be put back in the exact same place. Apparently, the seemingly random placement of bottles was anything but. Dakota had grumbled some colorful obscenities under his breath as he'd spent thirty minutes rearranging them after I'd mixed them up.

He'd been short with me most of the day. If I were in his position, I probably would have been short with me too. Still, it stung each time he snapped or barked an order. Not only because he was gorgeous and I was clearly driving him crazy, but also because each time it reminded me how foolish I must seem.

Dakota went to the dishwasher, slid out the top rack and pulled out two glasses now that they'd cooled.

"I can empty it." I rose from my seat, but he shot me a look that sent my butt back onto the stool.

"I'll do it. Just . . . rest your feet."

My shoulders fell. I'd hoped he hadn't noticed my limping steps over the past hour. "Sorry."

"Wear comfortable shoes tomorrow."

I nodded and sipped my water, wishing it were vodka. I hadn't brought any shoes along that didn't have a heel.

I'd have to borrow something from Thea, though I already knew we weren't the same size. I'd bought her a pair of Manolo Blahnik pumps last year for her birthday. I'd never seen her wear them and now I knew why. Four-inch stilettos with beaded embellishments were completely unnecessary here.

Just like me.

"You look like you're about to cry," Wayne whispered, leaning in close. "Everything okay?"

I nodded, blinking away a fresh onslaught of tears. "I'm out of my element."

"Ah, don't worry. You'll get the hang of things soon. You look like a smart gal."

His words made me want to cry even more. How was it that a man I'd met just moments ago had such confidence in me? The people I was closest to didn't think I'd ever amount to much.

"Excuse me." I slid off my stool, ignoring the ache in my feet as I hurried behind the bar. As soon as I reached the hallway, I covered my mouth with a hand. The sob that had been bubbling up to the surface escaped, echoing through the kitchen as I burst through the door.

I stopped next to the table in the middle of the room and closed my eyes. Then I let the tears flow free.

The first wave had barely cascaded down my cheeks when

a deep voice rang in the kitchen. "Oh, Christ."

The annoyance in his tone was too much to take. I spun, my chin no longer quivering now that my temper was on the rise. "Do you mind? Can I just have a few minutes to feel sorry for myself? Or am I not doing that right either?"

His stoic and stern expression cracked. His eyes softened, and he shied back a step. "Sorry."

"I'm sure my tears are silly to you." I swiped at them and sniffled. "I know I've been an inconvenience today. But I'm not going to apologize anymore. Working here wasn't my idea, okay? I don't know what I'm doing. With anything. It's all a mess. *My life* is a mess!"

My overdramatic outburst earned me a frown, one I recognized from the countless times my father had sent a matching one my way.

Before Dakota could speak, I held up my hand. "Don't say it. I already know what you're thinking. Spoiled little rich girl is having a bad day because she's had to work for a change. That's not what this is about. This is about me realizing that I've spent thirty-two years on this planet and have *nothing* to show for myself other than a no-limit Amex. *I* am nothing."

The frown on Dakota's face disappeared as the tears kept falling.

I hated them at the moment. Later tonight, when I was alone and vulnerable, I'd savor a good cry and the chance to let it all out. But at the moment, I didn't want to be a crier, not anymore.

Not in front of Dakota.

He took a step forward, coming right into my space. And just like he'd done in the bar earlier, he slid his hand up the curve of my jaw to cup my cheek. "Don't say that."

"But it's true," I whispered.

The magazine article had called me out as frivolous and petty. It had taken just over twenty-four hours for me to realize, despite all my efforts to change, there was truth behind that reporter's words. What did it mean that in only a day I'd realized she was right?

Maybe I'd been living in denial about myself for too long. Maybe I'd been ignoring the criticisms and advice from my family because making a change was so hard.

Maybe I'd just been playing the role everyone had put me in.

The reason didn't matter. My world had been turned on its head, and I could not get my bearings.

Yet with Dakota's warm skin touching mine, not all was lost.

With his dark eyes holding mine steady, the tears just stopped. It was like he'd commanded them to cease and they obeyed.

"I've never had a job before," I whispered.

"I know."

"I don't know how to do anything that means something. Does that make sense?"

"Yeah." He dropped his hand. "It does."

"What should I do?"

"Come on." He jerked his chin to the door. "Let me pour you a drink and get you something to eat. Then I'll teach you something else."

"What's that?"

"Bartenders are good listeners."

Whether it was setting some of the tears free or Dakota's comforting touch, I felt lighter as I came back out to the bar.

Wayne sent me another smile as I returned to the seat at his side.

Then Dakota made good on his promise to pour me a drink. As he made me a vodka tonic, I memorized his steps, from pouring the alcohol to adding the tonic and squeezing in the lemon. Had I ever really paid attention to the people making my drinks before? Had I ever thanked them?

"Thank you."

Dakota nodded as he put the drink in front of me. "Welcome."

I sipped my cocktail, keeping Wayne company as he finished his beer. When he was done, he shook my hand good night and promised to come back tomorrow. Then he left, nearly the moment the other pair in the bar paid their tab and left too.

Which left me and Dakota alone, sharing the pepperoni pizza he'd made after our customers had gone.

The bar was quiet and the darkness had settled outside hours ago, but the clock behind the bar read only seven o'clock. I'd been here for over eight hours and we weren't even close to the closing time listed on the front window.

"Do you always work this long?" I asked Dakota before taking my last bite of pizza. I didn't allow myself dairy or carbohydrates during the weekdays, but I'd earned some extra calories tonight.

"Usually. Me and Jackson and Thea split the hours. But since both of them are gone, I'll cover the place from open to close."

I did the math and the number I came up with nearly made me choke. "That's *fifteen* hours."

The corner of his mouth ticked up in an almost smile.

"Not every day. When it's dead like this, we close up early. We'll finish eating, give it another hour as we close things down, then call it."

My shoulders sagged. "Good. I don't think I can make it past midnight."

"You did good today."

"Don't lie. I was a train wreck."

He shrugged. "Could have been worse."

"True. I could have burned the place down."

Dakota's entire demeanor had shifted after my crying jag in the kitchen. I hadn't really felt like talking about my problems, so we'd sat there and let the television in the corner fill the silence with some sports newscaster show. And even though I hadn't confessed all of my problems, he'd been right about being a good listener.

He'd heard enough in the kitchen to know that what I'd really needed was a reprieve.

So there had been no more lessons. No more cleaning instructions. No more tips on how to best deliver drinks. He'd just let me sit on this rickety stool and rest my weary bones.

God, I wanted a bed.

I'd planned on moving my things into the boathouse tonight, but that was before Thea and Logan had surprised me with their vacation. Now I was glad I didn't have to pack up my things. I could just go back and crash in their guest bedroom.

I wasn't even going to wash my face.

Yet as exhausted as I was, as easy as it would have been to lay my head in my arms and fall asleep on the bar, my eyes were wide open. And they were locked on Dakota.

He really was something incredible. I'd seen some rather handsome Native American men before in the city. There was an Apache gentleman I'd met last year who was becoming a go-to model for some top fashion designers.

That man had the same black hair and high cheekbones as Dakota. He was absolutely beautiful, but he lacked Dakota's utter brilliance. The model didn't have the same depth to his eyes, the endless black orbs that stripped you bare. He didn't convey the same level of intimidation that was terrifying and dangerously sexy.

Watching Dakota work over the last hour had been torture. The fit of his jeans, the way his shirt strained across his biceps and chest as he moved were nothing short of erotic.

I so badly wanted to see more of his tanned, smooth skin. Just the thought of raking my nails across his bare back sent a shiver racing down my spine.

"You done?" Dakota asked, pointing to my half-empty cocktail.

"Yes, thank you." I shuffled my empty plate and crumpled napkin, hoping Dakota hadn't noticed me staring.

He swiped up my glass, my plate and the pizza pan, taking them all to the kitchen. I listened to the sound of him rinsing the dishes and putting them in the washer, glad to have a moment to compose myself.

And chastise myself.

Same old tricks. Wasn't this how it always happened? I'd be feeling lonely or sad or confused, and within a week, I'd find a man who'd give me some attention. I'd find someone who would provide a distraction, like I had with both of my ex-husbands.

My first husband, Kevin, had been working as a stockbroker on Wall Street. We'd met through a mutual acquaintance my senior year in college, just a month before graduation.

At the time, I'd felt so much pressure to find a job and put my interior design degree to use. Everyone had been waiting, expecting me to make these monumental life decisions. All of my classmates had accepted offers and were planning the next stages of their lives.

But me? I hadn't planned a thing. All I'd wanted was to get my diploma and never talk about the differences between artistic, bohemian and retro styles again.

So when Kevin had come along, he'd provided the excuse I'd been searching for. We'd fallen in love, fast and hard—at least, I had with him. He'd fallen in love with my last name. But when he'd asked me to marry him, I'd accepted immediately.

From that point on, I hadn't had to answer questions about my future. I'd told everyone I'd start my career after the wedding.

Start to finish, my relationship with Kevin had lasted only nineteen months before I'd come home early one day from a yoga class and found him fucking our neighbor from three doors down on the kitchen counter.

I'd recovered from that broken heart by marrying Bryson, the artist, four months later. My union to him ended just shy of our three-year anniversary, when I discovered he'd been stealing jewelry and trinkets from my parents' and grandparents' estates at our regular dinners. He'd been pawning them to help pay his mistress's rent.

The ink on my divorce papers had barely dried when I'd met Jay.

Here I was again, recovering from a breakup, my self-image shredded to pieces. The first thing I'd done was latch on to my handsome companion for the next ten days.

When was I going to learn?

One thing I'd figured out from years of watching Jay play poker? All that really mattered was the number of chips in your stack. When it came to my heart, I'd been losing chips for years.

The smart thing to do would be to hoard the few remaining.

But as Dakota came striding out of the kitchen, once again holding a white towel in his long fingers, those chips were his for the taking.

Maybe he was different. Maybe I was just as foolish as ever. Maybe people didn't really change.

All I knew was that if he asked, I'd be all in.

four

DAKOTA

"Like this?" Sofia gingerly crushed the mixture of sugar, lime, mint and huckleberries with the cocktail muddler in the bottom of a glass.

"Yep. Get after it."

She gripped the wooden tool harder as she dug in, smashing the remaining berries. "Okay, now what?"

"Fill it with ice. Shot of rum. Club soda to the top. Then stir."

She nodded, her eyebrows set in a focused line as she concentrated on the glass and followed my instructions exactly.

I'd been teaching her how to make drinks all afternoon.

We'd started with the easy stuff, pouring draft beers and making two-ingredient drinks. But when she'd mastered those quickly, I'd started giving her more complicated cocktails. She whipped them out like she'd been working behind the bar for months, not a day.

Today had gone so differently than yesterday it was hard to believe.

After we'd eaten dinner last night, I'd left Sofia on her stool and gone back to clean up the kitchen. It had taken me less than ten minutes, but when I'd come back out, she'd been asleep on the bar with her face resting peacefully on her arms.

She was beautiful when she slept—angelic, delicate and fragile. I refused to think about the minutes I stood there watching her. Because that was fucking creepy.

I went about cleaning, wiping down tables and putting up the chairs. Then I closed out the till and finished handwashing a few straggling glasses before shaking her shoulder gently to wake her up.

She stayed in a sleepy haze as she pulled on her coat and followed me out the rear door to my truck in the alley. I helped her into the passenger side, barely closing the door before she was resting her head on the freezing glass window. She was asleep again not five hundred feet from the bar.

I didn't even bother waking her up when I pulled into Thea and Logan's driveway. I hustled out into the cold, found the spare key under the mat and unlocked the door. Then I collected Sofia and carried her inside, laying her on a couch and covering her with a blanket.

Her murmured *good night* echoed in my ears the entire drive home on the dark, snow-covered streets.

Normally, I would have crashed just as hard and fast once my head hit the pillow. Mom always said I could sleep through an earthquake. But for once, I tossed and turned throughout the night. Thoughts of Sofia kept popping in and out of my head, keeping me awake.

She was an enigma. A puzzle.

She was a woman who had everything in the world at her fingertips and yet seemed so . . . miserable and lonely. She seemed so lost.

I didn't pity her. But I was intrigued. I ached to get closer and solve her riddle.

I ached for her.

The second the image of her long legs wrapped around my hips popped into my head, I knew there was only one way for me to fall asleep. So I took my cock in my hand and got off to the mental picture of her soft lips parting on a gasp as I slid deep inside her.

Sleep shouldn't have been hard to find after that. But it was. Because I felt like a pervert for jacking off to thoughts of my boss's sister-in-law, the woman I'd been entrusted to watch over.

Finally, I climbed out of bed and went to the gym I'd set up in my garage. After running five miles on my treadmill, I collapsed on my bed and passed out until my alarm blared through the room at ten the next morning.

Showered and dressed, I drove over to pick up Sofia.

I was certain she'd still be asleep, but when I pulled into the driveway, she was waiting just inside the door.

She seemed almost eager as she hopped into the truck. Maybe she was just a morning person. Maybe the shock of her situation had faded, and she'd found a better attitude.

I hadn't asked. I'd just enjoyed the ride.

And praised the fucking heavens there hadn't been any more tears.

Her excitement carried us through the lunch hour and into our bartending lessons. Sofia finished stirring her huckleberry mojito and added a lime wedge. Then she dunked a straw into the glass and handed it over.

I brought it to my lips and took a sip. "Tastes like a huckleberry mojito."

She smiled. "Thank god."

I pulled out my straw, putting a new one in its place, then

handed over the glass. "Give it a try."

As she took the drink from my hands, I looked away. I'd made the mistake earlier in the day of watching as she sipped from a straw, and I'd had to excuse myself so she wouldn't notice the growing bulge behind my zipper.

"It's really good. Sweeter than a regular mojito with the huckleberry."

"They'll be popular tomorrow night." There were about ten ladies around Lark Cove who ordered one of my huckleberry mojitos every time they came in.

"What's next?" Sofia dumped out the drink and rinsed the glass.

"What's your favorite drink?"

She shrugged. "I don't know if I have one."

"Really?" Fancy women like her always seemed to have a signature drink.

"I don't like beer," she told me.

"Why am I not surprised?"

Sofia's eyes twinkled as she giggled. "I like drinks with citrus tones. Or champagne."

"Then tomorrow night you'll be in charge of champagne."

"What?" Her eyes widened. "You're going to let me serve drinks?"

"Uh . . . yeah. That's kind of why you're here, isn't it?"

"I-I don't know. I didn't think you'd actually give me important things to do."

"Then what did you expect me to have you do?" Maybe she'd thought I'd just have her chasing down empties all night.

"I don't know," she muttered, toying with a spoon on the bar. "Maybe take out the garbage. Or clear dishes. Hand out peanuts. Stuff that doesn't matter when I mess it up."

I blinked twice as her words soaked in. Then I considered kicking my own ass. I'd been such a dick yesterday, criticizing her every move in an attempt to hide my attraction. But she wasn't useless. And when I wasn't harping on her, she picked things up quickly.

"You're good at this," I told her. "Not gonna lie and say it didn't surprise me. But you're a fast learner. I could use your help during the party."

"You really think so?"

"Wouldn't say it if I didn't."

The look on her face said she didn't really believe me. How was that possible? Logan was one of the most confident people I'd ever met. It rolled off him in waves. But his younger sister was a damn mess of self-doubts.

Was I the only one who saw this? How could that be?

Maybe others didn't see past the front. They couldn't look beyond the sexy clothes, fancy hair and stunning face.

But I saw underneath that superficial layer to a woman who was questioning everything at the moment. Thea had mentioned something about a magazine article. Had it shaken her up? Or had it just exposed the insecurities she'd been hiding from the world?

"Huh." Her eyebrows furrowed. "I guess all those years spent at dinner parties and galas wasn't for nothing. I've seen so many drinks mixed before, maybe I've picked up more than I realized."

"That's not the reason."

She was smart. Smarter than she gave herself credit for.

I'd taught a few people how to mix drinks before, and they always needed a few reminders about the ingredients before they had it down. But not Sofia. For her, I only had to list them once.

"Well, I'll do whatever you need me to tomorrow." She filled up a glass of water and added a couple lime slices. "But promise to tell me if I get in the way."

"Promise."

She smiled and walked around the edge of the bar.

I dropped my eyes, not letting my gaze wander down her legs.

She was wearing a pair of tennis shoes today that I'd seen Thea wear a hundred times. They were forgettable when my boss wore them. But on Sofia, those shoes accentuated the tight fit of her jeans, which were only slightly less sexy than the leather pants she'd been in yesterday. Didn't she own anything looser?

I studied the fruit tray as she slid onto a stool across from me. I'd cut twice the limes as usual this morning while I'd been doing prep because yesterday I'd noticed that she liked them in her water. Why? Because I was a good bartender, that's why. It had nothing to do with the woman with another goddamn straw to her mouth.

"How did you learn all of this?" she asked.

"It's kind of a long story."

"I've got nine days left on my sentence, so you have time."

I chuckled and filled a water glass of my own. "I grew up on a reservation about two hours away from here. After I graduated high school, I wasn't sure what I wanted to do so I took a job working at a casino in town, dealing poker."

"Poker," she grumbled under her breath.

"Not a fan?"

"My ex was a professional poker player."

"Ah. Well, this was small stakes. One day this guy came in

and sat at my table. It was a quiet night so it was just the two of us for a couple hours. We got to talking. Hit it off. He worked at a dude ranch, and before he left, he told me if I ever wanted to try something different to give him a call."

The business card he'd tossed on the felt table was still in my wallet.

Because of that man and that card, I'd taken a risk. I'd left the reservation despite my family's protests. I'd taken a job that paid three times what I'd been making at the casino plus free room and board. And I'd had the chance to meet people who lived a different life.

All of the guests at the dude ranch had money. The ones I found the most interesting were those who'd started small. The men and women who'd come from humble beginnings, like mine, and made it big.

Maybe I wouldn't be a self-made millionaire. But at thirty-two years old, I was working my ass off to hit that goal. And it had all started on that dude ranch, where I'd squirreled away a stash of money that I'd put to work for me these last five years.

"I called him the next day," I told Sofia. "He got me hooked up with the ranch manager and they hired me to work at the main lodge. Started off washing dishes during the day and dealing cards to the guests at night. The bartender had me help him whenever I didn't have a game. When he quit about six months later, I took over."

"How long did you work there?"

"Three years. I was one of the few year-round employees. Most of the ranch's crew worked in the summer only. So I took on other jobs in the winter besides bartending. Clearing snow. Taking care of animals. Whatever needed to be done."

It was an awesome job for a guy my age, but once I'd

turned twenty-one, I'd been ready to live somewhere on my own. I'd been sick of bunk beds and communal showers.

"Then what?" Sofia propped her elbow on the bar, her chin in her palm. Her attention was locked on me as she soaked up my every word.

It was unsettling to have a woman so refined give me her fullest attention. So much so that I nearly forgot her question.

"I, uh, went back home."

What was wrong with me? I'd been around rich women before. They'd rotated in and out of the dude ranch week after week, and we got a lot of wealthy out-of-towners in Lark Cove. But unless a woman wanted me for something more than to mix her a drink, I only got the normal courtesies people paid their bartender.

Sofia's attention made me nervous. The last time I'd felt like this had been for my job interview with Thea and Jackson five years ago.

"What did you do at home?" she asked.

"Took another bartending job." I busied myself by filling a glass with some ice and soda as I spoke, hoping it would keep me calm. "Worked there until I decided it was time for another change."

"What kind of change?"

"Location mostly. My uncle Xavier had been living here for years, so I called him up to see if I could crash with him until I figured out what I wanted to do."

"But you stayed?"

I nodded. "I stayed."

I had planned to make Lark Cove just a temporary home base until I found a town where real estate was on the rise. I hadn't considered staying here for the long term. But then I'd started watching the housing and rental markets in Kalispell out of sheer curiosity.

They were perfect for a guy like me.

This area had a heavy influence of out-of-state money, which brought growth and development to this corner of the world. There were other places in the country I could have gone, towns expanding so fast it made your head spin. But why leave when opportunity was just thirty minutes away?

Buying in Montana wasn't as risky as the oil-boom towns in North Dakota that could dry up at a moment's notice. My money went further here than it would in California or Florida.

And the truth was, I liked it here. The cost of living was damn cheap, and for a guy with no higher education, I made good money working at the bar.

"How'd you end up working here?" Sofia asked.

I shrugged. "Thea and Jackson were looking for some help, and it was a no-brainer."

Because of Xavier's relationship with Thea and Jackson, the pair had hired me based on his referral alone. The fact that I'd known how to serve a drink had been a bonus.

They'd been the only ones happy about my move.

Five years later, my family was still upset I'd left the reservation. The fact that I'd moved in with Xavier, my dad's older brother who had also left the reservation behind when he was young, had been like pouring salt on an open wound.

My family didn't understand my ambition. They didn't see the end goal where I retired early and had the flexibility to travel the world. To them, there was no better place than amongst our people.

It wasn't like I didn't value my heritage. It had always been an important part of me, which was another reason I hadn't moved out of Montana. I admired my culture, my family traditions. But I wanted more. I wanted freedom.

And freedom cost money. A lot of money.

I wanted to explore a Mayan ruin and tour the Colosseum in Rome. I wanted to walk along the Great Wall of China and snorkel in the Caribbean. I could spend months just exploring my own country, seeing as much of America as possible.

I didn't want to live in the same neighborhood where I'd been born. I didn't want to go to work with the same guys I'd met in grade school. I didn't want to marry a woman just because she had an acceptable genealogy and could ensure our children had the appropriate blood quantum.

I wanted to live the life of my choosing.

Right now, that meant working here in Lark Cove, biding my time and forcing myself to keep that wanderlust in check so I didn't spend my savings on frivolous travel before it was the right time.

That was the plan.

The only person in my family who'd bought into it was Xavier.

"I owe my uncle a lot." I took the gun and refilled Sofia's water. "He set me up when I moved here. Helped me get this job. He even sold me his house when he and Hazel got married. Have you ever met him?"

She nodded. "Just once. He and Hazel spent Christmas Eve with us one year when all of us Kendricks came to Montana. It was the year they got married, I think. Two years ago?"

"Sounds about right."

That was the Christmas Hazel and Xavier had invited me to join them at the Kendricks' place. Instead, I'd driven home to spend it with my family. When I'd arrived, I'd found my ex-girlfriend sitting at the dinner table between my two sisters. They'd tried to pair me up with her again, spending the entire night talking about how great we'd been as a couple.

After a few hours, I'd had enough of the not-so-subtle hints to return home, get married and have a dozen kids to carry on the family line. I'd left, taking the icy roads back to Lark Cove in the middle of the night.

I'd toasted Christmas at midnight, alone on the dark and empty highway. Then I'd celebrated the holiday by gutting the basement bathroom in my house.

When I'd told Xavier about the unrelenting pressure from my family, he'd gotten furious and called my father. That argument had been the last time they'd spoken, to my knowledge. I wasn't sure if they'd ever speak again.

Hazel had been so fired up that she'd made it a requirement to spend all holidays at their cottage. My name had been on gifts under the Christmas tree ever since.

"So what else?" Sofia reached into the tray and plucked out another lime.

"What else what?"

"What else about you? What do you like to do for fun?"

Fun? I was too busy working and managing my investments for fun. Thea had told me once that the Kendricks had made their fortune in real estate. If I was even a fraction as successful in my ventures as they were in theirs, I'd call it a win.

I worked my ass off to make sure that happened.

"I don't have a lot of time for fun."

"Now you sound like my dad." She rolled her eyes. "There's got to be something you do for fun. What is it?"

Her eyes pleaded for an answer, like she didn't want my life to be filled with only work. There was desperation on her face as the silence dragged on. Her frame deflated as I racked my brain for something to say.

If I didn't come up with something, *anything*, she'd shove me into the same category as her dad, and I'd crush her hopes along the way.

"I play basketball."

Her shoulders perked up. "That's fun."

"Not a lot of games this time of year, but once a week I'll meet some guys at the school gym and shoot around. In the summer, we have a game going every day at a park."

"I'm glad you have that."

"Me too." I hadn't really thought about my basketball games, but they were something I looked forward to every time.

"It's important to not just work all the time." She slid off her stool, bringing her water glass with her. "It consumes my dad's life. My sister's too. Though I probably shouldn't criticize since I've never worked. I'm guessing you agree with them."

"You're working now."

She came around the bar, stopping next to me and shrugged. "Does this really count, though? I'm not *really* working. I'm not even getting paid."

"Hey. Look at me." I took her glass from her hand. "This counts. And whatever tips you make while you're here are yours. You'll have earned them on your own."

To emphasize my point, I put down her water glass and walked over to a cabinet down the bar. It was full of a bunch of junk that we'd tossed into one place so it was out of the way. Every few months, that cabinet would annoy Thea so she'd spend an afternoon cleaning it out. Then she'd tell me and Jackson if we piled it full again, we had to clean it ourselves.

We never did.

The cycle just went on and on. Lucky for me, it was overdue for a clean out, but Thea hadn't done it yet.

I riffled through one of the shelves and found an empty olive jar. I took it over to Sofia, grabbed a Sharpie from the can of pens by the cash register and handed them both over. "That's your tip jar. Write your name on it."

She hesitated, her eyes locked on the marker. I was just asking her to write her name on glass, but she looked at it like I was asking her to doodle on the *Mona Lisa*.

Finally, she took the marker and carefully wrote out *Sofia* in swirly, flowing letters.

When she was done, I took it and set it on the bar, making sure that it was front and center. My tip jar was next to Thea's and Jackson's by the register, but I wanted hers to be visible.

Because she was visible.

She had more potential than she knew. She had more intelligence than most—in spades.

If I did anything in the next nine days, I hoped to show her that at least one person believed in her, that one person didn't expect her to conform to a certain role because of her heritage or last name or birth order.

Like Xavier had for me.

The Lark Cove Bar wasn't glamorous, but I was starting to see why Thea had pushed for Sofia to work here. Not because she needed to be taught a life lesson. Not because she needed to learn about hard work and blue-collar life.

But because she needed to find a purpose.

There was something to be said for serving others. A good day's work in this bar made me feel valuable. It made me feel like I had something to offer.

Sofia needed to feel those things too.

"Ready for another lesson?" I asked.

"Yes." She inhaled a fortifying breath and picked up a tumbler from the mat next to the dishwasher. Then she set it out on the rubber spill mat.

She looked up to me, waiting for my instruction.

But the drink recipe I'd made a thousand times escaped me. The ingredients got lost in her rich, brown eyes.

With her chin tipped up, her breath wafted between us, the citrus from her water lingering in the air. The scent grew stronger as the heat between us kicked up a notch.

When had we gotten so close? Her chest was just inches from mine. The tips of our shoes were nearly touching beneath us. And her lips . . . with just one tug, I'd have her breasts smashed against my chest and my mouth on hers. One tug and I'd find out exactly how that lime tasted on her tongue.

Sofia's breath hitched, her eyes locked on my mouth. Her eyes were hooded as she silently begged me to give in.

I leaned in, a split second away from ruining her lipstick. My fingers were hovering beside her cheek, ready to dive into her thick hair, when a voice filled the air.

"If you're pouring, I'll have a whiskey ditch."

We flinched, breaking apart. I spun around as Xavier led the way in from the back door, down the hallway, Hazel and the Kendrick kids trailing behind. His hair hung long over his shoulders. His black Stetson, the one he always wore, covered the gray strands.

"Sofia!" Charlie shoved past Xavier, running straight for her aunt's legs. The younger two plowed by too, all three children dressed in snow bibs, boots and puffy coats.

"Hey! You guys all have red noses." She touched Camila's tiny nose. "Were you playing in the snow?"

"Yep." Charlie pulled off her gloves. "We went sledding."

"That sounds like fun." Sofia smiled at them then looked up at Hazel and Xavier. "Nice to see you both again."

"Yeah. Didn't hear you come in." I shook Xavier's hand. "What's up?"

"Nothing much, bud. We were just out and about with the kids and thought we'd say hello."

Hazel made her way past the kids to give Sofia a hug. "How's this place treating you so far?"

"Well, I haven't broken anything today, so that's a plus. And Dakota's been teaching me how to make drinks."

"He has, has he?" Hazel turned to me, her eyes narrowing as she looked me up and down.

Fuck my life. She was worse than a damn bloodhound when it came to sniffing things out—gossip, trouble or romance. If not for my uncle's interruption, there was no doubt in my mind I would have kissed Sofia.

Hazel knew it too.

"Can we have some pizza, Dakota?" Collin groaned. "I'm starving."

"You got it."

The kids ate here enough I knew exactly what kind of pizza they all liked. Collin loved ham and pineapple. And since he'd interrupted Hazel's inspection, he'd be getting extra of both.

"Sofia, you're the bartender," I announced as I walked away from the group and toward the kitchen.

"What?" she gasped. "O-okay."

I retreated to the kitchen, hoping for a second alone to shake off that heated moment, but my uncle's footsteps followed me.

"How goes it?" he asked.

"Good. Slow today." I opened the fridge and took out some pizza dough. "Tomorrow will be a shit show."

He hummed. "Call the station if anything bad goes down. Don't try to handle it yourself."

"Don't worry, I'll call."

As the town's former sheriff, Xavier had spent many New Year's Eves out patrolling the streets and making sure everyone made it home safely. But I had no doubt that if trouble did break out, there would be no need for a phone call. This was Lark Cove's one and only bar. The deputies would be hanging around anyway.

"Hey, um, sorry." Sofia appeared in the doorway, giving Xavier a wary glance as she walked my way. She crossed into my space, practically standing on my toes as she motioned me lower.

"What?" I asked.

She waved me even closer until my ear was next to her lips. "What's a ditch?"

"Huh?" I leaned back, taking in the flush of her cheeks.

"A ditch?" She angled her head to the side, hiding her face from Xavier as she spoke. "Hazel told me to make Xavier a whiskey ditch. I didn't want to ask her what that meant."

"Oh." I should have known what she'd meant, but the woman had scrambled my brain. "It's water. One shot Crown Royal in a highball. The rest ice and water."

She nodded, backing out of the kitchen as quickly as she'd approached, hurrying out to the bar to make my uncle his favorite cocktail.

Xavier watched her leave, giving her a few moments to disappear. Then he crossed his arms over his chest. "She's beautiful."

"I know that." I went to the fridge and took out various tubs of pizza toppings, cheese and sauce.

"She lives in New York."

"Know that too."

"What are you thinking here, bud?"

"I don't know." I closed the refrigerator door. "She's . . ."

Sexy. Enchanting. Rich as hell and way the fuck out of my league. But there was so much heat between us, it could level this whole place to the ground.

"Just make sure you do right by the both of you."

I nodded. "Got it."

Without another word, Xavier walked out of the kitchen and left me to make the kids' pizza.

My uncle was my confidant. He was the man I'd looked up to ever since my father and I had gotten into a fight the day before I'd left home for the dude ranch.

Normally, I'd tell him everything about how I was feeling. But *women* wasn't a topic we delved into much, mostly because I hadn't had a girlfriend in a decade. I had no idea what he'd say, especially since he was in love with Hazel.

The last thing I needed was for him to push me into a relationship because he'd found one of his own. I didn't need him telling me to settle down and find someone to share my life with.

I'd dealt with that shit from my parents for years. Though their "advice" had always come with the understanding that the woman I chose shared our heritage.

Christ. If my parents saw me and Sofia together, they'd be crushed.

Which meant if something did happen between us, it needed to stay quiet. I didn't have the energy to deal with my family if they found out I was hooked up with a woman like Sofia.

Though I would take Xavier's advice. I'd do right by us both.

Was I considering making a play for Sofia Kendrick? Despite my better judgment, the fact that she was my boss's sister-in-law and the slew of other reasons this was fucking stupid, the answer was yes.

I was considering it.

Maybe if we could come to an understanding, a kiss in the bar wouldn't be out of the question. Maybe Sofia and I could have a little fun for the next nine days, then go our separate ways.

Though I doubted I'd ever see a lime wedge again and not think of her smile.

five

SOFIA

"Hi, how are you?" I asked as Aubrey answered my call.

"Hello. And I'm good." The sound of fingers flying over a keyboard echoed in the background. I didn't need to see her to know that her headset was on in one ear, her eyes were on a computer screen, and her brain was focused on something other than my phone call.

"I was just calling to tell you I won't be able to make our lunch date next week."

"Fine."

The clicking in the background continued, this time with more fury. I felt bad for the person on the receiving end of whatever response she was hammering out.

"I'm in Montana."

"I know. Dad told me you took the plane on a spur-of-the-moment trip." Her tone was full of annoyance, like it was an inconvenience for me to use the *family's* private jet.

Maybe she thought I hadn't earned that privilege, unlike her. Except the only time she needed the Gulfstream was when she had a business meeting to attend and the company's plane was already spoken for.

Someone should use the plane. Why not me?

"I've been, um . . . working," I told her.

The clicking stopped. "Working?"

"Yes. I'm helping at the bar while Thea and Logan are in Paris."

There was silence on her end for a few moments, then the clicking continued without another word.

Seriously? That was her reaction? I didn't expect Aubrey to throw me a parade for doing two days' worth of work, but she could at least acknowledge I was completely out of my comfort zone.

No, all I got was more background typing, reminding me that my life would never be as important as the job she'd married at twenty-one.

"Are you doing anything for New Year's Eve?" I asked, still trying like I always did with Aubrey. Though I think my efforts just annoyed her more.

"No plans." Her lips were pursed, I was sure of it.

"Oh. Um, are you seeing anyone new?" Or anyone at all?

The last time there had been a man in Aubrey's life was three years ago, and he'd only lasted six months. He'd quickly learned that he'd always come in second place to her job.

Clearly the man was smarter than me.

I was still trying to compete.

"No, I'm not seeing anyone," Aubrey huffed. "I don't need to have a guy in my life to feel satisfied."

That's your thing, Sofia. Not mine.

The words were unspoken, but I heard them loud and clear nonetheless. I'd heard them many times before, and just like always, they burned.

Aubrey frowned upon me because I was always in a

relationship—well, it was *one* of the reasons she frowned upon me. In her eyes, it made me weak and dependent.

Maybe she was right.

"Okay." I sighed. "You're busy. I'll let you go. Happy New Year."

"Thanks. Same to you." And the line went dead.

I stared at my phone for a moment, replaying our short conversation. Was it time to give up? We were in our thirties. Maybe it was time I just accepted I would never be friends with my sister.

Aubrey and I had never been close. Even as kids, we'd never shared that sisterly bond. We hadn't played Barbies or braided one another's hair. We hadn't fought over the same toys or what to watch on TV. At times, she felt more like an acquaintance than my sister. When we met for our monthly lunch, she'd spend most of the hour checking messages and emails while I scrolled through social media or texted.

She was too much like my dad, driven and competitive. My lack of enthusiasm for the things they found most important exasperated them.

What *was* my passion?

I searched for an answer but came up empty.

Scrolling through my contacts, I passed by my friends' names, not feeling like texting any of them. Not one of them had called me even once since the magazine article had been released.

Friends was probably too fond a word for most of the names in my phone.

Over the last few years, I'd made it a point to cull toxic friendships from my life. After I'd treated Thea so badly during our first introduction and Logan had threatened to cut me off from my trust fund, it had been a wake-up call.

I'd played games. I'd lost.

I was just lucky it hadn't cost me my brother.

Most of the girlfriends I'd been hanging out with at the time hadn't wanted friendship. They'd wanted access to my social connections or my handsome, billionaire brother. It seemed my taste in friends was as good as it was in men.

So I'd ghosted the ones who loved to use others and play games. They were probably planning a brunch to get together and toast my demise by magazine article.

Whatever. In truth, there hadn't been many to trim. I'd always had a lot of acquaintances, women who ran in the same circles as my family so we'd see each other at functions. But they'd never been true friends.

Still, my breakup with Jay had been hard, not only because we'd been together for so long, but because I hadn't had anyone to talk to.

Sometimes, even a bad friend who listened was better than no friend at all.

Aubrey was only two years older than I was and would make a wonderful best friend.

If we could get along.

I carried my phone across the living room at Thea and Logan's house to sit in one of the overstuffed chairs positioned by a window. The front of the home was filled with huge glass panes that overlooked their snow-covered yard and Flathead Lake beyond.

It was frozen now, but in the summer, the lake was magical, with glassy blue water that begged me to run my fingers over its smooth surface.

Right now, it just looked cold and empty.

Like my life.

I turned away from the view and let my eyes travel around the living room.

This house was so different than the sprawling estate where Logan, Aubrey and I had grown up. This home was beautiful, with its cedar shakes and tall roof peaks. Logan had bought one of the most expensive homes in the area. But it wasn't ostentatious. It had a casual, homey feel, which was probably due to Thea being so down-to-earth.

The furniture was high-end, but it was functional. The coffee table held books that were actually being read. The throw blankets on the couch had been snuggled under on movie night. There wasn't a coaster in sight, because here, you set your coffee mug directly on the end tables.

There was green crayon on the wall by the television. Thea's own artwork adorned the walls, her dimensional pieces the shelves. A basket in the corner overflowed with baby toys.

This home was alive and full of personality. It was full of love.

It was the polar opposite of my penthouse apartment in the city.

My housekeeper cleaned rooms every week that hadn't seen a person, other than her, in months. I hadn't thought a thing of it before. So why did that seem so silly at the moment?

Outside, evergreens towered over the road running around the edge of the lake. Their faces were taking the full force of the sun's morning rays, making their ice-covered needles sparkle.

Malcom had added that same sparkle to the photo for the magazine.

That goddamn magazine.

Since that article had landed on my doorstep, I'd been

questioning everything about my life.

Every. Single. Thing.

I lived in a high-rise penthouse in a glitzy neighborhood in SoHo. I had a trust fund that would keep me living in finery for the rest of my life. I had complete freedom with no job or responsibilities.

So why wasn't I happy? What was I missing? Normally, I would have blown the magazine article off by now. Why was it still niggling at me?

I'd been trying so hard these last few years, giving up nasty friendships and helping more with Mom's charities or family functions. Yet no one in my family seemed to see it. I'd had such high hopes that someone from the outside would.

That reporter's words would not stop haunting me. *Superficial. Gaudy. Flighty.*

"I'm not those things," I mumbled to no one. Was I?

Shaking it off, I unlocked my phone, pulling up Mom's number in the hope that talking to one of my parents would give me a sense of normalcy.

I hadn't talked to Dad since the magazine had come out. And as much as I would like to make sure he wasn't still upset with me, I knew better than to call him during work hours. Really, I'd been lucky that Aubrey had answered.

Maybe we weren't as hopeless as I'd thought.

Dad would have sent me straight to voicemail. But Mom, as always, answered immediately.

"Hi, Mom."

"Sweetheart, how are you? Are you enjoying your vacation?"

"Uh . . . yeah. Though it isn't much of a vacation. Believe it or not, I'm working at Thea's bar."

"I'm sorry, Sofia. I think your connection must be spotty. What did you say?"

"I said, I'm working at Thea's bar."

A wave of panic hit as the other end of the phone went completely still. Was she disappointed? Had I stooped too low? Mom didn't discriminate against blue-collar jobs, but then again, they'd never been held down by her youngest daughter.

The family's image was always paramount.

To my knowledge, Mom had never worked. She'd met Dad in college and they'd married young. It was ironic that my siblings had condemned me for never getting a job when our mother had never had one either.

Though Mom did volunteer with select charities and was a member of numerous clubs. Plus, she was a mother.

I'd always considered it lucky I hadn't gotten pregnant since my exes had all turned out to be awful men. I was fortunate not to be tied to any of them forever. But maybe if I had children, that reporter would have left me alone entirely. Maybe there wouldn't be the tension between me and my family members.

Maybe there wouldn't still be silence on the other end of the phone.

"Mom?"

"I'm here." She cleared her throat. "You just took me by surprise."

"Sorry."

"It's fine. I'm . . . you're really working?"

"Yes." Harder than ever before. "Just helping while Thea and Logan are on their trip."

"That's wonderful. I'm sure they're happy to have you."

I laughed. "I don't know about that. But I'm trying."

Not just for myself, but for Dakota. I had this powerful

urge to make up for my awful first impression. Not only because he was a man who made my heart race and my palms sweat. But because he'd become my chauffeur, mentor and keeper. My presence had put him out, and I guess I wanted to make it easy on him if I could.

When I'd gotten up yesterday morning, I'd promised myself I would keep a positive attitude at the bar. I'd make the best of the situation.

And to my delight, we'd had a good day.

Some might even call it fun.

"When are you coming home?" Mom asked.

"As soon as Thea and Logan get home. The plane will be here already so that way the pilot won't have to make a special trip back for me."

"I'm sure he wouldn't mind."

"It's okay. It'll be time for me to come home anyway." Hiding in Lark Cove wasn't a long-term solution to my problems.

"Let's have dinner when you return."

"I'd love that. Anyway, I'll let you go. I just wanted to say hello. Happy New Year. I'll give you and Dad a call tomorrow."

"All right." But before I hung up, she stopped me. "Sofia?"

"Yes?"

"I'm proud of you for helping Logan and Thea."

My chest swelled. "Thank you."

"Good-bye."

I was smiling as I took the phone away from my ear. When was the last time she'd said she was proud of me? It had to have been a while. The rush of pride running through my blood, warming me from head to toe, felt foreign.

Lillian Kendrick, a woman well-known for her social

stature, exquisite taste and impeccable manners, was proud of her daughter for working in a rustic, Montana bar.

I can't wait to tell Dakota.

That thought jolted me in my seat. I'd only known the man a couple of days, yet he was consuming my thoughts.

The same thing had happened when I'd met my second husband, Bryson.

I'd been recovering from my divorce with Kevin, keeping a low profile because I'd just been made a fool, thanks to my cheating husband. But a friend had begged me to attend her art gallery exhibit. *Get back out there. Show him he didn't deserve you in the first place.* That's what she'd told me.

Looking back, I realized her motives were entirely selfish. She'd wanted my attendance to create a buzz for her show. The only time I'd heard from her since was when she was hosting another event.

Bryson had been there that night. He'd introduced himself, handed me a glass of champagne and flashed me his sexy smile. I'd fallen into him instantly. And he'd consumed my thoughts from that moment on, holding them captive until we'd unraveled so spectacularly.

According to the gossip circle, he'd married his mistress after our divorce and they now had a little girl. They were living comfortably, thanks to the check I'd written Bryson to go away forever. I didn't know how long the pair had been playing me—I hadn't asked—though I assumed from the very beginning.

I'd been a blind fool. Again.

So as much as I wanted Dakota to kiss me up one side and down the other, his uncle's timing had likely saved me from another mistake. I didn't need to get wrapped up in a man right now, not after my last three disasters.

Though, Dakota seemed different. Even with my track record, I knew he was nothing like Kevin, Bryson or Jay. Dakota didn't pander to me. When I annoyed him, his voice was full of irritation and he'd snap. He clenched his jaw when he was losing his patience. When he did give me a compliment, it was short and sweet. None of my exes would have ever let on that I was driving them crazy. And their gushing praise was always over the top.

Dakota was different because he had pride. It was part of his makeup, like bones and muscle. It ran through his blood.

It was insanely sexy.

I checked the time on my phone. I had about ten minutes before he was due to pick me up. It was going to be hectic and stressful at the party, but I was giddy with excitement for tonight. Not just for the festivities, but to show Dakota that his faith in me wasn't misplaced.

I was going to be at my absolute best tonight. I'd make him proud. Maybe I'd make myself proud along the way too. I was facing a new year from a strange place and a strange position. But maybe this shake-up was long overdue.

Maybe it was time to start a year off in tennis shoes instead of stilettos.

I stood and left the living room, heading toward Thea's closet to borrow another pair of shoes. I was just passing the front door—the locked front door—when the deadbolt flipped and the knob turned.

I gasped, staggering backward as my heart lodged in my throat. I was about to scream my head off when Piper swung open the door.

"Hi!" She came inside with a stack of papers tucked under her arm.

My entire frame fell, my heart dropping back into its normal place from my throat. "Oh my god. You scared the hell out of me."

"Sorry." She winced. "I should have rung the doorbell first."

"It's fine." I waved it off as she came over and gave me a quick hug.

Piper was Logan's assistant at the Kendrick Foundation, our family's charitable organization. She'd worked for him for years in the city and was his most trusted and favorite employee. When she'd gone through a nasty divorce a while back, he'd convinced her to move to Montana and work with him out here.

I'd figured the move would be temporary, but then she'd met her handsome husband, Kaine, and Montana had become her forever home. They had twin boys who were almost one.

"You look happy."

She tucked a strand of her chestnut hair behind an ear. "Thank you. And you look beautiful, as always."

"Thank you."

I'd known Piper for a long time and had always thought she was gorgeous. But her happiness had taken her to a whole new level since she'd moved to Montana. Her skin glowed and her smile radiated through the room.

"So how are you doing?" she asked.

"I'm good. You?"

"I'm fantastic. I just wanted to swing by and drop off some paperwork."

"On New Year's Eve?" I asked. "My brother isn't even here. He needs to cut you some slack."

"He sure does." Her eyes scanned me up and down, looking

over every inch twice.

"What?" I inspected my clothing. "Why are you looking—wait. You're not here to drop off paperwork. My brother sent you here to check on me, didn't he?"

She hesitated a moment but nodded. "Sorry. He was worried."

"Ugh." I rolled my eyes. "It's been two days. I'm fine."

"I tried to tell him that too, but he just wanted to be sure. He loves you."

"Yeah," I muttered. "I love him too."

And this check-in was irritably kind. Logan had always been protective of me, even if he did claim that I gave him gray hair.

"Okay, now that I've seen you're alive and still standing, I can report back to Logan. I'll just drop these papers in the office before Kaine comes in search of me. The boys are probably going nuts in their car seats since we've been stopped for ten seconds. They don't like being trapped. Stop lights are stressful right now."

"They're all outside?" I peered past her.

"Yep. Kaine's talking to Dakota. Be right back."

She hurried down the hallway toward the office as I rushed to put on some shoes. Then I stole a heavy ski coat from Thea's coatrack, shrugging it on just as Piper came back. "Ready?"

"Ready." I nodded. "Are you guys coming to the party tonight?"

She smiled. "We'll be there. Kaine's mom is coming up this afternoon to watch the boys so we can have a night out."

"It'll be nice to see a familiar face. Dakota put me in charge of pouring champagne, so I'll make sure your glass is always full."

"Perfect." She laughed. "How's it going with work and Dakota?"

"Good. He's sweet." That word slipped right out. It was not the one I'd meant to say because *sweet* revealed way too much. I turned and walked to the door, hoping Piper had missed it.

"Hold up."

Damn. I sighed and spun back around.

"He's sweet?" she repeated. "Dakota Magee has never been described as sweet. What's going on?"

If this had been Sean, Logan's other assistant, I would have been able to avoid this conversation. But Piper had become an extension of Logan's family over the years, and I'd known her for way too long. She'd keep me inside until I told her all about Dakota and the last two days.

"Nothing. It's not like that. Kind of. I don't know. He's . . ." I tossed my hand in the general direction of the men outside, looking at them from the window next to the door.

They were standing by the hood of Dakota's black truck, talking. Dakota had his arms crossed over his broad chest. His canvas coat did nothing to hide the bulk of his arms. His faded jeans molded around his thick thighs, his boots planted wide in the snow.

My mouth went dry.

"Hot," Piper finished.

I nodded. "Super hot."

"Hmm. And this is a problem?"

"Yes. The last thing I need is another relationship."

"Why does it have to be a relationship? You know, casual sex gets a bad rap. There is nothing wrong with a woman having some fun with a sexy man."

"Really?" My mouth fell open. I bet Logan wouldn't want

Piper checking up on me again if he knew she was encouraging me to have casual sex with Thea's employee.

"Kaine and I jumped right into something crazy and wild. It was so out of character for me and the best decision I've ever made in my life."

"Yeah, but you got married and had cute babies. I'm not looking for a husband. Been there. Done that twice. Clearly, my taste in partners cannot be trusted."

Piper's face softened. "Sofia, don't be so hard on yourself. You've had some bad luck with men. But honestly, I don't think any of that was your fault."

"You don't?"

"No, I don't." She put her hand on my shoulder. "Here's what I know. Dakota is a good man. He's honest. I think a relationship, even a brief one, with a good man is just what you need. He can teach you what it feels like to be with the right kind of someone."

"I'm leaving as soon as Thea and Logan get back."

"Logan always says you're a fast learner."

Huh? "He does?"

She winked and let go of the door, forcing me out of the way as she stepped outside.

I followed, shielding my eyes from the bright winter sun and locking the door behind me.

Kaine spotted Piper and left Dakota's side, coming to her side and making sure she didn't slip on the snowy sidewalk.

"I can walk on my own," she told him. "I've been doing it for over thirty years."

"Just let me help you." He didn't let go of his wife as he opened her door on their SUV. Just as she'd expected, two tiny and unhappy voices were shouting in the backseat.

"Bye!" Piper waved at me as Kaine jogged around and got in the driver's side.

"See you tonight." He gave me a jerk of the chin, climbed into the driver's seat and pulled away, leaving Dakota and me standing outside in the snow alone.

"Good morning," I said. It felt awkward. Why were we awkward?

Because you almost kissed yesterday.

"Hey." Dakota's breath billowed around his handsome face as he walked me to the passenger side of his truck. He stayed a foot away, but the heat between us was enough to chase away the winter chill.

"It's the big day."

"It is. You ready for this?" That deep voice paired with those dark eyes sent a rush of desire down my spine. It pooled between my legs and made me slightly dizzy.

There was no ignoring my attraction to Dakota. Forcing it away was impossible. The magnetism between us was going to keep pulling us together until one of us finally gave in. Maybe Piper was right. Why resist it?

This didn't have to be anything serious. A kiss, or something more, didn't mean we'd be walking down the aisle. For once, maybe I would give casual a try.

I'd show myself that I didn't need a man. But that didn't mean I couldn't enjoy the company of a hot one for a few days.

Was I ready for this?

"Hell yes."

six

DAKOTA

"I FOUND ONE MORE BAG OF CONFETTI HIDDEN UNDERNEATH the streamers."

"Goodie," I deadpanned.

"Oh, stop." Sofia laughed, opening it up to sprinkle the confetti across the bar.

I'd hoped to keep Thea's box of decorations a secret, especially the confetti. That shit was a pain in the ass to clean up. But Thea must have known I had no plans to decorate because she'd sent Sofia a text on the drive to the bar this morning. The first thing my *helper* had done was find the decorations and start decking the place out.

Thea had bought so much crap, it had taken Sofia hours. Not that there had been much else to do. The lunch hour had been dead, and I doubted we'd see a soul until seven or eight, when the party was scheduled to begin. The decorations had at least kept Sofia busy.

And as much as I didn't want to spend the extra time taking it all down, it was nice to see her so excited. Sofia's eyes sparkled brighter than the plastic gold tiara she'd put on her head.

"What do you normally do on New Year's Eve?" she asked,

wadding up the now-empty confetti bag and tossing it into the garbage.

"Work." If I wasn't bartending here, I was somewhere else. There were always one or two out-of-staters who wanted a private bartender for their intimate parties. They were boring as hell, but the money was stupid easy. "What about you?"

"Normally, I'd spend the day getting ready for a party or two."

"I'm scared to ask what that entails."

She sighed. "Facial. Massage. Pedicure. Manicure. Makeup. Hair. Dress. The works."

"Guess today you'll have to settle for dressing up the bar instead."

"I guess so." She adjusted the tiara on her head. "This is different but better than I'd expected. So far, today has been one of the best New Year's Eves I've had in ages. I'm not usually the one who decorates for parties. This is fun. Really fun, actually."

Damn. I reached into my jeans pocket and pulled out the last bag of confetti I'd stolen earlier to throw away when she wasn't looking.

"Here." I tossed it to her. "Go nuts."

Sofia's smile hit me square in the chest as she tore into the bag. Those eyes shone bright, like I'd just handed her keys to a new car, not a ninety-nine-cent bag of confetti.

She'd gone all out today, arranging items for maximum visibility. Hats and tiaras, like the one she was wearing, were placed in various spots around the room. We'd find a bunch of them trampled on the floor by the end of the night. A banner announcing the year was strung across the jukebox. The chances of it surviving to midnight were slim. Gold foil horns that were going to drive me crazy by ten o'clock were on every table.

But I wouldn't tell her any of that.

"Looks good in here."

"Thanks." She spread out the confetti on a cocktail table. "You're the third person to give me a compliment today."

"And the first two?"

"Piper when I saw her earlier. And my mom when I talked to her this morning. She said she was proud of me for working here."

"She should be proud."

"Well, I don't get compliments like that much. It felt good." She finished with the confetti and came to sit across from me at the bar. "Did Thea and Logan tell you about the magazine?"

"They mentioned it."

"It was humiliating." Her shoulders fell. "It *is* humiliating. I guess I'd always just thought that my family saw me as useless, no matter what I did. Then the article happened, and I realized the world saw me that way."

"Don't say that."

She shrugged. "But it's true. Or was. I don't know. But I guess what I'm trying to explain is that in my family, I'm not the child my parents are proud of. I'm the one who makes bad decisions in husbands and friends. In life. My mom saying she is proud is . . ."

"Huge."

"Epic." Sofia nodded. "It was nice to get recognized for something right for a change. And I needed it. I didn't even know how much."

Sofia slid off her stool and plucked the tiara from her head. Then she did something that nearly short-circuited my brain. Instead of walking over to put the tiara on the cocktail table, she danced.

Raising her arms above her head, she lifted to her toes. The muscles in her legs, those toned thighs and calves, bunched underneath her tight jeans. Her sweater rode up above her hips, giving me a glimpse of her belly button and the diamond jewel in its center.

On one foot, she spun in a graceful twirl, her hair whirling around her shoulders in loose curls that hung down her back.

One spin.

That was all she did. One spin and I was dizzy.

She set down the tiara on the table, like that spin midstep was as easy as walking, and came back to the bar and stood across from me.

She was so graceful. She was whimsical, like a fairy without her wings.

Add in that sexy navel piercing, her expressive brown eyes, and I was standing next to an enigma.

Every time I thought I had her figured out, she surprised me. Every damn time.

As Sofia approached, I snapped out of my stupor and dropped my eyes to my boots.

My fingers itched to pull up the hem of her sweater just to make sure I'd seen that piercing. But if I spotted it again, it would be impossible not to run my tongue over the gem. To suck it into my mouth and wet the warm metal on my tongue.

I closed my eyes, taking a breath and willing my blood to cool. *One. Two. Three.* I counted up to ten. Then backward to zero. When I opened my eyes, I expected to see Sofia watching me, wondering what the hell was my problem.

But she wasn't in front of me.

She'd quietly climbed on top of the bar.

"What the fuck? Get down." My heart stopped and my

arms shot out to grab her. But she took a step away. "Sofia, get down."

"I have to hang these up." She wiggled the spirals of silver and gold foil in her hand.

"Let me do it."

She waved me off. "I'm fine."

"Be careful." I stepped closer, keeping my arms out in case she stumbled and fell.

She rose up on her toes and taped a streamer to the iron beam that ran the length of the room. Sofia took a few steps, taped up another, then continued until she'd spaced them along the length of the bar.

The entire time, I followed her with my arms outstretched.

When the last one was hung, she smiled at her work and dropped her gaze to me and my arms. "I'm not going to fall."

"You might."

"Then you'd catch me."

Without question.

I wouldn't let her fall, not while she was here. I had no idea how I'd done it, but somehow in the last few days, she'd gotten that message too.

Sofia bent lower and held out her arms.

I stepped up, gripping her at the waist. Her hands dropped to my shoulders. And then she just fell forward, trusting that I'd deliver her safely to the floor.

Her chest dragged down mine as I lowered her. Her eyes stayed locked on mine the entire time.

The moment her toes touched the floor, I should have let her go and backed away, but my hands were glued to her hips. My fingertips dug in harder to her jeans, not wanting to let go.

"Thanks." Her hands stayed on my shoulders.

"Welcome."

Her lips were parted as she breathed. She hadn't worn lipstick today, just a light-colored gloss that made them look wet.

I wanted to lick it off, clean those lips so the only thing on them was me.

Sofia let out a breath, and the words *kiss me* lingered in the air.

So I did.

I crushed my lips down on hers, hard. I moaned, letting the sticky gloss wet my lips and the softness of her mouth mold against mine.

Sofia gasped, wrapping her arms tighter around my neck. Her fingers dove into the strands of hair at my nape, digging her manicured nails into my scalp.

I loosened my grip on her hips so I could wrap my arms around her back, then I pulled her to me, smashing our bodies together. I slanted my head to delve deeper, my tongue exploring every corner of her mouth.

Her taste exploded in my mouth, her own flavor mixing with a hint of lime. It was as delicious as I'd expected. Better, even.

Sofia Kendrick was a sweet creature. The sweetest I'd ever tasted.

"More." Sofia grappled at my shoulders, pulling us even closer.

I let my hands drift down to cup her ass, tilting my hips so she could feel the entire length of my arousal.

"Uh, are you guys open?"

The voice broke us apart. Sofia and I both panted. I shook my head, blinking furiously to get out of my lusty haze as I turned to the door. A man I'd never seen before was hovering just inside, looking awkward and ready to bolt.

"Yeah, we're open." I dragged a hand over my lips, wiping away the signs from our kiss and Sofia's lip gloss. "Come on in."

Sofia's face turned bright red as she turned her back to the customer.

"Sorry to interrupt." The man crossed the room and sat at one of the tables. He plucked the menu from the stand and started to read it.

I raked a hand through my hair, muttering, "Shit."

Sofia looked over. The redness in her face was gone but her cheeks were still flushed. "Back to work?"

"In a sec."

Her eyes drifted down my body, widening as they landed on the bulge behind my zipper. "Oh. I-I'll just go take his order."

"Thanks." I nodded, closing my eyes and taking a few breaths. But it was impossible to get my dick under control with the taste of her still on my tongue.

Fuck my life. I'd just crossed a line and there was no going back.

Kissing her was the best bad idea I'd had in years. She was rich and beautiful and the type of woman who sucked men in and held them captive.

Sofia took the man's order and came back around the bar. Without a word, she poured his beer and delivered it with a coaster and tray of peanuts.

I was still fighting to get myself back under control.

"I'm going to see if there are any more decorations." She walked past me and down to the office.

"Fine." I went straight for the bottle of whiskey on the back shelf, poured a shot glass full and tossed it back.

"Need me to take this to go?" the man at the table asked,

grinning as he sipped his beer. "You could lock up and help her look for decorations."

"We're good."

He raised his eyebrows.

I sent him a glare, making it clear that if he brought up Sofia or the situation he'd walked in on again, he wouldn't have to leave. I'd throw him out the fucking door.

"This is the last of the decorations." Sofia returned with another two bags of confetti and a box labeled in Chinese.

"What's in that one?" I pointed to the box.

"Noisemakers."

I took the box from her hands but saw that it was unopened. "How do you know it's noisemakers?"

"Because it says so on the box."

"You can read Chinese?"

She shrugged. "Not well, but enough. I had lessons in high school. I'm much better at Spanish because I spent a month in Barcelona after graduation. Though I haven't used it since. Both are rusty."

I blinked. "You speak Spanish and Chinese."

"I don't really *speak* Chinese. I haven't since I stopped taking lessons. But I can read it well enough to get by."

Christ. I didn't need more turn-ons. A woman whose mind was as sharp as the bite of her fingernails was impossible to resist.

The door to the bar opened again, and this time a familiar face came walking in.

"Hey, Wayne." I jerked up my chin.

"Dakota. Hey, Sofia. How are you two getting on?"

The man at the table choked on a peanut as he laughed.

"We're fine," I muttered. "Want your usual?"

"Sure."

I poured Wayne a beer as Sofia went to sprinkle more shit on the tables we'd just have to clean up later. I didn't have the heart to tell her she'd probably be the one to sweep up all that confetti.

"How are your feet holding up?" Wayne asked Sofia.

"Much better." She kicked up a heel of the Chuck Taylors I'd seen Thea wear frequently. "These are comfortable. Though I look silly in sneakers."

I frowned. "No, you don't."

Her skinny jeans and simple white V-neck tee were much more appealing than the fancy shit she'd worn the last two days. Today, she looked like she was comfortable here.

Confident. Every move was made with more surety, whether she was picking up glasses or using the soda gun. She walked around this bar like she owned the place.

It was the confidence I recognized from her siblings.

Add to that her beauty, and it was hard not to stare. For the rest of her "internship," I'd be more focused on her than I would the bar.

"Big party tonight." Wayne sipped his beer. "I might have to break my one-beer rule and stick around for a little bit longer."

"You should." Sofia adjusted a spray of stars and foil strings she'd put on one table. "It's going to be fun."

Her excitement was palpable, her anticipation contagious. Fuck the drinks. Screw the customers. All that mattered tonight was that Sofia had a good time.

I wanted her to leave here tonight feeling like she'd made a difference. That I couldn't have done it without her help.

I wanted her to feel like *she* mattered, at least for one night.

To make that happen, I'd need to be as methodical as

possible. I'd need to make sure I didn't get too busy and shove her out of the way. So I spent the next hour doing added prep while Sofia talked to Wayne. I made us all a pizza so we could eat early, and then I closed up the kitchen.

Thankfully, Thea had learned from her mistakes the previous year. She'd tried to run both the bar and kitchen last year, and it had been chaos. This year, she'd advertised the kitchen would be closed, giving me one less thing to worry about for the night.

By seven o'clock, we were prepped and waiting. Wayne had decided to stay and was in the bathroom. Which left me and Sofia standing behind the bar as the first customers came in the door.

"Ready for this?" I asked her.

She blew out a shaking breath but smiled. "So ready."

"What a rush!" Sofia did her twirly thing around one of the tables. "I don't think eight hours has ever gone by so fast before. That was crazy!"

I grinned as I locked up the front door. I'd announced last call an hour ago, but it had taken people a while to filter out. The clock behind the bar, which was always twenty minutes fast, read three in the morning.

"You did good tonight."

Sofia had been more of a help than I could have ever imagined. I hadn't needed to make sure she'd contributed. She just had.

I'd set up the champagne for her to pour, which she had, but at one point when we'd been slammed, she'd been mixing drinks nearly as fast as I could.

The two of us had kept up with the drink orders all night, and as much as I hated to admit I couldn't run this place alone, I'd needed her. Sofia had mostly mixed drinks all night while I'd run the register and managed the other orders. But just having her fill some orders had been huge.

The entire time, she'd done it with a smile on the lips I'd kissed.

She'd been nervous at first and hesitant as people came in. For the first few hours, she'd hung out on the far end of the bar, hovering near Piper and Kaine. I think she'd just been trying to stay out of my way.

But finally, I'd whistled for her to come and mix a couple of drinks, hoping she'd loosen up.

From then on out, she'd relaxed and come into her own.

She had the same charisma as her brother. It didn't shine through as quickly, but she'd charmed everyone in the bar tonight with her laughter and quick wit.

"Want some more champagne?" I asked as I went behind the bar. There was still half a bottle left. I'd made sure she had a glass in her hand as the crowd counted down to midnight. Since then, we'd both been sipping it on and off.

"Yes, please." She came behind the bar, depositing the last few dirty glasses in the sink.

I filled her glass then poured myself a bit more. As much as I wanted to kiss her again, I resisted the urge, just like I'd done at midnight too. "Happy New Year."

"Happy New Year." We clinked glasses and I downed mine. Champagne wasn't really my thing but the occasion called for it.

When I looked back up, she was guzzling her glass dry. She

laughed as she set it down empty. "I was thirsty."

I smiled, noticing a drop hanging on the corner of her lip.

She wiped it away, looked at me, then froze.

"What?"

"You're smiling. You don't smile that much. But when you do . . . it's crazy hot."

I chuckled. "Maybe that's enough champagne."

"Maybe you're right." She giggled. "I'll get to work on cleaning up the confetti."

We spent the next hour cleaning and putting things away. Busy nights like this were a high, and it was always hard to wind down. It would take hours for the exhaustion to sink in.

Sofia was riding the excitement too, cleaning as I took out the trash. When I came back from dumping six bags, I found her on the bar, ripping down the foil spirals.

"What the fuck?" I jogged down the hallway. "Careful."

"I'm fine. See?" She rose up on her toes and did the same twirl she'd done on the floor earlier. Except this time, her footing wasn't quite as steady or her movements as tight.

"Sofia, get down. You're going to fall and hurt yourself."

She ignored me as she ripped down another spiral. "It was so fun tonight."

"Down," I ordered only to be ignored again. So like I had earlier tonight, I followed along with her, my arms extended to make sure I'd catch her if she fell.

"I can't remember the last time I had that much fun." She rose up on her toes then lifted one leg in the air as her arms floated up toward the ceiling. "My feet feel great too, even if these shoes look silly."

"Sofia," I barked. "Both feet on the bar or get the fuck down."

"Okay," she drawled, putting her feet back on the bar and walking to the final spiral. "What's your passion?"

"My passion?" What did that have to do with her getting off the bar?

"Yes, your passion. What do you love? What gets you excited?"

"Right now? Keeping you from breaking your damn neck."

She pulled the last foil spiral from the ceiling, but instead of getting down, she paused and smirked at me. Then she rose up on her toes, kicked out a leg and spun in two fast circles. When she landed, a hand covered her laughing mouth.

"Do that shit on the floor." I put my hands on my hips. "Get down. Now."

She crouched. "I took ballet lessons my entire childhood, all through high school. I'm not going to fall."

"You might."

"And you'll catch me if I do."

"This is dangerous." We both knew I wasn't talking about her standing on the bar.

With one fast move, Sofia fell forward, her arms extended. I caught her at the waist, helping her down to the floor.

She didn't step away, and I didn't let her go.

"You kissed me," she whispered.

I nodded.

"But you didn't kiss me at midnight."

"We were busy."

"We're not busy now."

I dropped my forehead to hers. "I'm not sure it's a good idea."

"Me neither," she admitted. "But I don't know if I can stop."

She leaned in, pressing her lips to mine in a soft kiss. Her tongue darted out and traced my lower lip.

Without any hesitation, I hoisted her up into my arms, only remembering to hit the lights as I carried her out of the bar. We forgot everything else that needed to be cleaned or cared for in the race to get her into my truck.

The need to drive was the only reason we broke apart. But our separation only lasted the short drive to my house. Where I parked, lifted her back into my arms.

And carried her into my bed.

seven

SOFIA

A SMILE STRETCHED ACROSS MY FACE AS I BURIED MY FACE IN Dakota's pillow, inhaling his woodsy scent. My arms extended to the headboard, and my toes pointed toward the base of the bed. I still hadn't opened my eyes, wanting just a few more seconds to savor the stiffness kinking my muscles.

Dakota had worked some parts of my body last night that I hadn't used in a while. A long while.

My triceps were stiff from bracing against his wooden headboard as he pounded into me from behind. My quads were tired from riding him like my own personal stallion. My ankle had a tender spot from where he'd bitten me as he'd come.

Aches aside, this was the best I'd felt in months. Years even.

Piper's advice to just go for it with Dakota had been spot on.

Last night had reminded me that sex could be fun. Dakota and I had gone at it hot and heavy the moment he'd pulled me into his home. His mouth had latched on to mine, never taking it away as he'd stripped me bare on our journey to his bedroom.

My clothes were still littered all over the house.

I took one last breath of his pillow and rolled onto my

back, my naked breasts covered loosely by the sheets. My nipples had never felt better than when he'd had them in his hot mouth, his tongue dragging over the hardened buds until I'd begun shaking. Just thinking about how his cock had filled me so completely had me squirming for more.

Damn, that man knew how to treat a woman's body.

The sheets were warm on my side of the bed. I slid a foot to his side, finding the cotton cold. When had he gotten up? How long had I been sleeping?

I cracked my eyes open, clutching the sheet to my chest as I sat up. The window blinds were closed, but sunshine streamed through the gaps in the wooden slats. I squinted, waiting for my eyes to adjust to the light.

Then I inspected Dakota's bedroom.

The bed sat right in the middle of the room across from a door that led to a bathroom. The closet was to my left. One of the bypass doors was open, revealing Dakota's shirts on wire hangers and his jeans folded and stacked on the top shelves.

That closet wouldn't hold a tenth of my clothes, let alone my shoes. In fact, this room was about the size of my entire walk-in closet in my penthouse.

But it was a nice room. The floors were wooden, stained a warm, light brown. The walls were a simple off-white offset by white trim. Clearly, these weren't the original finishes, meaning either Dakota or Xavier had made some upgrades. I was guessing Dakota.

His bed sheets were a stark white, his quilt a thick and heavy charcoal cotton. This room had only the basics—a bed, one nightstand and a reading lamp. There wasn't even a television. It was masculine and simple, much like the man himself.

Honestly, the decor didn't matter much. I was just glad he'd had the essentials for a night of debauchery. His condoms were stashed in the nightstand. The mattress was soft and he'd used a down pillow to prop up my hips as he knelt above me, sliding into my deepest places with long, languid strokes.

A rush of desire settled in my core. Where was he?

Swinging my feet over the edge of the bed, I dropped the sheet and let the cool air rush over my bare skin as I tiptoed to the bathroom. I did a little spin before the doorway. The floor was smooth and my bare feet skimmed across its surface like ice.

On the vanity next to the sink sat a tube of toothpaste and an unopened toothbrush. I smiled as I ripped it open and used it to brush my teeth with Dakota's minty toothpaste.

Did he do this a lot? Did he bring women home from the bar often? Was that why he kept extra toothbrushes on hand? Curiosity got the best of me and I opened the three drawers on each side of the vanity.

They were filled with extra hand towels, some shaving cream, a box of Q-Tips and some other bathroom necessities. But there wasn't a stash of new toothbrushes anywhere to be found.

Smiling that this one must have just been an extra, I went back to the mirror with my toothbrush. When I was finished, I dropped it in the container next to his.

Maybe I'd use it again this week.

I hoped so. Because now that I'd had him, I was addicted to Dakota. More so than I'd ever been to a man, including both of my ex-husbands.

He'd given me the best sex of my entire life, and I *had* to have more. I needed something to satisfy me for a while, because when I went back to the city, I was taking a long break from men.

Memories of Dakota were going to keep me company for the foreseeable future.

After my divorce from Bryson, Logan had encouraged me to lay off men for a while. His advice had fallen on deaf ears because I'd already met Jay and was completely infatuated in my new relationship.

And look how that one had ended.

So it was time to try a new tactic, and since my brother was one of the smartest people I knew, I was giving his advice a try. Once I left Montana, I was going to be single for a change.

Dakota wasn't the right man, but he was a good man. He was refreshing. If I found a good man once, maybe I'd find another someday.

Or he could find me.

I walked back to Dakota's room, smiling at the rumpled bedsheets. They were definitely going to need washing. But I didn't know how to use a washing machine or a dryer, so I'd have to ask him for help.

Or, better yet, we could just get them even dirtier. Then he could teach me how to do laundry.

I walked over to the column of drawers inside his closet and opened the top one, searching for something to wear. I found a pair of thick, brown wool socks. I took them, along with a long-sleeved flannel, and pulled them both on.

Then I grabbed one last thing from the nightstand before going in search of my new lover.

At the door, I looked both ways down the hallway, reorienting myself with the house. One direction led to another bedroom and bathroom. The other led down a long hallway that opened up into a living room.

I skimmed my hands over the cool leather sofa as I passed through the living room. All of the furniture was angled at the large television mounted on the wall. Surround sound speakers were flush mounted on the walls and ceiling. The two lounge chairs facing the TV made me cringe.

They weren't exactly ugly—but they weren't pretty either. Their brown leather matched the couch, clearly part of a set. But they were lounge chairs, complete with handles to kick up the footrests and built-in cup holders.

They were probably comfortable and obviously practical for watching Monday Night Football. None of those qualities had ever ranked high on my interior design checklists.

With no sign of Dakota, I kept exploring.

I walked toward the kitchen located at the front of the house. It was a galley style with clean white cabinets and quartz countertops. At the far end, there were two doors. I assumed one led to a basement and the other to the garage.

We'd come through the exterior back door last night and through the living room. He'd parked his truck in a detached shop behind his house. I doubted he'd left me here alone, and since going to check to see if his truck was where we'd left it meant walking outside in the snow, I opted for the basement first.

The temperature dropped as I opened the door and took the first few stairs. Through the darkness, I could make out a landing at the bottom in the faint light. A chill ran over my arms, and I wrapped them around my middle.

"Dakota? Are you down there?"

When I didn't get an answer, I turned and scurried back upstairs, closing the door behind me quickly. Basements had scared me ever since I was nine and I'd snuck into our theater room at home where Logan and some of his friends had been watching a horror movie.

I'd hidden behind a couch, watching the movie even though I was supposed to have been in bed. Logan had found me when I'd screamed at the woman getting hacked to pieces on the screen.

My brother had whisked me away to my room, then stayed with me all night simply because I'd asked him to. He'd missed his sleepover with his friends to care for me.

I wasn't sure where I'd left my phone last night, but as soon as I found it, I was going to send Logan a text. I'd never said thank you for that night.

Thank you had been missing a lot from my vocabulary.

With no sign of Dakota in the basement, I walked to the other door. The moment I got close, I heard music blaring from the other side.

Carefully, I pulled it open and peeked through the crack.

Dakota was in the center of his garage, lying on a workout bench. He'd converted the garage to a gym.

Free weights were all lined up on racks against one wall. He'd put in mirrors on a few walls and mats all across the floors. An elliptical machine squatted in one corner, a treadmill by its side.

I opened the door farther, leaning against the frame as Dakota bench-pressed a bar with two black weights on each end.

He wore only a pair of shorts, leaving his sweaty chest bare. The muscles of his arms bunched and shook as he brought the bar to his pecks, then pushed it up on an exhale. I swallowed hard, my pulse racing at the sight of his washboard abs.

Last night, we'd had sex with the lights off. Today, I wouldn't be making the same mistake. I wanted the visuals to go along with the feelings.

Rep after rep Dakota pushed himself. Finally, he set the bar on the rest behind his head and sat up. He dragged his fingers through his sweaty hair, separating the black streaks with his fingers.

He reached for the floor, swiping a towel to dry his face. Then he swapped it for the water bottle by his feet, squirting a long stream of water into his mouth.

His tennis shoes were on, but he hadn't done up the laces. The white strings draped loosely down to the black rubber mats.

"Morning." His greeting carried over the loud music. He didn't turn, but he must have caught me in the mirror.

"Hi." I pushed off the doorway and went down the three steps to the garage floor. I walked to the speaker in the corner, pausing the angry rock music.

The silence in the room was instant and startling. I could hear Dakota's chest heave as he took another drink of water and regained his breath.

"This is nice." I swung a hand out to indicate the gym.

"There aren't any gyms in town. Had to make my own." He turned away from me, watching me from the mirror. "Nice shirt."

"It's a little big." The sleeves hung past my fingertips and the hem hit me midthigh.

"Your clothes are in the laundry room."

"Okay." Was that a hint for me to go put them on? If it was, I pretended to miss it.

I went right to the bench and put a knee on the seat

between Dakota's legs. It forced his gaze away from the mirror.

He leaned back, his dark, assessing eyes holding mine. They didn't give anything away, just like the first time I'd seen him.

Dakota had put up some guards since last night. Maybe he'd disappeared to this gym so he wouldn't wake up next to me in his bed.

"What time do we have to be at the bar?" I ran my fingertips through the sweaty strands of his hair by his ear.

"We're closed today." His voice was rough and hoarse.

I hummed. "So are you in?"

"In for what?"

"A week of me."

His eyes flashed, the wariness turning to heat. "Think that's smart?"

"I can walk away from this as friends. Can you?"

He nodded. "Not a problem."

"Then it's brilliant." I dropped my mouth onto his, playing at it with my tongue. The sweat on his top lip was salty.

Dakota's hands dug into my hips, kneading my soft curves before slipping under the hem of his shirt. When he found nothing but bare skin, his tongue dove into my mouth.

I ran my hands down his shoulders and over his back. I towered over him on the bench, forcing him to rise up to meet me.

The skin on his fingers was coarse against the soft flesh of my ass as he palmed it, urging me closer. His spicy scent surrounded us, stronger now that it was mixed with sweat.

My hands slid down the damp plains of his back, fitting to the muscles that were just as chiseled as his abs. Then I picked my knee up and straddled him before dropping my center to his.

The mesh fabric of his shorts didn't conceal the iron rod

between us. I slipped a hand down his front, diving under the elastic waistband and gripping his silky shaft, stroking as he moaned into my mouth.

"Condom." Dakota started to rise but I gave him all my weight, squeezing his cock harder.

"Shirt pocket," I panted into his mouth.

The corners of his lips turned up against mine as he went for the pocket. The sound of ripping foil, racing hearts and shuddered breaths echoed through the room.

Dakota lifted up slightly, using one arm to keep me pressed against him as the other moved around in hurried motions to strip down his shorts.

I let go of his shaft, took the condom from his fingers and rolled it onto his hardness. When it was in place, he gripped my hips, steadying me, before lifting me up and planting me right on his throbbing cock.

"Fuck," he groaned as I gasped.

"You feel so good." My head lolled to the side as I stretched around him. "So, so good."

His luscious mouth latched on to my collarbone, pushing the flannel out of the way. He sucked hard as he picked me up and brought me back down onto his cock again. Hard.

That move earned him a hiss.

He did it again five times before his arms dropped to his sides and he let out a huff. "My arms are dead. Let's shift."

"Okay," I breathed.

He picked me up, spun us both around and laid me down on the bench, hovering over me with his thick, long cock still rooted deep. Then he tilted up my hips, testing the angle with one long pull and deep plunge.

"Yessss." My entire body nearly came off the bench. How

he'd figured out so quickly to keep my hips up I had no idea. But it was the only way he'd fit that deep.

Last night's escapades had made me sensitive this morning, but the little bit of pain mixed with the intense pleasure had me coiled and ready to explode.

If Dakota lived in New York, I'd be tempted to have this every single day. So it was a good thing we had a limit on this. It was a good thing that a relationship was out of the question.

It's a good thing.

His strokes got faster, his arms holding my legs just underneath my knees. With every thrust forward, he pulled me onto him. The sound of slapping skin, his grunts and my gasps chased away the silence from the gym.

The collar of my flannel dipped over a shoulder as Dakota rocked us back and forth on the bench. With every bounce, the material fell sideways until one of my nipples worked free.

Dakota spotted it and planted himself deep. Then he bent over me, taking my nipple in between his lips and sucking it hard.

"Oh god." My hands went right into his hair, tugging at the silky strands.

He nipped at the side of my breast, then licked my skin before standing tall again. As he withdrew from me, a wicked gleam settled into his black eyes right before he slammed home, shaking the bench and the bar behind it.

"Touch yourself," Dakota commanded. "Come around me."

I nodded, letting one hand drift to my exposed nipple. Then the other slipped down my stomach to my clit. I put the pad of my middle finger on the hard nub, circling just twice before the shaking in my legs set in.

"That's it, babe. Again."

I circled again, this time moaning through shallow breaths. My eyes squeezed closed as I rubbed my clit again, feeling the build.

"Come."

I did on command, letting go as white spots consumed my vision. My back arched off the bench, the hand on my nipple flying to the bar behind my head to hold on so I wouldn't fall over.

Dakota shuttered as I clenched around him, the pleasure washing over me in body-racking waves. The grip he had on my calves tightened as he thrust one more time and roared his own release into the condom.

We were both boneless and weak when he set my legs down. I watched through the mirror as he kicked off his shoes and shorts, then walked naked to a trash can in the corner to dispose of the condom.

He came back, still semihard. My eyes widened at his big cock hanging thick down his thigh.

"Had enough?" He held out a hand and helped me from the bench.

I grinned and shook my head.

That wicked gleam turned into a smirk as he reached for the collar of my flannel shirt. One rip and the few buttons I'd done up went popping. He yanked hard enough for the seams to split. The flannel was stripped from my shoulders and went floating to the floor.

The corner of his sexy mouth lifted. "I never liked that shirt."

"This is much better." I giggled. "Now we match."

He chuckled, circling me with his arms and bringing his

mouth to mine. Then he picked me up and carried me back inside and to his bed.

Where we did not do laundry with his sheets.

"You want to go home?"

I shook my head against his chest. "Can I stay here?"

"Sure." He drew another circle on the small of my back.

I traced an invisible star around one of his brown nipples.

After we'd spent the rest of the morning in bed, we'd gotten up to shower and eat. I'd never had macaroni and cheese from the blue box before, something Dakota had told me was important. So he'd made me lunch and we'd eaten it in his lounge chairs.

I hated to admit they were comfortable and the drink holders convenient.

Dakota and I had done the dishes, then he'd taken me back into the living room. He'd flipped on the TV and pulled me on top of him on the couch as an action movie played in the background.

After our shower, I'd paired one of his T-shirts with a pair of sweats that were rolled three times at the waist. He'd donned nearly the same. But even clothed, we'd found a way to touch one another's skin.

I had my hand up the front of his T-shirt while he had his under the back hem of mine.

Neither of us paid much attention to the movie. I expected in another thirty minutes I'd be fast asleep.

"How'd your family make their money?"

My hand froze on Dakota's chest.

Money? He wanted to know about my money? Had I really read him that wrong?

I'd been so confident that he was different than the others. I'd been sure he hadn't cared at all about my money. But he hadn't waited long at all to bring it up.

I guess in that regard, he was different. My exes had all waited at least a month before asking about my money. They'd pretended to be interested in me.

But Dakota just cut right to the chase.

I pulled my hand from his shirt and moved to leave the couch, but the moment he sensed me about to stand, his arms pinned me tight to his chest.

"What's wrong?"

"Nothing." I tried to get away again but he had me trapped.

"Sofia," he warned.

"Dakota," I mimicked.

"Talk to me, babe. I just asked a simple question. Why are you trying to bolt?"

"Was it a simple question?"

"What are you talking about?"

"Money," I huffed. "It always comes down to money."

Dakota relaxed his arms, but only so he could twist us around, pinning me beneath him on the couch. "You think I want your money?"

"Why else would you ask about my family's money?"

He frowned. "Before me, have you ever been fucked by a real man?"

"What are you talking about?"

"A real man. Have you ever fucked one?"

"I'm confused."

"Then the answer is no, you haven't. By the end of this

week, I'm going to be inside you enough so you can start to tell the difference."

I blinked up at him, completely baffled. "What?"

"A real man doesn't fuck you for your money. He fucks you because you're gorgeous. Because you come like a rocket. Because you have eyes that show him everything you're feeling. He fucks you because nothing has ever felt better."

"Oh."

"Yeah, *oh*. I don't give a shit about your money." With that, he let me go and stood, his fists clenched at his sides. "I was just curious. But I'll just ask your brother someday."

Damn it. He *was* different. I wouldn't make the mistake of misjudging Dakota again.

Before he could walk away, I reached out and took his wrist. Then I looked up to him, hoping what he'd said was true—that he could read the apology in my eyes.

He sighed, shaking his head and relaxing his fists. Then he lay back down on the couch, positioning us both back in the place we'd been before.

I curled back into his side, slipped my hand under his shirt and placed my palm on his heart.

"My great-great-grandfather bought a small bakery in the city at the turn of the century. When that business made a profit, he bought another. And another. Until he'd built up his wealth."

He'd started small with that bakery and then a flower shop. After some restaurants, he'd expanded into real estate developments. That had bloomed into investments in steel factories and shipping companies. Now, Kendrick Enterprises had billons of dollars under its umbrella and businesses of all shapes and sizes.

"I like that." Dakota slipped his hand back under the hem of my shirt, redrawing circles. "One guy building that legacy for his family. Starting small. Earning it all himself."

"I like that too." It was something I'd always taken pride in, that my family had amassed such wealth because so many of the Kendricks were driven and smart. It may have missed me, but that didn't mean I wasn't proud of my name and the accomplishments of my family.

Each generation had doubled the fortune from the previous company's leader. My father had nearly tripled Pop's success. And Aubrey was poised to put all the Kendrick men to shame.

I was proud of my sister, something—like thank you—I hadn't said enough.

But while I'd missed thank-yous simply because I was more concerned with myself than others, I was scared to tell Aubrey that I admired her success. Because while I could compliment her for hours, she had nothing to compliment back.

I'd done nothing to make Aubrey proud.

So far, I had gone through life existing off my family's money and, since I'd turned thirty, my multimillion-dollar trust fund. It was something all of the direct descendants of my great-great-grandfather received.

I liked to imagine that my great-great-grandfather was a lot like Dakota. Ambitious. Hard-working. An opportunist.

Maybe he'd teach me more than what it was like to be with a real man. Maybe he'd teach me a little something about those qualities too. Maybe he'd teach me to stop hiding behind my money and do something with my life.

Maybe, in a small way, he already had.

"Thank you," I said against his chest.

"For what?"

"I don't know. But I wanted to say it."

eight

DAKOTA

"IS THERE A REASON YOU'RE CRAWLING ON ME?" I STOPPED IN the middle of the staircase leading to the basement.

Sofia was on the step behind me. Her hands were clinging to my shoulders and her front was pressed against my back like she was ready to hop on up. "I don't like basements."

I peeled one of her hands off my T-shirt then threaded my fingers with hers. "Come on."

After she'd told me about her family's history, we'd fallen asleep on the couch. When we'd woken up, she'd asked to see more of my house, so I'd followed her around as she'd explored. When she'd hit the kitchen, Sofia had shot a wary glance at the basement door.

I'd practically had to pull her through its frame.

She clung to my hand, staying close all the way to the bottom step.

I flicked on the lights, illuminating a short hall on our right. "There's another guest room and bathroom on this side."

"It's nice." She walked down the hall, going into the bedroom. As she looked around, she ran her fingers over the quilt I'd put on the bed. Then she peered into the attached bathroom. "Did you remodel this yourself?"

I nodded. "Yep. Took me forever, but I saved a fortune doing it myself in my free time." I didn't need the room for guests. I rarely had them. But I'd fixed it all up in case I wanted to sell the place one day.

"You're very . . . handy." She wagged her eyebrows, glancing at my fingers.

I'd had them all over her intimate places earlier. And I planned to have them there again after we regained some energy.

"The other side isn't as nice." I turned away from the room, walking down the hall toward the other half of the basement. If we stayed in that bedroom, we'd be using it. So I went to a room that had no temptations other than the woman herself.

Sofia followed, staying close to my back as she waited for me to turn on the lights. When I did, she peered past me and giggled. "Oh my god. You're a hoarder."

I chuckled as she stepped into the storage room. It was dark, despite the bare light bulbs in three sockets. The ceiling was raw and unfinished. The walls were just pink insulation batting between two-by-four studs. The cement floor was barely visible underneath all of the stuff I'd shoved in here.

"What is all of this stuff?" she asked.

"Junk mostly. I've got a few rental properties up in Kalispell. I bought each cheap and part of that was because they'd been full of old shit. Anything I thought could be salvaged I brought here."

"Wow." She took in the mirror propped up against a wall then the antique clock I'd stacked on a dresser. Neither was expensive, but with a little cleaning, I'd be able to sell them to someone who wanted that vintage look.

"One of the places I bought *was* owned by a hoarder," I told her. "The woman died and it took days for anyone to notice."

Sofia's face soured. "Gross."

"Yeah. Smelled pretty bad. Almost everything she had was trashed, but there were some good pieces in there."

"This is cool." She stopped in front of a piano. "Does it work?"

I shrugged. "Don't know. It makes noise but I don't know if it's any good."

She pulled out the bench, but when she saw the thick layer of dust on the seat, she pushed it back in. But the dust didn't scare her away from the keys. She lifted up the cover, bent at the waist to set her hands in place and played the beginning of an unfamiliar tune.

"It just needs to be tuned." She pulled her fingers away, then returned the cover before wiping her hands clean. "But it has a nice tone."

"Good to know." That piano hadn't been a priority, but now that I knew it worked, I'd get someone in to fix it up. Maybe paired with a few other sales from my storage room, I'd have enough to get an offer in on my next property.

"You're good." I gestured to the piano.

"Not really. I haven't played in ages."

"Why not?"

"I don't know." She shrugged. "I took lessons for years."

"When was the last time you played?"

She thought about it for a moment. "My last lesson."

That was the same thing she'd said about her foreign languages. Sofia had taken all of these lessons to learn incredible things, but I doubted it was because she'd wanted to.

"Rental properties, huh?" she asked, still maneuvering through the crowded room.

"Yep." I leaned against the door.

"So you buy these gross places, fix them up and rent them out?"

"Pretty much. Eventually, I hope to have the capital to just buy them. Fixing them up is a bitch." But for now, I did it all to save up for the next property since I couldn't afford a construction crew.

"How long will you keep the rentals?"

I shrugged. "Depends on the market. As long as the rental income can pay for the mortgage, I'll keep them. Let them appreciate. If we have a boom in the market, I might sell."

"There's a lot of opportunity in real estate. That's smart."

"Hope so." I was counting on it to fund my future. I liked working at the bar, but I wasn't going to do it past my thirties. In fifteen years, I wanted to have enough properties that managing them was my only job. "They're going to fund my retirement. Free me up so I can quit bartending and maybe do some traveling."

"I like it." Sofia passed a stack of boxes, scanned the room once more, then walked to me at the door. She placed her hands on my waist, sliding them underneath the hem of my T-shirt. "Anything left to show me on the tour?"

"Nope. You've seen the whole place." I ran my fingers over her hair then stole a soft kiss.

She leaned into my body, deepening the kiss. Her hands drifted down to my ass, squeezing hard. "Want to show me your bedroom again?"

I grinned against her lips. "After dinner."

"I'm not hungry."

"Then we'd better go back to Logan and Thea's."

"Oh." Her hands dropped away from my sweats. She

backed away, her gaze falling to the floor. "O-okay. Right. I should get back. Get some sleep."

I took her hand, pulling her back into my arms. "You're sleeping here. I just thought you might want to stop by and pick up a change of clothes for tomorrow."

"You're not kicking me out?"

"Until you leave for New York, you're in my bed. You good with that?"

She smiled. "Perfect."

With Sofia staring out her window of my truck, I drove us through the quiet streets of Lark Cove. Most people were probably at home, enjoying the holiday. It had snowed this morning and the streets hadn't been plowed. Ours was the only set of tire tracks in the fresh powder.

"I haven't spent much time on this side of town." Sofia scanned the homes as we passed them by.

"It's where most people who are here year-round live."

The highway divided Lark Cove in two. Most of the homes along the lake were larger and owned by people who came here for summer or winter vacations. But the locals and businesses were located on my side of town.

The seventies- and eighties-style ramblers and split-level homes were organized in square blocks. Homes were close enough that you could smell your neighbors' barbeque from three houses down.

These were safe streets, where kids rode their bikes down the roads and played until sunset. The school was in the center of it all. The playground was open to the kids year-round.

The basketball courts were available for us adults to use for our games.

In a way, this part of Lark Cove reminded me of my home-town on the reservation. I'd grown up on a street similar to the one where I lived now. My family hadn't felt the poverty that so often plagued my people.

One day, I wanted to give back to that area and those not as fortunate. Maybe fix up a couple places on the reservation and rent them out to a couple families who'd fallen down on their luck.

If they'd let me.

It was one of the many reasons my father was so upset that I'd left the reservation. He'd expected me to follow in his foot-steps, to take a job improving the lives of our tribal members. To help those Blackfeet people who needed it get back on their feet.

In Dad's eyes, I'd left and turned my back on those respon-sibilities. He couldn't see that I might be able to do more for them if I wasn't actually living there.

That being two hours away meant I could help twice the people.

We reached the highway and I drove toward Logan and Thea's place. The evening sun had almost set, and there was only a little light left on the frozen lake. The quiet road to their house was just as peaceful as the sleepy streets in town.

"I forgot to tell you thanks the other night," Sofia said as we pulled into the driveway.

"For what?"

"For carrying me inside. That was sweet."

"You were dead to the world, babe. There wasn't much sweet about it. I needed you out of my truck."

She laughed. "Liar. You're sweet."

I winked, opening my door first. Then I hustled around the truck to help her out. She shivered as we went to the door, and she pulled a key from her pocket. The minute we got inside, I took a deep breath.

Thea and Logan's house always smelled good. The few times I'd been here, I hadn't been able to get enough. I wasn't sure if it was the housekeeper's doing, but it always smelled like fresh wood polish and vanilla.

"I'll hurry." Sofia walked through the kitchen, going right for the guest bedroom down a hall.

"Take your time," I said, but before she was out of my sight, I called her name. "Sofia."

"Yeah?"

"Pack all your stuff."

She nodded, blushing a bit. "Okay."

I was determined to enjoy the rest of our days together, and she wasn't sleeping anywhere but in my bed.

I wandered through the house as she disappeared to collect her things. I went into the living room, circling the room until I stopped in front of the fireplace. Thea had filled the mantel with a row of framed pictures. They were mostly pictures of the kids, but there was one of her, Hazel and Jackson at the bar from way back when. And there was one group shot of the Kendrick family.

I found Sofia in the photo instantly.

She had a smile on, but it was different than the one I'd gotten used to in the last few days.

She wasn't showing her teeth, and it didn't reach her eyes. The smile was posed and perfect—too perfect.

Her chin was extended and her head tilted ever so slightly to the right, giving the camera a certain angle. Her shoulders were pinned back, and her arms were poised at her sides. Everyone else in the picture looked relaxed with their arms around the people next to them.

But she stood apart from her family.

Her parents were in the middle of the photo. Aubrey was next to their father. Logan and Thea were on the other side with an elderly woman I assumed was Sofia's grandmother. The kids were scattered around the adults' legs.

Everyone was together, except her. There was a visible space between Sofia and Aubrey. Between her and the rest of the family. Why was that?

The woman in the picture looked like the princess I'd seen walk into the bar on that first day. She wore the role proudly in the photo, flaunting her black dress and thick jewelry while the rest of the family wore light clothes and pants. It was like she had this image she had to portray, even with her family.

Maybe especially with her family.

"Ready." Sofia came into the living room with two large suitcases in tow.

I left the picture and went to get her bags. "Why am I not surprised you packed more clothes for a ten-day vacation than I own altogether?"

"I was gone the day they taught packing light in charm school."

I laughed, leading the way out of the house. While she climbed inside the truck, I loaded up her bags into the backseat. Then I drove us to Bob's Diner, the only other place in town that served food besides the bar.

And the only place in town open on New Year's Day.

We walked into the restaurant, and I waved to the waitress

as we slid into a booth. The place was deserted except for us, but I picked a place along the far back wall because Edith was known for gossiping. I didn't want her to overhear anything Sofia and I had to talk about.

She came over and took our cheeseburger order then went back to the kitchen, where I assumed Bob was holed up. The man loved cooking, but he hated dealing with customers.

"So your uncle lives here. Do you have other family in town?" Sofia asked after Edith brought over our water glasses. Sofia frowned at the lemon wedge on its rim.

"No, my family all lives on the reservation." I took her lemon wedge and plopped it into my glass.

"Thanks. I prefer lime."

I chuckled. "Figured that one out two days ago."

"What do they do?" she asked. "Your parents?"

"My dad works for the Blackfeet Land Department and is on the tribal council. My mom is retired now and watches my sisters' kids during the day, but she used to run the heritage center."

"Interesting. I've never been on a reservation before. What's it like?"

I shrugged. "Like any other town. It's got its good parts and bad."

"You have sisters?"

"Yep. Two younger sisters. Rozene and Koko."

"Then you're like Logan. Do your sisters cause you stress too?"

"They do. It's . . . complicated."

Sofia nodded, settling for my one-word explanation.

Her questions were innocent enough, but only a few people knew about the dynamic in our family. I didn't talk about it to anyone in Lark Cove except Xavier and Hazel, mostly because it was difficult for outsiders to understand.

But I had an urge to delve deeper, to let Sofia see beneath the surface.

"My family doesn't approve of me living off the reservation."

Her eyebrows came together. "Why?"

"There's a bunch of reasons. Tradition. Loyalty. Politics. Take your pick."

"Politics?"

I nodded. "Have you ever heard of blood quantum?"

"No."

"It's basically the amount of pure Blackfeet blood you have. My family has one of the strongest bloodlines left in the world. To keep it simple, you could say I'm as close to a full-blood Blackfeet, which is very rare these days."

"Interesting." She sipped her water. "How does that lead to complicated?"

"There has been an ongoing debate on the reservation for the last decade about who can enroll with the tribe, who can be officially deemed part of the Blackfeet Nation. In the Blackfeet constitution, it's based on blood quantum. Basically, you have to have a certain percentage of Blackfeet blood to be considered part of the tribe. Others are fighting to amend the constitution and remove the blood quantum requirement. Make it more inclusive just based on lineal descent."

"Why is that important?"

"Because if you're an enrolled member of the tribe, you get certain benefits. Subsidized health care. Educational grants. Payments. The right to vote in tribal elections or hold an elected office."

"I see." She nodded. "Which side of the argument are you on?"

"Neither. I see pros and cons to each side of the argument. But since my parents are strongly opposed to open enrollment—removing the blood quantum stipulation—me not picking their side caused a rift."

"So because of political reasons, you don't get along with your family?"

I sighed. "That's a piece of it. My parents had hoped I'd eventually become part of the tribal council. Support their argument. But mostly, they want me to carry on the family line. Before my sisters got married, they were each given a list of the men they could have children with that wouldn't dilute our heritage."

"What?" Her mouth fell open. "That's insane. What if they fell in love with someone else?"

"They wouldn't have even let themselves get close to someone who wasn't an option. Their husbands are both nice guys. They have the same stance on things. So it works for them."

"But not you? Did you meet someone they didn't approve of or something?"

I shook my head. "No. But I didn't want the pressure to get married or get the right job or get on board with the right political beliefs. As I got older, it just got more suffocating. My family, they're good people. They just have this idea of how life should be. I had a different idea. We clashed."

We clashed about things so fundamental it was hard to find common ground anymore.

As a young man, I'd always thought I'd have kids. Children were an important part of our culture and heritage, and I'd always pictured myself as a father one day. But then the pressure to have them with the right woman had set in.

I'd only been a freshman in high school when Dad had sat me down and told me that when I was ready to mate, I had to be sure to wear a condom with the women who weren't the right ones.

Two of his friends on the tribal council had daughters around my age. Dad had told me that if I happened to forget a condom with them, it wouldn't be the end of the world.

That had just been the beginning.

"When I came back from the dude ranch, things got worse and worse at home. Dad and I were arguing almost every day about things. Mom and my sisters were constantly nagging at me to settle down. Finally, I couldn't take it anymore. So I left."

I'd called up Xavier and he'd given me an escape.

His reasons for leaving the reservation had been similar. The pressure from my grandmother and his brother—my father—to be a certain person and do certain things had driven him away.

So when I'd called him out of the blue, he'd understood.

Xavier hadn't been around a lot when I'd grown up, but he'd made it a point to know me and my sisters, even though he'd had his own rift with my father.

I wasn't sure what Dad hated more: that I'd left, or that I'd called Xavier for help.

"Is it like that for everyone on the reservation?" Sofia asked.

"No. I don't mean to make it sound like they're prejudiced. They aren't at all. They just love our people. Our culture is ingrained in them so deeply, to them it's everything. And they fight to protect it. Part of that is defending it fiercely. A son who defies it gets put through his paces, if that makes sense."

"It does." She nodded. "So what would happen if you had

kids who weren't—I don't know if it's the right term, but—full blood?"

"Nothing," I muttered. "That's the thing. They'd be kids. They'd be free to live however they wanted. They'd have enough blood quantum to be part of the tribe. But my parents don't see it quite like that. They were raised to believe that marrying a Blackfeet partner was the best way. Just like their parents before them. And their parents before that. They don't see why I *wouldn't* want to do the same. They're blinded by tradition and pride. By fear. They're terrified that our people's traditions are being forgotten."

"That's so sad."

"Yeah. It is."

She reached across the table and covered my hand in hers. "Sorry."

"I've come to terms with it."

I'd made my decisions and set my future in stone.

No wife. No kids. It was easier that way.

Edith came over carrying two large plates, each with a mound of fries stacked next to a thick cheeseburger. She set them down, ending the conversation about my family.

"This is bigger than my face." Sofia eyed the cheeseburger, unsure of how to pick it up.

"Like this." I gripped my burger with both hands, squishing down the bun. Then I opened wide and took a huge bite. Grease dripped onto my plate as I held the burger and chewed.

Sofia stared at me for a long moment, then hesitantly copied my movements until her cheeks were bulging, and she moaned at that first bite.

"Good?"

She nodded, swallowing that bite. "I haven't had a

cheeseburger in years."

"I have one at least once a week."

"I'm going to need to use your gym in the morning." She dove in for another bite.

"Don't worry. I'll work it all off of you tonight."

She raised an eyebrow as she chewed. A sexy smirk played at the corner of her lips.

If I were to ever break my own rules and have kids, Sofia would be fun to share that adventure with.

I took another bite, shaking that thought away. Blocking it out for good.

My future was planned. I knew what I wanted and where I was going.

There was no use questioning it.

Not even for a woman like Sofia Kendrick.

nine

SOFIA

"YOU DON'T SMILE ENOUGH."

Dakota kept his eyes on the cutting board as he diced a green pepper. His mouth was set in a serious line. "You smile too much."

I forced the corners of my mouth down. "You can't criticize someone for smiling too much."

"But it's okay to tell someone they don't smile enough?"

"Yes."

"Why?" he shot back.

"I, uh, I don't know. It just is. Smiling is nice."

He shrugged, sliding the pieces of green pepper off the cutting board and into a bowl. Then he took the onion he'd set out earlier and began dicing it too. "Grab the eggs. Start cracking them into a bowl."

"Not until you smile."

"I'm not smiling."

I crossed my arms over my chest. "Then I'm not cracking eggs."

"I'll just do it myself."

"If you do it yourself, that kind of defeats the point of a cooking lesson, don't you think?"

"Then grab the eggs, babe."

"Not until you smile."

He shook his head.

"Why?" I asked. "You haven't smiled all morning."

"Wrong. I smiled at you in the shower. Remember? It was right after I came all over your tits."

My cheeks flushed as I remembered the feel of his hot spurts coating my nipples. I'd been on my knees, ready to swallow his release when Dakota had pulled his cock out of my mouth and surprised me with a shower of his own.

"Whatever." I ignored the pulsing in my core. "That was a grin, not a smile. A smile includes teeth."

The corner of his mouth twitched, but he still wouldn't give it up.

"Smile."

"No."

"Smile," I insisted.

"Now I'm not going to smile all day."

"What? Why?"

He smirked. "Because you want it so bad, it'll be fun torturing you."

"Fine." I pushed away from the counter and went to the refrigerator, grabbing the carton of eggs. "But you should know I'm withholding sex until you smile."

Dakota's chest shook with a silent laugh. There was a tiny dimple forming at the corner of his mouth, but he took a breath, shoving all humor aside and concentrating on the onion.

"You're the worst," I muttered, taking a bowl from the cupboard.

"Yeah? And you'll break first."

"What?" I cocked a hip. "Never."

He put down his knife and turned to me. Then he took one step forward, coming right into my space and forcing me to lean back. His abs pushed against mine. His hips pressed flush against my own so tight I could feel the bulge beneath his sweatpants. And his nose hovered just a fraction of an inch away from my cheek.

"I'll smile after I fuck you on the counter."

My heart skipped as his breath floated across my skin.

"What do you say, princess?" He dropped his mouth and slowly licked the shell of my ear. "How badly do you want that smile?"

"Damn you," I whispered.

His chest rumbled with a laugh. "That a yes?"

I shook my head as my fingers toyed with the hem of his T-shirt. "Smile first, then fuck me on the counter."

"Nope." In a flash, he was gone, the cold air rushing into the space where he'd been standing, causing goose bumps to tickle my forearms.

"Wha—seriously?"

He picked up the knife and went back to the onion. "Hustle with the eggs. They need to go in first."

I scowled. "This is the worst cooking lesson in the history of the world."

I wasn't sure how the man could laugh without smiling, but he did. Dakota's rumble filled the kitchen, echoing off the cabinets.

The corner of my lips turned up as I took an egg from the carton. I cracked the shell on the side of the bowl, like he'd showed me how to do two mornings ago, then plopped the yolk and whites in the dish before tossing the shell into the sink.

We'd started with the basics for breakfast lessons over the

past two days, simple scrambled eggs, bacon and toast. But to-day, he was graduating me to an omelet.

"How many?" I asked.

"Do six. We'll make one and split it."

I nodded, concentrating on the eggs so I didn't get any shell in the bowl. When they were cracked, I splashed in some milk then whipped them up with a fork.

My personal chef, Carrie, would be so proud if she could see me now. I thought about taking a selfie and sending it to her, but then I realized she was on vacation too. She probably didn't want to hear from her boss.

"What's next?" I asked.

"Dump those into the pan, but instead of stirring them, we'll let them sit until they firm up."

"Okay." I followed his instruction, pouring the beaten eggs into the pan where he'd already melted a tablespoon of butter.

From the fridge, Dakota pulled out some ham and a block of cheese. I dug out the grater, having learned how to use it yesterday, and began shredding some cheese onto a plate.

"Why do you want to see me smile?" Dakota asked as he diced some ham.

"Just because."

The real reason was going to stay my little secret.

Because I'd been trying to memorize it over the past three days. I wanted to see it enough while I was here that I could picture it when I was gone.

When I remembered Dakota years from now, I wanted it to be with him smiling. But he didn't smile often, and I wasn't the type to see something once and commit it permanently. A picture would be better, but if he wouldn't smile for me, the chances of getting it on my phone weren't good.

He put down the knife again and covered my hands with his own, interrupting my cheese grating. "Tell me."

"It makes me happy to see you smile."

It was the truth. Part of it, at least.

Dakota's eyes searched mine for a long moment, then his soft lips parted, revealing his straight, white teeth in an easy smile.

My heart stuttered, thumping hard as it worked back to its regular rhythm.

Dakota's smile was something else. It was beautiful. It was as bold and mesmerizing as everything else about the man.

And he'd given it to me because it made me happy.

The sharp burn in my throat made me panic—this was not the time to cry. So I concentrated on one detail of Dakota's smile, committing it to memory.

He had such nice teeth. I didn't need a thousand more smiles to remember them. Like most people, the canines were pointed and slightly longer than the front four. But Dakota's were more pronounced.

"You have vampire teeth."

He chuckled, his smile widening. "What?"

"These ones." I reached out and touched the sharp tip of his incisor. "They're long. Almost like vampire teeth."

Dakota's tongue darted out and touched my finger. I dropped it from his mouth as he lowered his head, ducking under my chin and setting his lips on the soft flesh of my neck. He nipped at me with his pointed teeth, my breath catching as he licked the spot of the careful bite.

"Do it again," I whispered.

He lifted, moving in a flash to the other side of my neck. Then he nipped and licked me again. "Breakfast?"

I shook my head, letting my eyes fall shut and my head loll to the side.

Dakota stepped away from me for a moment, turning off the stove's burner. Then his heat returned as he picked me up and set me on the counter.

I pushed the cheese grater and cutting board out of the way then wiggled to the edge so my center was right up against his growing arousal.

He latched on to my neck, sucking just below my ear as he ground his thickness into my damp center.

I moaned, wrapping a leg around his hip just as he broke away.

"Fuck. Need to go grab a condom."

My hands shot to his shoulders, keeping him from leaving. "Wait. Do we need one?"

His eyes went liquid black. "I got tested six months ago. Always used condoms since."

"I haven't been with anyone since my last checkup."

His smile turned sexy and a bit dangerous, like I was going to be his breakfast. He could eat me for lunch too, I wouldn't protest.

I reached for the waistband of my silk pajama shorts, rocking on the counter until I had them off my hips and down my thighs. Dakota didn't step back or give me space as he shoved the elastic of his sweats to his knees and kicked them away. Then he dragged my shorts down so I could swing them off my feet.

He whipped my tank off, grabbed a fistful of his T-shirt from behind his neck and yanked it over his head. His cock was a steel rod between us, poised at my slick entrance.

My hands gripped his bare shoulders, my eyes closed and

heart racing as I waited to feel him without any barriers. But Dakota didn't move.

I waited two thundering heartbeats then dared to crack my eyelids.

Dakota was waiting, his chest heaving, as he silently asked if I was sure he could have me bare.

"Yes."

One word and he thrust forward, pulling my knees onto him as he impaled me.

"Fuck," he groaned as I cried out.

I collapsed forward, giving him my weight. He stayed rooted, pushing me back so my ass was on the counter as I stretched around him.

"So good," I moaned. "So, so good. Keep going."

"I need a sec or I'm gonna come already."

I smiled into his neck, squeezing my inner muscles around him.

"Goddamn it, Sofia," he grunted. "Knock that shit off. I'm not going to last as it is."

"Sorry." I wasn't.

Making Dakota lose control was my latest obsession.

He pulled out slowly then eased back inside, making my legs shake as they dangled by his thighs.

My breaths were jagged. My heartbeat erratic. Dakota wasn't the only one who was ready to come. The man's silken flesh inside my tight heat was the best—the most incredible—sexual moment of my life.

"Give me your mouth."

I straightened from the crook of his neck, lifting my chin so he could claim my lips.

His tongue slid inside my mouth at the same time his cock

thrust deep. The two of us were fused together, clinging to one another as he moved in and out, setting the pace.

Dakota liked control when we were together. It was something I'd learned over the last three nights spent between his bedsheets. The dominance was a different experience, something I hadn't had with another man. It was thrilling to just let go and trust that he'd get me to my peak.

Not once did I have to ask him to do something different. I didn't need to worry that he'd get so focused on chasing his own release that he'd forget about mine. Every one of my orgasms had been real.

Even with my hair in a messy knot, still wet since I'd showered and hadn't dried it yet. Even without a swipe of makeup. He made me feel like the sexiest, most desired woman on earth.

We fucked on the counter, just like he'd promised. He brought me higher and higher until I exploded around him, coming with so much force my entire body felt like it was breaking apart.

Dakota came at the same time, groaning against my skin as he bit down on my shoulder, hard enough I hissed at the sting but not so hard that it hurt. It just made the pleasure spike for one more delicious second.

We held on to each other with sweaty limbs as we came down from the high. Our bodies stayed connected until Dakota's release began to slide out, slicking down my inner thighs.

The sticky drops made me smile. "I need another shower."

"Me too." He kissed my temple then slid out. "You take the first one. I'll finish breakfast and hop in after you."

The clock on the oven showed we still had forty minutes before we had to be at the bar for work, but a rush of alarm had me jumping off the island. To do my hair, get dressed and put on makeup, I needed at least an hour.

I scurried out of the kitchen naked, my pajamas left piled on the floor with Dakota's clothes.

My shower was fast, but it took time we didn't have. I'd only just gotten my hair dried and curled in the time it took Dakota to take his own fresh shower, get dressed in some jeans, his boots and a long-sleeved Henley and finish our omelet. He brought me in a plate with half the omelet, the cheese oozing from the egg wrap. I devoured bites as I swiped on some foundation.

"We gotta go soon."

"I'm hurrying." I put my finishing powder away and got out an eye shadow palette. I glanced in the mirror to see Dakota leaning against the doorframe of the bathroom, a steamy mug of coffee in his grip.

"You don't need all that. We're just going to work."

I took out a brush from my case. "I don't go out in public without makeup."

I didn't even go to the gym or the spa without makeup first. I'd sweat through it or my technician would wipe my face clean.

"No one at the Lark Cove Bar is going to care that you aren't all done up today."

"But I care."

He pushed off the door, coming right into my space. He set his mug down next to my plate and pulled the hair off my shoulder. I was only wearing a towel wrapped around my chest, so he lowered his head and kissed the spot where he'd bitten me earlier. The faint outline of his teeth was still pink.

"Don't you feel beautiful without it?" he asked.

"Yes. I don't know." No one had ever asked me that

question before. I don't think I'd really even asked myself. "I've just always worn makeup."

"If it makes you feel good, put it on. We can be a few minutes late." He ran his knuckles over my cheek. Then he kissed my hair, picked up his coffee cup and walked out of the bathroom with my empty plate.

My insides swirled, my lungs unable to get full. I used a minute I didn't have to stare at the makeup brush in my hand. Then another minute to take a hard look at my reflection in the mirror.

My entire reflection.

Did makeup make me feel good? Yes. Did I feel beautiful without it?

I pulled my shoulders back and lifted my chin. My cheekbones hadn't been contoured or highlighted. My eyes were still naked, and my lips were their natural pale pink.

Do I feel beautiful?

Yes. Yes, I did.

Except I'd been wearing makeup since I was twelve. It was more than just a habit, it was part of how I presented myself to the world.

Though, thanks to the magazine article, I had new doubts about that presentation.

Did I need it today? Not really. This was Lark Cove. There were no reporters or photographers here. I'd just be in the bar where the dark lighting was forgiving.

I put my brush away and rolled up my case, packing my makeup away. But before I put it all on the shelf Dakota had cleared for me during my stay, I grabbed my mascara, quickly swiping a single coat over my lashes.

Baby steps.

I hustled out of the bathroom, leaving the mirror before I could change my mind. I got dressed in some skinny jeans and a V-neck black sweater that cut low in the center, nearly to my pink lace bra. I tugged on Thea's shoes, having claimed them for the rest of my trip, and walked out of the bedroom.

Dakota was waiting by the back door, his coat already on and mine in his hands.

The corner of his mouth twitched when he saw my face. He helped me into my coat and outside, across the icy walk to the door of his garage.

Then he drove us to work with a smile on his face.

Two hours later, Dakota and I were at the bar and little boots were running down the hallway from the back door.

I was standing around the corner, unable to see down the hallway, but I smiled as I waited to greet my nieces and nephew. Except the child that emerged was not a Kendrick.

It was Willa and Jackson's little boy who came rushing in wearing a police officer's costume. As he ran up to Dakota's leg, I scrambled to remember his name.

Ryder was Jackson's teenage brother. Their son was—*it starts with an R*—Roman. His name was Roman.

"Hey, bud." Dakota ruffled his hair. "How's it going?"

"Went skiing wif Daddy and Wyder!"

"Yeah?" Dakota grinned at him just as Jackson, Willa and Ryder emerged.

"Hey guys." Jackson nodded to me and shook Dakota's hand. Ryder did the same.

"How was vacation?" Dakota asked.

"Went skiing!" the little boy repeated. "On snow."

"Yes, Roman went skiing on the snow." Willa ran her fingers through her son's blond hair, which matched her own, and came over to give me a hug. "It's good to see you again."

"You too."

Since Jackson was practically Thea's brother, Willa was a pseudo sister-in-law. Whenever there was a family event in Lark Cove, they were there, and I'd gotten to know her a bit over the years. She was sweet and shy.

And enormously pregnant.

"What are you guys doing here?" Dakota asked.

"Just wanted to stop by and see how things were going." Jackson looked me up and down the same way Piper had days ago.

"Let me guess." I rolled my eyes. "Thea and/or Logan called and asked you to check up on me."

Jackson grinned. "You'd be right."

"Those two need to learn how to take a vacation and stop worrying about me."

I'd talked to both Thea and Logan on New Year's Day. They'd called to see how the party had gone, and I'd assured them it had been a success. I'd also assured them I still had all my fingers and toes.

They must have thought I was lying.

"How did the party go?" Willa asked. "Was it fun?"

"It was a blast." I smiled. "One of the best I've had in a long time."

I ducked my head, hoping she wouldn't be able to read my thoughts, which had quickly turned dirty as I thought back to how much of that night's fun had been spent in Dakota's bed.

"The place was packed," Dakota told Jackson. "Ran out of

Crown about eleven. Next year, we'll have to stock up."

As Jackson, Dakota and Ryder spoke about the upcoming NFL playoffs, Roman walked over to stand at his mother's side.

"I like your costume," I told him.

He pointed to his badge. "Cop."

"This is Xavier's doing." Willa sighed. "He's obsessed with this costume. Xavier convinced him he had to be a cop for Halloween, and he doesn't want to wear anything else now. It's a fight to get him into regular clothes for daycare. Since it's just us today, I gave in and let him wear the costume."

"It's cute. Maybe he'll join the police when he grows up."

"Maybe." Willa smiled down at her son. "Did you ever have a favorite Halloween costume?"

I thought over all of them and shook my head. "Princesses. There were a lot of princesses."

"I was a princess once. Then I went through a long streak where I dressed up as a science teacher, complete with my safety goggles and white lab coat, because I wanted to grow up and be a teacher like my dad."

"I wonder if Roman will stick with the cop costume."

She shrugged. "Who knows? But he's dedicated."

I'd never had any excitement for a job, pretend or real. I envied Roman, the two-year-old boy who had more conviction for a costume than I'd had about much of anything lately.

If I could pick any job in the world, what would it be?

I had the freedom to go back to school if needed. I had complete financial flexibility to start my own business or make an investment. But what would it be? What was I so obsessed with that I'd be willing to make it a huge part of my life?

Nothing came to mind.

Was this how other people felt? I doubted everyone was

satisfied with their job.

I was sure there were grocery store clerks and gas station attendants who hated going to work every day. A part of me hoped I wasn't alone in my lack of enthusiasm. How bad was it that I hoped people hated their jobs?

Bad.

I didn't have to work. In last names, I'd gotten lucky. But as I looked down at Roman, I knew for every person who hated their job, there was someone who loved it. Like Dad or Aubrey or Logan or Thea or Willa.

"I hope Roman is always this excited about whatever job he has."

Willa gave me a sidelong look. "Are you okay?"

"Yeah!" I said, too loud and with too much excitement. "Yeah. I just mean, it's nice he has a passion at such a young age."

I'd never had that.

"How are things at the camp?" I asked, wanting a change of subject.

"Great! We're all shut down for the winter so I'm just working for Logan until the baby is born. But I'm already excited for the summer season to start."

Willa ran a children's camp in town. Besides her own children, it was her pride and joy.

It was her passion.

Everyone in this room seemed to have one except me. Even Ryder, who was still in high school, had his sights set on a college football scholarship.

"Hungry." Roman tugged on Willa's coat.

"Okay, sweetheart. We'll go home and get some lunch."

"I'll be here tomorrow," Jackson told Dakota. "Just leave

me a note if there's anything I should know."

"Will do."

"Thanks for your help, Sofia," he said.

"It's been fun." I waved good-bye to Ryder then Jackson, who'd hoisted Roman onto a hip before taking his wife's arm to escort her out the back.

"You good?" Dakota asked as the door shut.

"Yep. What can I do?"

"We need to prep some more pizza dough. There's only enough left to last through dinner and maybe lunch tomorrow."

"Lead the way."

An hour later, when my hands were sticky and my sweater dusted with flour, I couldn't get Roman and his costume out of my head.

What was my passion?

It wasn't working at a bar. I was enjoying my time here, but that was because of Dakota. Working in this job wasn't something I could do every day with a smile.

What was I going to do? It had to be something.

In the last six days, I'd realized that my family had been right all along. It was time for me to do more with myself than stay a career socialite. It was time to stop being the superficial, petty and naïve woman who'd been portrayed as nothing more than tinsel in that magazine article.

It was time to find a purpose.

I just had no idea how.

ten

DAKOTA

"WHAT ARE WE DOING TODAY?" SOFIA SNUGGLED deeper into my side.

I hooked my leg over her hip, rolling her onto her back and pinning her into the bed. Then I kissed the fuck out of her, pressing my erection into her core.

When she was breathless, I broke away. "That answer your question?"

"Uh-huh," she panted into my neck before latching on to the skin and sucking hard.

I'd been looking forward to spending another day together in bed since New Year's. We'd just been learning that day, exploring and testing. But now that I knew Sofia was good with me taking control, that she could relax and let go of any inhibitions when it came to her body, today we were going to play.

I dropped a hand to the waistband of her shorts and slid them down. The woman loved her silk pajamas, but today she was going to be sleeping naked except for that jewel in her navel. If we slept at all. And for the rest of this vacation, she'd be naked as much as possible.

I was bewitched. Addicted after only days.

In another life, I'd do more than chase her around.

I'd catch her.

My hand slipped between us, instantly finding her clit. Her hips bucked off the bed with my slight touch and her eyes flared.

Those dark irises were just as expressive in the bedroom as they were anywhere else. I knew exactly what she was feeling, how close she was to an explosion and how badly she wanted me.

And right now she wanted me to fuck her nine ways from Sunday.

Still naked from the night before, I took my cock in my hand, positioning it at her entrance. I was about to slide inside when the phone on my nightstand rang.

"Damn it."

"Don't answer." Sofia shook her head, her eyes pleading.

"Sorry, babe." I rolled off her and grabbed the phone. It was Dad's ringtone, one I hadn't heard in over a month. If he was calling, something was up.

"Hello." I shifted off the bed, dropping my feet to the floor. My hard-on was just as pissed as Sofia.

"Dakota." He didn't sound upset or angry for a change. Maybe this was a call I could have ignored.

"Dad."

"Your sister had her baby."

"What?" I shot off the bed. Koko wasn't due for another six weeks. "Is everything okay?"

"Ten fingers. Ten toes. You've got a new niece."

"And Koko?"

"Just fine."

I sighed, sinking back to the edge of the bed. Behind me, Sofia was sitting up with the sheet clutched to her breasts. "That's good."

Koko had four other kids so it wasn't like this was her first experience with childbirth. But you never knew what could happen.

"I'll call her later," I told Dad. "And I'll send some flowers to the hospital."

"Just bring them."

"Bring them?"

"Koko wants you to be here for the naming today."

I ran a hand through my hair. "Dad, I, uh, I can't come over there today."

"Are you working or something?" he asked, his tone bitter.

Dad was one of the hardest workers I knew and had taught his kids how to hustle. But since I wasn't working on the reservation, I could put in hundred-hour weeks and I'd still be slacking.

"No, I'm not."

"Then drive safe." Dad hung up the phone.

I hung my head, my shoulders hunched forward, heavy with guilt.

Koko had been the one to start this tradition. Ever since her first son was born, she wanted all of us around when she and her husband announced a baby's name. Then we'd pass the newborn around, introduce ourselves so he or she would know we were family.

I hadn't missed a naming ceremony for any of my sisters' kids. Something Dad knew.

"Fuck." I tossed the phone on the mattress. I hated wasting a day with Sofia with her leaving so soon.

"What?" Sofia walked across the bed on her knees, placing her hands on my shoulders. "Is everything all right?"

"I need to go home. My sister had a baby today, and we do

this thing where we all have to be there when she announces the name."

"Oh, okay." Her hands fell away and she climbed off the bed. Then she dug through the sheets to find her pajama shorts. "I'll toss on some pants and pack up some stuff, and you can drop me at Logan's on your way out of town."

I didn't want her to pack up her stuff. I'd told her that she was staying here for the rest of her trip, and her suitcases belonged in the corner of my bedroom, right where they were until our time was up.

"Wait." I snagged her hand before she could walk away, pulling her between my knees. Her floral scent hit my nose, chasing away good reason. "Do you want to come along?"

She side-eyed me. "To the reservation?"

"Yes." *What the hell am I thinking?* This had disaster written all over it in Sharpie. But I wasn't spending the day without her.

"Is that okay? Isn't it a family affair?"

I nodded. "It is. But it won't take long. We'll go to Browning. Say congrats. Deliver some flowers and do the naming. Then we'll come back."

"Are you sure?"

No. "Yeah."

"Okay. I'll hop in the shower." She bent, planted a kiss on my lips, then sauntered to the bathroom, stripping off her tank top as she walked and tossing it into the pile of dirty clothes she'd been making next to one suitcase.

As the water turned on in the bathroom, I rubbed my face in my hands, wondering if I should take back the invitation.

My family would take one look at Sofia and instantly be on alert. Not because she was a white girl on the reservation. But because she was a white girl on the reservation who'd arrived in the passenger seat of my truck.

I stood and took one step toward the bathroom. Dread churned in my gut. No way this day ended in happy smiles.

I didn't want to go home, but I didn't have a choice. And since I had to go, I didn't want to go alone.

It probably wasn't fair to let Sofia walk into this situation. It really wasn't fair to let her go without a warning.

I walked down to the bathroom, watching her blurry form from behind the frosted glass of the shower's door. "I think you need to know what you're getting into here."

"What's that?" she called.

"You know I've got a beef with my family. They probably won't be too happy to see me."

She laughed. "You mean, they won't be too happy to see *me*."

"Well, yeah."

The door slid open and she peeked her wet head outside. "Do you want me to stay here?"

"No," I admitted.

"Then consider me warned. Your family is going to be surprised I'm there. My family would be surprised if I brought you home too."

I hadn't thought of it that way. It was a nice fantasy to think social barriers didn't exist, that rich people weren't wary of poor people and vice versa.

Though I think of our two families, hers was the one we were selling short. From what Thea had told me, they were fairly down-to-earth, considering their wealth.

The only one she'd ever been wary of was Sofia.

No worries there.

"They'll be civil," I promised.

"Even if they're not, I'm fine. I'd like to see where you're from."

We'd be driving through the worst part of town to get to the hospital. That probably deserved another warning of its own, but I wasn't going to completely scare her away.

Selfish as it was, I wanted every one of Sofia's minutes for the rest of her trip.

Even if that meant taking her along to meet my family.

"Congratulations, Koko." I bent to the hospital bed and kissed my sister's cheek.

She didn't really notice the hug I tried to give her. She was too busy staring at Sofia with a slackened jaw. Just like all the other women in the room.

Dad was the only one looking at me. His stare etched my skin like a laser beam.

I ignored them and rubbed a knuckle against the pink cheek of my niece, who was sleeping in her mother's arms. "Hi, little one." *Good luck.*

I was ashamed to admit I didn't know my nieces and nephews well. Koko had five kids now. My sister Rozene had four boys. The youngest ones I hadn't seen in months. Rozene's youngest was ten months old, and I'd only seen him twice, his naming ceremony and now. The kid was sitting on the floor in the corner, chewing on a plastic rattle.

This baby girl wouldn't know me any better. Hell, I didn't even know if they talked about me. Given the way Dad was still glaring, I doubted they would much after today.

I touched the baby's nose then left their bedside to greet

everyone else.

"Hi, Mom." I kissed her forehead. Her black hair had more gray hairs since the last time I'd come home. Her long braid was tied off with one of the leather straps Dad always made for her hair.

"Dakota." She leaned in closer to speak softly. "Today is for family."

Dad grumbled and from the corner of my eye, Rozene nodded vigorously. These hospital rooms didn't only smell like antiseptic, their acoustics meant everyone had heard Mom's statement.

Including Sofia.

"This is Sofia Kendrick. She's—"

"A coworker." Sofia stepped away from the doorway and farther into the room. Her shoulders were pulled back and her chin raised. She looked like the Sofia I'd seen in her family pictures, like she'd put up her guard.

Smart.

"I just came along to see your town. I'll step outside." She looked to me. "I'll be in the waiting room."

I nodded, keeping my eyes on her as she retreated out into the hallway. She'd worn her high-heeled snow boots again today. Her jeans were black, and her sweater was another cashmere number. She'd gone for the diamond studs today that probably cost more than the medical equipment in the room. My warning in the shower must have inspired her to put on some armor.

For Sofia's sake, I was glad for it. But where my family was concerned, it probably just made things worse.

The moment her footsteps were no longer audible, my family converged.

"Why would you bring a strange woman here?"

"This is a family function."

"Seriously, Dakota? I just had a baby."

I was opening my mouth to tell them this was a one-time guest when another voice filled the room.

"Hello."

My spine stiffened as I slowly spun around to see my ex-girlfriend, Petah, walking into the room with a bouquet of pink roses.

"You're just in time." Koko gave her a one-armed hug after Petah placed the flowers on a side table. "Dakota just got here, so we can start."

Petah met my eyes, her gaze familiar from the years we'd spent together. Familiar, but not comforting. It wasn't home.

"Hi." She smiled and walked over.

"Hey." I bent to kiss her cheek except she went for my lips. I was lucky to dodge it and brush the corner of her mouth.

It was awkward and we both broke apart. Her eyes darted to the floor while mine went to my sister in her hospital bed.

Koko had her hair braided in a long flow over one shoulder, much like Mom's. She was smiling, but it wasn't because of her new baby. It was because of me and Petah, standing side by side.

No matter how many years went by, Koko was set on the two of us together. To her, Petah was the big sister she'd always loved and wanted to keep.

Koko had put more pressure on me than anyone to come home, hoping I'd marry Petah. The only time she'd backed off was when Petah had gotten married to one of our high school classmates a few years after we'd broken up. I'd been on the dude ranch at the time, glad she'd found someone else.

But then they'd gotten divorced about a year later. Koko swore it was because Petah was still in love with me. Maybe she was.

I'd always been fond of Petah. But love? I'd never been in love.

"You look good," I told her.

Her eyes came up from the floor. They were filled with longing, and I regretted my compliment. "You too. You always do."

"Thanks," I clipped, keeping my expression blank. I didn't want to give her any false hope.

Petah was beautiful. One of the most beautiful women I'd ever seen. She had long, thick black hair that hung to the middle of her back. Her eyes were round and as black as coal. Her lips had a pout that my sisters had always envied.

And she was a sweetheart.

Petah was kind and soft-spoken. When we'd dated in high school, she'd lived to serve my every whim. If I said I was thirsty, she'd hurry to get me a glass of water even though I hadn't asked. She'd sit and watch every basketball practice, every track meet. She didn't make plans because she did whatever I was doing.

As a high-school kid, it was a thrill to have that kind of devotion. But that thrill had faded after three years together. I'd broken up with her a few months before I'd gone to work at the dude ranch.

I hadn't wanted to hurt her, but it had been for the best. I'd known it after my first summer at the dude ranch. I'd see these powerful women walk through the door and capture the room. The idea of being with a woman like that sent electricity through my veins.

Petah never challenged me or pushed me to see things in a different light. For the right man, she would be the perfect partner.

But I wasn't the right man.

Not when one look at Sofia gave me more energy than years with Petah had ever done.

I'd tried to make it clear to my family that Petah and I were never going to happen. She wouldn't ever be my wife. We'd never have babies. But did they hear me? No. Here she was for a *family function*.

"Should we get started?" I asked Koko.

She frowned. "In a hurry to leave?"

Yes. "No. Just excited to learn her name."

"We can't start until the guys come back." Rozene dug a bowl of crackers out of her purse for the little one on the floor. "They went to get the other kids."

My brothers-in-law were both good guys. They were involved with the tribal council along with Dad. Koko's husband worked as a lead prosecutor for the tribal court. Rozene's husband worked for the Bureau of Indian Affairs.

I liked them both. But when they were in the room, Dad was reminded that his only son was just a bartender. His disappointment would suck the happiness out of any occasion.

We stood around in silence for a few minutes except for the noises coming from the hallway as nurses walked by and a man in a walker shuffled past the door.

"Are you here for long?" Petah asked me quietly.

"No, I'm heading back today."

"Would you like to have dinner before you leave? I made a casserole this morning; it's the kind you like. It would be nice to catch up."

The minute Koko's baby was born, I bet she went right to the store to whip up that casserole. It was guaranteed I'd be home.

I sighed. "I can't. I didn't come alone."

Dad was leaning against the far wall of the room next to some kind of monitor. He crossed his arms over his broad chest and shook his head. "You shouldn't have brought her."

Petah flinched at my side. "Her? Oh. I, um . . . sorry. I didn't realize you were seeing someone."

"I'm not." I corrected because the pain radiating off her was hard to stomach. "She's a coworker." *And my lover.*

Clearly, Dad had derived that already, but I wasn't going to spell it out for Petah.

If I was lucky, I could get out of here without Petah and Sofia seeing one another. I had no doubt Sofia could handle a run-in with my ex. But I wasn't going to add insult to injury for Petah. I wasn't going to rub it in that Sofia had the one thing Petah wanted so desperately.

My undivided attention.

The sound of little feet echoed down the hallway, and I held my breath, hoping it was one of my nieces or nephews. Sure enough, a familiar face rounded the corner and hurried into the room.

"Mama!" The little girl climbed right up on Koko's bed, crawling up to the baby.

Her hair was tied back in the same leather strap as Mom's. No doubt Dad had made all the girls in the family those hair ties, along with the boys who'd chosen to wear theirs long too. Just like their grandfather and great-uncle Xavier.

One by one, the room filled with children. My brothers-in-law walked in with wide grins on their faces.

"We're here!" Koko's husband, Ty, went right to her bedside and scooped up his new daughter, smiling brightly at his
baby. "Ready to spill our secret?"

My heart thumped too hard as I watched the man gaze
upon his latest creation. There was so much love and adoration
in those eyes, I turned away.

Stop that shit. I'd made my decision. I'd chosen to follow
my own path. And that path didn't include children, so there
was no point in getting soft at the sight of a proud father.

"Okay, you guys know how this works." Koko shifted on
the bed, sitting up higher and straightening the red robe around
her shoulders. "We'll pass the baby around and you have to introduce yourself to her."

"I'll go grab a coffee from the cafeteria." Petah took a step
for the door, but Koko shot out an arm.

"No! You should stay."

"Oh, no. I don't want to intrude."

"Please? I'd like you to stay." Koko's eyes pleaded with
Petah. "You're like her aunt."

Fuck my life. I clenched my jaw, trying to keep cool. The
room was packed with people and even though I refused to
look around, I knew they were all sending their thoughts my
way.

Marry Petah. That came from Mom, Rozene and Koko.

Come home and take responsibility for who you are. That was
from Dad.

Who is that guy again? That came from the kids.

"Koko and I flipped a coin and she lost. So I get to tell you
guys this precious one's name." Ty came to my rescue, not for
the first time, and brought the attention back to his new daughter. "Kimi. It means secret."

"I love it." Rozene clutched her heart then looked to her husband. "Let's try for a girl."

He just smiled at her—a smile that said I'd be here again in about nine months.

My father stepped up first, taking the baby in his arms and rocking her back and forth until her momentary fussing stopped. "Kimi. I am your grandfather, Joseph. Burn bright, little star."

It was something Dad always added. I wasn't sure if the rest of my family wished the babies anything. If they did, they didn't say it out loud.

"Kimi." Mom was next to take the baby. "I am your grandmother, Lyndie."

She turned to me, bringing the child over. I took her in my arms, careful not to bounce her too much as I cradled her.

I wasn't like other single men who were nervous around babies. We'd always had kids in and out of our house growing up. My mother or sisters were always babysitting for a relative or neighbor and I'd pitch in.

I liked kids. I liked this kid.

Her eyes were open and dark, staring at me without blinking.

"Kimi, I am your uncle, Dakota." *Be free.*

It was the same thing I'd wished for all of them after they were born.

If they ever needed some help finding that freedom, I'd be the guy they could call. Even if I didn't live down the block or attend every holiday, I'd be there.

Like Xavier had been for me.

"My turn." Rozene swept the baby from my arms, cooing as she rocked her side to side. "Kimi, I am your aunt, Rozene.

And this is your other aunt." Rozene handed the baby to Petah.

She hesitated a moment after the baby was in her arms, then she introduced herself. "Hi, Kimi, I'm Petah."

At least she hadn't added the *aunt*.

Petah rocked the baby back and forth, smiling at Kimi's round face. Then she looked to me with the words *I want one* written all over her face.

I took a step away from Petah, nearly knocking over one of my nephews who'd come over to stand close.

My family had all but convinced her I'd come home eventually. No matter how many times I stressed that I wasn't coming back, that Petah and I would never be together again, they'd fooled her into thinking there was still a chance.

Petah handed the baby to Rozene's husband next. When he was done with his introduction, Kimi went back to Koko. Each of the kids climbed up on the hospital bed for their introductions. As I waited for each to say their name to the baby, I maintained the foot of space between me and Petah.

When was she going to get the hint? The shoulder I'd always tried to keep lukewarm needed to turn icy cold.

The moment the naming was done, I walked to Koko's side and dropped another kiss on her cheek. "Congratulations. Get some rest, okay?"

"You're leaving?"

"The roads are icy," I lied. "Don't want to drive on them in the dark."

Koko frowned. "Fine. I guess we'll see you when we see you."

"Yep."

I bit my tongue so I wouldn't point out for the tenth time they could always come and visit me. I'd lived in Lark Cove for five years and not once had a family member made the two-hour drive to see where I lived or where I worked.

I hugged Mom and Rozene good-bye. The embraces weren't returned since they were just as pissed as Koko. Then with a nod and wave to the guys, I strode out the door.

"Dakota." Dad followed me into the hallway.

I stopped walking and turned, fisting my hands on my hips. "Dad."

"They're looking for a new director at the economic development office."

"Great. Hope they find someone." Because I had a job.

Dad didn't seem to remember that little fact. Each time I came home, he'd list off all the available jobs in the area.

"It's time you came home," he said. "Hasn't it been long enough? You belong here."

"I have a home. I belong there."

"With your uncle," he grumbled.

"He supports me."

Dad didn't have a response.

So I spun around, striding down the hallway and leaving him behind.

Every time this happened. I'd come here, and all I'd get was pressure. Not a single person asked me how I was doing. Not a single family member asked me if I was happy.

"Dakota, wait," Petah called after me.

"Christ," I groaned, looking at the ceiling as I stopped once again. The waiting room was only three feet away and around the corner. So close. But my escape was stopped again.

Petah caught up, brushing a lock of hair away from her face. "I just wanted to say I'm sorry. I didn't know you'd be here. Koko called and said she'd had the baby, and I asked if it was an okay time to bring flowers. Please don't leave because of me. I can go."

As frustrated as I was with the entire situation, I didn't blame Petah. I knew her well enough to know she wasn't into games or manipulations. She didn't realize that she was part of one. My sisters were using her as bait, a beautiful woman who might entice me to come home.

"No. It's fine. It's not you."

"My offer for dinner is still on the table. You could bring your friend."

At that exact moment, Sofia rounded the corner from the waiting room. "Oh, hey. Are you done? I was just going to find a vending machine for a soda." She smiled at me then noticed Petah. "Oh, I'm sorry. I didn't mean to interrupt."

"It's fine." *Fuck*. I waved Sofia over. "Sofia Kendrick, this is Petah Tatsey."

"Hi." Sofia stepped up and held out her hand. She stood so close to me that our elbows were touching.

Petah was sweet and soft-spoken, but she wasn't oblivious. She noticed how easily Sofia had merged our personal bubbles. Her face fell as she shook Sofia's hand. Then she looked up to me, her hopes shattering before my eyes. "Your coworker?"

Fuck. Fuck. Fuck. "Yes, we work together."

The pain on her face was heartbreaking. I'd never brought another woman home. It had only ever been her. I hated what I was about to do, but I sucked it up, hoping it would hurt Petah in the now so she could heal in the long run.

So she'd stop waiting around for me.

I wrapped my arm around Sofia's shoulder and pinned her to my side. Then I kissed her temple.

Sofia stiffened, not missing Petah's sharp breath.

I swallowed down the disgust, holding tight to Sofia as Petah stared at us both for a long moment.

Then she did something that surprised me. She straightened her spine and forced a polite smile. "Nice to meet you, Sofia. Travel safely home."

"Shit." I let Sofia go as Petah turned on a heel and hurried down the hallway. "I need to get out of here."

Sofia crossed her arms over her chest, glaring at my profile. "Look, I—"

She didn't wait for my explanation. She walked away from me too, right through the sliding doors and outside into the cold.

I caught up to her quickly, keeping pace as she marched through the parking lot to my truck.

Her arms were still crossed as she waited for me to unlock and open her door. She didn't take my hand when I offered it to help her inside the cab.

Shutting the door on her side, I jogged around to the other and climbed in. The truck roared to life, the heat quickly chasing away the winter cold as we sat in the parking lot.

It didn't do much to thaw out my passenger.

"Is that why you invited me along?" she asked. "Am I just the someone you needed to piss off your family?"

"No."

"Then why did you shove me in that woman's face? So I could break her heart?"

"I'm sorry." I sighed. "That was my ex-girlfriend."

"I figured that one out."

"She needs to move on."

"Then be a man and tell her to move on," she snapped. "I've played every game in the book, Dakota. Every. Single.

One. I'm done with that. If you need a pretty face at your side to send a message, find a different one."

"I didn't know she was going to be here."

"Doesn't matter," she fired back.

"You're right."

She huffed and stared out her window. The air vents in the dash blew a loose strand of hair around her cheek.

"Sofia." I reached for her hand, taking it off her lap. "I didn't mean to use you. That's not why I brought you today. I just wanted someone here who was on my side. But you're right, I played a game with Petah. The end game. She's gotta move on. Maybe now she will."

Sofia blew out a long breath and laced her fingers with mine. "I guess . . . I guess it just surprised me. Besides, it's probably better to make me the bad guy since I'm never coming back."

"Right."

The one woman I'd brought along to meet my family was leaving.

My family would probably be glad to know she'd be gone in three days.

But me? I wasn't sure how I'd go back home and not wish she were by my side.

eleven

SOFIA

"THIS IS IT." DAKOTA PARKED HIS TRUCK ON THE STREET in front of the rental property.

"It's nice."

The duplex was older, but Dakota had updated it recently. The siding had been freshly painted a mushroom beige, the trim a clean white. And the black shutters matched the front door, giving it a dash of character.

One side of the property had a quiet, snow-covered lawn and a sidewalk that hadn't been shoveled. The other side hadn't been shoveled either, but a path had been worn into the snow with lots of footprints.

"Hang tight." Dakota left the truck running as he opened the door. "Let me shovel."

He hopped out, shutting the door quickly to keep in the heat, grabbed the snow shovel from the back and went to work clearing the walkway.

It had been three days since our trip to Dakota's hometown. We'd worked those days at the bar and were going in late this afternoon to relieve Jackson for the night. For my last shift at the Lark Cove Bar. But first, we'd come up to Kalispell to check on one of his tenants.

Things had gone back to normal after we'd gotten home from the reservation. After the two-hour drive back to Lark Cove, I'd shrugged off my mood, determined to enjoy my time with Dakota, since it was about to come to an end.

Dakota hadn't been kidding about the welcome I'd receive from his family—or the lack thereof. One death glare from his dad, and I'd regretted getting out of bed and making the trip.

But it hadn't been the first time I'd been on the receiving end of disgusted frowns and harsh glares. I'd weathered them with a well-practiced smile then gone to the waiting room, where I'd caught up on social media.

My so-called friends had been busy over the last week, sharing the magazine's article on every platform possible. When Dakota had pulled that stunt with Petah, I'd already been irritated. His play had sent me over the edge.

Years ago I would have volunteered to help Dakota send a message to his ex-girlfriend. Games and tricks had been my forte. But those days were over, and I was done being used by people.

I felt awful for Petah. And Dakota too. He was a good man. I believed his actions had been spur-of-the-moment and made with her best interests at heart.

But I'd felt her pain in that hallway. She was in love with him, and he'd slashed those feelings apart.

On the drive home, I hadn't had the courage to ask him about their relationship and why they hadn't worked. I'd been too busy dealing with some insecurities on the trip. Petah was beautiful, stunningly so, with a face that photographers like Malcom would salivate over. And she was from the right heritage. If she wasn't his one, who was? Who would eventually win Dakota's heart?

It wasn't me. We were just a casual and fun affair.

I'd been reminding myself of that ever since he'd pulled out of the hospital's parking lot.

I was not getting into a relationship, a long-distance one at that. Despite my growing feelings for Dakota, despite the fact that he'd slipped past my flimsy barriers faster than any man in the past, I was not getting into another relationship.

The trip had been a good reminder.

It had been interesting to see where Dakota had grown up. The town itself had been more rundown than I'd imagined. I'd never visited a reservation before, but according to Dakota, his was one of the poorest in the country. Over half of the buildings and homes along the highway were falling apart. Broken down and beat-up cars crowded driveways. More than a few businesses had boarded up doors spray painted with *CLOSED* on the face.

The neighborhoods had gotten nicer as we'd driven off the main highway and into town. The hospital itself was nice though small, and the homes in the surrounding area reminded me of Dakota's Lark Cove neighborhood.

But there were no wealthy parts of town. There were no booming businesses. It made sense why he'd left to find a better-paying job.

And why he'd chosen to invest in properties here, where he could charge a higher rent.

Dakota finished shoveling and came back to the truck, stowing the shovel before opening my door. The icy air blasted me in the face.

"Will you reach over and shut it off?"

"Got it." I leaned across the console, turning the keys and taking them out of the ignition. Then I plopped them into his gloved hand.

As I hopped out, he opened the back door to start loading up grocery bags. We'd filled seven at the store this morning. Dakota handed me three and kept the others for himself along with a case of Mountain Dew.

With our arms loaded, we walked up the narrow path to the front door. We didn't need to knock before the door swung open and an elderly man waved us straight inside.

"Arthur." Dakota clapped the shorter, elderly man on the shoulder. "Good to see you. I've got a guest with me today. Meet Sofia."

"Hello."

He smiled, tilting his black-rimmed sunglasses toward me. "Welcome."

I stepped inside as Dakota elbowed the door closed. Then I followed him past the living room off the front door and into the square kitchen at the rear of the house.

As I put the grocery bags on the counter, I inspected the place. The interior had been painted a soft white, and the cabinets in the kitchen were deep gray. Dakota had an eye for clean lines with a farmhouse style, something that went perfectly in a place like this. My interior designer heart loved him for his taste.

I thought we'd just leave the groceries, but Dakota began to unpack, quickly putting things in their place. He'd clearly done this many times before.

"Thank you both." Arthur stood at the entrance to the kitchen. "Can you sit and visit for a minute?"

"We'd love to. You guys sit. I'll be right in."

I followed Arthur to the living room, my tennis shoes sinking into the shag carpet as I walked to the couch.

Arthur went right for his recliner in the corner, sitting down and shifting until he was comfortable.

Dakota didn't waste any time in the kitchen. I was just settling into the seat when he came in and sank down next to me.

"Thanks for shoveling the walk," Arthur told him. "I couldn't keep up with the snow last week."

"Sorry I didn't get up sooner to take care of it for you."

"You're busy. Don't worry about me." Arthur relaxed in his chair. He was a small man, about as tall as my five foot six. He wore a plaid shirt and loose, brown polyester slacks with black suspenders holding them up.

His hair had long since fallen out and his bald scalp was dotted with freckles. I'd expected now that we were inside, he'd lose the sunglasses. But he kept them on, maybe because the room was so bright due to the picture window between us.

"So what's new?" Dakota asked him, relaxing deeper into the couch and tossing an arm around the back.

"Oh, not much." Arthur sighed. "New Year's Eve was interesting."

Dakota stiffened. "What happened?"

Arthur hooked a thumb over his shoulder, pointing to the shared wall between the two units in the property. "He had a party."

"Shit," Dakota grumbled. "Sorry. I'll go over and give him a warning. I know this sounds bad, but I hope he does it again. Then I can kick him out."

"I wouldn't complain. Especially if you found a nice old gal who needed a man around to keep her company." Arthur snapped one of the straps on his suspenders, wagging his eyebrows.

Dakota and I both laughed. "I'll make sure to include it in the ad."

"Good." Arthur reached into the drawer on the side table next to the recliner and pulled out a checkbook and pen. Then with careful precision, he wrote Dakota a check. "I can mail these. Save you a trip. I know you're busy."

"Not too busy to visit." Dakota stood and crossed the small room, taking the check from Arthur. "I wish we could stay longer, but I've got to work this afternoon. The roads were slow on our way up."

"Go. Don't let me keep you. Next time, maybe we'll fit in a quick game." Arthur nodded to the chessboard set up on the dining room table off the living room.

"I'd like that." Dakota shook Arthur's hand, pulling him up from the recliner.

"Will I see you again?" Arthur asked me as he followed us to the door.

"I'm afraid not." I gave him a sad smile. "I live in New York. I'm just tagging along with Dakota for a few days."

One more day to be exact. Thea and Logan were due back tomorrow. The thought of leaving so soon made my stomach twist.

"Well, it was nice to meet you, even for a brief moment. And thank you for delivering my groceries." He held out his hand, his fingers shaking a little. He was too far away from me so I stepped up and took his hand.

"Call if you need anything at all," Dakota said.

"I will."

With that, Dakota opened the front door and waved me outside. Then he shut it behind him and handed me the keys to his truck. "I need to go over to the other unit."

"Okay." I took the keys then started down the sidewalk as Dakota stepped into the snowy yard and went to the other unit.

The vibrations from his fist pounding on the front door echoed down the street.

A few seconds later, the door whipped open and a tall, thin man in jeans and a dirty white T-shirt jerked up his chin at Dakota. I couldn't hear everything Dakota said, but as I shuffled to the truck, I glanced over my shoulder and saw the other man's face twisted in an angry scowl.

His eyes darted my way just as I reached the truck. He was staring at my ass as he asked Dakota, "Who's your lady?"

Dakota ignored the question, turning and leaving the man on the stoop alone. But not without one last warning. "Keep it down. Or you're out."

The man shrugged, his eyes still raking over my legs, giving me the creeps.

I yanked the door open, getting in as quickly as possible. When I was closed in, I shuddered, wanting another shower.

Dakota wasn't far behind me, throwing his door open and getting into the driver's seat. "Fucking asshole. I need to kick his ass out."

Dakota pulled away from the curb, navigating us down the quiet neighborhood street with homes similar to his property. Three houses down, two kids were attempting to build a snowman. Another three down, a dad was outside pulling his little one in a blue sled.

His creeper renter did not belong here.

"Was he always like that? Even when he moved in?"

"Yep." He sighed. "That place was a mess when I bought it. The guy selling it wanted out of it bad so he slashed the price as long as I let his friend stay in that unit. I agreed because I wanted the deal. But now I wish I had kicked him out or found someplace else to buy. He's been nothing but a headache for the last six months. Every time I come up here it's something."

"And you can't evict him?"

"I can. I should have already. But now I've waited too long. Montana has some pretty strict regulations about evicting someone in the winter months. Since he pays his rent, I doubt I'll be able to get him out until spring. And I need the money. I can't have a property sitting empty all winter, because no one wants to move in the snow."

"Sorry." Being a landlord sounded, well, awful. Unless you had only nice tenants.

"Lesson learned."

"What's Arthur's story?" I asked.

"He's a great guy. He doesn't have family close, so I come up about every week or ten days and bring him junk food since he's homebound."

"Why's he homebound?"

"He's blind."

My mouth fell open. "What? No way."

Arthur had navigated his house without using a cane. He hadn't touched the walls for guidance or to get his bearings. He'd walked right up to his chair, sitting without feeling for it first. Though that did explain the sunglasses.

Dakota nodded. "He's been blind since Vietnam."

"Wow. It's really kind of you to bring him groceries."

"Like I said, he's a great guy. Grew up in Kalispell. His kids left ages ago for their own lives. He just doesn't want to leave. One of them saw my ad for a place and they jumped on it. They have a service to clean and help him cook. But the cook only does healthy food. I bring Arthur the good stuff."

I giggled, thinking of the cookies, popcorn and potato chips we'd bought earlier. "Where are your other properties?"

"All right in this same neighborhood." Dakota took a left down another side street. About halfway down the block, he pointed to a green single-family home. "That one there."

"It's cute."

"I'm not going to tell the bodybuilder who rents from me that you called his house cute."

I smiled. "And the other? You have three, right?"

"Yep." He drove down the rest of the block and on to the next one. This time the house he pointed out was on my side and painted a soft beige with chocolate trim. "That one was my first. It's the one that makes me the least amount of money."

"Why's that?"

"Because the previous owner is the tenant. She's a single mom with two teenaged boys. The bank was going to foreclose on her, so she put it up for sale before they could. I bought it, rented it back to her at a discount, and she works two jobs to pay her bills. She's never missed a rent check. She didn't want to lose the house where her kids are growing up."

"That's an amazing thing for you to do."

He shrugged. "She just got down on her luck. It happens."

"Thank you," I told him.

"For what?"

"For bringing me here today. And for showing me your properties." It was a glimpse deeper into the man behind the wheel, confirming what I already knew.

Dakota Magee wasn't a good man. He was *the* good man. I doubted I'd ever find another who would live up to his standards.

"I know they aren't much. But I'm proud of them."

"You should be. You'll accomplish great things."

"I don't know about great. But I have my goals."

I wanted goals.

I didn't need to conquer the world—I'd leave that to Aubrey. I just wanted more excitement in my life, more happiness and fulfillment. More pride.

I wanted to be more like Dakota.

He was one of a kind, a man who knew down to his fiber the difference between right and wrong. A man who made his own destiny.

A man who I would miss terribly when our affair was over.

"Is today your last day?" Wayne asked me from across the bar.

I gave him a sad smile. "Yes, Thea and Logan should be back tonight." Then I'd be leaving tomorrow morning.

"Don't tell me you're going to miss sweeping floors and wiping up spilled beer."

I smiled. "Maybe just a little."

The jukebox changed to a faster country song, and Wayne stood from his stool. "I haven't heard this one in ages. How about a farewell jitterbug?"

"Huh?"

"The jitterbug. Want to dance?"

Dakota laughed from over by the register, where he was taking stock of the liquor bottles in a spiral notebook. "Watch your feet. The last time a woman danced with Wayne, she almost lost a toe."

"To be fair, that woman was drunk, and she stepped on me first." Wayne got off his stool, waving me around the bar.

I set down the glass I'd been rinsing and hurried around

to his side.

Wayne grabbed my hands, holding them out at our sides. Then he pulled us together, me going to one side of his body before stepping back. Then he did it again, turning us in a circle.

I'd learned the jitterbug as a kid when my ballet teacher had been on maternity leave and her substitute had wanted to teach us some other basics, like the waltz, mambo and two-step. That substitute had been fired not long after the lead instructor's maternity leave had ended.

And even though those lessons had been a long time ago, it wasn't hard to follow Wayne as he pulled me around and spun me in a few easy twirls. By the time the song ended, we were laughing and smiling, both out of breath.

"Thanks," I panted.

"Thank you." Wayne kissed the back of my hand, bowing as he let me go. "I'd better get on home. It was wonderful to spend time with you, Sofia. Don't be a stranger the next time you're in town."

"It was lovely spending time with you too."

"I hope we get to dance another day." Wayne went to his stool to collect his coat and hat. Then with one last wave to Dakota, he was out the door.

My eyes flooded as he disappeared outside. I wiped the tears away before they could fall, determined not to let myself cry over something so silly. It wasn't like I would never see Wayne again. I came to Lark Cove to visit.

But he'd been so nice to me that first day when I'd broken all those glasses. He'd been the first in a long, long time who'd seen me as something different.

So had Dakota.

"You know what I think is interesting?" he asked.

I swallowed the burn in my throat and blinked away the tears before turning around. "What?"

"Of all the lessons you've told me about in the last ten days, dancing is the only thing you still do."

Was that true? My mother had insisted that all of us be involved and busy. My extracurricular activities had always been on the artsy side. Language. Music. Dance.

That last one was really the only one that had stuck into adulthood.

What did that mean?

Before I had a chance to ask, the door to the bar opened again and three children rushed inside, followed by their parents.

Parents who were back from their trip to Paris.

"So where are your suitcases?" Thea asked.

I blushed as she handed me a glass of wine.

After they'd come to the bar this evening, it had been a whirlwind. The kids had been anxious to go home with their parents. Thea and Logan had been excited to be with the kids. Before I'd even had a chance to say a proper good-bye to Dakota, they'd swept me along with them.

He was at the bar, finishing the night alone.

I hadn't even thought about my suitcases in all the commotion. They were still lying in the corner of his bedroom.

Dakota and I both knew today was my last day in Lark Cove, yet neither of us had thought to pack my things. We both knew I'd be in his bed tonight.

One last night.

"They're at Dakota's house."

She choked on her sip of wine and coughed. "What?"

"I've been staying there." Since I was planning on going back tonight, there was no use in denying it. And I wasn't going to pretend Dakota and I hadn't had a glorious affair.

Logan would have an opinion. I wasn't sure how Thea was going to react. But right now, it didn't matter. The kids were in bed. The bar was probably quiet, and Dakota was likely closing it down. They could lecture me later.

Right now, I just wanted to leave.

As if he knew what I was thinking, a truck rumbled up the driveway outside. I shot off my chair in the living room and rushed to a window, peering outside in the dark and seeing Dakota's truck pull up.

"Get out of here." Thea smiled, sighing as she sipped more wine.

"Have a good night." I smiled back, hurrying out of the room. "Oh, and Thea?" I paused, turning back. "Thank you. I'm glad I trusted you."

"Me too."

With one last smile, I ran to the front door just as my brother was coming out of Charlie's room down the hallway.

"Where are you going?" he asked.

I ignored him.

Thea appeared in the entryway, her wine in hand. "Do we need to take you to the airport tomorrow?"

"Yes, please." I pulled on the coat of hers I'd been borrowing all week. "I'll be back in the morning before eight."

"What?" Logan crossed his arms over his chest. "Where are you going?"

"Have fun." Thea winked at me as I kissed Logan's cheek then opened the door.

"Sofia—"

I shut the door on him, knowing Thea would explain. Then I hurried to Dakota's truck, going straight for the passenger side door and hopping up.

The second I was inside, Dakota's long arms reached for me, taking my face and pulling my lips to his. He kissed me with abandon, his tongue diving into my mouth and retracing the same path he'd made a hundred times in our time together.

We were starved and reckless, lost in the hot and wet kiss that went on for what felt like hours.

Finally, he broke away but kept my cheeks in his hands. "I didn't bring your suitcases."

"I don't want my suitcases."

Not yet.

He kissed me again, slanting my face one way as he devoured me again. When I was breathless and aching for more, he drove us to his home.

Neither of us slept as we savored the last hours together, linked until the sun began to rise.

I didn't cry as I packed my suitcases or after Dakota kissed me one last time in his truck. I didn't cry as I hugged my family good-bye at the airport. I didn't even cry as the jet lifted into the air, leaving Montana behind. I saved all of my tears for the moment I stepped inside my penthouse apartment in New York City, alone.

My holiday vacation was really over.

And the life I'd returned to wasn't much of a life at all.

twelve

SOFIA

"IS THERE ANYTHING IN PARTICULAR YOU'D LIKE FOR LUNCH today, Ms. Kendrick?"

"No, thank you, Carrie." I set down the magazine on my lap and smiled at my personal chef as she stood outside the living room. "Whatever you'd like to make will be lovely."

"Your trainer called me this morning and mentioned we needed to limit carbs for a few weeks. With the weather being so cold, I was thinking a variety of soups, if that would please you."

I frowned. When I'd had my workout this morning, my trainer had been less than pleased when I'd stepped on the scale. Ten days in Montana of eating whatever I wanted had "softened" things.

When I'd gotten home two days ago, I'd contemplated asking Carrie to cook only healthy foods. Instead, I'd decided to wallow. So I'd given her an extra two days paid vacation and asked my doorman for recommendations for the best, greasiest takeout places in Manhattan.

"Miss?" Carrie cleared her throat. "The soups?"

"That's fine." I sighed. The sooner I got back into my regular diet, regular schedule, regular . . . life, the sooner I'd snap out of this somber mood. "Thank you."

"Can I get you anything? I'd be happy to call your massage therapist or get you scheduled for a facial. You have one tomorrow, but I'm sure they'd be able to move you up."

"No, but thank you. Tomorrow will be fine."

Carrie had started off as just my chef, but her job had expanded over the last year. She actually did the tasks I paid my assistant to do, like coordinate with the housekeeper, give my schedule to my driver and arrange for my laundry to be done.

My paid assistant, Sandrine, had become quite lax in her duties over the last year. She was using me. And she was using Carrie, knowing that Carrie would cover for her shortcomings.

"I'll just be off to the market." Carrie turned for the kitchen, but before she got too far, I called her back.

"I appreciate all that you do for me."

Her entire body froze, like she was expecting my next statement to be *you're fired*.

I smiled widely, hoping to ease her fears, and tossed my magazine aside before gesturing to the chair across from my sofa. "Would you mind?"

Carrie hurried to the seat, sitting on its edge with her hands placed in her lap. She had better posture than I did after years of etiquette lessons.

"I'd like to offer you a job."

She blinked. "A job?"

"I'm consolidating staff." For a decision I'd made a second ago, my voice was surprisingly confident. "I'd like to hire you on full-time. Benefits. Four weeks paid vacation. And I'll pay you three times what I do now, but you'd have to drop your other client."

Carrie also cooked for another man in this building, a

loathsome gentleman who didn't hold the elevator and always smelled of stale cigar smoke. He paid her well, at least I assumed so, which was why she worked for him. Plus, there was the added convenience of us living in the same building. But I'd overheard her on the phone about six months ago complaining that he was a pig.

I'd had enough pigs in my life. Carrie shouldn't have to deal with them either, especially since it was time to make a change.

She thought about it for a minute, but then the corner of her mouth turned up. "What is the job?"

I scooted forward on the couch, already excited about this possibility. "You'll still have to cook, and I'd like you to keep coordinating with the cleaning and laundry staff. In addition, you'd coordinate my travel and any preparation for events. You'd make appointments for me when needed, that sort of thing. In short, you'll assume all of the duties that Sandrine does now."

Carrie rolled her eyes at my personal assistant's name but caught it halfway through the loop. "Sorry."

"It's okay." I wanted to roll my eyes too. "So . . . think about it. Let me know."

"I'll put in my notice downstairs today."

"Oh, uh . . . do you need to talk about it first with . . ." A husband? Boyfriend? I didn't even know if she was in a relationship.

"My wife has been begging me to quit him for years." She pointed to the floor, where her other client lived five floors down. "I'm sure she'll be thrilled with this change."

"Wonderful." I stood from the couch and held out my hand. "Then as your first official duty as my new assistant, please get in touch with my business manager and tell him to give you a raise."

She smiled and took my hand. "Thank you, Ms. Kendrick."

"Please, call me Sofia. And thank you." A rush of joy surged as she left the living room. But I stopped her again. "Carrie?"

"Yes, Ms. Ken—Sofia?"

"It would be my pleasure to meet your wife one day. Please bring her by."

"I'm sure she'd love to meet you too."

"Oh." I held up a finger before she could leave. "And can you add bread to the menu? I'd like some sourdough or a rye to go with the soup."

In the morning, I'd tell my trainer he was going to have to find a balance between a workout and a diet where I could eat carbs.

Carrie smiled wider, nodded and disappeared from the room.

I sat back down on the couch, too giddy to go back to thumbing through the magazines that had piled up while I'd been in Montana.

I made a mental note to ask Carrie to cancel all but a handful. Then I picked up my phone and emailed my business manager, informing him of my change with Carrie and requesting he terminate Sandrine.

Once the email was sent, temptation got the better of me. I thumbed through my contacts and pulled up Dakota's name just to see it on the screen.

I hadn't talked to him since I'd left Montana.

I'd thought about him constantly though, wondering if he was working or maybe on a trip to visit Arthur.

Did he miss me at all?

I missed him, certain things especially. I missed the way it felt to lean against his chest and have those long arms wrapped around my back. I missed burying my face in his pillow and soaking up his scent. I missed his easy nature, how steady the world felt when he was around.

God, I wanted to call him. I wanted to hear his deep voice and feel it in my bones. I wanted to hear some longing in his voice.

Our good-bye hadn't been enough. Those moments in his truck had been cut too short. This was supposed to have been a temporary thing. An easy New Year's fling. Not ten days where I'd nearly given away my heart.

It's over now.

As much as I wanted to dial his number, I kept scrolling through names, up and down in a mindless motion. The loneliness closed in on me, like it had in quiet moments like this for the past two days.

My finger paused over my sister's name. Without second-guessing myself, I pushed her number.

"Hi," she answered on the second ring. Her usual typing in the background was missing. "Are you back?"

"Yes. I'm certain you're at work, but I was wondering if you'd like to have dinner with me tonight?" Another split-second decision that felt surprisingly easy.

"Where?"

"Would you want to come over here? I was thinking pizza." With extra cheese because it made me think of Dakota.

"I could eat pizza. My trainer won't be happy though."

"Screw the trainers," I muttered.

She laughed. "I tried that once, remember? It didn't end well."

"Oh, yeah." I giggled, remembering one of Aubrey's few

relationships. She'd fallen for her trainer during her junior year of college, and they'd hooked up a few times. They'd gotten adventurous one quiet Saturday night, and he'd met her in the empty weight room. Her one and only failure had been getting caught on her knees by a custodian.

She'd sworn off men for the rest of college.

"I have a meeting until seven," she said. "Then I'll be over."

"I'll be here. Bye." I hung up the phone, surprised at how well that had gone. I'd honestly expected to be blown off.

I stood from the couch, wanting to stop Carrie before she left so she knew I didn't need her to make dinner. Just as I was about to walk out of the living room, I paused and took stock of the decor.

With my latest redesign, I'd gone for a classic, contemporary look. My couches were beige. I had an upholstered black and cream striped settee and matching ottoman. The enormous black cube that served as my coffee table had a tasteful arrangement of white roses and gardenias.

Collectively, it was gorgeous, my favorite of all the designs I'd done for this penthouse. But it was missing something.

What was it missing? I frowned as I glanced around the room. Maybe some color? I scrunched my nose at the idea. Textures? With the stripes, the jacquard pillows and my faux fur throw, any other textures would be overkill.

So what was it? I'd never second-guessed my design decisions before. But I couldn't shake this feeling that it was wrong. What was this home lacking?

I sighed, hating the funk I'd been in for the last two days, knowing it was because I was missing a man.

But it had been worth it.

My Dakota hangover had been so completely worth it.

"You're different." Aubrey gave me a weird look before taking a bite of our cheese pizza. We'd gotten the best brick oven crust in SoHo, according to my doorman.

I shrugged. "I'm in a funk."

"Because of the magazine?"

"Yes and no. It's made me do some soul-searching. But my funk is mostly because I met a guy in Montana."

"What? But I thought you were 'working.'"

"Don't do that." I scowled. "Don't use air quotes. Just because I don't have an important job like you doesn't mean I wasn't working."

"You're right. Sorry." She tossed down her slice onto her plate. "I've been a bitch lately, haven't I?"

"You said it first," I muttered.

"I'm in a funk too."

"Why?" I took a huge bite, savoring the cheesiness. It was a good pizza. But it wasn't nearly as good as the ones Dakota made in the bar.

"I got dumped."

I choked on my bite and sauce dribbled out of my lips. "What?"

"Swallow." Aubrey rolled her eyes. "That's gross."

I chewed as fast as humanly possible, chased the bite down with some water and wiped my mouth. "You got dumped? By who?"

"My boyfriend. We were together for about five months."

"Five months?" I'd brought Kevin to a family function five *days* after we'd started dating. "Who is he? Why didn't we meet him?"

Her face twisted in nothing but misery. "He's a lawyer at the firm where Logan used to work when he lived here. We met a few years ago and bumped into each other this summer at a work function and started dating. I couldn't tell anyone because I signed a contract."

"Like *Fifty Shades of Grey*? Because if so, stop right now. There are things I really don't need to know about my sister."

"No." She laughed, swatting me away. "Like a nondisclosure contract with his firm. Technically, I was a client. So we kept it secret. And that was the reason we never worked. He wanted me to make an announcement. I knew it would cause a lot of trouble with the company, so I told him we needed to keep it secret for a while longer. He got upset and decided we'd just end it altogether."

"Oh." I reached across the table in my dining room and took her hand. "I'm sorry."

"It's okay." She gave me a sad smile. "He wasn't the one. I just . . . I really liked him."

"Did you love him?"

Her chin quivered. "I think so. It's hard. I love my job. The company is my life. I wish he had understood that too."

I didn't have any advice to offer so I just held her hand. In true Aubrey fashion, she pulled herself together quickly and kept eating. Aubrey would never quit her job or put it at risk, especially for a man, but for the first time, I think she resented it some.

"Can I ask you something?"

I nodded. "Sure."

"Have you ever gotten your heart broken?"

"Huh?" How did she not already know the answer to that question?

"Have you ever gotten your heart broken?" she repeated.

"Yeah. A lot. Do you not remember that both of my husbands were with other women during our marriages?"

"Yeah, but you didn't love them."

"What?" My mouth fell open. "Of course I loved them."

"You did?"

I shook my head, dumbfounded. "Why would I have married them if I didn't love them?"

"I just thought it was for show."

For once, I'd thought my sister and I would be able to talk without arguing. But now I was angry, and I'd had just about enough of her judgment.

"No," I huffed. "It wasn't for show. And yes, I've had my heart broken. They might not have turned out to be good men, but that didn't make it hurt any less when they betrayed me."

"I'm sorry, Sofia. I'm really sorry. I didn't know. You moved on from Kevin so fast. The same with Bryson. I didn't realize you were hurting."

Her apology cooled my rising temper. "I was."

"Are you still?"

"No. I did love them, and it was painful. But looking back, I don't think I was as in love with them as I let myself believe." I guess her observation wasn't entirely off-base after all. Probably why it was easier to let it go.

"We're a pair. It's a good thing Mom and Dad have Logan. He's their only shot at grandchildren."

"That's the truth."

We both laughed, but then Aubrey's smile fell away. "Why aren't we friends?"

My heart clenched. "Because you don't really like me much."

"That's not true." She looked me right in the eyes. "I love you. But I don't understand you."

"Why?" The reporter had pegged me after a one-hour interview. Aubrey should have figured me out years ago. "What don't you understand?"

"You have so much potential, and you waste it. That baffles me."

"I'm not you. Or Dad. I've never wanted work to be my life. You guys keep trying to shove me into your idea of what I should be doing. But don't you see? That's not me."

"We don't do that."

"Aubrey," I said gently. "You do."

She thought about it for a few moments. The air in the dining room whirled in the silence as I waited. Then she slumped her shoulders and nodded. "Maybe you're right. But you hold my job against me just as much as I hold your lifestyle against you."

"I do," I admitted. I'd fought so hard to make sure I *wasn't* like them that their professional success had become something I judged. "I'm sorry. Can't we just accept one another as we are?"

She nodded. "I'd like that."

"I'm kind of lonely."

Aubrey huffed. "You and me both."

"You are? But you're always with people."

"Yeah, work people. I'm not their friend though. I'm their boss. Do you know the last time I actually had a friend? It was in college. As soon as I started working, people were wary of me because I was the boss's daughter. Then I became the boss. I'm not complaining, because I really do love my job. But it's lonely at the top."

"I'd like to be your friend." This was a strange conversation to have with my sister, but I was on the edge of my seat, waiting and hoping she wanted more of a relationship.

"We've made it through one meal without getting into a fight." She grinned. "I'd say there's hope."

"Me too." I blew out the breath I'd been holding and took another huge bite of pizza.

Aubrey did the same, and we ate with smiles until we were both full.

"Do you want to go get a drink?" she asked as we stared at plates full of leftover crust. "It's been a long week."

"Sure. But I'm not changing."

My sister looked at me like I'd grown two heads.

I hadn't done much with myself today. I'd showered and dried my hair, but it was hanging straight and limp. I hadn't used my curling iron or styling products since I'd come home. I'd also put on my new minimalist makeup after I'd gotten home from the trainer's this morning.

On top of that, I was in my Montana apparel: skinny jeans, a hoodie I'd unearthed from my closet and the tennis shoes I'd stolen from Thea even though they were too big.

They reminded me of Dakota.

"Who are you?" Aubrey asked.

It was a simple question, one I should have been able to answer. "I don't know."

That was the problem.

I didn't know who I was. The version of myself I used to know, I didn't like.

Aubrey gave me a sympathetic smile and stood. She was wearing a navy pencil skirt, a blue pin-striped shirt and nude patent pumps. Her blazer had been discarded over the back of a spare chair. "Let's go somewhere low-key."

"Sounds good." I stood and gathered our dishes. Instead of putting it all in the sink for Carrie to deal with in the morning, I trashed the box and rinsed the dishes, putting them in the dishwasher.

"Your driver or mine?" Aubrey asked, taking out her phone.

"Yours. Or we could get a cab, maybe?"

Her jaw dropped. "I'm worried about what happened to you in Montana."

Neither of us had been in a cab in decades because . . . germs.

I laughed. "Then call your driver. I don't want to bother Glen. He has young kids, and it's already dark. I'm sure the last thing he wants is to come and pick us up so we can get a drink."

"But it's his job. We pay them to be on call at all times."

"Then call yours."

She already was. Her fingers flew over her phone as she messaged him for a ride.

Thirty minutes later, we were at a small bar not too far from my building. It was quiet and dim, and we chose a booth in the corner.

"What can I get you?" the server asked.

"I'd like a huckleberry mojito."

Now it was his turn to look at me like I'd grown two heads. "What's a huckleberry?"

"Never mind," I muttered. "I'll just have a glass of red."

Before I'd gone to Lark Cove the first time, I hadn't known what a huckleberry was either. They were a berry local to the Pacific Northwest.

"Same." Aubrey held up two fingers.

As the server left to get our drinks, I looked over to the

bar, hoping to see a snack tray. I wasn't hungry, but I wanted a peanut.

My Dakota hangover was getting worse.

"We kind of got off topic at your place." Aubrey stowed her phone in her handbag, giving me her full attention. "Tell me about this guy you met in Montana."

"Did you ever meet Dakota? He works for Thea at the bar."

Her eyes turned to saucers. "Black eyes, dark hair, scorch-the-earth hot Dakota?"

"That's the one." Though she'd forgotten sweet, kind and unforgettable. "We had a fling."

"You don't do flings."

"No, I don't." I had relationships. Always. "But you know, it was good. We ended on good terms—also something I don't normally do."

I spent the time it took us to drink two glasses of wine telling Aubrey all about my time in Montana. I told her about Dakota and how he'd shown me a different side to the world. How ten days in his simple lifestyle had been more fulfilling than the elaborate charade I'd created in my thirty-two years.

"Do you think you guys could try something long-distance?" Aubrey asked.

"No. We totally connected, you know? But we have such different lives. I think we were perfect for a fling. Long-term, we'd probably end up hating one another."

"What are you going to do?"

"Nothing. Something." I just didn't know what yet.

We sipped the dregs of our wine, and I glanced at the clock above the bar. "It's late. I guess I'd better let you get home. You probably have early morning meetings."

Aubrey smiled, not groaning like I would have at the

prospect of getting up at five to be at work by six. "That's probably a good idea. I'm tired."

We slid out of our booth, leaving some cash on the table for the drinks. Then we went outside and into the cold, where her driver was waiting.

The ride home was short, and I hugged Aubrey good-bye from the back of her town car before hustling inside my building and upstairs. The moment the penthouse door closed behind me, I leaned back against it and smiled.

Because I had a sister.

She'd always been there, but tonight, I'd had a friend too.

I dug my phone from my purse, not questioning or doubting my actions, and pulled up Dakota's number.

My heart raced as it rang once then twice. When he didn't answer on the third ring, I panicked, ready to hang up and forget it had ever happened. But then his voice came on the line and all my worries went away.

"Hey."

That voice. I twirled in a circle as I walked down the hall to my bedroom. "Hi. Am I bothering you?"

"Nope. Just at the bar. It's dead. I'm watching the game on TV until it's time to close."

"You should go home."

"Yeah," he muttered, sounding melancholy. Lonely.

He sounded hungover too.

The corner of my mouth pulled up, loving that my misery had company. "How have you been?"

"Meh. Fine."

"Is this okay? Me calling you?"

"Yeah. Thought about calling you yesterday too."

My heart soared. "It's weird to just shut things off, isn't it?"

"I was thinking the same thing yesterday." He chuckled. "You glad to be home?"

"Yes and no. I feel off, like I need to make some changes."

"Find your passion?"

"Something like that." I smiled at how well he knew me.

"Will you call me when you find it?"

When I discovered my passion, the person I would undoubtedly talk to first was Dakota Magee. "Count on it."

thirteen

DAKOTA

Four months later . . .

"CONGRATULATIONS, BUD."

I clinked my beer bottle with my uncle's. "Thanks."

We were sitting on the back porch of his and Hazel's lake cottage. The snow in the yard had finally melted away, revealing the soggy grass underneath. Across the yard, the water from the lake lapped the gravel shoreline.

"Five properties. Proud of you."

I was proud of myself too. It had been a long-ass winter in Lark Cove. The property I'd had my eye on since before Christmas had been the hardest one I'd ever bought. The negotiations had taken forever and the seller had nearly backed out. Twice. But we'd finally landed on a price and closed.

Then two weeks later, I'd stumbled across a screaming deal in the classifieds. I'd drained my savings, sold everything I could from my basement and managed to make a down payment.

The titles to both places had become mine within ten days of one another. I'd signed papers on the second this morning.

I was in, committed one hundred percent, praying that my renters would all stay put for the next twelve months until I built back up my savings cushion.

It was always exciting diving into another house, let alone two. The stress was mounting, but these two purchases had been smart. They were each the worst house on a nice block. I'd be putting more sweat equity into my investments than ever before, but it would be worth it in the long run.

If the market kept going up like it had over the last couple of years, I'd be able to sell both and turn a nice profit.

And I'd have something to do this spring and summer. I was aching for a distraction.

The last four months had been long and tiresome. I was hoping by throwing myself into another property, I'd get back to normal.

Maybe I'd get through a day without Sofia constantly popping into my mind.

"So what's next?" Xavier asked.

I blew out a long breath. "Paint. Lots of paint. See if I can get them both livable. Then I'm hoping to get a couple renters who won't mind me making updates while they're living there."

"Good plan."

"Xavier?" Hazel called from the kitchen.

My uncle turned his head over his shoulder, looking to the screen door that led inside from the porch. "Yeah, baby?"

"Would you start the grill?"

"On it." He stood from his chair and went to the grill on the other side of the porch. It was still cool outside, but like a lot of folks around here, the second the weather stayed above freezing, Hazel and Xavier busted out the grill.

They'd invited me over for steaks to celebrate my new property.

This had become a sort of tradition for us. As nice as it would be to see them, what I really wanted was to talk to Sofia.

The overwhelming urge to call her after I'd walked out of the title company today had nearly knocked me over. But had I called her? No.

Over the last four months, I'd become a chicken shit.

I'd spent the thirty-minute drive from Kalispell to Lark Cove taking out my phone only to put it away. A move I'd perfected since she'd left.

Fear, something I hadn't felt in a long time, had become a quiet companion.

Would she want to hear from me? I was terrified that I'd call her and she'd brush me off. Or worse, that she'd tell me she'd found someone new.

Christ. It wasn't like we'd been together. We weren't even really friends. But the hold that woman had on me after ten days was impossible to shake.

Hazel came outside with a plate of raw steaks. She handed them to Xavier, gave him her cheek for a kiss, then perched herself on the railing across from our chairs. Settled, she took out her pack of cigarettes and lit one up, blowing a stream of smoke toward the yard.

"You doing all right?" she asked.

I nodded. "Doing great."

She studied my face, her eyes narrowing on my own. "You've been off."

"Yeah." I shrugged. "It's just the winter. I'm ready for sunshine."

Hazel frowned. "Don't give me that bullshit. Your mood has nothing to do with the damn weather."

"Doesn't it?"

"Dakota. Spill."

I chuckled, taking a sip of my beer. "You never beat around the bush, do you? Why are you asking if you already know?"

"It's Sofia."

There was no use denying it so I nodded. "She's in my head."

And in my heart.

No woman had ever crept in there, not even Petah.

"What are you going to do?" she asked.

"Nothing to be done. We had fun. She's back in the city. I'm here. I'll always remember her though, you know? She'll stick with me."

Hazel's face softened as Xavier came over and resumed his seat. "Who'll stick with you?"

"Sofia," I told him.

"Hmm. You talk to her lately?"

"Nope." Which didn't matter. She was still on my mind.

I thought about her whenever I worked, if I was unloading the dishwasher or sweeping up the floor. I thought about her when I was at home and on the couch watching TV. She'd fit well with me on that couch. I thought about her when I was in my truck, and the kiss I'd given her good-bye the morning I'd dropped her off at Logan and Thea's place.

It hadn't been enough. I hadn't kissed her enough.

Because over the last four months, I'd forgotten what she tasted like.

Xavier and Hazel shared a look, one I ignored because it was full of pity. I didn't want to be fucking pitied. I hadn't gotten my heart broken. I hadn't gotten hurt.

I just missed her.

I missed that connection with another person. Maybe I

needed to go on a date. Get laid. It wasn't like I hadn't had the opportunity. But the idea of another woman in my bed, taking Sofia's place, didn't sit well in my gut.

Maybe this shitty attitude of mine was because I hadn't had sex in four months.

"So what's new with you guys?" I leaned forward on my elbows, more than ready for a change of subject.

Hazel and Xavier didn't answer my question. Instead, the pair shared another look. The two lovebirds had basically mind-melded over the last three years.

"Would you two stop that shit?" I grumbled. "I'm fine. We're celebrating."

Xavier put his hand on my knee, and I braced, ready for him to keep hold of the Sofia topic. "Want another beer?"

"Please."

"I'll get them." Hazel snubbed out her cigarette and slid off the porch rail, going inside as Xavier went back to the grill.

Thankfully, the conversation about Sofia was over. For now.

We enjoyed our meal at their small kitchen table, talking mostly about my new properties and the plans I had for improvements.

"I think I'll take a walk." I patted my stomach. "I ate too much."

"Sounds good." Xavier stood from the table at the same time I did, each of us clearing our plate to the sink. "I'll help my wife with the dishes."

"I won't be long." I went out the patio door, glad for the cool spring air as I walked outside. In early May, there was still the chance that we could get a late snow, but the weather was turning. It had rained this morning and the smell had lingered all day. As I set out across the yard, the woodsy scent from the evergreens towering over the shoreline filled my nose.

Montana was in my blood. The open plains. The brutal mountains. The sky, wide and blue. I ached to stretch my wings and explore, to experience what other places and people had to offer. But my roots would always bring me back here, where it smelled like home.

As I walked down the narrow road that wound around this cove of the lake, a weight lifted from my shoulders.

I'd been cooped up in the bar, working as much as possible to float that last property purchase. I needed to make more time to get outside, reset myself and take a breath.

I spent the next ten minutes walking in one direction before turning and heading back to the cottage. But instead of going back inside, I took a turn and went to the end of the dock that jutted out into the lake that abutted Hazel's property.

The dock was old. The boards had completely grayed and were warped at the edges. But it was a cool spot. Thea still waxed on about how much she missed this dock. It had been her spot to unwind when she'd lived in the cottage with Hazel.

I reached the end and looked out over the water. The sun was nearly gone behind the mountains in the distance, and soon the oranges and pinks would fade to black.

Above me, a few stars had already come out for the night.

I closed my eyes and took a long breath.

Maybe it was time to move on. Go on a date or something. Willa had come into the bar the other day with her and Jackson's new baby daughter Zoe. One of her old friends from high school had tagged along. Hannah was her name. She was good-looking and lived in Kalispell. She'd eye fucked me for nearly twenty minutes. No doubt she'd say *yes* to a night of fun.

I dismissed the idea instantly. I didn't need a local woman getting attached when all I really wanted was to blow off some steam. I'd wait until the summer when the tourists flocked to the bar. I'd never been short on action before, and this summer wouldn't be any different.

It wouldn't be long before I'd be back to myself.

I opened my eyes and watched the sun set. It was nearly dark and I was about to head back inside and say good night to Hazel and Xavier when my phone rang.

I fished it out of my pocket, not sure what I was expecting, and nearly fell face-first into the lake at the name on the screen.

Sofia.

She'd put her number in my phone the night before she'd left. I'd only seen it once, four months ago when she'd called me after getting back to the city.

My heart was nearly pounding out of my chest as I answered, "Hello."

"Hey." She was nervous. Just that one-word greeting and her voice shook.

"How are you?"

She blew out a breath. "I'm good, I think. I-I've been meaning to call you. But I've been nervous to tell you something."

My racing heart stopped cold. And I blurted the first nightmare that popped into mind. "You're pregnant."

"What? No! No, I'm not pregnant." She giggled. "But thanks for that. I needed to laugh."

Fuck. Me. She wasn't pregnant. My head was spinning so I took a step away from the edge of the dock, not wanting to end up in the water. Would it have been the worst thing in the world if she had been pregnant? *No. Yes.* Whatever. It didn't matter because she wasn't pregnant.

"Are you good? You're okay?" I asked.

"Yes, I'm good. On the cusp of great."

My heart had just started beating again, but with that, it flatlined. This was the part where Sofia told me she'd met someone. That she was getting remarried or she was in love with another man. This was the part where I lost her for good.

"What's up?" My voice was cold.

"Are you busy?" she asked. "I can call back later."

"No. Tell me."

"Okay. Here goes." She paused. "I found it."

"Found what?"

"My passion."

Her passion? What was she—*her passion*. How could I have forgotten? I'd told her to call me when she'd found her passion. "You found it?"

"Yes. I'm opening a dance studio."

A smile split my face. "That's fantastic."

"I'm really excited. I've been renovating this studio over the last three months and it's almost ready. I'm opening it in two weeks. On May fifteenth."

"I'm happy for you, babe."

"Happy enough to come over for the opening?"

I blinked, replaying her sentence. Had she just invited me to New York? Yes, she had. And there was no way I could afford to go.

If I hadn't just bought two new properties and sunk all of my reserves into a down payment, I would have blown some extra cash on a flight, no problem. But in two weeks? I couldn't swing it.

"I don't know if I can."

"Please? I'm not above begging. I really want you to be here."

"Why?"

"Because so much of this is because of you. I've felt different since I left. That magazine article. Working with you in the bar. I guess it inspired me to do more with my life. And honestly, I've missed you. I can't imagine opening this place without you here to see it too."

Saying no wasn't an option now. "I'll see if I can get some time off."

"Thank you. Let me know."

I hung up the phone, staring out over the water.

She'd found her passion. The smile on my face wouldn't go down.

A trip to New York City meant something in one of my new rentals would have to get delayed. Maybe new carpet. Maybe I'd find a renter who didn't care if the fridge was pea green.

I was brainstorming ideas for coming up with plane-ticket money as I turned and walked back down the dock. I said a quick good-bye to Hazel and Xavier, thanking them for dinner. Then instead of going home, I went to the bar.

Thea gave me a funny look as I walked through the front door. "Hey. What are you doing here?"

"I need a favor."

"Okay." She set down the sketchpad in her hand. Whenever it was slow, Thea drew pictures. I'd seen a couple sketches with my own face in them before, but tonight's was one of Camila.

"Can you trade me weekends in two weeks? I need it and the following Monday and Tuesday off." I hadn't asked for a day off in years. And I never changed the schedule. It felt strange asking for something.

"Um, of course." She nodded. "I'm sure either Jackson or I can be here. Is everything okay?"

"I'm good. Just had a last-minute vacation come up."

"Good for you. You never take vacations. Going anywhere fun?"

I tensed because there was no way I could hide this. "I'm actually going to New York."

"New Yor—the studio." She gave me a knowing grin. "You're going to Sofia's studio opening."

"I'd like to."

"I honestly didn't think you guys were still talking. Sorry. I should have thought of it sooner."

"It's fine. We haven't been talking. But she called and invited me. Sounds important to her."

"It is. She actually didn't tell us about it until last week. I think she's really nervous about what we'll all think. It's nice of you to be there for her."

"She'd do the same for me." I shrugged, not wanting to make a bigger deal about it than it was. I was just going over as a friend. *Right.*

Thea and I hadn't discussed all that had happened with me and her sister-in-law. So it was no surprise that she hadn't told me about Sofia's studio. It had become this non-discussion topic, probably because everyone thought we'd just been a fling.

No one knew how much I still thought about her.

"Take as much time as you need," she said. "Logan is going too, so you might as well fly over with him."

"Nah, that's okay. I can get a ticket."

"Or you can fly in a private jet for free." She rolled her eyes.

"The Kendricks have money, Dakota."

"I'm aware," I muttered.

"There's no shame in letting them do something nice for you."

"It's not that."

She cocked a hand on her hip. "Don't be that man."

"What man?"

"The one too proud to be with a rich woman. Because it's not Sofia's fault she was born wealthy."

"That's not . . ." I stopped myself before I could deny it. Because maybe there was some truth in what Thea was saying. And I really could use a free flight. "Okay. Thanks."

"You're welcome. I'll let Logan know you're hitching a ride."

I nodded, waved good-bye and left the bar. The second I got in my truck, I pulled out my phone and called Sofia. She answered on the first ring.

"Hi. So? Are you coming? Please tell me you're coming."

I grinned. "I'll be there."

"Shit. You guys are loaded, aren't you?"

Logan chuckled as we left his private jet and walked down the private runway toward a private helicopter pad where a chopper was waiting. "Friday night in the city. Traffic will be a nightmare."

I shook my head, trying to figure out what alternate reality I'd stepped into where a middle-class kid from a poor reservation was hanging with one of the richest men in America. From the moment I'd stepped into their cushy Gulfstream, I'd been waiting for someone to pinch me awake.

We loaded up our bags, got into the helicopter and put on some headphones. I'd never been in a helicopter before, so as the pilot made an announcement and took off, my jaw was on the floor.

I wanted a helicopter. I mentally scratched it on the list of things I'd buy if I won the lottery.

"You ever been?" Logan asked as the pilot flew us toward the towering skyscrapers in the distance.

"To New York? No." I glanced at him as I spoke, but it was nearly impossible to take my eyes off the view.

Pictures of New York City did it no justice. The sheer magnitude of the buildings beneath us, the number of people all living in a few hundred square miles, it made my pulse race.

This was what I was working for. *This.* To see the world. To experience things firsthand and get this rush of energy.

When I retired, I wouldn't be flying in private planes or taking helicopters instead of taxis. But I'd get to see the world.

In the distance, I spotted the Statue of Liberty, her arm raised high. That statue was a marvel. As an American, I appreciated her as a symbol for my country and my freedom, something my grandfather had fought to preserve in World War II. But as an American Indian, my ancestors hadn't come through Ellis Island. They'd been here long before, living off the earth.

The pilot signaled we were approaching our destination, forcing my eyes back to the buildings beneath us.

"That is the Kendrick Enterprises building," Logan spoke into the headset, pointing out the window to where we were headed. It wasn't as tall as some of the massive skyscrapers in the surrounding blocks, but it was wide with gleaming glass windows from top to bottom. "My family's company. My father and sister Aubrey work there."

I nodded, not having much else to say as the pilot began his descent to the landing pad.

The Kendrick fortune was unfathomable. It was impossible for me to wrap my head around that kind of money. I owned hundred-thousand-dollar rental homes in Kalispell, Montana. They owned a tower in Manhattan.

The pilot put us down on the rooftop, the blades whirling above us as we opened the door and stepped out, taking our bags with us.

The duffel bag I'd packed for the trip was a cheap thing I'd picked up years ago in a department store. One of the straps was broken and I'd duct taped it back together. When I'd handed it over to the flight attendant at the runway this morning, I'd regretted not buying a new suitcase. As I walked beside Logan into the elevator off the helipad, I covered the tape with my hand.

This was so damn intimidating.

At the elevator, instead of pushing the button to the ground floor, Logan pulled out his wallet, held it to a pad next to the buttons and pressed P. The access card in his wallet lit up the button on the board.

"Thanks for letting me tag along," I told him.

"Anytime." It was the same response he'd given me the other six times I'd said thanks.

The ride was short, but before the doors opened, Logan looked over and grinned. "See you on Monday."

The doors opened with a ding. He took a step out first, waving to a receptionist before walking to a huge glass office in the corner. Aubrey stood from her desk and hurried to the door to greet her brother.

"Hey."

My head whipped the other direction toward that sweet voice.

And there she was.

I swallowed hard. "Hey."

Sofia's face was made up flawlessly. Her hair was curled and falling down her chest, draping over the curve of her breasts. She'd worn black slacks today with a white silk blouse tucked into the waist.

I was in jeans and a blue button-down shirt I hadn't thought to iron. My brown boots were scuffed, like they'd been for years. But the nerves and insecurities I'd battled all day went away.

I didn't give a fuck what I was wearing. I didn't give a fuck where I was standing.

Not with Sofia Kendrick racing across the lobby.

And right into my arms.

fourteen

SOFIA

"I NEED." I PANTED TWICE. "MY KEY."

Dakota tore his mouth away from my neck, growling as I dug into my purse for the keycard to the penthouse. I found it and reached behind me, pressing it to the space above the handle.

My back was pressed against the door, my legs wrapped around Dakota's hips as he used an arm underneath my ass to hold me up.

The moment we'd stepped off the elevator into my private space, we'd attacked each other. The lobby outside my door was private, a waiting space for any visitors, which was good considering I'd torn Dakota's shirt over his head two seconds ago and my blouse was open and hanging loose, showing him the sheer lace bra underneath.

Both of us had swollen lips, and I'd scratched the skin on his shoulders, clawing my way up his body. He'd left a bite mark above my collarbone.

Four months without him had been too long.

With the door unlocked, Dakota turned the knob and pushed it open, carrying me inside. I dropped my thirteen-thousand-dollar handbag, not caring that the calfskin had never once touched a floor. All I cared about was getting Dakota's mouth back onto mine, feeling his soft, wet lips as his tongue pushed hard against my own.

His erection was digging into my core, the heat of my center permeating through my slacks and his jeans.

"Need. You." I was barely able to breathe as I slid a hand between us and went for his zipper.

He set me down on the hand-carved table in my entryway. My ass was barely perched on the wood, but it was enough that he could reach between us and free himself from his jeans.

My heart jumped as I saw the enormous bulge trying to break free from his black boxer briefs.

His calloused fingers went to the tab on my slacks, pulling them roughly apart. The zipper ripped open as his hands gripped the fabric on my hips, yanking them away along with my panties.

The movement pulled me off the table and right into his chest. I held on to his shoulders as he stripped me down, the wide-leg slacks pooling around my heels as I kicked them free.

I hopped back up into Dakota's arms and wrapped my legs around his back. My trainer had added a yoga regime over the last few months to help me manage stress. The results were mixed for my anxieties. But if this flexibility was a side benefit, yoga had just become a permanent practice.

Dakota yanked down the fabric of his briefs between us, fisting his cock and positioning it at my entrance.

I was primed and ready for his thrust, to be filled and stretched, but at the last second, I stopped him. "Wait."

His eyes snapped down to mine, his chest expanding in heaves. "What?"

"Condom?"

His eyes narrowed and the sudden tense of his jaw made me scramble.

"I haven't been with anyone," I blurted. "Have you?"

"No." And with that, he thrust forward, impaling me.

I cried out, my head falling backward as my eyes slammed shut. I shuddered as sheer pleasure rolled down my spine. My inner thighs trembled as he stayed rooted.

His arms were shaking as he held me up. His shoulders quivered as he held back his own release.

"Missed you." I dropped my chin and put my forehead onto his shoulder. "God, I missed you."

Dakota took two steps, maneuvering around the table so he could plaster my back up against the wall. When I was secure, he let go of my ass with one hand and brought it up to my face, cupping my cheek. "Missed you too."

I smiled then gave him my lips for a soft, sweet kiss. That was the only tender moment between us.

The frenzy that had brought us barreling into my penthouse returned, and we went at each other like animals.

My first orgasm came fast and with such force that my skull banged into the wall behind me.

After that, Dakota moved a hand to the back of my head, keeping it in place the entire time he fucked me with a relentless rhythm until I shattered around him once more, coaxing his own orgasm free.

With a spinning head and wobbling legs, Dakota put me down, his come dripping down my legs. That sexy smirk of his, the one he had whenever I was marked with his release, made him look so devilishly handsome.

"Thank you for coming."

He raised an eyebrow. "Don't have to thank me. The

pleasure was all mine."

I laughed. "Thanks for coming *to New York*."

"Welcome." He grinned. "From what I've seen, it's an awesome city."

"Do you feel like doing some sightseeing?"

"Yeah." He dropped his gaze to his bare cock, standing thick and glistening, ready for another go. "Let's start with your bedroom."

"Where do you want to go first?" I asked Dakota as we slid into the town car parked along the curb of my building.

"Your studio."

I smiled and looked to my driver, Glen, in the rearview mirror. "To the studio, please."

"Yes, Ms. Kendrick." He nodded and rolled up the partition between us.

Dakota and I hadn't left my penthouse yesterday after he'd arrived. We'd spent the rest of the day in my bed, remembering how it felt to be together. We'd ordered in dinner and eaten it at my kitchen island. Then he'd fucked me again, this time on the beige couch in my living room.

Surrounded by my classic furniture and a spring mix of white flowers on my coffee table, I'd finally figured out what had been bugging me for four months. I'd realized what had been missing from my home.

Him.

I'd been missing him, and he hadn't even been in my apartment before.

But sitting on my couch alone was miserable compared

to cuddling into his chest. Standing in the kitchen was lonely when he wasn't there, teaching me how to cook. My bedroom was too quiet at night without his heavy breathing into my hair.

Not so deep down, I'd known it for months. Which was probably why I'd thrown myself so completely into the studio. It had given me a reason not to be at home. Not here, where I was alone.

I'd gotten into a routine over the last three months, one that kept me away as much as possible. I'd get up, go to the gym then come home and get ready for the day. I'd have a latte and visit with Carrie before heading out. Then I'd spend the rest of my time at my temporary office at Kendrick Enterprises, the one I'd been using up until my office at the studio was finished just last week.

Working two floors down from Aubrey had become extremely convenient since she'd managed to cut some things from her schedule in order to give me advice on starting up a business.

Still, with all of my planning, I had never been this nervous.

"It's not much," I warned Dakota.

"Doesn't have to be. Tell me about it."

I took a deep breath. "It's in Midtown, not all that far from my family's building."

Aubrey lived about five blocks from the studio. She'd chosen a sprawling penthouse in Midtown rather than SoHo or Tribeca because she wanted to be close to work, whereas I'd chosen my neighborhood because celebrities flocked to those areas.

"So, dance?" Dakota asked. "Ballet?"

"Originally, I'd thought just ballet. But then I decided to

offer all kinds of dance. My jitterbug lesson with Wayne was an inspiration."

He chuckled. "I like it. What else?"

"It's just for kids eighteen and under. I might expand it someday for adults, but this is where I thought it would be best to start."

"Good thinking."

I looked up at his profile, studying the stern, straight set of his nose. That his serious brow and naturally narrowed eyes had once intimidated me now seemed funny.

I leaned closer, threading my arm through his and hugging it against my chest. Then I rested my ear on his shoulder as we navigated through the busy Manhattan streets.

"Thank you for coming."

He kissed my temple. "Wouldn't miss it."

Traffic was busy this morning, and the trip took more than twice as long as usual, but thirty minutes later, Glen dropped us off in front of the corner space I'd purchased in a midsize building.

"This is it." I swung my hand out at the front door as we stood on the sidewalk, my stomach in my throat as I waited for his reaction.

The pair of us were reflected in the floor-to-ceiling windows on the front of the building. Inside, the mirror-covered walls and wooden floors gleamed in the sunlight. A sign with details for the grand opening on Monday hung on the entrance.

"Midtown Dance Studio." Dakota read the name written on the glass in classic white blocked letters. Underneath was the website address and phone number.

"Too boring?" I asked.

He shook his head. "No, not at all. It's clean. Simple. Easy to remember and google. Except you don't have your name anywhere."

"I didn't want my name on this place."

His forehead furrowed. "Why not? You should be damn proud of this."

"It's not that. I just . . . I didn't want it to be showy. I didn't want it to be about me."

"Huh?"

I pulled his hand and led him to the front door, where I got out my keys and unlocked the latch. Inside, the place still smelled like fresh paint. The crew had just finished up the lobby two mornings ago. I'd had a final walk-through with the foreman yesterday, a couple of hours before I'd gone to Kendrick Enterprises to wait for Dakota.

Flipping on a light, I walked up to the reception counter, where I had stacks of our intake paperwork.

I pulled a flyer from behind the counter and handed it over to Dakota, shifting back and forth on my wedged heels as he read the sheet.

I worn jeans today, knowing he'd be in them too. I'd reverted back to my normal New York style over the last four months, wearing clothes that fit better for a future businesswoman and philanthropist.

But today, I didn't need to dress for meetings. Today, I was dressed for pure fun. Something else I'd missed. Starting the studio had been exhilarating, fun at times, but also full of strife. I had no doubt that today would be one of the best I'd had in four months.

I'd fallen back into old routines since leaving Montana. I'd developed some new ones, namely this business and throwing myself into it headfirst, but since my drinks with Aubrey all those months ago, I hadn't left the penthouse without makeup. I'd dressed impeccably each day.

Maybe that was why it had taken so long to call Dakota. I'd been worried that this version of Sofia, the one who was still trying to find herself, wouldn't be the one he wanted.

I'd been worried that he'd already moved on.

When I'd called him two weeks ago, it had been from this very spot.

The walls in the studio hadn't been painted their cream yet. The Sheetrock had just been taped and textured. The floors had been draped in plastic and splattered with drywall compound. My office had been a mess of supplies and things waiting to get put away.

When I'd called Dakota, I'd been close to panic. I'd been so sure this would be a failure I'd nearly had a breakdown.

But just one hello from him and it had all gone away.

I'd stood there, staring at my mess, and had known I could see it through.

"It's free?" Dakota asked after he finished reading the flyer.

"Yes, it's free. Kids from low-income families don't have to pay. We ask those who can afford lessons to simply make donations when they are able."

I wanted all kids to get to have dance lessons. Somehow, my lessons had been the thing to stick with me. They'd been the quiet passion I'd kept for all these years. I didn't want to deny that to any child in the city just because they couldn't afford one of the pricey studios nearby.

"So you're running a business and a charity?"

I shrugged. "Well, not *me*. At first, I was going to try and do it all myself, but then I had a couple of meetings with Aubrey and, well, I saw some shortcomings. If I really wanted this place to be a success, I needed help from people who are better at the business side. So I hired an operations manager who is going to run the day-to-day. And there are teachers who will teach the actual dance classes."

I knew my limitations well enough to know that, while I found the business strategy interesting, it wasn't my forte. If we were going to grow, I needed help. I was the creator and artistic director. I would play a key role in fundraising. But my staff would take on the rest. That way, I could keep my freedom and wouldn't have to commit to being here every day.

"So far we have about a hundred kids signed up," I told him. "That's enough to fill most of the evening classes. But I'm hoping we'll get more. The manager and I were talking about reaching out to inner-city children's programs and having kids bussed here, since their parents might not be able to afford transportation."

Dakota nodded and pointed to the glass separating the parent observation area and the actual dance room. "Can we go in?"

"Sure." I led him past the reception counter and down a hallway, pointing to the various doors as we walked. "Locker rooms are on the right, one for boys and one for girls. Next is my manager's office. And mine is at the end of the hallway."

I took a left through the open, double doors into the dance studio. It was dim, only lit up by the sunshine streaming through the front windows. But it was wide and open. Along the back wall ran a bar for the ballet classes.

"This is something." Dakota walked deeper into the space, taking it all in as he lapped the room. "Why'd you decide to do it for free?"

"It's not like I need the money," I teased. "But mostly

because I didn't want to risk turning my passion into something negative."

"What do you mean?"

"My dad worked all the time when I was growing up. He still does. He never made it to one of my dance recitals because there was always a conflict, a meeting or an event. My grandfather worked just as hard as Dad does, right up until he died. My sister is worse than both of them. So I guess I've always seen work as this bad thing. Up until you."

"Me?"

I nodded. "You showed me that even working in an old bar in Montana can be fun. That there is joy to be found in a job. I've never had one. So for my first real job, I want to make sure it's something that won't ever ruin my passion. The best way I could think of doing that was to make sure it never became about the money."

Dakota nodded but didn't say anything as he continued to walk the room in a slow circle, inspecting every inch. My anxiety grew tenfold with each of his steps.

"Do—" I swallowed hard, dreading his answer. "Do you think that's stupid?"

"No." He stopped walking and leveled me with his gaze. "It's brilliant."

The urge to cry hit hard, and I choked on the lump in my throat. I so wanted to share this opening with Dakota. He had been such an inspiration to me. But more than I wanted him here, I wanted him to think my idea was special.

Because I thought everything about him was remarkable.

I blinked away the tears prickling the corners of my eyes. My chin fell, hiding my watery gaze as Dakota's footsteps came closer.

His boots stopped close to my toes as his hand came to my cheek, cupping it and turning my face up to his.

"I'm such a crier." I sniffled. "I'm pitiful."

"Don't say that," he whispered.

Just like that, we were out of my studio and back in Lark Cove, where he'd said the same thing to me over a pile of peanut shells. Back to the place where I'd fallen for him.

A tear dripped down my cheek without permission, but he caught it with his thumb. "I'm proud of you. So damn proud."

"Stop," I pleaded. "You'll just make me cry more."

"Then cry, babe."

I fell forward, my head collapsing into his chest. His long arms wound around my back, and he held me until I let go of a few more tears and then fought the rest back.

There were so many emotions swirling, I didn't know how to deal with them.

He was here. I'd missed him.

He was leaving. I'd miss him again.

I was excited for the studio to open. I was terrified that the studio would fail.

"What if it does?" I asked quietly into his black shirt.

"What if what does?"

I looked up. "What if the studio fails?"

"It won't. You won't let it fail."

"But what—"

He pressed his finger against my lips, cutting me off. "When I bought my first rental, I asked my uncle the same thing. You know what he told me?"

I shook my head.

"He told me to ask a different *what if*. What if I hate being a landlord? What if a tenant asked to buy the place, and I sold it sooner than I'd planned? What if a house got struck by lightning and burned to the ground? Would those things make me a failure?"

"No."

"No. It just means that you live and learn. This might not be the thing you do your entire life. But if you give it your all, you'll never be a failure."

I sagged against his chest again. "Thank you."

He had no idea how much I'd needed to hear those words.

My biggest fear wasn't just failure but disappointment. If this studio flopped, I had no idea how my family would react. I was so nervous I'd sworn Aubrey to secrecy months ago, making her promise to let me tell the rest of them in my own time. I'd even managed to avoid Dad at Kendrick Enterprises when I'd gone into work.

But a week and a half ago, with the opening looming, I finally had to confess and tell them about what I'd been up to. Their excitement had just made my anxieties worse.

"I don't want to let my family down," I whispered. "Not again."

"You might."

"What?" I stood back, making sure I'd heard him right.

"You might." He nodded. "You might not do exactly what they want or how they want it. But take it from a guy who has disappointed his family for years. It doesn't matter. Don't do this because you want to make them proud. Do this because it's going to feed your spirit. My guess? They'll be damn proud, no matter what happens."

"I hadn't thought about it that way." I let his words sink in then gave him a smile. "You always know the right thing to say."

He chuckled. "Glad you think so because I'm just winging it."

"Come on." I took his hand and led him out of the studio and back to the hallway. "I'll show you the offices. Then we can explore the city. Is there anywhere you'd like to go?"

"How about you take me to your favorite places? Give me the Sofia Kendrick tour of the city."

I smiled. "You don't want to see the tourist stops?"

He shrugged. "I can hit them another time."

My heart leapt. "You're coming back?"

"Maybe someday. It's a cool city. I'll have to hit up the landmarks one day."

"Oh." My excitement died. Of course he wouldn't be back to visit me. He was here as a one-time favor because I'd practically begged him to come.

The sex was a bonus, though if I'd taken it off the table, he still would have flown over. This was nothing more than a weekend affair. Wasn't it?

So why had he gone through a four-month dry spell? Why had I? Was there more here than just occasional, long-distance lovers?

Maybe there was a future. Maybe this short-lived affair didn't have to be short-lived. Maybe we had something real.

For once in my life, I'd found a man who was worth my attention.

Except when I looked into the future, I couldn't picture us together. I couldn't see myself living in Montana. I couldn't see him here with me in the city. Was there an in-between? A lifestyle that fit for us both?

My mind came up empty.

What did that mean?

I didn't have time to dream up answers. We reached my office and I gestured for him to walk in first. "Here's my office. It just got finished the other day."

"Nice." Dakota walked in and ran his fingers over my white desk. Then he turned and perched his ass on a corner.

"I like it."

I stared at him as he took in the bookshelves along one wall and the painting on the other. He'd be the finest man I'd ever have in this room. Dakota was more than just a good guy. He was top-shelf. His moral fiber ran so deep it was ingrained in his very being. With him, there were no games. No tricks. No ulterior motives.

He was just pure and honest.

If he wanted more of a relationship, he would have told me so. If he saw a future between us, he'd have clued me in.

Which meant this was it. This weekend in New York would be our last together.

And I was going to make it count.

I walked over to him, fitting myself between his bulky thighs. "Would you mind doing one more thing for me before we go exploring?"

"Shoot."

I ran my hands up his chest, wrapping them around his broad shoulders. Then I leaned in and ran my nose around the shell of his ear. "Let's break in my desk."

fifteen

DAKOTA

SOFIA AND I SPENT ONE OF THE BEST WEEKENDS OF MY LIFE IN the city.

We walked through Central Park along a path she said was once her favorite running trail when she'd lived on the Upper East Side years ago. She took me to the Met, her favorite museum, and showed me her favorite paintings, some of which were tucked away in corners I wouldn't have found myself. We spent hours strolling along the city sidewalks, her arm linked with mine as she pointed out places here and there that held a memory for her.

It was an adventure, exploring and getting a glimpse into her life. Even though she'd lived outside the city at her family's estate on Long Island as a child, she'd lived in the city ever since high school. And it was a part of her, like Montana was a part of me. It was where her roots had come from. Her culture and heritage.

During the day, we went sightseeing, but at night, we were in her bed. I made sure to get my fill of her taste, that sweetness on my tongue I'd forgotten over the last four months.

After this weekend, I wasn't sure when I'd get to see her again.

I sure as hell couldn't afford a trip to New York, and with her dance studio opening, she'd be tied up here, unable to visit Montana.

It was for the best. Wasn't it?

We were destined for different lives.

As I stood outside the bathroom in her penthouse, watching from the doorway as she put on her makeup, I couldn't ignore the sinking feeling in my gut. I'd been pushing it away all weekend.

This trip would be the end.

But not quite. In an hour, we were going to the studio. Then we'd be heading to dinner with her family. First thing tomorrow morning, a car was picking me up outside her building to take me back to the airport where I'd be flying back to Montana with Logan.

This was it.

So I studied her, watching as she leaned in closer to the mirror to swipe some mascara on those eyes. Eyes I'd never forget, no matter how many months or years or decades had passed.

Those eyes, I'd remember for the rest of my life.

Sofia was going all-out glam for tonight, though the grand opening, I'd learned, wasn't going to be all that grand of an affair. Sofia had invited her family to come down and watch the first class. Her business manager and dance instructors had also invited some friends and family.

In all, it would be a quiet event with some cookies for the kids and refreshments for the rest of us. Sofia had arranged to do a champagne toast before the first class started.

The big fanfare was to come in three weeks. She'd been organizing a gala to fundraise for the studio. It would be a glamorous event with ball gowns and tuxedos, catering to some of New York's richest.

I was glad she hadn't invited me to that one. Tonight's simple get-together would serve me just fine.

"Are you going to just watch me?" Sofia smiled in the mirror, her eyes catching mine.

"Yep."

"Well, I'm about to put on my lipstick. So you'd better come get a kiss while you still can."

I strode into the room, stepping up behind her in front of the vanity. She tipped her chin, looking over her shoulder just in time for me to set a soft kiss on her lips.

When she turned back, she smiled at me in the mirror then dropped her gaze to the lipstick next to the sink. But she didn't reach for it. Instead, she just stared blankly at the marble underneath her palms.

"There's only going to be a few kids tonight. Just so you know."

"It's the first day. I didn't expect a packed house."

"We're only doing the one class."

"I know." Sofia had already told me that when she'd explained the evening's plan. "What's going on in your head, babe?"

She blew out a long breath. "I just don't want you to expect this big show. It's probably going to be small. Nothing major."

"Are you worried about me? Or your family?"

Her shoulders fell. "I'm worried about everything."

"Hey. Look at me." I waited until her dark eyes found mine in the mirror. "You got this."

"I don't," she whispered.

"You do. You. Got. This. And I can't wait to be there tonight when you realize it too."

A flicker of confidence sparked in her eyes, chasing away the fear. Her back straightened against my chest as she stood taller. "Thank you."

I dropped a kiss to her temple, ran my hands up and down her bare arms and left her in the bathroom to finish getting ready.

There wasn't much I could do for a woman who had everything in the world. But for tonight, I could be here. I could boost her up until she felt capable of flying on her own.

An hour later, we were getting out of her town car in front of the studio. As Sofia stepped onto the sidewalk, a whole crew of women—all dressed similarly to her in fitted cocktail dresses—rushed out of the studio's front door to greet her.

I stepped out behind her, grinning as she laughed with her staff. She shot me a look over her shoulder, her eyes bright, as they ushered her inside.

"Thanks for the ride." I jerked my chin to Glen, who was standing by the driver's side door, smiling at Sofia.

He nodded. "Tell her good luck for me."

"Will do." I waved and walked inside the studio.

The second the door opened, the hushed whispering inside stopped, and the room went dead silent.

"Everyone, this is Dakota. We're—"

"Coworkers." I smirked, remembering how she'd introduced herself to my family.

A slow smile spread across her gorgeous face. "Coworkers."

"Are there more of him where you used to work?" one of the women asked Sofia.

The entire group burst out giggling except for the tall, lean Asian man behind the reception counter who shook his head.

"Can we please focus? We have one hour. Let's make sure everything is ready to go."

With a chorus of agreement, the reception area cleared, leaving just me, Sofia and the man.

"Dakota Magee, meet Daniel Kim," Sofia said. "Daniel is my operations manager here at the studio."

I shook the man's hand over the reception counter. "Good to meet you."

"Same to you." He nodded. "I've heard a lot about you."

"That so?"

Daniel chuckled. "I have you partly to thank for my job. She gives you a lot of credit for this place. Or the motivation to try, at least. I'm glad you could be here today."

"So am I, but I get no credit for this. It's all her." I held Sofia's dark eyes, making sure she heard this next part. "You did this. It's all you. And it's incredible."

"It hasn't even opened yet," she mumbled, dismissing the compliment.

"Doesn't matter. It's still true."

This studio would be a success, I was sure of it. But Sofia would need time to find that confidence.

She'd spent too many years sitting idle. Too many years believing that she was nothing more than the woman others told her she was.

This place would change it all.

"I've been trying to give her compliments for weeks." Daniel walked around the counter. "She brushes mine off too. Doesn't mean I won't keep trying." He went right up to Sofia's side and threw his arm around her shoulders.

With that move, Daniel got my full attention. My eyes narrowed, looking him up and down. He wore a fitted black suit, the dress shirt under his jacket also black, and two buttons from the collar were open.

Unbuttoned that far down, I should have seen some chest hair. But Daniel must believe in waxing because his skin was smooth. Was that what men did here in the city? Waxed to get the attention of a woman like Sofia Kendrick?

They worked together. I knew firsthand how easy it could be to fall for Sofia when she was your coworker. If I called her in a few months, would she be with Daniel? Would he be the one watching her get ready in the bathroom mirror? My jaw ticked as jealousy brewed like a thunderstorm inside my chest.

Daniel must have sensed it, because he grinned and let her go, discreetly flashing me his left hand and the gold band on his ring finger.

I breathed, glad there was one less man in Manhattan I had to worry about when I left.

Sofia came over and slid into my side, unaware of the exchange.

My arm went right to the place where Daniel's had just been. This weekend, she was mine.

The door behind us opened, and Sofia's parents, her sister and Logan came inside the studio. Logan was escorting an older woman who was smiling wide as she took in the room.

Sofia unhitched herself from my side, dragging in a steadying breath as she turned to greet her family. "Hi, Mom and Dad. Thanks for coming."

Her mom came over and kissed Sofia's cheek. "This is wonderful, sweetheart."

"I love everything you've done here." The elderly woman came over and gave Sofia a firm hug.

"Thank you, Granny. I'm glad you could be here."

"Me too. Pop would be so proud of you."

Sofia nodded, blinking a couple of extra times. No doubt she was on the verge of tears, but she was holding strong, keeping them back. Later tonight I'd probably find her in her closet, shedding the emotion from the evening.

"Congratulations!" Aubrey came over next, giving Sofia a quick hug before waving at me.

I nodded my silent greeting. It never failed to surprise me how much Aubrey looked like Logan and Thea's oldest daughter, Charlie.

"The place looks fantastic." Sofia's father was still inspecting the place as he spoke and walked toward the counter. He picked up one of the flyers, the same one I'd read when I'd first come here. "Smart. This entire setup is so smart."

"Thanks, Dad." She swallowed hard, her eyes glistening. "I'm glad you could make it."

"I missed a lot of stuff when you were a kid. I'm trying to do better. I wasn't going to miss this."

I took a step toward Sofia, ready to give her a reassuring hug, but her brother beat me to it.

"I wouldn't miss it either." Logan let his sister go then shook my hand. "How was the weekend?"

"Good. This is quite the city." And spending it with Sofia had been the experience of a lifetime.

"Mom, Dad, Granny," Sofia swung her arm out to me, "I'd like you to meet Dakota Magee. He works with Thea in Lark Cove. He flew out with Logan for the opening. These are my parents, Thomas and Lillian Kendrick. And my grandmother, Joan."

I shook Thomas's hand first, hoping he couldn't feel my own tremble. "Sir."

"Dakota, welcome."

Thomas was an older version of Logan. He wore an expensive suit that was tailored around his broad shoulders. The man had probably worn suits every day for the last forty years. His gray hair was styled and combed, and the smell of his aftershave wafted between us like he'd been freshly shaved.

"Thank you for coming." Lillian came over next. After a slight embrace, she stayed close and offered me her cheek.

I hesitated, every second getting more awkward as she waited, then it dawned on me what she was after. I dropped a kiss on her cheek, she smiled and walked away. It was the strangest greeting I'd ever had, since I'd never kissed a stranger's cheek before. It was just as strange to repeat it with Sofia's grandmother.

"You'll be joining us for dinner, won't you?" Lillian asked.

"Yes, ma'am." And thanks to Logan, who was wearing jeans, I wouldn't feel completely out of place.

The door opened again and other people shuffled inside. Sofia went to greet them as I stood back and watched her family. They were in awe of her accomplishment, unable to soak it all in. They wandered around the reception area, touching chairs and walls and counters to make sure it was real.

Sofia had confessed the other night she'd kept this place a secret from everyone but Aubrey. They'd only learned about it a week before she'd called me. And none of them, not even her sister, had gotten to see the place.

I'd been the first.

"Excuse me, Ms. Kendrick?" A woman with long red hair tied into a twist came into the reception area. "We're all set up with the champagne and appetizers in the common room."

"Thank you, Carrie." Sofia nodded then addressed the

room. "We're having a small toast for the opening before the first students get here. You are all welcome to some champagne as you meet the staff. Then please feel free to wander through the studio."

The room emptied as people migrated down the hallway, leaving just me and Sofia in the reception area.

Her smile stayed in place until she was sure we were alone. Then her guard fell and underneath, she looked ready to puke.

"You okay?"

She nodded *yes* but her face said *no*.

I held out my hand, palm up. She immediately put hers in mine, lacing our fingers together.

"You got this."

She took a long, deep breath then squared her shoulders. "I got this."

"You crushed it, babe."

"I'm trying my very hardest to be modest and not jinx myself here, but I so did."

Sofia laughed and fell into my side, letting her head rest on my shoulder as the car wove through the dark streets toward SoHo.

In just a long weekend, I'd gotten used to riding in this position. It would be strange going home and driving myself. It would be stranger not having Sofia at my side.

"I'm so full." Sofia sighed. "Dinner was delicious."

"Best steak I've had in years." Though if asked, I'd swear on my life nothing could beat Xavier's grill.

The opening had gone as well as I'd imagined. I'd stayed in

the wings, just watching and waiting. I'd kept my focus entirely on her in case she needed a reassuring nod.

She had at first, but then she'd stepped into her own.

And I couldn't have been prouder.

The studio had been filled with friends and family members, since most of the staff had invited their significant others to come for the opening.

Sofia started the evening by thanking each employee by name. She gave a short speech, expressing how much it meant that they'd take a gamble on a new company. Then she raised her glass of champagne and toasted Midtown Dance Studio.

The room cheered.

After that, she welcomed the entire group to the studio, opening it up for an informal self-guided tour. Most everyone had a flute of champagne in their hand as they walked through the studio, while Sofia kept a bottle in hers, refilling glasses until the reception was over.

There were ten kids for the first class, all girls in pink tights, black leotards and huge smiles. Besides the three instructors in the studio, the rest of us sat with the parents in the observation area and watched the girls learn about first, second and third positions.

When the class was over, Sofia handed the duties over to Daniel to close down, and we rode with her family in their limousine to dinner.

The restaurant we'd gone to had required jackets. They only took reservations. We'd walked in, not having either, and found ourselves in a small room at the back with a private waitstaff and bartender.

"Your family is nice," I told her.

"They are. I'm glad they got to meet you."

"Same here."

They were all down-to-earth and genuine. They used their wealth but didn't flaunt it. Not once had they made it known they stood about ten classes above mine. They were just . . . people. People with money.

Her granny was a kick, her attitude and sarcasm reminding me of Hazel. Lillian was sweet, a more sensitive soul than the others. Kind of like her youngest daughter. Her dad and Aubrey were a pair. They'd started to talk about work during the appetizers, but Logan had shot them a look and it had ceased immediately.

"My dad . . ." Sofia trailed off.

I waited for her to continue, but all I heard was a sniffle. "Your dad, what?"

"He didn't take his phone out." She leaned back and looked up with tears in her eyes.

"And that's a bad thing?"

"No." She wiped her eyes dry. "No, it's a good thing. He's always on his phone. But tonight, he wasn't just there, he was *present*. When I was a kid, he never once made it to my dance recitals. I never saw him at the dinner table without his phone in his hand. He was always working. I don't think I realized how angry I've been about that. But after tonight, it feels like I can let some of that go."

"Good for you."

She fell back into my arm, clutching it tighter than before. "I can't thank you enough for being here. I wish you could stay longer."

"Yeah, me too."

"Could you? I know you've got your new properties, but can they survive a few extra days without you?"

I sighed and shook my head. "No, I need to get back."

There was a ton of work to be done, and I needed to put some hours in at the bar. And though both of those things could have been pushed back a day or two, it was best we cut this short.

Glen pulled up outside her building and opened his door, ready to get out and open ours, but I stopped him. "I got it."

"Yes, sir." He turned back and smiled at Sofia. "Congratulations on your opening tonight."

"Thank you. Sorry to keep you out late."

"It's my pleasure." He looked to me. "Safe travels home, Mr. Magee."

I nodded, opened the door and helped Sofia out. Then we went inside, waving to her doorman as we passed through the lobby and right to the elevator.

The moment we stepped foot inside her penthouse, Sofia kicked off her heels and flew into my arms, wrapping them tightly around my waist.

I didn't hesitate, holding her right back.

"Am I going to see you again?" she whispered.

"Someday." I hoped.

"I don't want this to be the end."

I dropped my cheek to the top of her head, wishing we had more time and knowing we didn't.

Our futures followed two different paths. Paths that ran in two different directions. Our time at their intersection was over.

"Tell me something. Can you look into the future and see us together?"

I wanted her answer to be *yes*. I wanted her to paint me a picture of a future where Sofia Kendrick and Dakota Magee stayed together. Because for all the hours I'd spent trying, I sure as hell couldn't imagine one.

We were a void. An empty, black box.

Her frame slumped. "No. Honestly, I've tried. But I just can't see it."

"Me neither."

She sniffled, her chin quivering against my chest. "I hate this."

"So do I."

Sofia leaned back, giving me eyes full of unshed tears. "One more night."

One more night.

I bent, scooping her up under the knees, and carried her down the long hallway and up the stairs to her bedroom. There we spent the night together, forsaking sleep like we had during our last night in Montana. We spent the hours holding tight to those last precious moments.

When morning came, Sofia and I stood on the sidewalk outside her building. Her eyes were red rimmed and full of despair. I hated that when she let loose, when she cried after the car parked at the curb pulled away, I wouldn't be here to hold her.

"So, I'll see you when I see you." She forced a smile.

I nodded. "See you when I see you."

"You can call me. Whenever you want, call me."

"Same to you."

Neither of us would be making that call.

The first good-bye in Lark Cove had been hard. This one, nearly impossible. I wouldn't be able to walk away from a third. Phone calls and texts would only make things harder.

"Take care of yourself, Sofia Kendrick." I cupped her cheek, letting the warmth from my palm heat her skin. Then I dropped a soft kiss to her lips and another to her temple.

My temple.

Letting her go was the hardest thing I'd done in years, but I dropped my hand, turned and walked to the car.

I didn't look back. In the reflection of the car's tinted windows, she waved. She began to cry as she whispered, "Goodbye, Dakota Magee."

sixteen

SOFIA

Three months later . . .

"I THINK WE NEED TO HIRE ANOTHER BALLET INSTRUCTOR," Daniel said.

We were standing side by side in front of the observation window, watching the afternoon advanced ballet class.

"I could do it."

His face snapped to mine, but I kept watching as the girls practiced their pliés. "I thought you didn't want to be tied to a schedule."

I shrugged. "I'm here anyway. It would be fun."

In the three months since the studio had opened, something had happened I would have bet my trust fund would be impossible.

I had turned into a workaholic.

I was the first one here each day, coming straight to the studio after meeting with my trainer at six each morning. I'd make coffee, tidy up if needed, then settle into my office, working there until the instructors showed up at two each afternoon to prep for class. Once the children arrived, I'd visit with parents and loiter in the reception area. And when everyone had left for the night, I'd let Daniel escort me out, and

I'd lock up behind us both.

I wasn't sure if the studio's locks would accept anyone else's key but mine.

Work was the best thing for me, I'd learned. Staying home was too lonely and depressing. At least here, I was happy.

Or, happy-ish.

Was this why Dad and Aubrey worked so much? Were they avoiding things at home? Or did they just love their jobs?

At the moment, mine was a combination of both. I'd built ultimate flexibility into my job, but I had no desire to use it. So if I was going to be here anyway, why not teach?

"How about this?" Daniel turned his back to the glass. "What if we advertised for an instructor, and if we don't find one we want to hire, you can do it? If you feel like teaching, you can pop in and out. And if we need one and you're here, you can always be a substitute teacher."

"Or I could be *the* teacher."

"But what if you decide to take a vacation? Like an impromptu trip to, say . . . I don't know. Montana?"

I shot him a glare. "Would you stop with that?"

"Sorry." He held up his hands. "It was only a suggestion."

"You're worse than my parents."

My parents were quite enchanted with Dakota. It was a welcome change, considering their cold attitude when I'd brought home other men. My father had barely spoken to Bryson the first time I'd invited him to a family dinner.

But with Dakota, everything was different. My father liked his entrepreneurial spirit. Granny loved his ability to banter. Aubrey liked that he was hardworking. And Mom had simply appreciated he'd beat the waiter to pull out her chair at the dinner table.

Like me, they'd all fallen for Dakota. It had taken nearly all of the past three months to get them to stop asking when he'd be visiting again. They didn't understand why we weren't in a relationship.

Especially when the relationships I had chosen had been with such losers. Mom especially was bewildered that I'd let Dakota go.

What my family didn't realize was that we'd set each other free.

It was for the best. I kept telling myself that. If he couldn't see us together, we'd be doomed before we started.

As much as he was his own man who made his own path, I knew his family's influence played a part in his decisions—whether he wanted to admit it or not. For so long, he'd been taught to pick a suitable partner, a woman who shared his heritage.

I was not that woman.

Maybe the reason he couldn't picture us together was because I'd never be right. It was crushing. Soul crushing. For once, I'd found the right guy. And for once, I wasn't the right girl.

The irony had sent me into my new workaholic state. Was three months long enough for that self-appointed title?

Whatever. I was keeping it. Because that was *my* heritage.

"Fine. I'll settle for substitute teacher," I told Daniel then walked away from the window and down the hallway to my office.

"You are the boss." Daniel followed me and took the guest chair in front of my desk. "You can overrule me."

"No, you're right. We should hire an instructor. If we can find someone with a few professional accolades, that might help with fundraising too."

"If you keep raising money, we're going to need to expand."

"Should we?"

His face blanched. "I was joking."

"But what if you weren't?"

Daniel thought about it for a moment, pondering the idea. We'd only been open for three months, but our classes were full and I had a waiting list of schools with children interested in attending in lieu of an after-school program.

We'd raised three years' worth of operating costs at our grand opening gala, seven times what we'd projected. It put us in a great spot to run the studio for years. And worst-case scenario, if everything fell to pieces, I was not above using my trust fund to supplement the donations.

Expanding meant twice the cost. Maybe three times. And it meant finding a larger building or opening a satellite studio.

But the prospect of another huge project to consume my every waking minute was so tempting I was practically drooling as Daniel sat, silently contemplating my suggestion.

"It's so soon." He worried his bottom lip between his teeth, a nervous habit I'd noticed early on in our working relationship.

"Let's think about it. Hire your instructor. Run some numbers because I know you, and you won't be able to sleep until you have everything analyzed in a spreadsheet. Then let's talk. But I don't want to slow down. We have momentum right now, and I don't want to lose it."

The authority in my voice was surprising. Exciting, even. Usually, he was the one giving me orders, even though I was technically the boss.

Daniel nodded, still deep in thought. When he stood up from the chair, I knew I'd sparked an interest because he went to his neighboring office and closed the door.

Daniel only closed his office door when he needed to concentrate.

I had a feeling I'd be getting an email in the middle of the night with colorful graphs and charts showing me exactly what an expansion would entail.

Alone in my office, I spent the rest of the evening returning a few emails and handwriting thank-you notes to our latest donors. I said good night to the last class of children, waited for the instructors to grab their things and leave, then knocked on Daniel's office door.

"Time to go home."

"Huh?" He looked up from the mess of papers on his desk. He'd rolled up his shirtsleeves and gotten out his reading glasses.

"It's seven o'clock."

He looked at the clock on the wall, then frowned. "I'm not done. But if I don't leave now, I'll miss dinner and that would make my beautiful wife very angry."

"We can't have that." I smiled and left him to collect my things. With my new Chanel bag slung over my shoulder, I shut off the light to my office just as Daniel came out of his.

We walked outside together, stepping into the muggy evening air. This summer had been miserably hot, and even this late in the evening, mid-August was brutal. Dressed lightly in linen trousers and a sleeveless silk top, I was still sweating.

"Where's your driver?" Daniel asked after I locked up the studio's door, seeing that my town car was notably absent from the street.

"I told him to give me an extra thirty minutes. I'm going to go grab an iced coffee." I pointed to the coffee shop on the next block over. "See you tomorrow."

"I'll be here." He waved, setting off on the sidewalk in the opposite direction.

I started toward the coffee shop, though I didn't really need the caffeine. I just wasn't ready to go home.

It would be empty there. By the time I made it down to SoHo, it would be getting dark. Carrie had left hours ago after making me a dinner I could simply reheat. Which left me a huge, spacious penthouse with nothing but the television to keep me company.

Alone and bored, I'd no doubt stare at Dakota's name in my phone. I wanted to hear his voice more than I wanted the carbs I'd told Carrie to cut from the menu for the next two weeks.

As I walked to the coffee shop, a tall man with dark hair ducked into a cab across the street, and I did a double take. For a split second, I thought it was Dakota. It wasn't.

That old cliché was true. You saw the one you loved around every corner.

"Don't scream."

My ears registered the voice before my brain caught up in time for me to panic.

While I'd been looking across the street, a man had slid right into my side and wrapped his arm around my hips. He smelled like rotten eggs and cigarettes.

My feet froze on the sidewalk, my heels skidding as I tried to keep my balance. I pushed the stranger away, but he held on tighter, his fingertips biting into my flesh.

Something pointed was pressed into my side, but I was too scared to look down and see what it was. A gun probably, or maybe a knife.

Panic seized the air in my lungs, and my vision went blurry as he whispered in my ear, "It's a good evening to hand over that purse."

I stayed still as he stripped the gold-chain strap from my shoulder. Then he took a long, audible sniff of my hair, pressed a kiss to my temple and was gone.

Along with my purse, keys, phone. Everything I'd brought to the studio with me this morning.

I stood frozen on the sidewalk. The entire encounter had lasted thirty seconds at most, but I was struggling to comprehend it. *Did that just happen?* It wasn't dark. I wasn't in an alley or a sketchy part of town. I'd been walking to a coffee shop in a wealthy neighborhood. And I'd gotten mugged.

Police. I needed to call the police.

I took a step and my ankle gave way. I caught myself, standing upright again. I went to try another step, but the other ankle turned too. I was about ten seconds away from melting into a puddle of tears when a familiar black sedan pulled up to the curb, and Glen got out of the driver's seat.

"Ms. Kendrick?"

I looked at him, still unable to move my feet. "I-I got mugged."

His eyes went wide as he rushed over. He helped me to the car then sped off toward the nearest police station.

"Are you hurt?" Glen asked into the rearview mirror.

"What?"

"Are you hurt? Your temple?"

I dropped my hand, not realizing I'd had my fingers pressed to the place where the mugger had kissed me. "No, I'm not hurt."

But I had been violated. That thief had put his hands on me. His lips.

My hand went back up to my temple, rubbing the feeling

of his lips away.

The last man who'd kissed me in that spot had been Dakota. For three months I'd been able to feel his lips in that spot.

The bastard thief had stolen that from me too.

"All right, Ms. Kendrick."

"Sofia." We'd been sitting together for nearly two hours. The officer had earned first-name privilege.

"Sofia," the officer corrected. "I've got everything I need to file a report."

He'd already told me the chance of getting anything back was slim to none. My handbag had likely already been pawned, my phone wiped and sold too.

"Here's my card." Aubrey slid it over to the officer. "Since Sofia's phone was stolen, you can call me directly."

"Okay." He took it and tucked it into his uniform pocket.

"So what's next?" Aubrey asked. "How will you be investigating this? Do you expect to find the guy soon?"

Apparently, Officer McClellan's explanation had fallen on deaf ears with Aubrey. Or she just hadn't liked his answer.

Aubrey raised her eyebrow at the officer, and to my surprise he didn't cower. Most people did. Instead, the corner of his mouth twitched.

Not good.

"Do you think this is funny?" The room temperature rose ten degrees as anger blasted from her body. "My sister was violated. He touched her. He stole from her. And you're smiling?"

"It's not funny." Officer McClellan kept his easy smile as he leaned his forearms on the table. "But your expectations are.

Like I've told you, we'll do everything we can to track this guy down. But Ms. Kendrick's personal belongings will probably not be recovered. I'm just being real. Unless you'd rather I lied?"

"Yes," I spoke up before Aubrey could snap again. "Lie to me. Please."

"I'll find the guy today."

"Okay, great. What else?"

He grinned. "I'm sure your handbag is being treated with the utmost care. He probably took it to get cleaned."

"That's nice of him."

"I think so too. And it was nice of him to donate the cash in your purse to charity."

"It sure was." I smiled. "Thank you."

"I'm not trying to make light of this situation," he said. "It happens too often and unfortunately we don't have the man power to track down every petty thief. But I am really sorry this happened to you."

"It's New York."

"Still doesn't make it right," he said.

"No, it doesn't. Do you need anything else from us, Officer McClellan?"

"Landon," he corrected me this time. "And no. You're free to go. I have your number."

"Except she doesn't have a phone," Aubrey muttered, standing from her chair.

I stood too and held out my hand. Landon shook it then smiled as he waved us to the door.

"Are you going to be all right tonight?" He escorted us out of the office where we'd been sitting.

Aubrey marched ahead, down the hallway and past desks occupied by other officers.

"I think so. I just feel . . ." My shoulders shook with the shivers.

"Creeped out."

"Yeah." I nodded. "And dirty."

"Well, you don't look dirty. You look beautiful."

"Oh, um, thanks."

Did he just hit on me? His compliment came out more like a statement than a pickup line, but I was too out of practice with flirting to know for certain.

Landon was a good-looking man with dirty blond hair. He had a good-cop vibe going for him with a clean-shaven face, straight nose and crystal blue eyes. Add to that a muscular physique his uniform only accentuated, and he was prime precinct calendar material.

He was completely my type, and a year ago, I would have shamelessly flirted for his phone number.

But I wasn't that woman anymore. Now I wasn't sure who I was.

An entrepreneur? A philanthropist? A socialite?

There were hints of them all, and the mixture was unsettling. Nothing had been steady since Dakota had left three months ago.

"I'm sorry. That was stupid." Landon frowned at himself. "I shouldn't have said that. Now I made it weird. I just . . . you don't look dirty. I wanted you to know that. Still, it was out of line. I'm sorry."

"Please, don't be."

Landon had been a saint, patient and kind to me from the moment he'd been assigned my case. And now that I knew his compliment hadn't been a come-on, it made me even more grateful that he'd been the officer to call my name in the waiting room.

We caught up with Aubrey, who was standing by the door-way to the staircase leading us out of the building.

"I'll be in touch." Landon pulled a business card and a pen from his shirt pocket. Then he put the card on the wall and jotted down a phone number. "Here's my cell. If you need any-thing at all, someone to talk to, a coffee buddy, a cop who seems to piss off your sister, just give me a call."

"Thank you." I smiled. "Have a good night."

"You too, Sofia." With a wink, he turned and retreated down the hallway. He had that natural swagger that was hard not to watch. Even Aubrey couldn't take her eyes off his firm behind as he sauntered away.

"I don't like him," she huffed. "I think we should hire a private investigator."

I rolled my eyes and shuffled her out the door. Outside, Glen was standing stoically by the car. I'd told him he could leave when we'd arrived earlier, but I wasn't surprised to see him still here.

When he spotted us, he rushed forward. "How did it go?"

"It's done, and I'm ready to forget this ever happened."

"Can I take you home?"

"Actually," I looked to Aubrey, "would you mind some company tonight? I don't want to go home."

On the way to the precinct, Glen had called my doorman and told him my things had been stolen, including my keys. They'd probably already recoded the access points to my pent-house, so there was no way that the thief would be able to get inside. Still, I was uneasy. Night had fallen since I'd gotten to the station, and I wouldn't feel good going home until broad daylight.

"You're always welcome." Aubrey put her arm around my shoulder. "I'm glad you're okay."

I leaned into her side. "Me too."

"My car is down there." She pointed to the far end of the parking lot.

"Thank you, Glen. For everything." He was getting a raise for being early to the studio instead of waiting that extra thirty minutes I'd requested. Though, no matter when he'd arrived, I think he would have found me in that same spot on the sidewalk.

"My pleasure, Ms. Kendrick. I'll be waiting for your call in the morning to take you home."

I waved my good-bye and followed Aubrey down the sidewalk. It took hardly any time at all for us to get to her penthouse, a place she'd decorated with a modern minimalist touch. It was about as opposite to my mother's style as you could get and not nearly as homey as my own place.

But it was bright. I needed bright.

When we got inside, she busied herself with finding me some pajamas to wear while I went to the living room to call our parents from her phone.

I'd called them on the drive to the precinct using Glen's phone. My parents had been ready to drive into the city, but I'd assured them I was fine and urged them to save themselves a long trip. Aubrey had dropped everything and rushed to sit at my side.

After reassuring Mom and Dad that I was fine, I made a quick call to Logan and told him the same. Then I closed my eyes, wishing Aubrey had bought a more comfortable couch, and waited for her to return.

"I called for a massage therapist." Aubrey sat next to me on the couch, handing over some clothes. "We could both use a long massage before going to bed."

"I need to get a new phone." I closed my eyes. "And cancel my credit cards."

"I already emailed Carrie. She's taking care of your credit cards. A new phone will be couriered over in an hour."

"Sometimes being rich has its perks." Though if I hadn't been rich, would I have gotten mugged?

"What can I do?" Aubrey asked, taking my hand.

The sting in my nose, the one that had kept me company for hours, was sharper than ever. "I'm going to cry. And I need you to let me and not make me feel bad for it."

"Oh, Sofia, I'm so sorry," she whispered.

The dam broke loose. The tears I'd been holding back all evening, for months really, came forward.

My sister pulled me into her side and let me cry them all onto her shoulder. And when I was finally able to pull myself together, when the emotion had been set free, I looked at her and confessed something I'd been hiding for months.

"I miss him."

Collectively, Dakota and I had only been together for a couple weeks. But those weeks had meant more to me than any day in the months in between.

"Call him," Aubrey said gently.

"I can't. If I call him once, I won't want to stop."

"Why would you have to stop?"

I wiped my eyes dry. "Because it'll never work. He says he can't see us together. He can't see a future. And I don't think I can see one either."

"You might if you gave it a try."

"Maybe. But I'm scared this is all just me. I was going through a hard time, and I found a man to make it easier. I don't trust my feelings for Dakota."

"Do you love him?" Aubrey asked.

"Completely." *I love him.* "But I thought that about Kevin and Bryson and Jay. How can I know this time it's right?"

"Dakota is different than any man you've ever brought home."

"He is different. He doesn't want me for my money. He doesn't want me for my last name. He doesn't want me at all."

The Kendrick princess had finally been denied something. And unless I changed my ancestry, there wasn't a damn thing I could do about it.

Aubrey's hand clasped mine harder just as the doorbell chimed.

I started to rise from the couch, but she kept hold of my hand. "I wish there was something I could do."

"You're doing it." Heartbreak was easier to handle when you had a sister. And a friend.

If that was the only lasting relationship to come from this year, then I was more than okay with the outcome.

Aubrey and I got our massages then went to bed. Sleep didn't come easy and I woke with a heavy heart. But finally admitting to another person how I felt about Dakota, how I worried about my own feelings, was healing in a way.

Maybe it was the first step in letting him go.

Still in my borrowed pajamas, I came out to the kitchen to find Aubrey all dressed and ready for work. I also found a surprise guest.

Dad.

I rushed right into his arms.

"I'm glad you're all right." He held me tight. "We're going to look at getting you some security. Both of you. You girls have always been so independent, but I don't want to get another phone call like last night's."

I nodded into his suit jacket. "That's fine by me."

"As long as he or she stays out of my way, it's fine with me too," Aubrey declared before sipping from her cappuccino.

"Do you have some clothes I can wear home?" The clothes I'd worn yesterday were being donated to charity immediately. Or burned.

"Feel free to take anything you'd like from my closet."

"Well," Dad straightened his necktie, "now that I've seen you are in one piece, I need to get to work."

I smiled, knowing some things about Dad would never change. He worked. Maybe it wasn't as bad of a habit as I'd always thought. It didn't bother me as much, especially since he'd been making more time for family, like coming to my studio's opening. Or stopping by here when I knew it had probably meant reshuffling his day.

"I'll ride with you." Aubrey downed the rest of her coffee.

"Will you call your mother?" Dad asked.

"I need to set up my new phone first, then she'll be the first call." I hadn't had the energy to get it going last night.

With a kiss good-bye from Dad and a hug from Aubrey, they left me alone in her penthouse. I took a long shower, scrubbing extra hard at the place where the mugger had kissed me. Then I got dressed in one of Aubrey's yoga ensembles, choosing leggings and a light tank top for the day since there was no way I'd be going to the dance studio.

But I didn't really want to go home either. The irrational fear that the thief was inside my penthouse, waiting for me to come home, had been the reason I hadn't slept.

Glen would no doubt check the house for me. My

doorman would too. Carrie was likely already inside, making me breakfast.

But irrational fears were just that. So I sat at my sister's kitchen island, procrastinating going home by setting up my new phone. The minute it was active, voicemails and texts and social media notifications flooded the screen. But before I could clear them away, it rang with an unfamiliar number.

"Hello?"

"Sofia?"

I paused, trying to place the man's voice but couldn't. "Yes."

"This is Officer Landon McClellan."

"Oh. Hi." That's why he sounded familiar. "Did you find my purse?"

He chuckled. "No. Sorry. I was calling to check in. You were pretty shaken up last night."

"And here I was thinking I'd really kept it together."

He laughed again. "How are you holding up?"

"I'm all right. I was just building up the courage to go home," I admitted. "I keep thinking I'm going to walk into my closet and find that creep loading up more handbags."

"I'd be happy to do a sweep for you if it would put your mind at ease."

"Really?" A police officer checking my penthouse would make me feel so much better. But I didn't want to put him out.

"No bother at all."

"Hi." I waved to him as he stood next to my town car outside Aubrey's building.

"Morning." He wasn't in uniform but wearing a pair of

jeans and a simple white button-down rolled up his forearms. In his hand was a baseball cap he'd clearly taken off when he'd seen me coming.

I'd assumed he was at the precinct when he'd called me, which was why I'd suggested he meet me at Aubrey's and ride along to my penthouse. "You're not on duty today?"

He shook his head. "Day off."

"Now I feel bad for asking you to come along."

"Buy me a coffee and we'll call it square."

"I tried to get coffee yesterday, and that didn't work out so well for me. I'm boycotting all coffee shops at the moment."

He chuckled. "Fair enough."

"But my assistant makes the best lattes in Manhattan. After you appease my crazy fears that a creep is lurking underneath my bed, she'll make you whatever your heart desires."

"You got yourself a deal, Sofia."

I walked over to the car, and he opened my door for me before I could touch the handle. Then he climbed in behind me, buckling up as I greeted Glen and asked him to take me home.

Twenty minutes later, we were parked outside my building. My phone was still blowing up with messages, but I put it on silent, blocking out all of it until this walk-through was over.

"Thank you for doing this," I told Landon.

Landon nodded. "It's no problem."

He got out first then held out his hand to help me out.

"I'm going to be home the rest of the day," I told Glen. "Tomorrow too."

"Very well, Ms. Kendrick. Just call if you change your mind."

I wouldn't. As soon as Landon checked every corner of my place, I'd be staying in the safety of my lonely home until I felt more like myself and ready to get back to work at the studio.

I stepped out of the car, taking Landon's hand. Then I led him to the door to my building. But before going inside, I glanced down the sidewalk.

A man was walking the other way, a green backpack slung over his shoulder. He had the same stride as Dakota. The same black hair. I narrowed my eyes, studying him closer.

"Coming?" Landon stole my attention.

"Uh, yeah," I told him but looked down the sidewalk again in time to see the man turn the corner of the block and disappear.

My imagination was cruel. I wished it would stop conjuring the man I needed so desperately. The man I'd dreamed about last night. Everywhere I looked, I saw Dakota.

But he wasn't here.

He'd gone back to his life without so much as a backward glance.

seventeen

DAKOTA

I WAS LYING ON THE COUCH IN MY LIVING ROOM WHEN THE FRONT door opened. I didn't get up. My eyes stayed glued to the baseball game on TV, not that I was really watching.

"Dakota?" My uncle's voice carried into the room. "Is that you?"

"Yeah."

Xavier came into the room. "I, uh, thought you were in New York."

"Nope." Not anymore.

Not since I'd gotten there just in time to see Sofia with another man.

I hadn't worked at the bar last night, but I'd stopped by to pick up my paycheck. I was bullshitting with Thea when she got the call that Sofia had been mugged.

The minute I heard, I bolted out the door, came home and tossed some clothes in a backpack. Then I hauled ass to the airport, buying the only ticket available to New York City.

My flight had two different connections, putting me in after midnight. But my second flight was delayed, causing me to miss the third. After sleeping on an airport bench, I finally arrived in the city this morning.

It seemed like a month ago, not less than a day.

On the trip, I'd tried Sofia's phone a thousand times only to get sent straight to voicemail each time. Even if she had answered, I still would have made the trip. Talking to her wasn't enough. I had to see her. I had to know she was all right and hold her in my arms to feel that she was safe.

Damn the cost.

My flight was a thousand dollars, my cab ride to Sofia's building one hundred.

The cab ride back to the airport had been the same.

Timing was not on my side. I'd gotten out of the taxi, ready to beg Sofia's doorman to help me track her down, just in time to see her get out of her town car with her hand in another man's.

I turned away from them, unable to watch, and walked three blocks while my head spun in circles. Then I flagged down another cab, went back to the airport and spent the day flying home.

It was nearly dark out now, which was good. I was ready for this day to be over and to forget it had ever happened.

"What are you doing here?" I asked Xavier.

I wasn't angry that he'd come over. He still had a key, since this had been his house not all that long ago. But I really didn't want company. Not tonight.

"Needed to borrow your shop floodlight. Mine quit on me while I was trying to finish up a project on Hazel's garden. Saw your truck in the shop and came on over."

I nodded. "Did you find the light?"

"I did."

He took a seat in a recliner, settling in like he was here to watch the game. Really, he was just waiting for me to tell him why my trip had been cut short.

"I don't want to talk about it. But do me a favor, don't tell anyone I went to New York. Ask Hazel to keep it quiet too."

"Okay."

"Thanks."

It was embarrassing enough as it was without the whole town of Lark Cove knowing. Maybe if I was lucky, I could convince Thea to keep it under wraps too.

Xavier leaned forward and took the remote off the coffee table, turned up the volume, then relaxed back in the chair.

"I said I don't want to talk about it."

"Who's talking? I'm watching the game."

"Fine." I pulled my arms tight across my chest.

We sat for an inning, neither team scoring, until the commercials came on. Xavier shifted in his chair, chuckling at one of the ads.

I loved my uncle, but I did not feel like listening to him laugh at the moment.

"Did you need anything other than the light?" I asked.

"No."

"I thought you were working on a project for Hazel."

He shrugged. "It's not urgent."

"I'm sure she's expecting you home."

"She knows where I'm at."

Fuck my life. He wasn't leaving here until he got it all.

I took a deep breath, rubbed my hands over my face, swung my legs down and sat up. "She was with another man."

"Thought you didn't want to talk about it."

"I don't. But you aren't leaving here until I do, so we might as well get this over with."

Xavier muted the game then gave me his full attention.

"Ready when you are."

"I went to New York. She was with another man."

My uncle nodded but stayed quiet. After years of working as a cop and listening to confessions, he knew when to press for more. He also knew when his subject would spill willingly.

"I feel stupid. It was stupid to spend money I don't have and go out there. It was stupid to think she'd want me there. It was stupid to think she wouldn't eventually move on. We ended things. Parted ways. And now I feel fucking stupid."

"You're not."

I scoffed. "Come on. It was stupid."

"Why'd you two end it?" Xavier had been wanting to ask that question for months, but I'd never given him a window. But now that the door was open, he wasn't hesitating to walk right through it.

"There's no future there. We both know that. It was better to end things sooner than later."

"But you care about her."

"Obviously." I wouldn't have flown to New York City and back in twenty-four hours for anyone but Sofia.

"Then why not give it a shot?"

"Like I said, I don't see a future there." That black box had gotten bigger these past few months. "There's too many obstacles."

"Is it the long-distance thing?"

"That's one of them."

Xavier leaned forward, his elbows resting on his knees as he thought it over. "Is it her money?"

"Yes and no. It sets us apart, for sure. I don't want it. But I'm glad she has it."

"Then what is it? Gotta explain it to me, bud."

"I don't know." I sighed. "My head is so mixed up, it's hard to untwist it all."

"Just start talking."

I took a deep breath, knowing if anyone could help me make sense of these feelings, it would be Xavier. He was the one person who held no judgment about my life choices.

"Mom and Dad, they have this picture of what success looks like." Live on the reservation. Work for our people. Marry the right woman and have as many babies as I could make.

"But that's not the life you want."

"No, it's not. But it's still there. It's in here." I put my palm up to my heart. "I left that behind but it doesn't mean it hasn't come with me. That future, the one they wanted for me, it's bone-deep. It doesn't just go away because I moved off the reservation. No matter what life I choose to live, even if it makes me happy, something other than the one I was taught to want feels like a constant betrayal."

It was an invisible weight that was impossible to shed.

"I get it." Xavier nodded. "It took me a lot of years to let that go. I wish I could tell you it was easy. It's not. It'll take time."

"Yeah. Maybe in time I won't care anymore. But the fact is, right now, I do. I care that my parents see this life as a failure. That my sisters don't look up to me like they used to. Maybe if I can show them I'm successful, prove that this was the right choice, they'll see things differently."

"Bud." Xavier stood from the chair and came over to the couch. He placed his hand over my knee. "They might not. No matter how successful you are, they might never come around."

He was speaking from experience. He'd done everything he'd set out to. Xavier had become a cop and moved to a predominately white town. He'd fought stereotypes and prejudice to become sheriff. He'd been a damn good one at that. But no matter how long he'd held office, no matter how many accolades he'd won from the Lark Cove populous, it had never been good enough for our family.

None of them had even bothered to come and meet his wife.

If Xavier was bothered, he hadn't mentioned it. He'd lost hope in them ages ago.

But I wasn't ready to admit defeat. Not yet. I had faith that if I could convince Dad, everyone else would come around.

"It's worth a try."

"Then try." Xavier patted my knee. "How does this roll back to Sofia?"

"She has so much money. So much fucking money I can't even wrap my head around it. And if I was with her, how would I prove to Dad that I am successful on my own?"

The room went silent as Xavier let my words sink in. He thought on them for a few long minutes until, finally, he spoke.

"You're proud, Dakota."

"I am."

Xavier clapped me on the shoulder then stood from the couch. I thought maybe he'd go back to his chair, but he didn't. He walked out of the living room and to the front door.

"No advice?" I called.

He paused in the entryway, looking at me from over his shoulder. "You know what you have to decide. Choose your path."

I dropped my eyes to the floor as he opened and closed the door behind him.

Choose your path.

He was right. I had to choose and live with the consequences.

My family might not come around. They might not accept my lifestyle and choices, no matter how successful I became. But they might. There was still a slim chance they'd open their minds and come around.

If I involved Sofia, that chance was gone.

Why was I even stressing about this? It didn't matter, not anymore. Sofia Kendrick was no longer a factor because she'd moved on and found another man.

I'd seen it with my own two eyes this morning.

So I'd continue down my path, toward the future I saw clear as day.

I was going to work my ass off, do my best to get back in my family's good graces while still living in Lark Cove, then travel the world.

Sofia would someday be a distant memory. I couldn't let a woman who I'd spent a collective two weeks with make me question the decisions I'd made years ago.

I shot off the couch and ran a hand over my face. *She's gone. Moved on. Good for her.*

I swiped my phone off the coffee table and went to my contacts. I pulled up her name but couldn't bring myself to erase it.

Instead, I touched her number—the one I'd touched all through last night—and listened as it rang.

"Hello?" she answered.

"Hey."

She was quiet.

"Sofia."

"I'm here."

Yes, she was. She was in New York and out of my grasp. She was probably in the arms of whoever the fuck that guy was.

He probably wasn't set on proving something to his family. He probably didn't give a shit that Sofia was richer than sin.

He probably didn't know how lucky he was.

"You okay?"

"I got mugged," she whispered.

My heart cracked. "Are you okay?"

"He took my purse and my phone and stuff."

"But are you okay?"

"He kissed me." Her voice shook. "On the temple. Where you kissed me. He—"

"Sofia," I cut her off. "Are. You. Okay?"

I needed to hear the words. Just seeing her hadn't been enough after all.

"Yes, I'm okay."

My body sagged backward until my knees hit the couch, and I collapsed into the seat. I dropped my head into my free hand and pinched the bridge of my nose.

Where the fuck was her guy when she'd been mugged? How could he let this happen to her? How could *I* let this happen to her?

"I'm sorry."

"Why? Did you take my purse?" she teased.

The corner of my mouth turned up. "What color was it? Your purse."

"Black."

"Next time take your pink one."

She giggled, the sound so magical it filled the empty hole in my chest. "How are you?"

"Good." *Bullshit.* "It's been busy at the bar this summer so I've spent most of my time there."

"I've been working a lot too."

"How's the studio?"

"Great. We might expand."

I grinned. "See? You're killing it. I knew you would."

"Thank you." Her smile came through her voice. "How are your properties doing? How's Arthur?"

"They're good. He's good. Happy since I finally kicked out my other tenant. He's been kicking my ass at chess lately. I've been distracted, so my game is shot."

"Distracted? Why?"

Because of you. "Just a lot on my mind."

"Oh."

An uncomfortable silence stretched between us. I hated small talk. I wasn't good at it with anyone, let alone her. We ran too deep. And all I really wanted from her was the truth. I wanted her to admit she'd met someone. To put me out of my misery.

"Anything else new?" I was fishing.

"Not really."

"Hmm." *Liar.* The bright feeling her voice had given me dulled. The fog I'd been in for three months hadn't lifted long.

I waited a few more seconds, hoping she'd just spit it out. When she didn't, I got angry.

She couldn't know I'd seen them together. How would she? But she could at least have the decency to tell me. We meant that much to each other, didn't we? Enough for honesty?

Maybe not.

Maybe I'd gotten so drunk on her I'd seen everything wrong.

"Are you still there?" she asked.

"Yeah, but I gotta run. Take care, Sofia."

"Oh, oka—"

I hung up and tossed the phone aside. Then I dropped my face into my hands.

What was wrong with me?

Before I could dive into that wormhole of a question, my phone rang. I picked it up. Sofia?

"Hey," I answered.

"What the hell?"

My spine straightened. "Huh?"

"What the hell, Dakota?" she snapped. "Why did you just hang up on me?"

"Sorry."

"Are you? We haven't talked in months. You call to ask if I'm okay. Then hang up on me? After everything, we could at least be friends."

"Friends?" We were so past friends it wasn't even a speck on the horizon.

"Friendly. Or whatever. We could at least be honest with each other."

"Honest. You want to talk to me about honesty?" I huffed. "That's hypocritical."

"Hypocritical? What are you talking about? I've always been honest with you."

"Really?" I stood and paced in front of the couch. "Then how about you be honest and say you've moved on?"

"Moved on to what?"

"Jesus fucking Christ. You're really lecturing me about being honest, and you can't even admit you're seeing someone?"

"What are you talking about?"

"I'm talking about you and a guy getting out of your car this morning, holding hands. I'm talking about you being honest with me or at least not lecturing me to be honest with you."

My voice carried across the room, echoing on the far wall. Then it got quiet. Too quiet.

"You saw me," she whispered.

"Yeah."

"You saw me."

"Yes."

"It was you walking away this morning. I didn't dream it up."

I stopped pacing. "You saw me?"

"No, you saw me!" she yelled. "You were here! And you didn't come to me. You were here, and you left me."

"You were with another man. What the hell did you think I'd do?"

"Come to me!" Her shout made me wince. "I needed you. I needed you, Dakota. And you were here and you walked away. I'm not dating anyone. I'm so hung up on you I can barely see straight. That man was the cop who took my case. He was there after I got mugged. He talked me through it. He sat with me when my hands wouldn't stop shaking. He brought me water when I felt like passing out. I needed someone to come with me into my apartment because I was terrified and alone."

Oh. Fucking. Hell. "Sofia—"

"No. I needed you and you walked away. I thought I meant more to you than that. I really did. But this? We're done. You were right. We don't have a future."

"Sofia—"

"Take care, Dakota." She spat my own words back in my ear then hung up.

"Shit." I threw my phone onto the couch and raked my hands through my hair.

I stalked to the kitchen, looked out the window over the

sink to the yard. I needed to mow the grass today. I could prune one of the bushes along the driveway. I should refill my bird feeder with some seed.

I had plenty of better shit to do here in my life than worry about a woman in New York City.

But instead, I walked back into the living room, picked up my phone and hit send on her number.

"What?" she answered.

"I'm sorry."

"You came here."

"I was worried. I heard what happened, took the first flight out."

"I needed you." She sniffled and it cut me to the core.

She was crying. I was sure of it. I'd made her cry. "Fuck, I'm sorry."

"We can't do this anymore. I can't do this. If we don't have a future, we have to stop."

"I know." It gutted me but she was right.

"Maybe one day I'll see you again."

"I'd like that."

The next three heartbeats felt like nails being driven into my chest.

"Take care, Dakota."

"Same to you, Sofia."

I hung up, knowing that phone call would be the last. I'd let her down, broken her trust. Truthfully, I'd let myself down.

I shoved my phone in my pocket and walked outside, where I spent the day busting my ass in my yard.

Trying to forget Sofia Kendrick.

eighteen

SOFIA

Two months later . . .

"SO WHAT ARE YOU GOING TO BE FOR HALLOWEEN?" Landon asked.

I swallowed my bite of pasta and smiled. "A ballerina. A few of us are going to dress up at the studio that day."

"You're really branching out with that one."

I giggled. "What about you?"

"A firefighter."

"A cop dressing up as a firefighter. Yeah, you're really stretching yourself too."

We both laughed, our smiles white in the dark booth at the Italian restaurant where he'd brought me for dinner.

In the last two months, Landon McClellan had proved my first impression had been accurate. He was kind and caring. He was thoughtful. But his strongest characteristic by far was stubbornness.

I'd called him on it a week ago. He'd just laughed it off, saying he preferred to be called persistent.

Since the day I'd called and begged him to "sweep" my penthouse, he'd asked me out on countless dates. Breakfast. Lunch. Dinner. I'd declined all of his invitations except those to meet him for coffee on Sunday mornings.

Still, no matter how many times I said no to a shared meal, he kept asking.

At first, it hadn't been hard at all to refuse Landon. I'd been so crushed by Dakota, so confused, I hadn't wanted anything to do with men as a species. But Landon wouldn't take no for an answer. He kept meeting me for coffee on Sundays, pretending like my last rejection had never happened.

Sunday mornings had become a highlight of my week, because Landon had become one of my closest friends.

We had coffee. He'd even stop by the studio on occasion just to say hello. Two of the instructors there had told me in no uncertain terms if I wasn't going to date the officer, they'd be happy to accept his invitations on my behalf.

Last Sunday, when he'd asked me to dinner, there had been no hope in his voice. He'd still made a convincing pitch, swearing the breadsticks at this little hole-in-the-wall eatery were the best he'd ever tasted. The breadstick ploy had won me over. The shock on his face when I'd agreed had been an added bonus.

So here we were, eating pasta and drinking red wine. The breadsticks had long since been devoured. And like our Sunday-morning coffee breaks, we talked about nothing serious.

Maybe that was why Landon and I'd developed this friendship. Because nothing about him was overly serious, except his job. But personality wise, he was one of the most laid-back people I'd ever met.

And after everything that had happened with Dakota, I'd needed some light. Being around Landon was refreshing. Light. Casual.

Empty.

This dinner date had confirmed the feeling I'd had for a

string of Sundays. Landon McClellan was a good guy—I was better at spotting the nice ones now—but he wasn't for me.

There was no all-consuming, steal-my-heart desperation. There were no skipped heartbeats or full-body shudders. There wasn't the potential for love.

Still, I owed Landon a debt.

I was lonely and sad. I was missing a piece of my heart. And for the first time in my life, a man's attention hadn't filled that void. I hadn't jumped at the opportunity for another relationship. I was going through a hard time, a man had come along, and I hadn't fallen in love with him.

Maybe my feelings weren't as broken as I'd once thought. I'd told Aubrey I couldn't trust my feelings for Dakota.

I didn't then. I did now.

I was in love with Dakota Magee. I loved him with all-consuming, steal-my-heart desperation. My curse was falling in love with men who couldn't love me in return.

"See that man over there?" Landon leaned across the table to whisper, nodding to the man sitting alone three tables over.

I glanced over quickly. "Yes. What about him?"

"He's going to ask the waitress out."

"He is? How do you know?"

Landon shrugged. "Just a theory. I'm guessing he comes in here a lot. Alone. He always sits in her section. And he's working up the courage to ask her out."

"Interesting." I spotted the waitress a few tables over, clearing away some platters. "Do you think he'll ask her tonight?"

"I'd put money on it."

I smiled. "How much?"

"Winner buys dinner?"

I held my hand out across the table. "You're on."

We spent the rest of the meal watching the man, carefully so he wouldn't catch us staring. Although I'd bet Landon the opposite, I was secretly hoping the man would ask the waitress out.

He had a kind face and looked at her with such adoration. She looked frazzled as she rushed around, her hair falling out of her ponytail. She looked like she could use someone to sweep her off her feet.

By the time our pasta was gone and we'd each had a tiramisu, the man still hadn't worked up the courage. I was beginning to lose hope.

"Will you excuse me?" I set my napkin on the table as I stood from my seat.

"Where are you going?" Landon asked when I took a step across the restaurant and not toward the restrooms at the back.

I just winked and strutted over to the man's table.

"Sir?" I greeted the man.

"Uh, yes?"

"Can I offer you a piece of unsolicited advice?" I didn't wait for him to answer. "Ask her. I'll buy your dinner if she says no. But I don't think she will."

"I, uh . . ." He blinked at me then turned over his shoulder to make sure the waitress hadn't overheard.

"Just ask her. You got this." I winked at him too, turned toward the restrooms and walked out of the room. After reapplying some lip gloss and washing my hands, I came back to my table.

Landon was grinning, even though he was shaking his head at me. "Did you forget which side of the bet you took?"

"No. And it looks like I came back just in time." I slid back into my seat, turned and didn't even try to hide it as I watched the man flag down the waitress, stand from his seat and introduce himself.

After their handshake, the words *coffee* and *tomorrow morning* drifted over.

She blushed, straightening the apron on her waist. Then she nodded, smiling as she rattled off her phone number.

"What did you say to him?" Landon asked.

"Just offered up some advice." Advice that Dakota had given me not that long ago.

"You realize I'm not going to let you buy me dinner. I don't care if we made a bet. This was a date, and I'm a gentleman."

"Fair enough."

I hadn't let Landon buy me a thing over the last two months. Never coffee. Never a muffin or bagel. I'd drawn that line so he'd know our Sunday meetings weren't dates.

Except this was a date. The first. And the last.

Later tonight, when we left the restaurant, I'd have to draw another line. I wasn't looking forward to that conversation, but I hoped I'd be able to let him down easily.

The waitress came over, her smile brighter than it had been all night, and delivered our check. True to his word, Landon paid for our meal then escorted me outside.

"Care to take a walk?" he asked.

"Sure." It was dark and the idea of being out in the open still made me nervous. But we were in a quiet neighborhood—the Italian place was a small, local establishment—and I felt safe with Landon.

We set out at an easy pace, enjoying the warm fall evening. Though I made sure to button my wool coat and tuck my hands into its pockets.

"So . . . not to put you on the spot or anything." Landon

looked down at me with a side smile. "But to put you on the spot, what are the chances I'm getting a second date?"

"Not great."

"I expected that." His smile stayed in place. "We're missing something."

"You think so too?"

"Yep." Landon held up a hand. "Don't get me wrong. You're an amazing woman. But we're missing—"

"Passion."

He nodded. "That's a good word for it."

"We might not be couple material, but I could use a good friend. Interested?"

"Definitely," Landon said without pause.

We continued walking and after a few blocks he looked to me and hummed. He opened his mouth, but before he said anything, he shook his head and turned his attention forward again.

"What?" I pressed.

"Nothing."

I nudged his elbow with mine. "Tell me."

"I think it'll come out wrong."

"Uh, okay." I wasn't sure exactly what that meant.

"It's just . . . I was thinking about my ideal woman."

"Which I am not."

"No. Sorry." He chuckled. "But I was just thinking that if a gorgeous, intelligent woman like you isn't my type, who is?"

"It seems like it should be easier, doesn't it? Finding the right person to love?"

"You said it."

"This is probably weird post-date conversation," I said. "But we are *friends* now. So I'm curious. When you think of your ideal woman, what's she like?"

"You're right. This is weird post-date conversation." He laughed. "But we are friends."

"Yes, we are."

"I, uh . . ." He rubbed the back of his neck, hesitating. Then he said, "I don't want you to take this personally."

"I won't. I promise."

"Okay. Well, I think I need a woman who isn't as easygoing as you."

I stopped dead on the sidewalk. "You think *I* am easygoing?"

He stopped and turned. "Yeah. You're chill."

"Wait." I took my phone from my purse and opened up the camera. "Say it again, this time so I can record it. No one, and I mean no one in the history of my life, has *ever* called me chill. *Chilly* maybe. But not chill."

"Nah." Landon grinned, turned the phone so he was in the video recording, then said, "Sofia Kendrick. You are chill."

I smiled as I hit end on the recording. "I think our definitions of chill are different."

"Maybe." He nodded and we resumed walking, both with easy smiles. "Maybe chill isn't the right term. But I like ruffling a woman's feathers. I want someone who will meet me head-on in a debate. Someone who will get fired up on occasion. Someone stubborn and iron-willed. A challenge. Again, no offense. But I think tonight's bet was the first time we took an opposing stance on something. And you ended up taking my side anyway."

I understood now what he meant by chill. Though I think he mistook me for easygoing when really, it was just a mutual lack of passion for one another.

"So you want a woman who will keep you on your toes."

"Exactly."

My sister's face popped into my mind.

I looked up at Landon's profile, studying the straight bridge of his nose. He'd give Aubrey a run for her money, that was for sure.

"You should ask my sister out."

"Your sister?" he asked skeptically. "Wouldn't that be strange?"

"For me? Not at all. And if you want a challenging woman, there isn't anyone I've met in Manhattan who'd be more of a challenge than Aubrey."

I hid a smile at the thought of him asking her relentlessly out on dates. She'd make Officer McClellan run a gauntlet of obstacles just to get through the front door at Kendrick Enterprises.

But he'd chase her. Persistently.

Besides Landon, I couldn't think of a man who'd chased me—not that I would have made any of them chase far. One of many problems in all of my past relationships had been effort, or lack thereof.

My ideal man would pursue me with wild abandon. He wouldn't take no for an answer. There would be no obstacle, no family issue, no distance, nothing that would keep him away.

"Think about it," I told Landon. "You have her number. And not that you need it, but you have my blessing."

"Thank you."

"I think I'd better wish you luck too. Aubrey's one of a kind."

He chuckled again and didn't say much else on the rest of our walk. Had I sparked an interest? Had I planted the seed? I crossed my fingers, hoping a nice man like Landon could bust his way past all of Aubrey's roadblocks.

After a few more blocks, I texted Glen and he came to pick me up. Standing by the door of the car, I stood on my toes and placed a kiss on Landon's cheek. "Thanks for dinner."

"You're welcome. How about coffee one of these days?"

"I'd like that." I waved good night and got into the car, destination home.

The streets were quiet for a change, traffic was light, and not a single taxi blared their horn on the drive back to SoHo. When I got out of the car, it was almost peaceful. The leaves from the trees around my street had begun to fall, dotting the sidewalk with lemon yellows and cherry reds.

I nodded to my doorman as he opened the door for me. Then I went to the elevator, making my way up to my empty penthouse.

This was the worst part of the night. The part when I'd walk through my front door and wonder what Dakota was doing. I'd picture the two of us together against the entryway wall. I'd remember how it had felt to take him on my couch. I'd slide into bed and think of how cold it was without him beneath my sheets.

I hadn't heard from Dakota since our fight. The day I'd hung up on him, I'd made the decision not to call him again. If he had something to say, he could reach out.

He hadn't.

And the wound he'd inflicted just festered. He'd come to New York, he'd been right here when I'd needed him most, and he'd let me down. He hadn't cared enough about me, even as a friend, to come over.

That broke me.

Because I would move mountains for him if he was hurting

or in trouble.

Once again, I'd thrown myself completely into a lopsided relationship.

I went in search of a distraction. As I walked down the hallway into my kitchen, my only company was the click of my heels on the marble floor. Next to a stack of mail, Carrie had left me a stack of papers to review.

Over the last month, I'd been looking at new buildings in the city. As much as I loved SoHo, I was ready for a change. So I'd asked Carrie to start getting details on options. I wanted to live closer to the studio. Mostly, I wanted a fresh start.

That's what this year had become for me. Moving would bring it full circle. It would be my chance to put the old Sofia, the one I'd been running from since New Year's, finally in the past.

Though there were still pieces of that Sofia inside me. The good qualities, the ones that reporter had refused to see, had been there all along.

I was stylish.

I was charming.

I was witty and smart.

The personal changes I'd made this year had made those qualities shine a little brighter.

As I thumbed through the papers, my fingers paused on the item on the bottom. It was a letter, addressed to me. The return address had a name I recognized. One I'd thought often about over the last ten months.

One that made me cringe.

Anne Asher.

The reporter from *NY Scene*.

I hesitated over the envelope. Daniel had been working

with various publications throughout the city to feature the studio. This was most likely a notice that we'd been chosen for an article.

But why would it be sent here, to my penthouse? Curiosity won out and I carefully tore it open, nervous that I'd find another condemning exposé inside. Instead, there was a simple note card, white with pale blue lines. It was the kind children used when making flash cards to study multiplication tables.

The back was blank. Her clean, tiny and concise handwriting only took up four lines on the front.

> *Ms. Kendrick,*
> *I am rarely proved wrong.*
> *Congratulations on your success.*
> *AA*

"What the hell?" I turned the card over, making sure I hadn't missed something. Then I read it again before diving back into the envelope, but there was no more.

Was this a joke? Was she genuine?

I'd probably never know. I had no plans to become friends with a woman who'd single-handedly turned my world upside down.

Still, the corners of my mouth turned up as I read it again.

This felt a bit like revenge, sweet in its satisfaction. But more, it felt a lot like pride.

Anne Asher might have been the catalyst, but I'd done the work. I'd proved to her, and to myself, there was more to Sofia Kendrick than had met her eye.

I collected the envelope and card, then walked to the trash can, depositing both inside. Then I swept up the spec sheets on the apartments Carrie had laid out for my review, taking them into the living room.

I'd just gotten comfortable when my phone rang.

An unfamiliar number lit up, but it came with the area code for Montana.

"Hello," I answered.

"Sofia? This is Xavier Magee."

My heart leapt into my throat. His introduction was hoarse and sullen. Nothing about his tone conveyed this was just a friendly call. My mind immediately went to the worst, that something had happened to Dakota, and my throat closed so I was unable to speak.

"Are you there?"

I nodded, clearing away the lump as best I could. "I'm here."

"I, uh, I don't know if you heard. Dakota's dad passed away earlier this week."

"Oh my god." The world tipped sideways, and I planted a hand on the couch to keep from falling over.

How was I just finding out about this? Why hadn't Thea or Logan told me?

Probably because the last time I'd talked to Logan I'd told him in no uncertain terms I didn't want to hear about Dakota. That topic was off limits.

Still, his father had died. I'd deserved to know.

"Why didn't anyone call me?"

"No one is handling this well, Dakota included. He told us all there'd been a family situation and he went home. None of us here knew. Dakota called me only a day ago and told me about Joseph. His family, *my* family, didn't want me at the funeral. He went against them and invited me along anyway. We buried my brother this afternoon."

"I'm so sorry, Xavier." I closed my eyes, dropping my forehead into a hand. "How did he die?"

"Heart attack. No one saw it coming."

"And Dakota? How is he?"

"Not good. He won't admit it, but he's really having a hard time. He and his dad didn't have the best relationship these last five years. Now he doesn't have the chance to fix it."

My eyes flooded, my heart shattering for Dakota. "What can I do?"

"Feel like taking a trip to Montana?"

The smart answer was no. I was still hurt and angry at Dakota. We were broken.

But I loved him. With every beat of my heart, I loved him.

"I'll be there tomorrow."

nineteen

DAKOTA

"WHAT ARE YOU DOING HERE?" THEA ASKED AS I walked in the back door of the bar.

"I need to work."

"Dakota—"

I held up a hand. "I need to work."

She opened her mouth to protest again but closed it with a nod. "Okay."

"Thanks."

She gave me a sad smile. "I've got some office stuff to do today. I'm here if you need me."

"I'm fine."

She knew I was lying. But she kept quiet as she walked over, squeezed my arm for a long moment, then slipped past me and down the hallway toward her office.

I walked over to the sink, washed my hands and emptied the dishwasher. Thea had already done the morning tasks to get the place opened, so I found some cleaning supplies and decided the liquor shelves all needed a thorough dusting, even though I'd done it last week.

Later, I'd empty and clean out all of the drawers and cabinets. Then I'd dust all of the frames along the walls. I didn't care what kind of work had to be done, I'd invent tasks if needed. I just wanted to stay busy. I wanted to stay away from home.

Maybe then I'd make it through this.

Maybe.

I woke up this morning completely lost. Dad and I hadn't been close lately, but he'd been an anchor. A constant. Despite the distance, I knew he was there.

Now he was gone.

One phone call six days ago and I was set adrift.

Mom called to tell me about Dad's heart attack, begging me to come straight home. I went, in shock. I didn't think to call anyone, Xavier included. It took me over twenty-four hours to just comprehend what happened.

My dad died.

I'd lost him. And I was close to losing Mom and my sisters too. They were furious at me because I thought Xavier deserved to be at his brother's funeral.

But they wanted to keep him in the dark. As I held Mom's hand at the funeral home, listening to her arrange the services for Dad, she cried and pleaded for me to keep Dad's death from Xavier. How fucked up was that?

How fucked up was it that I agreed?

Mom didn't want to make the funeral about Xavier's appearance. She told me there were too many emotions as it was. It would be easier that way. *It was what Dad would have wanted.* Rozene and Koko helped shove that guilt down my throat.

So I went along with it . . . until the day before the funeral.

I drove back to Lark Cove, went straight to the cottage and told Xavier about Dad's heart attack.

Xavier and Hazel were two of the first to arrive at Dad's graveside. If looks could kill, Mom, Rozene and Koko would have put me six feet under beside Dad.

I did my best to help Mom and my sisters through the funeral service, as much as they'd let me. I shook hands and made small talk with neighbors and distant relatives. I didn't outwardly cringe when not two but three members of the tribal council asked if I'd be coming home to run for Dad's seat.

I was busy, too busy, to comprehend the earth's shift under my feet. But then I came home, where there were no distractions or grieving family members to comfort, and got hit with the magnitude of the earthquake.

My dad died.

I wanted to scream until my lungs bled, just something to release some of this pain from my chest.

My dad died.

The last time I saw him was at the hospital after Koko had her baby. We had shallow phone calls since, none lasting more than two minutes. They were mostly full of awkward silence.

What was the last thing I said to him on the phone? What was the last thing I said that day in the hospital? I'd been trying to remember for days, but I couldn't recall the words. All I knew was they'd been said in anger and frustration.

I couldn't take them back. I couldn't right the wrongs between us.

Because the clock had stopped.

Because my dad had died.

I pulled another bottle off the shelf, revealing a patch of mirror. My eyes caught themselves in the reflection. They were bloodshot and glassy. The dark circles underneath hung nearly to my cheekbones.

I hadn't slept in days. There was too much on my mind for sleep. There were too many decisions to make.

Come home.

After everyone went home from the funeral and my sisters retreated to their homes to cuddle with their husbands and children, I went with Mom. We sat at the dining room table, cloaked in grief, and she said, "Come home."

It hadn't been a suggestion or a plea. It had been an order. An ultimatum.

The first thing that popped into my mind was that if I moved back to Browning, I wouldn't be in Lark Cove to catch a glimpse of Sofia if she ever came to visit.

Even though our last phone call had been a definite end, my broken heart held fast to a shred of hope.

With every passing second, it faded. I wouldn't be here the next time Sofia Kendrick came to visit. I'd be back on the reservation. If I didn't want to drive my mom and sisters further away, I had to move home.

I took down five more bottles, dusting the scotch section for probably the last time. I hated leaving Jackson and Thea in the lurch, but what choice did I have?

Wait for Mom to die? Wait for another phone call or surprise heart attack? If I didn't go back, would they call me for the next family funeral? Or would I become the next Xavier?

At least he had a wife.

Why should I stay in Lark Cove when I had no one but my uncle?

It might take me a while to find a job, but eventually something would come up. I'd travel back and forth to manage my properties for as long as it made sense. Maybe I'd sell them off one by one if the market didn't tank.

I'd have to find someone else to deliver Arthur's junk food every week.

After finishing one wall of shelves, I went to the other and got started dusting those. I worked fast, hoping I'd have time to do a deep clean of that cupboard where we piled up everything extra. I'd save Thea from doing it for once.

I said good-bye to the Lark Cove Bar as I cleaned. I soaked it all in, knowing it wouldn't be my refuge for much longer. Here, I'd found an escape. I'd found a job.

I'd found a family.

But it was time I went home to my real family, to the people who shared my blood and name. To the people I'd forsaken in the name of freedom.

Shackles closed around my ankles at the thought of packing my things and leaving my home. Iron cuffs wrapped around my wrists.

But I'd learn to tolerate them. For Dad's memory, I'd find a way to carry those chains.

The door opened behind me. I put the last few bottles back in place and turned to greet my customer, dust rag in hand. "Morn—Petah?"

"Hi." She waved and walked across the room, scanning the bar as she came closer.

"What are you doing here?" I tossed down my rag.

"I wanted to check on you. We didn't get to talk much yesterday."

Petah had sought me out after the funeral. I'd been standing with Hazel and Xavier at the cemetery. The wind had been blowing hard, biting into our skin, so we hadn't lingered by Dad's grave long.

Petah had been one of the few people at the services to acknowledge my uncle. She'd greeted him and Hazel with a smile, which meant more to me than she'd ever know. Then she'd given me her condolences and a hug with tears swimming in her eyes.

"This is a nice place." Petah pulled out a stool across from me and sat down.

"Can I get you something to drink?"

She nodded. "I'll have a Coke, please."

"No ice?" Petah had always hated ice in her soda.

"You remember."

I shrugged. "You're the only woman in the world who prefers lukewarm soda to cold."

"I don't mind cold. I just don't like ice."

I filled up a glass for her, foregoing the straw because she didn't like those either. Then I set it down and walked around the side of the bar.

She kept her seat as I gave her a hug and settled onto the stool at her side.

"How you holding up?" I asked.

"I'm supposed to be asking you that."

"I'm fine."

"No, you're not."

"Okay," I admitted. "No, I'm not."

Her dark eyes met mine. "Once upon a time, you used to talk to me. You still can."

"Once upon a time."

Petah had been the person I'd confided in when I was pissed at someone at school or upset about a test grade or angry about a ref's call at a basketball game. For normal high school problems, she'd been my confidant.

But I'd never talked to her about the stuff that mattered. I'd never shared my desires to leave the reservation or my need to see the world and break free. She had no clue back then how much I'd felt smothered and trapped, even as a teenager.

For the real problems, the real feelings, I went to Xavier.

And Sofia.

In the days I'd spent with Sofia, I'd told her more about myself, my real self, than Petah had ever known.

Except Sofia wasn't here, and Petah was.

Would we find our way back to one another when I moved home to the reservation? There was no doubt that Mom would like that. My sisters too.

"Mom wants me to move home." I waited for a reaction, but she just stared at me. "So I guess I'll move home."

"You don't want that."

"Yeah," I muttered. "I don't. But everyone else does. And don't tell me you aren't in that camp."

"Would I like to see you more? Yes. I'm not going to lie. Do I wish things had worked out between us? Yes. We both know that. But did you ever think to ask what I wanted? You're not the only person who wants certain things in life."

I blinked, taken aback by her sharp tone. Petah had never snapped at me. Not once. "I, uh . . . you're right. Sorry. What do you want?"

"I want a home and a family. I want my kids to live close to their grandparents. I want to settle down and live a simple life with a husband who also happens to be my best friend. I used to want that with you because you are a good man who has always been kind to me."

"Used to?"

Her shoulders fell forward. "Once upon a time you were the man of my dreams. I held on to that dream for too long. It's time to let it go."

"I didn't mean to hurt you."

"I know. You didn't do anything wrong. As much as it would be nice to place some blame, I can't fault you for following your heart."

"I appreciate that."

"And for what it's worth, I think it would be a mistake if you moved home."

I sighed. "I have to."

My dad died.

"You don't belong there, Dakota." Petah laid her hand on my forearm.

"I know. But where?" My voice cracked, my eyes searching hers for an answer. "Where do I belong?"

It wasn't in Lark Cove. It wasn't on the reservation. I really needed someone to tell me because I sure as fuck didn't know where I belonged right now.

"With me."

The whisper echoed through the bar.

I spun around, searching for the voice I'd been hearing in my sleep for the last two months. I found the source just inside the door. Sofia. Standing in nearly the same place as she had been the first time.

Her hair was down, longer than it had been all those months ago. She'd curled the ends and they twisted down to her waist. Her eyes were full of tears.

Tears for me.

And she was wearing those goddamn snow boots again. In October.

I'd missed those goddamn boots.

"Excuse me." Petah stood from her seat and bent, kissing my cheek. "Good-bye, Dakota."

I gave her a fast glance as she walked away but mostly kept

my focus on Sofia.

Her eyes held mine, even as Petah passed her by and went out the door.

When it was just the two of us in the bar, I broke the silence. "What are you doing here?"

"Your dad died."

"My dad died." My throat burned like someone had shoved a branding iron past my tongue. I'd been repeating those three words in my head for days. Not once had they come out of my mouth.

Not until Sofia had walked through the door.

"I'm sorry," she said softly.

Tears flooded my eyes this time. She was blurry as she crossed the room.

Dad would have told me to suck it up. He had never believed much in crying—that was something a man did on his own. But the overwhelming relief that she was here when I needed her, even after I hadn't been there for her, was more than I could keep bottled up.

"My dad died," I choked out.

She threw her arms around my shoulders, holding me tight. "I know, love."

The flood came. The rush of pain and anger and hopelessness. I put it all on Sofia's shoulders, banding my arms around her back as I buried my face in her neck and cried.

Her hold on me never wavered. It never loosened. She took everything I gave her and then some more.

I don't know how long we were there, me sitting on a stool, her standing between my legs. The breakdown I'd been fighting wasn't small, and I was glad no customers had come in and Thea had left us alone. Finally, when I pulled myself back together, I leaned back and took her all in.

She was here. She was standing right here with my face in her hands, my tears on her thumbs as she dried them away.

"You're here."

She nodded. "I'm so sorry about your dad."

"Me too. Who called you?"

"Xavier." Xavier must have told Thea too because I hadn't said a word. I blew out a deep breath, then ran my hands up and down my face. "Thanks for that. Sorry."

"Don't apologize. You needed it."

No, I'd needed her. "I'm sorry," I told her again.

"Dakota, it's fine. You don't need to apologize for crying after a parent dies."

"No." I shook my head then cupped her cheek with my palm. "I'm sorry for New York. I'm sorry for not being there when you needed me. I'm sorry for the phone call."

She tilted her head, the weight of her face resting in my hand. "You're forgiven."

"Easy as that?"

"I've been mad at you for months, and I'm tired of being mad. I'm letting it go."

I breathed and months' worth of regret floated away. "How long can you stay?"

"As long as you need."

Years. I needed years with this woman.

I wasn't going to get them, so I took a kiss instead.

twenty

SOFIA

I WOKE UP ALONE IN DAKOTA'S BED, SOMETHING THAT HAD happened every morning for the past two weeks. And like I'd done each of those days, I shrugged one of his bulky sweatshirts on over my pajamas and went to search for him.

Most days I found him in the gym. Today, I found him in the living room, sitting in a recliner and staring off into space.

My heart seized at the expression on his face. It was of utter grief and despair. I walked to him immediately, touching his arm when I got close. "Hi."

He jerked, blinking a few times as he shook his mind out of where it had been. "Hey."

I rounded the chair and slid right into his lap, tucking my knees into his chest as I snuggled in tight.

He had a coffee cup in his hand. I took it and brought it to my lips. As expected, it was cold.

Dakota had probably been up for hours.

I rested my head against his shoulder. "What can I do?"

Dakota wrapped his arms around me tighter, cloaking me with their warmth. "You're doing it. Stay with me?"

"I'm not going anywhere."

I'd meant what I'd said in the bar two weeks ago. Dakota

belonged with me.

I hadn't really meant to say it out loud. I'd come into the bar, shocked to see him sitting with Petah. But when he'd asked her where he belonged, the words had spilled past my lips.

With me.

I loved him. I hadn't said the words yet. It wasn't the right time. But I could show him how much I cared by being here.

The future was still hazy, but every moment spent in his arms brought different pixels into focus. I saw us sitting together over Thanksgiving dinner. I saw us exchanging presents on Christmas. I saw a lifetime of midnight kisses to ring in the new year.

In time, the gaps in between would sharpen too.

"My mom called this morning," he said quietly.

"What?" I sat up off his chest, glancing over the back of the chair to the clock on the wall. It was only six in the morning and still dark outside. "What time?"

"About four."

"Is she okay?" An emergency was the only reason someone would need to call at four.

"Koko ran into Petah at the grocery store yesterday."

Oh no. "And Petah told her I was here."

"Yep. Mom's, uh, worked up."

Other than it not happening sooner, it came as no surprise. I'd been waiting two weeks for this kind of call from his family.

Dakota had spoken to his mom every day, but their conversations had always been short check-ins to see how she was holding up. He'd avoided mentioning my arrival and my open-ended departure.

The day I'd come to Lark Cove, Dakota had told me all about his mom's ultimatum to move home. He'd also told me how much he didn't want to go back.

I think talking to Petah had helped him. As much as it irritated me that his ex-girlfriend had been the one to make an impression, I think only someone from the reservation, someone who knew him before, could have reinforced what he already knew.

It was no longer his home.

But until he convinced his mother and sisters of the same, they wouldn't let up. They certainly wouldn't accept me into his life.

"What do you want to do?" I asked. "Should I leave?"

I held my breath as he thought it over. The last thing I wanted to do was leave him. Dakota needed someone—no, not someone, *me*—here to help him through this rough patch. But if his family was going to throw up roadblocks and make dealing with the loss of his father even harder than it already was, I'd disappear.

For a while.

"No." He pulled me impossibly close. "I don't want you to leave."

I sighed. "I don't either."

"We have to figure a lot of shit out. I need . . . I don't know. I've had this image of how my future looked for so long. It's what's driven me forward. Now, with you, it's different. I'm still not sure what it looks like."

I twisted to the side so I could set down the coffee mug. "I don't know all of the details. I wish I did. But do we have to tackle the future right now? Can't some of it wait?"

"Yeah. I don't think I could figure it all out right now."

I put my hand on his face, his stubble rough against my palm. Then I laid a soft kiss on his lips. "I'm here. For whatever you need."

"I need to work this out with my family. I don't want to lose them. You either."

"Then let's go. Today. Let's go see them together."

It wasn't going to be an easy day facing off with his family, but it was inevitable. The future was taking shape in my mind. Hopefully it was doing the same in Dakota's.

And it was time to find out if his family was going to be part of our picture.

"Nice," Koko deadpanned as she answered the door to Dakota's childhood home with a scowl. "Dad's gone so now you bring her home?"

"Koko," Dakota warned. "Don't."

"You really do hate us, don't you? That's what Dad thought."

Dakota flinched, hard.

I squeezed his hand tighter as I stood by his side, waiting for his sister to get out of the way so we could go inside. Her words were cruel. Too cruel. I understood she was grieving too, but she'd just crossed a line.

The pain on Dakota's face must have clued her in. Her angry scowl began to fade. But still, she didn't invite us inside.

It had rained the entire way from Lark Cove to Browning. The early November weather was gray and dreary. Its chill settled into my bones. My teeth threatened to chatter, but I clamped my jaw shut, pretending I was lazing on a sunny beach, not waiting for his sister to drop her attitude.

After what felt like hours, Dakota's other sister, Rozene, came to the door. She pushed in beside Koko, her pregnant belly protruding between us, then mirrored her sister's frown.

"Mom's having a bad day," Rozene said. "It's not the time for this."

"It's never going to be the time," Dakota shot back. "But we're here so how about you stop acting like brats and let us the hell inside? It's cold."

There was no arguing with his tone.

The sisters shared a look and moved out of the way.

Dakota barreled inside the house, practically dragging me along with him. We stopped in the entryway to take off our coats.

Koko and Rozene stood close watch, no longer blocking the door, but they weren't inviting us farther into the house either.

As I unwrapped the scarf from my neck, I stole glances at them both.

The women were beautiful, much like their older brother, with striking features. Their mouths were set in a natural line that was intimidating.

I steeled my spine, refusing to cower.

Rozene must have noticed because she stood taller too, crossing her arms across her chest and resting them on her belly.

A woman's voice called from down the hallway. "Koko, where is the diaper bag?"

"In the kitchen!" she called over her shoulder.

"No, it's not." The voice came closer. "What are you . . ."

Dakota's mother pushed her daughters aside and saw us by the door. Her eyes flared as she recognized me.

"Mom." Dakota bent and kissed her cheek. "You remember Sofia?"

"Hi." I extended my free hand. "I'm so sorry about your loss, Lyndie."

Koko scoffed and spun around, retreating into the house. Rozene kept her stance firm and unwelcoming as Lyndie looked me up and down until I finally dropped my hand. Her stare wasn't as harsh as her daughters', but it held no more warmth than the air had outside.

When Lyndie's inspection was done, she planted her hands on her hips to address Dakota. "Take off your shoes if they're wet."

He nodded and toed off his boots. I followed suit.

When we were both down to our socks, he clutched my hand once more and followed his mother past his sister and through the house.

We walked down a short hallway. The two-story home opened up into a great room on one side and a long kitchen at the end of a hallway on the other.

In the great room, cartoons played for the three little kids rolling cars and stacking blocks on the carpet. A baby girl in a pair of pink leggings and a matching tee crawled around the coffee table.

It had to be the same baby who'd been born after New Year's. She'd gotten so big. Had it really been that long?

The endless months apart from Dakota had gone by in such a blur. Without him around to mark each day special, they'd all melded together.

Dakota waved at the older kids then turned away from the great room and took the hallway that led to the kitchen.

Lyndie was waiting. She stood on the far side of the center

island, wearing black pants and a black sweater. Her eyes darted to the stools under the island, quietly commanding us to sit.

Once we were settled, the air in the room got heavy as we waited for her to speak. I kept my mouth shut but let my eyes wander, mostly to escape her scrutiny.

The Magee home was older, probably built in the seventies, but they'd done some remodeling. Maybe Dakota had helped. The white cabinets looked new. The quartz countertops were a soft gray. The maple floors had been sealed but left in their natural tone.

The kitchen reminded me of the farmhouse style popular on a dozen home interior shows at the moment. It went perfectly in this home.

A compliment came to mind, but I kept it to myself. I doubted Lyndie wanted to hear how this New York City–trained interior designer felt about her home.

The uncomfortable silence lingered, until finally Dakota stirred the room with a long breath. He let go of my hand, leaning his forearms on the counter. With a gentle tone he used often with me, he asked, "How are you doing, Mom?"

"How do you think?" she snapped. Dakota's tone must not work on her like it did on me. "Your father dies, I ask you to move home, to be with your *family*, and instead you stay away."

With her.

The unspoken words boomed in the kitchen.

Lyndie's eyes flooded and she turned her back on us, taking a Kleenex from a box next to the sink. Her shoulders shook as she wept.

"I'll let you talk." I touched Dakota's forearm and slid off my stool.

He'd asked me to come along, but this conversation was

not for my ears. Me sitting here would only make it harder on him. And his mom.

So I walked out of the room, glancing over my shoulder as Dakota stood too, walked over to his mother and pulled her into his arms.

Lyndie collapsed into him, clinging to him as she cried.

Wanting to give her that privacy, I started down the hall-way, planning on joining the children in the living room. But three steps away from the kitchen, Rozene came into view. She shot me a glare and shook her head, trapping me in my place.

I wasn't welcome in the great room. I wasn't necessary in the kitchen. So I loitered in the hallway, stuck in limbo.

With nowhere else to look, I examined the walls. They were full of collaged photo frames. Most of the pictures were older from when Dakota was a child. He'd been a handsome boy, lean and lanky as a teenager before he'd filled his broad frame with muscle. In most, he had a basketball in his hand.

There was one photo that caught my attention, drawing me in. Dakota was standing at the free-throw line, poised and ready to make his shot. His dad was standing off to the side, a proud smile on his face.

When had Joseph stopped smiling at Dakota? Maybe he never had.

The saddest part was Dakota would never know. Their conversations would remain unfinished, their wounds unhealed.

Dakota's heart had been broken by regret. If his mom pushed hard on him to move home, I didn't know if he had the strength or energy at the moment to resist. He wouldn't leave things undone with a family member again.

Don't push him, Lyndie. As I listened to cartoons in one ear and Lyndie's weeping in the other, I begged for it over and over again.

The future I was beginning to see with Dakota would be erased forever if he came back here. For selfish reasons, I wanted him to stay in Lark Cove until we could figure *us* out.

For Dakota's sake, he needed to be free to live his life. To make his own choices. To shine.

That beautiful man had wings. Why couldn't his family see them?

"I'm sorry, Mom," he said quietly as she wept.

"Are you coming back?"

"No."

After a few seconds, the sound of dishes being taken out of a cupboard and put on the counter echoed my way.

"I regret not making things right with Dad," Dakota said. "It'll haunt me forever. I don't want that with you."

"Then come *home*. Be with your family."

"I can't."

A bowl slammed down. "Why?"

"I love you, Mom. I love Koko and Rozene. I love the kids. But I can't. I don't mean this to sound like I'm running your choices down, but I don't want this life."

"And Sofia?" Lyndie asked.

"She's in my heart."

"For how long?"

"Forever."

My breath hitched, hope swelling in my chest. And like always, my eyes flooded with tears.

He loved me. He might not have said it. He might not see the details of our future either. But he loved me.

There had to be a future. There *had* to be a way. We'd touched one another's lives, leaving permanent marks neither of us would ever erase.

If this didn't work out, if we couldn't find a way, I'd never be the same.

Neither would he.

"Dakota." Lyndie sighed. "Your father's death, it has crushed us. We all have things we should have said. We have our regrets."

"Mom—"

"Let me finish." She cut him off. "I don't want that. You are my son, and I love you. I don't understand you. But I love you."

"Thank you."

"I don't know where we go from here."

"Neither do I," Dakota admitted. "I'm lost."

"So am I." Lyndie's voice broke and she began to cry again. Her muffled sobs meant she was once again in Dakota's arms.

I sniffled, swallowing tears of my own. Sometime during the past year, I'd stopped criticizing myself for crying. It was my release, and I wasn't going to feel ashamed for it. But I'd also learned how to staunch them when I wanted to, not when others did.

They were *my* tears. I chose when they were needed. For now, they were at bay.

Turning away from the kitchen, I braved the remainder of the hallway to the great room. The wooden floors were slick under my socks so I took it slowly, dreading what was waiting for me.

The front door tempted me momentarily. I gave it a longing glance before stepping off the wooden floor and onto the carpet, crossing into enemy territory.

I entered the great room unnoticed by the kids. They kept playing, only one of them sparing me a glance. Koko was seated in a chair, her baby girl in her arms lazily drinking a bottle. Rozene was on one end of the couch, closest to the kids.

With a coat and diaper bag on the other chair in the room, I had no choice but to take the free end of the couch.

Neither of Dakota's sisters spoke to me as I settled into the leather. So I watched the cartoons, recognizing the show from when Dakota and I'd gone over to Thea and Logan's place on Halloween to tag along for trick-or-treating.

"My brother is exploring. It's in his blood." Koko spoke over the show. "But eventually, he'll realize his place is here and come back home to settle down."

Is that what she'd told Petah for all these years? Is that why she'd never gotten over Dakota?

"I disagree. I think if you asked and listened, he'd disagree as well."

Rozene huffed. "This is not what Dad would want."

Meaning me. *I* was not who her dad would have wanted for Dakota.

"I love him." My voice was unwavering. "He is the love of my life."

Rozene and Koko shared a look. Either they didn't believe me, or they thought it wouldn't matter. They really believed Dakota would come back.

Like their mother, they didn't understand him.

How could three siblings raised together be so different? Though, looking at my own relationship with my siblings, maybe it was something that evolved over time.

"Babe." All of us turned, the kids included, when Dakota entered the room with Lyndie close behind. He jerked his chin to the door. "Let's go."

"Oh, already?" I jumped from my seat, joining him by the door.

He pulled on his boots then gave his mom a long hug good-bye before opening the door. No one said good-bye. No one waved from the porch. The moment we stepped outside into the rain, the door closed behind us.

Dakota's hand found mine as we hurried down the sidewalk to the truck. He opened my door for me to hop inside then jogged around to get in himself to drive us straight out of town.

It took nearly an hour for his jaw to unclench and his hands to stop strangling the steering wheel.

"Did you mean it?"

"Mean what?" I turned away from the window where I'd been watching the rain streak across the glass.

"That you love me?"

"Yes. I love you."

He nodded once and turned back to the road. His jaw still tense, his hands still iron clamps on the wheel. Dakota's foot pressed harder on the gas pedal.

With each green mile marker, my heart sank lower.

The minutes on the clock ticked by. That urge to cry, the one I'd held back earlier, came back with a vengeance. I fought it but was close to giving in when Dakota slammed on the brakes.

My arms shot out to brace against the door, and my chest pressed hard into the seatbelt as he took a sharp turn.

The truck bounced down a dirt road fenced by barbed wire and tall trees. I had no idea where we were going, but Dakota seemed to know. He raced us down the road, the wheels exploding puddles along the way.

Dakota hit a hard bump, jostling me in the seat, and I couldn't stay quiet. "Where are we going?"

He didn't answer. He drove for another few seconds then pulled off the road and right up to the trees. Ahead of us, the road wound deeper into the forest. Behind us, the highway had long since been hidden by the trees.

"Dak—"

He reached over the console, unbuckled my seatbelt and took my face in his hands. Then he pulled me to the middle of the cab and slammed his mouth down on mine.

So caught off guard, I sat frozen for a second. Then I caught up. I scrambled for him, climbing over the console, banging my knees on the way. My back collided with the roof, but I didn't stop.

With his help, I made it to the driver's seat, but the steering wheel was in my way. So I sat on it. My knees were shoved into his sides, my feet at odd angles. But I clung to him, sinking close, somehow managing to fit my tiny frame into the cramped space.

Not once as I wiggled and shifted did he let me go. Not once did he break away from my lips. Not once did he open his eyes.

He held tight as I came to him.

Then he held me, letting his tongue explore my mouth as he tried to fuse us together. We kissed until the windows were coated in steam. Until one of my feet had fallen asleep. Until I broke away, panting as I held his dark gaze.

"Did you mean it?" I whispered.

"Mean what?"

"That I was in your heart forever?"

He brushed a fallen hair from my forehead. "Am I the kind

of man who says things he doesn't mean?"

"No."

"No." He grinned. "I'm not."

"I love you."

He kissed me on the temple. "Love you too."

I wanted our future to be full of those words. I wanted our children and grandchildren to see him kiss me on the temple so often they'd know it was his spot.

That was the future I wanted.

Did he?

twenty-one

DAKOTA

"DAKOTA," SOFIA GASPED AS I SLID INSIDE OF HER. Those dark eyes opened lazily, still clouded with sleep. She blinked a couple of times, then let them drift closed again. The corner of her mouth turned up in a half smile as she shifted her hips, making more room for me.

My lady loved to be woken up with my cock.

I grinned, easing out before thrusting in again, this time going all the way to the root.

Sofia moaned, her head pressing back into the pillow as she offered up her neck.

I latched my mouth on to the side, sucking hard and biting down hard enough it was going to leave a mark.

My mark.

While Sofia was mine, I wanted the world to know.

I slid my hands up her hips as I moved in and out of her tight heat. I traced the line of her ribs all the way past her breasts and to her shoulders. Then I stretched her arms up, pulling them straight above her head. With my fingers laced through hers, I pinned her hands to the mattress, trapping her beneath me.

This was the place. This, right here, was the best place in the world. I didn't need to travel to find it.

When we were connected, all of the shit we still had to figure out disappeared. I could block it out and pretend this might last forever.

"Love you," I whispered into her neck.

Sofia hummed, turning her smile to my ear. "I love you too."

We'd been saying those words for two weeks now. They came first thing in the morning, when I woke Sofia up by making love to her, saying those words to start the day. I angled my hips, sending my cock deeper and pressing the root into her clit.

She shivered, her breath hitching as I eased off and did it again. Making her come was easier in the morning. I had no idea why, but she'd go off like a rocket. She would at night too, but it always took a few more of my tricks.

But like this, relaxed and pliable, she let go.

In the morning, the things we'd been ignoring for two weeks weren't hanging over us. Yet. That goddamn cloud would settle around breakfast and haunt us for the rest of the day.

I eased out, gliding inside again just as Sofia wrapped her long, toned legs around my hips. She was flexible enough to hook her ankles around my back. It allowed me just enough space to build up some momentum and it angled her pussy so I was hitting her in the right spot every time.

"Harder," she begged.

"No. Easy." Today was all about easy. This morning was going to be about easy. Because later today, we had to start figuring things out. We'd put it off too long.

Sofia moaned, half protest, half agreement. Her hardened nipples rubbed against my chest, sliding in the sheen of sweat across my pecks. Her heart was pounding, the rose flush creeping up her neck, and I knew it wouldn't be long before she came.

I pressed a kiss to her temple, then dragged my lips down her cheek, finding the corner of her mouth. I dropped one open-mouthed kiss there and continued down. Her hands were still intertwined in mine, her legs around my back.

We were threaded together.

I went back to the spot where I'd bitten earlier and latched on, tickling the teeth marks with my tongue. Then I thrust harder, giving her what she wanted.

"Oh god." Her head thrashed on the pillow, her hair flying loose.

"Come." I ordered it into her skin, already feeling her pussy clench around my cock. "Yes," I groaned, letting her draw me out as she released. The pressure at the base of my spine spiked, my balls tightened. And I let go, coating her with me as the world disappeared.

I stayed inside her after we'd both come down, letting myself leak out between us. I let go of her hands to wrap her up while she dropped her fingers to my back, splaying them over my damp skin.

Her legs tightened, pulling my softening cock even deeper into her body. "This is the best part of my day."

"Mine too."

We stayed like that for a few minutes, just breathing. Just feeling one another's heartbeats echo in different rhythms. But eventually, the light streaming through the blinds forced us up and apart.

I got off the bed first, extending a hand to help Sofia to her feet. She leaned into me, kissing the skin over my heart, before walking on unsteady feet to the bathroom.

"Are you coming to work with me today?" I asked, trailing behind her.

She nodded. "You don't have to go until three, right?"

"Yeah." I'd been back to my normal schedule this week, covering most of the nights at the bar. It was a schedule I'd always liked, having my mornings free for whatever I needed to do. But it was dragging on Sofia.

She'd work here during the day, trying to keep up with everything at the dance studio, then would come to work and hang out with me until we closed. The bar had been quiet, so we'd been able to close down well before two each night. But it was still late, and she was trying to manage two different time zones.

"You don't have to. You could stay here. Go to bed early."

She shook her head as she turned on the shower then smiled over her shoulder. "I want to stay with you."

She hadn't left my side in two weeks.

Dad's death had rocked me off my footing. I wasn't sure I'd ever completely recover, but there was no going back. I couldn't change what had happened. Would I regret where things had ended? Always. It was a weight I'd carry until my last day.

But I was okay.

"I'm okay, babe."

"I still want to be with you." She stepped into the shower, tipping her head back into the stream. Water ran down her nose and soaked her hair.

I got in beside her, waiting as she swiped the water from her face and spun so we could trade places.

Since she'd been here, Sofia and I had found this routine where we got ready together.

We'd shower together, a dance so easy and fluid it was like we'd never showered apart. She'd wet her hair. I'd wet and shampoo mine while she squirted body wash on a shower puff.

She'd shampoo her hair while I scrubbed. Then she'd put in some conditioner and let it soak while she washed.

I'd get out first, go to the sink to shave and brush my teeth. It was perfectly timed so that when she was ready to get out, I'd be done. I'd hand her two towels, one for her body and another for her hair.

She'd take my place at the sink, working on her hair and makeup while I got dressed.

When I looked into the future, trying to picture a life with this woman, all I saw was that black box. I couldn't picture us living together or getting married or having children.

The only thing I could make out was this morning routine.

It was something.

But not enough.

"I'll bring you some coffee." I kissed her bare shoulder then went into the bedroom to get dressed.

I pulled on some jeans and a long-sleeved T-shirt, then re-played the questions Mom had asked me two weeks ago.

Will you get married? Will you move away? Will you have children?

Mom's questions had been loaded with dread. My own mother was disappointed in me for finding a woman I loved. A woman with a good family, with an education, with a career and dreams.

A woman who could give her beautiful grandchildren she didn't seem to want. Dad had helped teach me percentages in grade school by using blood quantum analogies. It was so ingrained in our household, I understood Mom's disappointment. I didn't agree with it, but I understood.

It was madness.

"Goddamn madness," I muttered, sitting on the edge of

the bed and pulling on some socks.

"What did you say?" Sofia poked her head out of the bathroom, her pink toothbrush in one hand.

"Nothing." I shook my head.

She waited, knowing there was something bothering me. I think she'd been waiting for two weeks for me to tell her why we'd flown out of my mother's house so quickly.

The last thing I wanted was for her to feel unworthy. She wasn't. But my own personal hang-ups were fucking with me.

Her money was still an issue for me. Her heritage. If Dad hadn't died, maybe these things wouldn't be plaguing me. Maybe I would have had an easier time saying *fuck it all*, because he'd be around and I could try and win him over.

I loved her.

I needed her.

Sofia was my one, like Mom was for him.

But he wasn't on this earth any longer. His ghost wasn't going to change his opinions.

"It's nothing, babe." I stood and went over to her for a kiss on her bare lips, tasting a hint of mint. "I'll get coffee."

It hurt her when I shut her out. I saw the pain flash in her eyes. But I kept quiet, hoping I'd get my head lined up before we had our talk.

I left the room and went to get the coffee going. When it was done, I took her mug back to the bathroom, another part of our routine.

"What do you want for breakfast?" I set her coffee down on the vanity.

She found my gaze in the mirror. "The truth."

"Sofia." I sighed. "It's nothing."

"Don't do that," she snapped, diving into her makeup bag.

She spoke to me through the mirror as she furiously swiped on some moisturizer. "You know what I learned after two failed marriages? I never wanted to really talk to my ex-husbands. I didn't really care what they had to say. With you? Every cell in my body cares. Every word means something, I care so much. Do you?"

"You know I do."

"Then talk. Be honest with me. Please," she begged. "I've never had honest, and I'm aching for it."

Christ, I couldn't say no. This conversation was going to end one of two ways. Either we'd come out of it stronger. Or she'd be on a plane back to New York with my broken heart in her handbag.

I'd dealt enough poker games to understand odds.

These were not in my favor.

"I don't know where to start," I admitted, setting down my coffee cup. Then I went to the toilet seat, sitting down and letting my shoulders hunch forward.

"How about with the basics? Do you want to live in Montana?" she asked.

"Yes. Do you?"

"No. Not full-time."

I sighed. "I have to work. I have bills to pay. Which means I need to live here."

"I have money. We could pay off your properties and buy a hundred more if you want. You don't have to work at the bar unless you want to. Isn't that the goal of your properties anyway? To leverage your investments so you can travel and be free to come and go as you please?"

"Yes, it is. Which is why I have to work. I'm not taking your money."

Sofia was bent close to the mirror, putting on some foundation with a sponge. She froze at my statement, the sponge poised right next to her nose. "Really?"

"Yes, really. I'm not that man."

"Are you serious?"

I gave her one nod. "Yes."

She rolled her eyes, dabbing the tip of her nose and putting the sponge away. She yanked a brush from her makeup bag and a small black compact. She opened it, pressing the brush so hard into the powder that little pink dust particles flew around her hand. "I don't even know how to respond to that."

I sat there waiting, thinking she'd come up with something soon. But she just went about putting on her makeup.

She went for the eyeshadow next. The entire time she put it on her eyelids, her nostrils were flaring. After that, she swiped on some liner and then mascara.

I still waited, thinking words would follow the makeup. But she put her cosmetic bag away and got out her hair dryer. The noise it created blocked out any chance of conversation. With every angry stroke of her brush through her hair, I heard her though.

I knew better than to leave the room. So I sat on the toilet, biding my time.

She finished with her hair, put away the dryer and turned to me with a hand perched on her hip.

This was it.

Make or break time. She'd either understand I was a man and there were certain lines I'd drawn. Or this would be a hurdle we couldn't get over.

"Your pride is foolish." She was fuming, but her voice was eerily steady. "Foolish male pride."

"It's not—"

"It is." She stopped me with a hand. "I'm not giving up my money because you have some caveman, animalistic desire to be the provider in the house."

"Babe, that's not what I'm saying. I want you to have your money."

Her anger deflated, confusion taking over. "Then I don't understand."

"I'm never going to be able to provide you the life you're used to."

"That's what I mean!" She stood tall. "That's just prid—"

"Hold up." I stood from the toilet, walking to her and putting my hands on her shoulders. "I'm never going to be able to provide you the life you're used to. I made peace with that a long time ago. But that doesn't mean I'm going to take your money. I need to be successful. On my own."

"You already are," she whispered.

My heart squeezed that she saw me like that. "I'm not there yet."

"Where is there? You work so hard. You're so ambitious. And I thought you were doing it for yourself. To be free and travel the world or whatever you wanted. I can give you that. Right now. And that doesn't make you any less successful."

"It's not . . . it's not just for the money."

"Then why?" Her eyes pleaded with me for an explanation she'd understand.

"Because I want my family to see me as successful. So maybe they get why I left. That the life I've chosen isn't a bad one. And if I take your money, they'll never recognize my own accomplishments."

Even with Dad gone, maybe *because* he was gone, the

desire to prove myself was as strong as ever.

"Oh." Her eyes flooded, and she blinked them rapidly to keep the tears from ruining her makeup. "So you'll stay here. Struggling and working yourself to the bone. Making me watch as you refuse to let me help you."

"Sofia—"

She shook her head, stepping away from me and out of the bathroom. Stripping off her towel, she tossed it on the bed and went to the closet. With her back to me, she pulled on some panties and strapped on a bra. Then she dug through the hangers for something to wear.

She'd unpacked her things into my closet the week she'd come here after Dad's funeral. I'd been so fucking happy not to have her living in those suitcases this time around.

But after she pulled on a long sweatshirt-type dress that hung to her ankles and some stark-white tennis shoes, she paused. Her face was aimed toward the suitcase in the bottom of the closet.

Fuck.

She was going to leave.

I took a step forward, reaching for her just as she spun around. The tears in her eyes made me stop.

"If you asked, I'd give it all up."

"I'd never ask," I said gently.

"I know. But I'd give it all up. Every cent if it meant we could be together and on the same wavelength. Should I?"

"No." I didn't want that for her. She shouldn't be without, forced to work for an hourly wage with a small-town job just because I had something to prove.

"It's not fair." She wiped a tear away from one eye before it could fall. "Why is it that money is the reason I can't be happy?

My ex-husbands just wanted my money. My feelings and my heart were an afterthought."

I grimaced, hating those two bastards and the pain they'd caused her. Though today, I wasn't doing much better.

"And now you." She swung out a hand. "You want me but not my money. Why can't I have both? Why can't you just accept that it is part of who I am? Why can't we share a life?"

"We can." I hoped.

"How is that going to work?" She cocked a hip. "I decide to go on vacation. But you can't afford a last-minute trip so you stay behind? Or how about something is happening at the studio, and I need to spend a few weeks in the city, but you can't take off work because you need to make a few thousand dollars."

"I'll stay."

"And I'll go," she huffed. "Separate lives. We're doomed to live separate lives. You are so hung up on the version of your life you've been living for years, you can't see the new version, the better version, right in front of your face."

"Maybe you're right," I admitted.

"I am."

Without another word, she turned and walked out of the bedroom. I followed her down the hall and through the living room. But instead of going to the kitchen like I'd expected, she went to the front door, lifting her coat from the hook as she walked.

"Where are you going?"

"For a walk."

"Don't." I snagged her arm, stopping her before she could put on her coat. "Don't go."

It didn't take much coercing for her to drop her coat. Just a gentle tug on her elbow and she tossed it on the floor and came right into my arms.

"I don't want to fight."

"Me neither," she said into my chest.

"What are we going to do?"

"You have to decide, Dakota. You." She walked out of my hold. But instead of going to the door, she walked over to the couch and sank down on the edge.

I followed and sat by her side, relieved she hadn't left. After how I'd left things with Dad, I couldn't stomach leaving things undone with anyone, especially Sofia.

"I want to get married again." She said it quietly and without hope. "I want to have a marriage. A real marriage with my best friend. I want children."

I cringed, and she felt it.

Her eyes snapped to my profile. "You don't?"

"It's complicated." I closed my eyes and took a deep breath. If she had reacted like this to the money conversation, my issues with children were going to send her racing out the door. "I feel guilty."

"Guilty?"

"Yeah. Guilty. I wanted kids once. But then things got so twisted up. If we had kids . . ."

"Oh my god," she gasped, figuring it out so I didn't have to say it. "Your family. You can't have kids with me because I'm white? You'd feel guilty?"

Christ, it sounded awful when she said it out loud.

Sofia shot off the couch, but she didn't leave. She just stood above me, her chest heaving as she fought the urge to either slap me or cry.

Probably both.

"This is insane, Dakota. It's completely fucked up."

She wasn't wrong. It was fucked up. But that still didn't help me figure out how to un-fuck it up.

Sofia took a few steps, making a circle as she thought it all over. She dragged her fingers through her hair, pulling hard at the roots. "You have to choose. God, I hate even saying that. But I can't change who I am."

"I know. I don't want you to change."

She scoffed. "Someone has to give here, love."

"Can you see this is killing me?" I ran my hands over my face. "I know this is my burden. I know I'm putting it all on you. But you wanted the truth. That's where I'm at. That's my battle."

The battle I felt like I'd been fighting my entire life.

Choose Sofia, and I'd lose my family.

Choose my family, and I'd lose the love of my life.

I'd walked away from the reservation years ago. I'd convinced myself I'd forged my own path.

Except all of the things I'd shunned seemed more important now that Dad was gone.

"I don't want to lose you." Her voice broke. "But I don't want to lose me either. I feel like I've worked so hard to find myself this year. I don't want to give up the woman you fell in love with."

"Come here." I waved her over.

She came to me, dropping to her knees in front of me instead of sitting next to me on the couch. Her hands threaded through my hair.

"You are you. Maybe you feel like you discovered yourself this year, but I've seen *you* since the beginning. And I fell in love with you the moment you tripped and fell on a bunch of peanut shells."

She laughed, a tear falling from one of her eyes. "There has to be a way."

"We'll figure it out."

"We will?"

I had no fucking clue, so I lied. "We will."

"When? We can't ignore all of this."

"I know. Let's get through Thanksgiving with your parents. Let's just . . . it's out there." We both knew the choice I had to make.

"Okay." She nodded, the hope in her eyes dulling. "I think I'm going to take a quick walk. I have a call with Daniel in an hour, and I need to get my head clear first."

The last thing I wanted was for her to leave, but at least she'd stayed to talk. Not that anything was solved. She was still walking out the door. This time, it was only for a walk. Next time . . .

I didn't want to think about next time.

"Fine." I held out a hand to help her up. I walked with her to the door and grabbed her coat from the floor, holding it open as she put it on.

"I'll make breakfast. It'll be ready when you come back."

She nodded. "I'm not going far."

I kissed her quickly then turned for the bedroom to collect our cold coffee mugs.

"Dakota," she called, stopping me.

"Yeah?"

"I see it. I see it so clearly, and it's magnificent. It takes my breath away."

"See what, babe?"

"The future." She turned the knob on the door. "I wish you could see it too."

twenty-two

SOFIA

"IT'S SO GOOD TO SEE YOU, SWEETHEART." MOM HUGGED ME as she came into the living room at Logan and Thea's house.

Dad was next, pulling me into his arms before letting me go to shake Dakota's hand. "Good to see you again, Dakota."

"You too, sir."

"Please, call me Thomas." Dad waved him off. "I get enough sirs at work."

Dakota nodded, kissed my mother on the cheek and gave me a smile as Aubrey and Granny came into the living room to join us.

The chaos of their arrival had energized the whole house. Logan was busy hauling in some bags from their rented SUV. The kids were going crazy, excited to see their grandparents.

"Hi." I hugged Aubrey. "How are you?"

"Good. I'm—ugh." She was interrupted when her phone rang. She pulled it from her pocket, frowned, then silenced the call. "I'd be better if a certain cop stopped calling me. But you wouldn't know anything about that, would you?"

I fought a smile. "Me? I have no idea what you're talking about."

"He's relentless."

Since I'd come to Montana, I hadn't had a chance to catch up with Aubrey. But I was guessing that Landon had made it his new hobby to pester my sister for a date.

I was rooting for him to win her over. As she looked at her phone again, her eyes twinkled at his name on the screen. I suspected Landon wasn't far from wearing her down.

"Nice to see you again, Aubrey." Dakota hugged her then stood by my side as they all came and sat in the living room.

Charlie had already stolen Granny away to her room, where the pair would probably be for the next hour, reading books and catching up on their time apart. The little kids climbed all over my parents, wanting to know where their special presents were stashed while Logan and Thea looked on with happy smiles.

My heart sank, knowing there was a very good chance I'd never have that. Not if I wanted to stay with Dakota.

Since our argument last week, he hadn't brought up his family or his issues with my money again. He hadn't hinted I'd be his choice.

With every passing minute, the chances of me coming out of this without a broken heart were shriveling. My vibrant dreams had faded to gray.

The urge to cry came on so strong, I quietly fled from the room. I made it to the kitchen, hoping for a few moments alone to collect myself.

I didn't get them.

I'd just made it to the island when Dakota's heat hit my back. He wrapped me up in a hug, holding me as he bent to whisper in my ear, "What's wrong?"

"I have a headache." It wasn't a complete lie. I hadn't felt all that well since I'd woken up this morning. "A couple Advil and I'll be fine."

His arms banded tighter, holding me in place, until he let me go after a few seconds.

I went to my purse on the counter and took out my travel bottle of pain pills. I popped a couple, chugged down some water, and smiled, leading him back into the living room without a word.

Conversation between us had all but stopped this week. Tension and stress had chased away my desire to talk. We exchanged as few words as necessary to get through the day's routine.

Yet we clung to each other physically. Dakota didn't let me leave a room without following. At night, I slept burrowed into his side. While I worked during the day, he was always near. And at night, I was across from him at the bar.

We made love as often as possible, from the early morning hours until late into the night. Dakota and I soaked up every second together, savoring this time.

I'd lost track of the number of times he and I had broken apart. The number of times we'd agreed to go our separate ways only to find ourselves thrust together again.

But this time, if or when I left, there would be no coming back.

This split, the last, would devastate us both.

So here we were, struggling through the motions, forcing smiles and laughter, so our unhappiness wouldn't ruin Thanksgiving.

As we walked out of the kitchen, the front door opened and closed. Boots stomped off the fresh snow we'd gotten last night. Hazel's hoarse laughter carried down the hallway as she and Xavier came inside.

"Hey, bud." Xavier clapped Dakota on the shoulder as they greeted us first. Then he bent to kiss my cheek. "How are you guys today?"

"Cold," I teased. The air from the front door gave me goose bumps. This Thanksgiving was supposed to be the coldest the area had seen in the last two decades.

"I'll keep you warm, babe." Dakota put his arm around my shoulders, guiding me into the living room.

More greetings and handshakes as we piled into the space. The room full of people I loved would be my saving grace this holiday.

It made it easier to ignore the pain in my heart when there was so much to be joyous about.

"How was your trip?" I asked my parents as Dakota and I sat on the loveseat.

"We were lucky to get here," Dad said. "They closed the airport twenty minutes after we touched down because of visibility."

"Oh no!" Thea gasped. "What about the pilot and crew? Did they take off?"

Mom shook her head. "No. They'll have to wait to see if things clear up."

"But Thanksgiving is tomorrow." Thea looked at Logan. "You better call and invite them down here, just in case. I hate to think of them in a hotel on a holiday."

"We've got extra rooms at our place," Mom said. "If they have to spend the night, we'll have them come here."

Mom and Dad's Montana house was a couple of miles away on the lake. It was just as big as Logan and Thea's, but we didn't spend much time there. We all preferred to stay here where the kids were comfortable and had all of their things.

"I can stay here and free up a room," Aubrey offered.

I opened my mouth to offer her Dakota's guest bedroom but stopped myself. If she stayed with us, she'd sense the tension. I'd have a harder time hiding my feelings, and right now, I didn't want to talk about them.

I didn't want to talk about any of it. When I wasn't on the verge of tears, I was numb.

"I wonder if Arthur's son made it up," Dakota said quietly. "He was supposed to fly in today."

"Can you call him?"

He nodded. "Yeah. Be right back."

I listened to the various conversations in the room as I waited for Dakota to return. Logan asked Dad and Aubrey about work. Mom and Thea talked about how Collin was doing in school. Hazel had Camila on her lap, the two of them whispering to one another in their own little game.

Xavier's eyes kept wandering to me. He knew my smile was fake. He'd been a police officer for so long, I doubted Dakota and I were fooling him.

"Dakota's working tonight?" he asked.

I nodded. "Yes. He's covering the bar tonight and then gets the rest of the weekend off."

Jackson would be there on Friday and over the weekend. At first, I'd been excited for the break because it would give Dakota and me time together without a schedule.

But then everything had come out last week, and now I was dreading this weekend. Without work as an excuse, we'd have to talk.

Sooner rather than later, he had to choose.

Maybe I should pull the pilot aside this weekend and clue him in that I might be flying back to New York next week too.

Dakota came back into the room, his face etched with concern. "Arthur's son's flight was canceled. I invited him here, but he said he'd rather stay home and listen to the television. He said he doesn't even like turkey."

"But he'll be alone on Thanksgiving."

"Maybe I could run up there." Dakota looked at the time on his phone and frowned. "I'll never make it back for work though. I don't want to ask Thea to cover, not with everyone here."

"I could go see Arthur," I offered.

"Not on these roads." He shook his head. "You're not driving anywhere."

"I'll go slow. It's not snowing hard, and it's just a little foggy. I'll stop at the grocery store in Kalispell and get him some of his favorite junk foods. Then I can hang out with him for a little bit."

And I could use the break.

I could use the quiet drive to Kalispell to think. I'd asked Dakota to make a choice, but I had one of my own to make.

If he chose his family over me, would I be willing to give up my own dreams?

"Where are you going?" Logan asked, halting all other conversations in the room.

"One of Dakota's tenants is this really sweet elderly man. He's blind and his son's flight was canceled, so he's alone for Thanksgiving. I thought I would go there for a bit today and say hello."

"You can't drive to Kalispell." Logan spoke first, stealing the exact words that were written on Dad's face. "The roads are icy, and you barely drive as it is."

He wasn't wrong. I rarely drove my car in the city. It sat

in the garage collecting dust most days. And I'd only driven Dakota's truck a couple of times when I'd come to visit Thea while he'd been at the bar.

"I'll drive you up there." Xavier pushed up from the couch. "I know Arthur. Wouldn't mind saying hello myself."

"Thank you." I stood too, ignoring the waves of frustration coming off Dakota.

He didn't want me leaving, but he wouldn't leave Arthur alone either. Since he trusted his uncle more than any other person in the world, he didn't have any more excuses to keep me in Lark Cove.

"I'll be back." I went to the couch, kissed Mom and Dad, then waved to Aubrey.

They looked a bit baffled that I was leaving already, but they didn't comment.

Before anyone could talk me out of this trip, I hurried to the kitchen, grabbed my purse and went to the door, where I'd hung up my puffer coat.

With it on, I stood by the door, waiting for Xavier and watching as Dakota stalked my way.

"I don't like you going up there today." He came close and planted his hands on his hips.

"It's just a quick trip. And I need it." The happy face I'd put on for the last week was getting heavy to wear. "Some time apart will be good for us both."

"Yeah." Dakota sighed. "You're probably right."

I stood there, wishing for a glimmer of hope on his face. But there was nothing. He looked to the floor, his hands falling to his sides. Was he even considering me as an option? Or had he already given up on us?

I swallowed down my disappointment, let Dakota kiss me

on the cheek, then followed Xavier outside after he'd shrugged on his coat.

His and Hazel's SUV was parked in the driveway. I got in, glad it was still warm. Just the short walk from the front door had frozen my ears.

Xavier climbed in and cranked up the heat.

"Thank you for taking me."

"Glad to do it." He reached over and patted my shoulder before backing out of the drive and getting us on the road. "You doing okay?"

"Not great," I admitted.

"Want to talk about it?"

"No." I sighed. "Yes. I don't like your family much."

He chuckled. "They can be a hard bunch to love. What happened?"

"I'm pretty sure they've been grooming Dakota since birth. That sounds extreme, but I can't think of another way to describe it."

He hummed. "Their beliefs can be hard to understand."

"Has it always been like this?" I asked. "Has he always had this kind of pressure? I mean, it's like when he was born they already knew how his life was going to be lived. He has to live in the right place. Work in the right job. Marry the right woman. Have the right kind of kids."

In a lot of ways, his family's expectations reminded me of the stories I'd read about princes and princesses of the past. If he wanted to inherit the crown, he had to toe the family line.

As a child, I'd wanted to be a princess. I *was* the princess.

A princess who would never get her prince.

"Like I said, it's hard to understand," Xavier said. "They are fiercely loyal to our family's traditions. Which isn't a bad thing.

But it can make them too rigid. They can be closed-minded. And I'm afraid that some of what they're putting Dakota through is my fault."

"Your fault? How is it your fault?"

He sighed, shifting his grip on the steering wheel. He grimaced as he did, sucking in a sharp breath as his hand went to his sternum.

"Are you okay?"

He nodded. "Just heartburn. I've had a hell of a time with it this week."

"Should we stop somewhere and get some medicine?"

"I'll be fine." His hand drifted down his chest to his stomach, pressing in on the side. "I took a couple of Tums a bit ago, just waiting for them to kick in."

I watched him closely. "Should we go back?"

"I'm fine." He smiled through the pain. "It's only heartburn."

"Okay." I struggled to relax in my seat. Dakota had just lost his father. If he lost Xavier too, he'd be destroyed.

"Where were we?" he asked.

"You said all of this was partly your fault."

"It is." He nodded. "My dad worked for the tribal authorities. It was how I got interested in becoming a cop. As a kid, I dreamed we'd get to work together when I got older. But then he got killed on duty before I graduated high school. Drunk guy traveling through the reservation stopped on the side of the road and killed his wife with a shotgun. My dad was out on patrol. He pulled up, and the guy killed him too before he turned it on himself."

"I'm sorry."

"It's a risk we all understand. Doesn't make it easier to deal with, but it's there. My mom, Dakota's grandmother, had a hard time."

"That's understandable."

"Mom got skittish of everything and everyone not from the reservation. In her mind, outsiders couldn't be trusted. It became this thing with her, this belief that blinded her. I had a couple of white friends. She refused to let me spend time with them. I worked for a white rancher out of town, fixing fence in the summer; she made me quit my job."

I blinked, watching the icy road ahead of us as Xavier drove. I hadn't met Dakota's grandmother, though I knew she was still alive and living in a nursing home on the reservation. My heart hurt for her, losing her husband too early.

And her son.

My heart hurt that her grief had turned into such venomous discrimination.

"My brother didn't think the way Mom did," Xavier said. "Joseph wasn't a prejudiced man. But he put our people first. Above all else. When I decided to leave the reservation, he saw it as a betrayal of our culture. I was the first one in my family line to have ever left. Ever. Generations and generations, I was the one to break the chain. Joseph never understood because we had everything there we needed to live, get an education and a job. To him, leaving was unnecessary."

"But you felt trapped."

"That's right." He looked over, his dark eyes soft underneath the brim of his Stetson. "I felt trapped, so I decided to leave. I had a lot to prove back then. Prove to myself I could make it off the reservation. Prove to outsiders that an American Indian could be sheriff in a white town. But it drove a wedge between me and my family. My mom saw it as a betrayal to my dad's memory. My brother saw it as a betrayal to our people. I should have stayed there to serve them, to make their lives better. Not live two hours away and serve a strange community."

"And then Dakota left too."

"That's right. But it wasn't just leaving. Dakota left and came to *me*. Joseph never forgave me for leaving. And I made it nearly impossible for him to accept that Dakota needed to leave."

"What about all the blood quantum stuff?"

Xavier frowned. "There's not many families on the reservation who still think that shit matters. But unfortunately, mine is one that does."

"Is there any hope?"

"There's always hope." Xavier placed his hand on my shoulder. "Our people, we are proud of our heritage. That pride is good and bad. Dakota has to learn to keep his pride and set it aside at the same time."

"I told him he had to choose." I dropped my eyes to my lap. "Was that wrong?"

"No. He does have a choice to make. But you have to understand how hard that choice will be. As much as you want him to choose you? They want it just as bad. They love him."

The guilt for putting him in this position settled hard. "Why does this even have to be a choice? Can't we all just love him?"

Xavier smiled. "That's why he'll choose you."

"I don't know if he will," I whispered as my eyes flooded.

"He will. My nephew is his own man. He might be conflicted, but give him time. He'll work it out." Xavier shifted, rubbing his side again.

"Are you sure you're okay?"

He nodded. "Good as gold."

Gold. "Can I ask you something else? If I were poor, do you think it would be easier?"

Xavier shook his head. "His family doesn't care about the money. That's Dakota's own personal hang-up."

Once again, his pride was coming between us. "I—"

"Ooof," he grunted, stopping me from speaking as his face twisted in pain.

"Xavier?"

His hand went back into his side, pressing hard. "Damn, that hurt."

The car drifted to the right before Xavier corrected it. The lines on the winding road around the lake were hidden under the snow, but there was no room for error. Too far off to the side and we were going to get stuck in a snow bank.

"Why don't you pull over?" I asked. There wasn't a lot of room, but we could quickly switch places.

He blew out another sharp breath, wincing so hard his hand jerked on the steering wheel. Something was wrong. Incredibly wrong.

"Xavier." My heart was racing. "Pull over. Let me drive. You need to go to the hospital."

"I'm okay." His face paled and a sheen of sweat beaded beneath the brim of his hat at his temple. He ran his hand up his side, once again rubbing his chest as he struggled to breathe. "I'm okay. It's just heartburn."

"I don't know. It seems ser—" A flash caught my eye and I flinched. "Look out!"

But my warning came seconds too late.

twenty-three

DAKOTA

"DOES THIS MEAN YOU CAN COME HOME FOR DINNER tomorrow?" Mom asked hopefully into the phone.

"No. I'll spend it here with Sofia's family. They've already made Thanksgiving plans, and I don't want to cancel on them."

"Oh, okay."

"Have a good evening, Mom."

"You too, Dakota. We'll see you soon?"

"Yeah. Be home soon. Bye." I hung up the phone, setting it on the bar.

It was warm from being pressed to my ear for the last hour. But that phone call to Mom was a week overdue. Our conversation was one of the hardest I'd ever had, but it was one I should have had months ago.

I just wished I'd had that conversation when Dad was alive.

I looked at the time on the screen and frowned. I hadn't heard from Sofia yet. After she and Xavier had left for Kalispell, I'd come to the bar and taken over for Jackson.

Willa and the kids had been in with him today, hanging out while he worked. Roman had been running around the room in his police officer costume—a new one since he'd outgrown the original. And baby Zoe was trying to escape her mother's grip so she could explore, and probably put something she wasn't supposed to in her drooling mouth.

As expected on the day before Thanksgiving, it was dead quiet. They'd only had one person in for lunch.

So after the Page crew left to go home and start enjoying the holiday, I'd taken advantage of the time alone and called Mom.

It had been nearly three hours since Sofia had left, and I'd expected to at least get a text when they were on their way back home.

It was dark outside, and though I trusted my uncle to drive them home carefully, I didn't like Sofia out on a snowy night.

I shouldn't have let her go and wouldn't have if not for the pleading in her eyes. She needed time and space away from me.

That hurt. But the way I'd handled things, from the beginning, had been wrong. For that, I'd always be sorry.

I picked up the phone and sent her a quick text.

You guys on your way back?

I wandered around the quiet room, pushing stools back in place, waiting for a return text to chime. When five minutes had passed, I checked to make sure my phone wasn't on silent. Then I took it into the kitchen, making sure everything was put away. I doubted we'd get any dinner customers, and with everything stowed, I was closing early.

Sofia and I had a lot to discuss.

If she'd ever get back.

"Where are they?" Instead of a text, I picked up my phone and made a call. It went straight to her voicemail. Then I called

Xavier's phone. Same thing.

Something wasn't right. The knot in my gut confirmed it. I strode out of the kitchen and into the bar. I didn't care what time it was, I was closing. First thing, I'd head over to Logan and Thea's place and double-check she wasn't there. Maybe her phone had just died.

I grabbed my keys from the counter, rounding the bar for the front door just as it burst open and Hazel rushed inside.

"Get your stuff." Her face was pale, worry lines creasing her leathered skin. But her eyes, they were feral. "Let's go."

"Go where?"

"Xavier's in the hospital."

My air rushed out of my lungs, but I managed a single word. "Sofia?"

"She's fine. I'll explain in the car."

"Go."

Hazel spun and was out the door as fast as she'd come in.

I followed right into the cold, the air biting through the flannel of my shirt. But I wasn't wasting time getting a coat. I locked the door, went straight to my truck and got inside. Hazel beeped the locks on her Subaru Outback, leaving it in the parking lot, and hopped in with me.

I roared down the road, my hands tight on the wheel as I drove as fast as possible without putting Hazel and me at risk. "Talk."

"They were driving up and almost hit a deer. Xavier swerved to miss it."

My teeth ground together. He knew better than to swerve. He should have hit it. His life, Sofia's life, was more precious than a deer's.

"He lost control, spun around a bit but they didn't end up

in the ditch."

"If they didn't crash, then how'd he end up in the hospital?"

"He was having a bunch of pains. After the deer, Sofia put him in the passenger seat and drove to the hospital. She just called."

"Goddamn it." I never should have let her go. "But she's okay?"

"She sounded shaken up."

I was sure of it. On top of being concerned about Xavier, she didn't drive much. She wasn't used to snow-packed and icy roads. But my lady was strong—stronger than she gave herself credit for.

"What's wrong with Xavier?" *Please, don't say heart attack.*

"They hadn't told Sofia yet."

I gripped the wheel harder, driving as fast as I could for the conditions. Hazel sat stone still except for the nervous fidgeting of her right hand.

"Go ahead."

"Go ahead, what?"

"Smoke." I didn't let people smoke in my truck, but this was a special circumstance. And it would calm her down.

But Hazel shook her head. "No. I quit."

I risked a glance away from the road to see if she was serious. Hazel had smoked since she was in her twenties. "When?"

"Right now."

If she was giving up smoking, that meant she was terrified for Xavier's life.

My foot pressed harder on the gas pedal. He had to be okay. I couldn't lose him too.

The rest of the drive was in panicked silence. Hazel and I had the same questions in mind. There was no need to ask. We said the same silent prayers. There was no need to voice them.

It was pitch-black when we arrived at the hospital. The air was ice, a deadly cold. My teeth chattered by the time we raced inside and stood at the reception counter, waiting to get Xavier's room number.

"Xavier Magee. Room . . ." The nurse pushed the glasses farther up her nose, leaning into the screen like she wanted to torture us. "Room three oh nine."

We were off like a rocket, Hazel leading the way to the staircase since neither of us had the patience to wait for an elevator.

Hazel took the stairs two at a time like she was my age, not in her early seventies. We broke through the heavy metal door to the third floor and jogged down the hallway toward Xavier's room.

We heard his voice from two doors down and relief cascaded down my body.

"Do I need it?"

"No," a man's voice answered.

"Then take the damn thing out, and let's be done with this."

"It's an organ," Sofia hissed. "At least read the brochure. And wait for your wife to get here. Doctor, could we have just a minute?"

Before the doctor could agree, Hazel and I burst into the room.

My uncle's eyes immediately went to his wife. "Hey, baby."

"What's going on?" Hazel snapped at the doctor, like this was his fault, as she walked over to Xavier's bedside and clutched his hand.

"Gallstones," Xavier muttered. "Hey, bud."

"Hi." I looked him up and down. Besides looking a little pale and wearing a green hospital gown, he looked fine. Which meant I could focus on Sofia. "Babe."

She was standing in the corner of the room against the window. She held my gaze as I crossed the floor, and the moment I was close enough, she fell into my arms.

"You okay?" I kissed her hair as she burrowed into my chest.

"I'm holding it together. I can't promise I will for much longer."

"I've got you now."

I twisted us both so I could hold Sofia and see the doctor, a middle-aged man who was waiting patiently for us to all get situated.

"So what's wrong?" I asked him. "Gallstones?"

The doctor nodded. "The CT scan shows them clearly. Based on their size and how likely they are to reoccur, I recommend we remove the gallbladder."

"Is it dangerous?" Hazel's grip on Xavier's hand tightened.

"It's a routine surgery. He will have to be sedated, and there is always the risk of complications. I'd be happy to go over them with you."

"I've heard them. I'm good with it," Xavier said. "Like I said, let's do it and be done with them."

The worry on Hazel's face eased as she shot her husband a scowl. "Well, I haven't heard them. So you can just wait a damn minute while I get caught up."

She dropped his hand, taking a step away from the bed. But then she stopped, spun around and dropped a kiss on Xavier's mouth. With that, she nodded to the doctor and followed him into the hallway.

My uncle chuckled, but then winced and clutched his side. "Go with her, will you? Just so she's not alone when he lists off all the stuff that could happen but won't. I don't want her freaked out."

I made a move to leave, but Sofia stopped me. "I'll go. You can stay with Xavier."

"Okay." Her footsteps were quiet as she left the room, but she was okay. They were both okay.

I breathed for the first time in an hour and went to collapse in the chair next to my uncle's bed. "A deer?"

"Damn deer," he huffed. "Wasn't even watching for them, since it was snowing. I thought they'd all be hunkered down somewhere. That animal is lucky to be alive."

"From the sounds of it, you are too."

"It wasn't that bad. Fishtailed on the road. Scared Sofia, though."

"Scared all of us."

He sighed. "Between me and you, scared me some too. Thought for sure I was having a heart attack. But the doctor seems to think we can get these gallstones under control. He's putting me on a pill for the acid reflux too."

"I can't . . ." I pinched the bridge of my nose, taking a minute to swallow down the lump in my throat. "Just take care of yourself, okay?"

He gave me a sad smile. "I'm not going anywhere. Not for a while."

Dad had probably thought the same. Xavier was older than Dad and had lived a more stressful life. The truth was, you never knew when your time was up.

"I have a lot of regrets," I told Xavier. "With Dad. I don't want any with you."

"We're good, bud. We're good."

"I should have been nicer. When I saw him last, I should have been nicer. I should have called more. The last time I saw him was at Kimi's naming. I should have tried harder."

Instead, I'd held on to my anger. I'd held on to my pride.

I couldn't remember the last time I'd said *I love you, Dad*.

"You can't blame yourself, Dakota. It's just life. Your dad . . . we didn't end things on good terms either. He was my brother. I can't remember the things we said the last time we spoke."

"Why does it have to be like this?"

He stared up at the ceiling. "We're stubborn men. Stubborn to a fault. I've let it run my life. Your dad did too. We've both held on to feelings that we should have let go of a long time ago. Learn from our mistakes."

"I'm sorry. I wish I could tell him that. I'm sorry, for all of it."

"Dakota." He turned his gaze to me. "It isn't your fault."

"I left."

"You have to be who you are. There's no shame in that."

I dropped my gaze to the floor. If only he was right.

"Did I ever tell you about the day you were born?"

"No."

Xavier's face turned back to the ceiling, giving me his profile as he spoke. "Your dad came up with this idea. He wanted to have this naming ceremony so that all the family could meet his new son."

"Wait. What? I thought the naming thing was Koko's idea."

"Nope, it was your dad's. He did it for all you kids. He even went against our mom and invited me. It caused a big stir, but he didn't care. I think he always had hope I'd come home. That things would be different. You know what he said that day when he announced your name?"

I shook my head, waiting.

"He looked at you with so much love. He said, 'Dakota. My son. Burn bright, little star. Burn bright.'"

My jaw dropped. That was the same thing Dad had said to all of his grandchildren when he'd introduced himself.

"Your dad, he wanted you all to succeed," Xavier said. "But I think he always knew you were too big for his idea of success. Deep down, I think he knew he was destined to lose you."

"He never lost me."

"It didn't make it any easier to watch you walk away. He loved you. He wouldn't have fought so hard to get you back if he didn't love you. Never forget that. Your dad loved you."

The fire in my throat began to choke. "I miss him."

I'd always miss him. Every day. All I could do now was hope that one day, I'd find some peace with his death.

And, like Xavier had said, learn from his mistakes.

"You're getting your gallbladder removed." Hazel marched into the room, her chin held high as she made the declaration. "Today."

Xavier chuckled. "Good idea."

"I'll leave you two alone." I stood from the chair, hugging Xavier and Hazel before walking out of the room and shutting the door behind me.

I found Sofia in the hallway, her arms wrapped tight around herself.

"I didn't make it to see Arthur." Her chin quivered. "I forgot to call him too."

"It's okay." I tucked her into my side with one arm around her shoulders and walked us down the hallway until I found a quiet corner at the end. "Thanks for getting Xavier here."

She blew out a long breath. "I'm never driving again."

I grinned. "I'll do the driving from now on."

"What if you're not with me?"

I let her go, angling myself in front of her. "I talked to my mom today."

Her frame locked tight. "And?"

"I told her I'd be pissed if she didn't come to our wedding."

Sofia blinked, letting my words sink in. Then her eyes began to fill with tears, the happy kind. "You did?"

"I did. And I told her I was going to make babies with you."

A sob escaped her lips, a tear dripping down her smooth cheek. "You picked me?"

"I'll always pick you. You're my family." I cupped her cheek, holding the weight of her face in my palm.

Her smile was blinding, but it didn't last long. Another sob choked free, one so full of relief and happiness it sent her face crashing into my chest so she could cry freely.

I wrapped her up as she clung to me, the weight of two different worlds lifting from above us. We didn't have to carry them anymore. We just had to hold up one another.

I'd told my mother today I would always choose Sofia. I gave her a choice: gain a daughter, or lose her son. I'd told her this would be the last time we spoke if she couldn't let go of the idea I'd move home and marry Petah.

It took her less than a second to realize just how serious I was.

Mom had lost enough. We all had.

It was time to pull together.

"We have to go to my mom's for Christmas," I whispered into Sofia's hair.

"Okay." She nodded. "Do you think if I bought your sisters

some Chanel handbags, it would help win them over?"

"Couldn't hurt."

She hiccupped a laugh, her arms hugging me tight. Then she tipped up her chin, resting it on my chest. "What about the money?"

"I want to work. It's part of who I am. But you are right. That money is a part of who you are. If this is going to work, we need to find a middle ground."

It still felt strange to not have earned the money myself. But like Sofia had said, it was just stupid male pride. I'd get over it eventually. Especially if her money could go toward a passion project. Dad wasn't around to see it, but with her resources, we could make my hometown a better place for the generations to come.

"You've got the studio. I was thinking maybe we could make some investments in the reservation. Give back to my people."

"Yes." She didn't hesitate. "I think that's a perfect idea."

I dropped my lips to hers. "Love you."

"I love you," she whispered back. "You saw it, didn't you?"

"I saw it." I smiled, the kind she'd begged me for all those mornings ago. The smile that was hers and hers alone.

I didn't know exactly what the future would entail, but the black box was gone. Sofia and I would wake up together. Sleep in one another's arms. We'd have passion for every day, simply because we were together.

I saw it.

And it was burning bright.

epilogue

SOFIA

One year later . . .

"WHERE ARE THEY?" I HUFFED TO DAKOTA. "IF THEY don't hurry up, we're going to have a screaming baby on our hands, and my boobs are going to explode."

I jostled Joseph in my arms, silently cursing myself for encouraging Landon to chase after Aubrey.

The pair of them had finally announced they were a couple about six months ago, but ever since, they were always sneaking off to grope one another.

"Relax, babe." Dakota put his arm around me, kissing my temple. "I'm sure they'll be here soon."

"Will you go find them?" I pleaded.

"No. I'm not walking in on your sister and Landon going at it." He glanced over his shoulder and chuckled. "Speaking of people going at it."

Thea and Logan came walking down the back hallway of the bar. My brother had a huge smile on his face. Thea's hair, which had been up when we'd gotten here, was now hanging down her back. Her cheeks were flushed a hot pink.

I rolled my eyes. "What is it with people tonight?"

"It's New Year's Eve. We're all just celebrating. We celebrated earlier so you can't hold it against them."

"Yeah, but we did it before the naming ceremony. Can't they do it on their own time? It's my time now."

Joseph opened his mouth and let out a squawk. He was a tiny clone of my husband, and his dark eyes were locked on mine. I hadn't known babies could glare until I'd met my son. This boy wanted a snack and he wanted it now.

The naming ceremony had been scheduled to start at five o'clock. It was now six.

Thea and Jackson had closed down the bar for two hours so we could have this family function before opening back up for the annual New Year's Eve party. If I left to nurse Joseph, we'd be gone for at least thirty minutes and the ceremony would be rushed.

"I should have fed him an hour ago."

"It'll be fine," Dakota said. "He's not starving."

Joseph grunted again, calling his father a liar.

Dakota grinned and took our two-month-old son from my arms. The instant he settled the baby on his shoulder, Joseph's fussiness stopped.

Dakota was the Joseph whisperer.

Our baby loved his father completely. He tolerated me, but that was mostly because I was necessary for food. The kid had become an eating machine these last few weeks. His fat rolls had fat rolls, and I'd turned into his personal milk machine.

Dakota and I had gotten pregnant a month after our wedding, on our extended honeymoon. We'd decided to marry on New Year's Eve last year, just a month after Xavier had gotten released from the hospital after having his gallbladder removed.

My family teased me for once again sending my wedding planner into a frenzy on short notice. But this time, it was all in good humor. They were just as anxious for Dakota to officially join our family as I was.

The doctors had cleared Xavier for travel, but we hadn't wanted him to fly across the country. So instead of a lavish wedding in the city like my previous charades, I opted for an elegant gathering of close family and friends here in Montana.

My dress was simple, with a third less material than either of its predecessors. It was the one I'd keep and pass down to a daughter if we had one. Made entirely of chiffon, its loose sleeves flowed to my elbows while the bodice gathered at the waist and the skirt billowed to my toes. Other than the deep V cut in the front and back, some would call it plain.

I called it perfect.

Dakota and I married in a small event hall on the lake. It wasn't a country wedding—I'd told my wedding planner she'd be fired if there was a horseshoe or wagon wheel in sight. It was us, a mixture of Dakota's simple roots and my touch of glamour.

I walked down the aisle on Dad's arm for the last time, not noticing the greenery and white flowers adorning the hall. I didn't notice the golden glow of the lights strung across the ceiling or the smiles on my friends' faces. I missed the happy tears in my mother's eyes.

All I saw was Dakota, standing at the altar.

Waiting for me.

The chase was over.

Now it was time to play for keeps.

We said our vows and timed the ceremony to kiss at midnight. And that kiss had started the best year of my life.

Dakota quit working at the bar a couple of weeks after the wedding, and we went on a long honeymoon. After a stop in the city to check in on the dance studio, plus approve the new site for the second location, we set off for three weeks in Europe.

Violent morning sickness cut our trip short, and we went back to the city to wait out those first few months of my pregnancy.

Then we came back to Montana to spend time with his family and start on Dakota's passion project.

In the last year, he'd rehabilitated ten different homes on the reservation. He'd overseen the entire operation, coordinating construction companies and property management companies to help the right families get into new homes.

A week before Christmas, the tribal council had given him an award for Tribal Member of the Year. They were also going to honor him at their annual powwow and rodeo next summer. His mom was making me a beaded buckskin belt to wear for the occasion.

Lyndie had asked if she could keep the plaque next to the same award his dad had won years ago. They were side by side on her living room wall next to the family picture we'd all taken this summer.

It hadn't been easy to work my way into their family. I wasn't there yet. Koko still had the hardest time accepting I was a permanent fixture in Dakota's life, but with every visit to Browning, things got easier.

They'd begun talking to me, asking questions about growing up in New York and how the dance studios were doing. And they both doted on Joseph, usually stealing him away the moment we stepped through Lyndie's front door.

It would take time to get closer to Dakota's sisters, something Logan had told me this past summer. He'd reminded me that Thea and I hadn't gotten off to a great start either, and now she was one of my best friends, along with Piper and Willa.

They were all a close second place to my best friend.

My sister.

"Sorry!" Aubrey rushed through the front door of the bar, followed by Landon, who was wiping her lipstick off his mouth. "We, uh—we were just—"

"We know what you were just," I snapped. "Can you please pull up your dress so your bra isn't showing and we can get started?"

Her face flushed as Landon came up behind her, chuckling. Aubrey turned her back to the room, adjusting her red dress so the black lace underneath was hidden again.

"Anyone want another drink?" Jackson called from behind the bar.

Logan raised his hand, taking his empty tumbler and Thea's glass over for a refill. With them full, Jackson joined Willa, who was talking to Kaine and Piper.

"Okay." I clapped, getting the attention of the room. "I think we're finally ready to start." I sent a glare my sister's way.

She just smiled back and settled into Landon's side as everyone in the bar gathered in a circle.

"Okay, everyone know how this works?" Dakota asked the room, getting a hum of agreement. "Great. Xavier, do you want to start?"

"Please." Xavier stood by Dakota's side, smiling up at him as he handed over our son.

With Joseph transferred, Dakota put his arm around my

waist, tugged me close and bent to give me a soft kiss. "Love you."

"I love you too."

We'd decided to carry on his family's tradition with Joseph. Though it was a bit different, since he'd been born in New York.

We'd named Joseph and told everyone but had planned this event specifically around New Year's Eve. We knew we'd be in Montana. It was where our hearts were.

Neither Dakota nor I wanted to spend New Year's Eve anywhere other than the Lark Cove Bar.

But we were here now, ready to make it official. We'd already had one naming ceremony with Dakota's family on the day we'd spent on the reservation earlier in the week. And now we were doing it here with our friends and family.

The only thing different this time around was that we'd asked that everyone say something either silently or aloud for Joseph.

"Joseph. My name is Xavier. I am your great uncle." Xavier kissed Joseph's forehead, his eyes wide as he took in the new face.

Xavier closed his eyes after his introduction, touched his forehead to Joseph's as he wished him something silently. Then he smiled and handed him over to Hazel, standing by her side.

"Joseph, I am Hazel. Your gran." She smirked, bent and whispered something into the baby's ear.

I scanned the room, seeing loving eyes all aimed at my son.

Two years ago, I wouldn't have believed this was possible. My eyes landed on the spot by the front door. The same spot where I'd stood that first day, aghast that I'd been asked to sweep.

The same place where our dear life had started.

I looked up at Dakota, my eyes glistening with happy tears.

He just smiled down, hugging me closer to his side. "Good?"

"Magnificent."

Dakota winked then watched as Hazel handed Joseph over to Willa and Jackson.

"Joseph," Willa started. "I'm Willa. This is Jackson." The pair shared a loving look, then looked down to him and said aloud, "Be bold."

They were the first ones to say something aloud. And knowing Jackson and Willa's love story, no words could have been more perfect.

Kaine and Piper took Joseph next. "Joseph," Kaine said, "I'm Kaine. And this is Piper." The couple shared a look and Piper stroked her pregnant belly. She was due with their daughter in a couple of months. Then, in unison, they smiled and said, "Find your magic."

I smiled, thinking of the magic cake recipe Piper had given me months ago. Those two had a lot of magic, but she swore up and down that cake could cure all ailments.

Aubrey and Landon were next in line. Though my parents had stayed in the city for New Year's, Aubrey had decided to bring Landon out for his first trip to Montana.

"Joseph, I'm your aunt Aubrey." She smiled up at Landon. "And this is your soon-to-be uncle Landon."

"Soon to be what?" Logan asked. "Uncle?"

As the room broke out into excited whispers, Dakota smiled wider at Landon. The pair of them had become friends over the last year, meeting occasionally for beers and to watch a game in the city.

I guess he knew about the engagement ring I was just now

noticing on Aubrey's finger.

It was a lot like the solitaire ring Dakota had given me, modest but striking, much like the men who'd given them to us.

"Congratulations," I mouthed to her across from me in the circle.

"Thank you." She dropped her head to Landon's shoulder, still holding Joseph in her arms.

Before we could find out more about their engagement, Joseph reminded us all with a wail that we were stealing his thunder.

Aubrey handed him over to Logan and Thea, who were the last in the circle. Besides my parents, they'd spent the most time with our son, since we balanced our time between Montana and New York.

This trip was the beginning of a three-month stay in Lark Cove. We were back in Dakota's house, settling in for some time to relax. We'd be working on some of his projects on the reservation and spending more time with Lyndie.

Joseph would be getting quality time with his cousins too. Once the ceremony was over, he'd be going with Hazel and Xavier to spend the night at their cottage and relieve the babysitter who was watching Logan and Thea's kids.

"Joseph." Logan smiled at his nephew. "I am your uncle Logan."

"And I'm your aunt Thea." She stood close to her husband, settling one of her hands over his. Then she bent close to his tiny ear, whispering loud enough that only Logan and I could hear her say, "Chase the impossible."

Be bold.

Find your magic.

Chase the impossible.

I wasn't sure what Xavier and Hazel had said to Joseph. Aubrey and Landon either. But those three sentiments were perfect.

They would complement what I knew was coming next. The same thing Dakota had told Joseph on the day he was born.

Thea handed me back my son, and I held him in my arms as Dakota bent over us both. Then he looked to me and I nodded, knowing he'd been waiting two months to say this again.

"Burn bright, little star."

He said the same thing when our second son, Xavier, was born two years later.

And again for our daughter, Penelope, the year after that.

BONUS
epilogue

SOFIA

"I THINK I'M GOING TO PUKE," AUBREY MUTTERED.

"Sorry." I adjusted my sister's veil. "Drink that ginger ale."

She swallowed hard and sipped the soda Thea had called for twenty minutes ago.

"How are those crackers sitting?" Thea asked.

"Ugh." Aubrey gagged. "Not so well."

"I need to finish your eyes." The makeup artist was hovering over Aubrey with a palette and brush.

"Go ahead." Aubrey nodded, swallowing again. "I'll be okay."

We were running thirty minutes behind because of Aubrey's queasy stomach. She'd had to take three breaks while a stylist had been doing her hair in order to rush to the bathroom and get sick.

She was in the throes of early pregnancy sickness, nauseated almost around the clock.

"I'm going to look awful for the pictures," she groaned.

"You look beautiful." Thea and I smiled as we said the

same thing.

"I should have postponed the wedding, but with Landon's schedule and mine, I knew if we put it off, this baby would be born before we made it happen."

"Chug that ginger ale." Thea pushed it closer to her. "You'll make it."

Aubrey obeyed, interrupting the makeup artist again. When the glass was empty, she put it down and belched.

Her eyes went wide, searching in the mirror for our mother. Mom's biggest pet peeve was burping.

I giggled. "She went out to check on the flowers."

"She thinks this is stupid. But it was Landon's idea." She gave us a small smile. "I can't say no to him."

She'd tried for months when they'd first gotten together, but once he'd worn her down, she was his. The two of them were getting married tonight, a few months after he'd proposed in Lark Cove on New Year's Eve.

Instead of a fancy ballroom or a church, they were getting married in Aubrey's office at Kendrick Enterprises.

Landon thought his idea was hilarious. He'd told us all six or seven times. His reasoning was that since she'd been married to her job for so long and he didn't want them to break up, the two would have to share Aubrey.

Hence, the office wedding.

It was good she had such a large office, second in size only to Dad's. Her thousand-square-foot room had been cleared of all its furniture and staged with an altar and seats for the guests.

We'd been using Dad's office all day to get ready. By now, the guests would be in the lobby, waiting. And nearly all of Landon's precinct would be here, preparing for their little surprise.

The officers were forming an aisle for Aubrey, but she didn't know it yet. I'd snuck out earlier to check on Joseph, and I'd caught them practicing their lineup—uniforms and all. I thought it was sweet how they'd all come here to support Landon.

I'd found him in her office, pacing, waiting for the wedding to start. He'd asked me three times in ten minutes if she was feeling all right. I promised him she was fine. She wasn't, but she would be. Landon looked so handsome in his tuxedo, Aubrey would take one look at him and forget all about being sick.

A knock sounded on the door, and we all turned just as Dad walked in. He took one look at Aubrey in her white strapless gown and his breath hitched. He blinked a few times too many, then cleared his throat and stepped inside.

"We're all set."

The makeup artist held up a lipstick brush. "I'm almost done."

Two minutes later, her face was finished.

"Okay." Aubrey blew out a deep breath and stood from her stool in front of the mirror. She smoothed out the skirt of her silk gown then walked over to Dad, looping his arm with hers.

"You look beautiful." He kissed her cheek.

"Thanks, Daddy." She sucked in a shaky breath. "I think I'm ready."

"Are you sure?" Thea asked. "We can take a minute if you're feeling sick."

Aubrey shook her head. "I don't want to keep Landon waiting."

I don't think any of us thought she would get married, Aubrey included. But Landon had been her game changer.

Like Dakota had been for me.

She'd been working less and enjoying life more since she'd met him. Just us family members knew she was pregnant. With their baby on the way, she'd told me a week ago that she'd be cutting down at work even more.

Aubrey was taking a page from my book and using her wealth to buy her the freedom to enjoy her happiness.

"You do look beautiful." I handed Aubrey her bouquet of roses.

"I'm not going to puke during my wedding," she declared.

I smiled. "You're not going to puke during your wedding."

"I'm ready."

I grabbed my own bouquet of roses and followed Thea out of the room.

She shot me a smile over her shoulder as Logan met us outside the door, looking dapper in his tux. They linked arms and waited at the beginning of the aisle of police officers that led from Dad's office all the way across the lobby and into Aubrey's.

When she spotted them, she laughed, shaking her head.

I smiled, just as a deep voice stole my attention.

"There's Mommy," Dakota told Joseph as they walked my way.

Dakota in a tux was a sight to see, especially with a baby in his arms. When I'd come out earlier and spotted him talking to Mom, it had taken all of my willpower not to pull him into the elevator and have my way with him.

The Italian wool had been tailored to perfection around his broad shoulders. The crisp white shirt underneath was fitted to his narrow waist. We'd be celebrating later when Mom took Joseph for the night. I was going to strip that bow tie off with my teeth.

"You look gorgeous, babe." He kissed my temple, staying close to whisper, "But that dress isn't going to survive the night."

I shivered, already anticipating how he'd shred the black silk with those large hands.

"You look beautiful, Aubrey," Logan told our sister as we lined up in order for the procession. "Everyone set?"

Aubrey nodded fast. "Lead the way."

"Okay, guys." Logan smiled at his kids, who were standing close by. "You heard the bride. Let's go. Charlie, you're first."

"Okay, Daddy." She beamed as she started down the aisle. Charlie, our gorgeous tomboy, had surprised us all by saying she'd prefer to wear a dress rather than the suit Thea had planned on getting her.

She was growing up. So were Collin and Camila, who, hand-in-hand, followed Charlie down the aisle with their parents trailing behind.

"Our turn." I looped my arm through Dakota's, smiling up at him.

He smiled back. He looked so gorgeous in his tux, but I knew he hated it. The bow tie. The shiny shoes. The pants he thought had been tailored too short. He'd gladly shed it all for me later. But he wore them tonight, for Aubrey and Landon.

He wore them because it was important to me. He wore them for our family.

Dakota escorted me past one officer, then the next, carrying our son as we walked down the aisle.

Landon stood stoically at the end, waiting for his bride. As we all stepped to the side—me on Aubrey's side to join Thea, Dakota on Landon's to stand by Logan—Aubrey came into his view. Landon's megawatt smile brought tears to my eyes.

I blinked them away, not wanting to ruin my makeup, and watched as my sister joined her man. Her face was full of color and joy; no one would know she'd been sick all day.

Dad gave her away by shaking hands with Landon as the officers from the hallway filed into the office, taking up every available seat before the pastor began the ceremony.

"Dearly beloved—"

"Wait." Landon tossed up a hand. "I need to say something before we start."

Aubrey's smile fell and her bare shoulders tensed. "What?"

"You look stunning."

"Thank you." She laughed. "Shall we keep going?"

The pastor nodded. "Dearly—"

"Wait." Landon stopped him again. "One more thing."

"Yes, Officer McClellan?" Aubrey's voice dripped with annoyance.

He grinned. "I'm just really happy your sister is so boring."

The entire room erupted into laughter, Aubrey included. He did that for her. He gave her that levity and reasons to smile.

Something Dakota did for me every day.

Landon took Aubrey's hand, kissing the back of it, before nodding to the pastor. "Please make this beautiful woman my wife."

As the pastor began to speak, I found my husband's waiting gaze.

"Magnificent," I mouthed.

He looked down at our son, who'd somehow in the commotion fallen asleep in his arms, then back over at me. "Magnificent."

Enjoy this preview from *The Birthday List*,
the first book in Devney's Maysen Jar series.

the
birthday
a love
story
list

prologue

"Poppy!" Jamie came rushing out of the office and into the kitchen.

The grin on his face made my heart flutter, just like it always did, which meant I'd been a mess of flutters since the day I'd met him five years ago.

We'd run into each other on the first day of our sophomore year at Montana State. Literally. I'd been rushing out of an economics lecture, my arms overloaded with books, notepads and a syllabus. Jamie had been rushing in, too busy looking over his shoulder at a buxom blond to see me in the classroom's doorway.

After the two of us had recovered from the crash, Jamie had helped me off the floor. The moment my hand had slipped into his, the buxom blond had been all but forgotten.

That was the day I'd met the man of my dreams.

My husband.

James Sawyer Maysen.

"Guess what?"

"What?" I giggled when he picked me up and set me on the counter, fitting himself between my open legs. Excitement radiated from his body and I couldn't help but smile at the light shining in his eyes.

"I just added a couple things to my birthday list." He pumped his fist. "Best ideas yet."

"Oh." My smile faltered. "Please tell me these ones aren't illegal."

"Nope. And I told you, the fire alarm one might not be illegal. I might *legitimately* need to pull a fire alarm before I turn forty-five."

"You'd better hope so. I have no desire to bail you out of jail just because you're determined to mark an item off your crazy list."

Jamie's "birthday list" had become his latest obsession. He'd started it a couple of weeks ago after he'd gotten the idea from a sitcom, and ever since, he'd been dreaming up these grand ideas—though some were more ridiculous than grand.

This list was Jamie's version of a bucket list. Except, rather than one long list to work through in retirement, Jamie had been assigning himself things to do before each of his birthdays. He didn't want to tackle some daunting list when he had all but lived his life. Instead, he wanted to tick things off the list every year before his birthday. So far, he'd filled in nearly every birthday until he turned fifty.

We had our own "couples" bucket list—places we wanted to travel and things we wanted to do together. This birthday list wasn't for that. It was just for Jamie. It was filled with things *he* wanted to do, just for him.

And though I may have grumbled about some of the riskier and crazier items, I supported it wholeheartedly.

"So what did you add today?"

He grinned. "My best idea yet. Here goes." He raised his arms, drawing them out wide and framing an invisible marquee. "Before I turn thirty-four, I want to swim in a pool of green Jell-O."

"Okay." I smiled, far from convinced it was his best idea yet, but it was Jamie. "But why Jell-O? And why green?"

"Don't you think it would be cool?" He wiggled between my legs, smiling even wider as he dropped his arms. "It's one of those things every kid wants to do but no parent will let them. Think of how fun it would be. I can squirm around in it. Squish it between my fingers and toes. And I picked green—"

"Because it's your favorite color," I finished, surprised I'd even asked the question in the first place.

"What do you think?"

"Honestly? It sounds like a mess. Besides that, Jell-O stains. You'll be a walking alien for a week."

He shrugged. "I'm cool with that. My students will think it's awesome, and I have you to help me clean it up."

"Yes, you do."

I'd help him scrub his skin back to its normal tan and dispose of a pool filled with green Jell-O because I loved him. Some items on Jamie's list seemed strange to me, but if they made him happy, I'd do what I could to help. For the next twenty-five years—or for however long he wanted—I'd be by his side as he crossed things out.

"What else did you add today?"

He slipped his hands around my waist and moved in a little closer. "I actually added one and crossed it off at the same time. It was for my twenty-fifth birthday. I wrote a letter to myself in ten years."

"That's cute." If I had a birthday list, I'd steal that idea for myself. "Can I read the letter?"

"Sure." He grinned. "As soon as I turn thirty-five."

I frowned but Jamie erased it with a soft kiss.

"I need to go run some errands. Do you need anything while I'm out?"

Errands. Riiight. Tomorrow was our one-year wedding anniversary and I'd bet good money his "errands" were to find me a last-minute gift. Unlike me, who had bought his present two months ago and stashed it in the laundry room, Jamie was always shopping on Christmas Eve or the day before my birthday.

But instead of teasing him about his tendency to procrastinate, I just nodded. "Yes, please. Would you mind going to the liquor store for me?" We were hosting a spring barbeque tomorrow to celebrate our anniversary and the only booze we had in the house was Jamie's favorite tequila.

"Babe, I told you. We don't need to have fancy cocktails. Just pick up some beer at the grocery store tomorrow and we'll drink my stuff."

"And, honey, I've told you. Not everyone likes to do tequila shots."

"Sure they do. Tequila shots are a classic party drink."

I rolled my eyes and laughed. "We're not having a frat party tomorrow. We're adults now and can afford some variety. At the very least, we could get some margarita mix."

"Fine," he grumbled. "Do you have a list?"

I nodded, but when I tried to move off the counter, he kept me trapped.

"Can I ask you something?" His eyebrows came together as his grin disappeared.

"Of course."

"We've been married for almost a year. What's your favorite thing about being married to me?"

My hands came up to his face, brushing the blond hair away from where it had fallen into his blue eyes. I didn't even have to think about my answer. "I love that I get to say I'm your wife. It fills me with pride every time. Like whenever we're at your school and parents come up to tell me how much their kids love your class, I'm so proud that I get to call you mine."

The tension in his face washed away.

I wasn't sure where his question had come from, but it was a good one. Especially today, the eve of our anniversary.

Jamie backed away but I grabbed the collar of his shirt and yanked him back into my space. "Hold up. It's your turn. What's your favorite thing about being married to me?"

He smirked. "That you have sex with me every day."

"Jamie!" I swatted his chest as he laughed. "Be serious."

"I am serious. Oh, and I love that you do all the cooking and my laundry. Seriously, babe. Thanks for that."

"Are you kidding me right now?"

He nodded and smiled wider. "I love that I get to be the one to watch you grow more beautiful with each and every day."

My heart fluttered again. "I love you, Jamie Maysen."

"I love you too, Poppy Maysen."

He leaned forward and brushed his lips against mine, teasing me for the briefest moment with his tongue before he stepped back and let me go.

"I'll get your list for the liquor store." I hopped off the counter and got the sticky note I'd made earlier.

"Okay. Be back soon." Jamie tucked the list in his pocket and kissed my hair before he walked out the door.

Three hours later, Jamie still hadn't returned. Every time I called his phone, it rang and rang and rang until his voicemail kicked in. I was doing my best to ignore the knot in my stomach. He was probably just shopping. Any minute, he'd be home and we could go out to dinner. Knowing Jamie, he'd just lost track of time or bumped into a friend and they'd gone out for a beer.

He's fine.

An hour later, he still wasn't home. "Jamie," I told his voicemail. "Where are you? It's getting late and I thought we were going to dinner. Did you lose your phone or something? You need to come home or call me back. I'm getting worried."

I hung up and paced the kitchen. *He's fine. He's fine.*

One hour later, I'd left him five more voicemails and bitten off all my fingernails.

One hour after that, I'd left fifteen voicemails and started calling hospitals.

I was looking up the number for the police department when the doorbell rang. Tossing my phone on the living room couch, I ran toward the door, but my feet stuttered at the sight of a uniform through the door's glass pane.

Oh, god. My stomach rolled. *Please let him be okay.*

I opened the door and stepped out onto the porch. "Officer."

The cop stood tall, his posture perfect, but his green eyes betrayed him. He didn't want to be knocking on my door any more than I wanted him on my porch.

"Ma'am. Are you Poppy Maysen?"

I choked out a yes before the bile rose up in my throat.

The cop's posture slackened an inch. "Mrs. Maysen, I'm afraid I have some bad news. Would you like to go inside and sit down?"

I shook my head. "Is it Jamie?"

He nodded and the pressure in my chest squeezed so tight, I couldn't breathe. My heart was pounding so hard in my chest that my ribs hurt.

"Just . . . just tell me," I whispered.

"Are you here alone? Can I call someone?"

I shook my head again. "Tell me. Please."

He took a deep breath. "I'm sorry to inform you, Mrs. Maysen, but your husband was killed earlier today."

Jamie wasn't fine.

The cop kept talking but his words were drowned out by the sound of my shattering heart.

I don't remember much else from that night. I remember my brother coming over. I remember him calling Jamie's parents to tell them that their son was no longer in this world—that he had been killed in a robbery at a liquor store.

I remember wishing that I were dead too.

And I remember that cop sitting by my side the entire time.

chapter 1

30th Birthday: Buy Poppy her restaurant

POPPY

Five years later . . .

"ARE YOU READY FOR THIS?" MOLLY ASKED.
I looked around the open room and smiled. "Yeah. I think so."

My restaurant, The Maysen Jar, was opening tomorrow.

The dream I'd had since I was a kid—the dream Jamie had shared with me—was actually coming true.

Once an old mechanic's garage, The Maysen Jar was now Bozeman, Montana's newest café. I'd taken a run-down, abandoned building and turned it into my future.

Gone were the cement floors spotted with oil. In their place was a hickory herringbone wood floor. The dingy garage doors had been replaced. Now visitors would pull up to a row of floor-to-ceiling black-paned windows. And decades of gunk, grime and grease had been scrubbed away. The original red brick walls had been cleaned to their former glory, and the tall, industrial ceilings had been painted a fresh white.

Good-bye, sockets and wrenches. Hello, spoons and forks.

"I was thinking." Molly straightened the menu cards for the fourth time. "We should probably call the radio station and see if they'd do a spotlight or something to announce that you're open. We've got that ad in the paper but radio might be good too."

I rearranged the jar of pens by the register. "Okay. I'll call them tomorrow."

We were standing shoulder to shoulder behind the counter at the back of the room. Both of us were fidgeting—touching things that didn't need to be touched and organizing things that had been organized plenty—until I admitted what we were both thinking. "I'm nervous."

Molly's hand slid across the counter and took mine. "You'll be great. This place is a dream, and I'll be here with you every step of the way."

I leaned my shoulder into hers. "Thanks. For everything. For helping me get this going. For agreeing to be my manager. I wouldn't have come this far without you."

"Yes, you would have, but I'm glad to be a part of this." She squeezed my hand before letting go and running her fingers across the black marble counter. "I was—"

The front door opened and an elderly man with a cane came shuffling inside. He paused inside the doorway, his gaze running over the black tables and chairs that filled the open space, until he saw Molly and me at the back of the room.

"Hello," I called. "Can I help you?"

He slipped off his gray driving cap and tucked it under his arm. "Just looking."

"I'm sorry, sir," Molly said, "but we don't open for business until tomorrow."

He ignored Molly and started shuffling down the center aisle. My restaurant wasn't huge. The garage itself had only been two stalls, and to cross from the front door to the counter took me exactly seventeen steps. This man made the trip seem like he was crossing the Sahara. Every step was small and he stopped repeatedly to look around. But eventually, he reached the counter and took a wooden stool across from Molly.

When her wide, brown eyes met mine, I just shrugged. I'd poured everything I had into this restaurant—heart and soul and wallet—and I couldn't afford to turn away potential customers, even if we hadn't opened for business yet.

"What can I do for you, sir?"

He reached past Molly, grabbing a menu card from her stack and rifling the entire bunch as he slid it over.

I stifled a laugh at Molly's frown. She wanted to fix those cards so badly her fingers were itching, but she held back, deciding to leave instead. "I think I'll go finish up in the back."

"Okay."

She turned and disappeared through the swinging door into the kitchen. When it swung closed behind her, I focused on the man memorizing my menu.

"Jars?" he asked.

I grinned. "Yes, jars. Most everything here is made in mason jars." Other than some sandwiches and breakfast pastries, I'd compiled a menu centered around mason jars.

It had actually been Jamie's idea to use jars. Not long after we'd gotten married, I'd been experimenting with recipes. Though it had always been my dream to open a restaurant, I'd never known exactly what I wanted to try. That was, until one night when I'd been experimenting with ideas I'd found on Pinterest. I'd made these dainty apple pies in tiny jars and Jamie had gone crazy over them. We'd spent the rest of the night brainstorming ideas for a jar-themed restaurant.

Jamie, you'd be so proud to see this place. An all-too-familiar sting hit my nose but I rubbed it away, focusing on my first customer instead of dwelling on the past.

"Would you like to try something?"

He didn't answer. He just set down the menu and stared, inspecting the chalkboard and display racks at my back. "You spelled it wrong."

"Actually, my last name is Maysen, spelled the same way as the restaurant."

"Huh," he muttered, clearly not as impressed with my cleverness.

"We don't open until tomorrow, but how about a sample? On the house?"

He shrugged.

Not letting his lack of enthusiasm and overall grouchy demeanor pull me down, I walked to the refrigerated display case next to the register and picked Jamie's favorite. I popped it in the toaster oven and then set out a spoon and napkin in front of the man while he kept scrutinizing the space.

Ignoring the frown on his face, I waited for the oven and let my eyes wander. As they did, my chest swelled with pride. Just this morning, I'd applied the finishing touches. I'd hung the last of the artwork and put a fresh flower on each table. It was hard to believe this was the same garage I'd walked into a year ago. That I'd finally been able to wipe out the smell of gasoline in exchange for sugar and spice.

No matter what happened with The Maysen Jar—whether it failed miserably or succeeded beyond my wildest dreams—I would always be proud of what I'd accomplished here.

Proud and grateful.

It had taken me almost four years to crawl out from underneath the weight of Jamie's death. Four years for the black fog of grief and loss to fade to gray. The Maysen Jar had given me a purpose this past year. Here, I wasn't just a twenty-nine-year-old widow struggling to make it through each day. Here, I was a business owner and entrepreneur. I was in control of my life and my own destiny.

The oven's chime snapped me out of my reverie. I pulled on a mitt and slid out the small jar, letting the smell of apples and butter and cinnamon waft to my nose. Then I went to the freezer, getting out my favorite vanilla-bean ice cream and placing a dollop atop the pie's lattice crust. Wrapping the hot jar in a black cloth napkin, I slid the pie in front of the grumpy old man.

"Enjoy." I held back a smug smile. Once he dug into that pie, I'd win him over.

He eyed it for a long minute, leaning around to inspect all sides of the dish before picking up his spoon. But with that first bite, an involuntary hum of pleasure escaped from his throat.

"I heard that," I teased.

He grumbled something under his breath before taking another steaming bite. Then another. The pie didn't last long; he devoured it while I pretended to clean.

"Thanks," he said quietly.

"You're welcome." I took his empty dishes and set them in a plastic bussing tub. "Would you like to take one to go? Maybe have it after dinner?"

He shrugged.

I took that as a yes and prepared a to-go bag with a blueberry crumble instead of the apple pie. Tucking a menu card and reheating instructions inside, I set the brown craft bag next to him on the counter.

"How much?" He reached for his wallet.

I waved him off. "It's on the house. A gift from me to you as my first customer, Mister . . ."

"James. Randall James."

I tensed at the name—just like I always did when I heard Jamie or a similar version—but let it roll off, glad things were improving. Five years ago, I would have burst into tears. Now, the bite was manageable.

Randall opened the bag and looked inside. "You send to-go stuff in a jar?"

"Yes, the jar goes too. If you bring it back, I give you a discount on your next purchase."

He closed the bag and muttered, "Huh."

We stared at each other in silence for a few beats, every ticking second getting more and more awkward, but I didn't break my smile.

"Are you from here?" he finally asked.

"I've lived in Bozeman since college, but no, I grew up in Alaska."

"Do they have these fancy *jar* restaurants up north?"

I laughed. "Not that I know of, but I haven't been home in a while."

"Huh."

Huh. I made a mental note never to answer questions with "huh" ever again. Up until I'd met Randall James, I'd never realized just how annoying it was.

The silence between us returned. Molly was banging around in the kitchen, probably unloading the clean dishes from the dishwasher, but as much as I wanted to be in there to help, I couldn't leave Randall out here alone.

I glanced at my watch. I had plans tonight and needed to get the breakfast quiches prepped before I left. Standing here while Randall pondered my restaurant was not something I'd figured into my plans.

"I, um—"

"I built this place."

His interruption surprised me. "The garage?"

He nodded. "Worked for the construction company that built it back in the sixties."

Now his inspection made sense. "What do you think?"

I normally didn't care much for the opinions of others—especially from a crotchety stranger—but for some reason, I wanted Randall's approval. He was the first person to enter this place who wasn't a family member or a part of my construction crew. A favorable opinion from an outsider would give my spirits a boost as I went into opening day.

But my spirits fell when, without a word, Randall pulled on his cap and slid off the stool. He looped the takeout bag over one wrist while grabbing his cane with his other hand. Then he began his slow journey toward the door.

Maybe my apple pie wasn't as magical as Jamie had thought.

When Randall paused at the door, I perked up, waiting for any sign that he'd enjoyed his time here.

He looked over his shoulder and winked. "Good luck, Ms. Maysen."

"Thank you, Mr. James." I kept my arms pinned at my sides until he turned back around and pushed through the door. As soon as he was out of sight, I threw my arms in the air, mouthing, *Yes!*

I wasn't sure if I'd ever see Randall James again, but I was taking his parting farewell as the blessing I'd been craving.

This was going to work. The Maysen Jar was going to be a success.

I could feel it down to my bones.

Not thirty seconds after Randall disappeared down the sidewalk, the door flew open again. This time, a little girl barreled down the center aisle. "Auntie Poppy!"

I hurried around the counter and knelt, ready for impact. "Kali bug! Where's my hug?"

Kali, my four-year-old niece, giggled. Her pink summer dress swished behind her as she raced toward me. Her brown curls—curls that matched Molly's—bounced down her shoulders as she flew into my arms. I kissed her cheek and tickled her sides but quickly let her go, knowing she wasn't here for me.

"Where's Mommy?"

I nodded toward the back. "In the kitchen."

"Mommy!" she yelled as she ran in search of Molly.

I stood just as the door jingled again and my brother, Finn, stepped inside with two-year-old Max in his arms.

"Hi." He crossed the room and tucked me into his side for a hug. "How are you?"

"Good." I squeezed his waist, then stood on my tiptoes to kiss my nephew's cheek. "How are you?"

"Fine."

Finn was far from fine but I didn't comment. "Do you want something to drink? I'll make you your favorite caramel latte."

"Sure." He nodded and set down Max when Molly and Kali came out of the kitchen.

"Mama!" Max's entire face lit up as he toddled toward his mother.

"Max!" She scooped him up, kissing his chubby cheeks and hugging him tight. "Oh, I missed you, sweetheart. Did you have a fun time at Daddy's?"

Max just hugged her back while Kali clung to her leg.

Finn and Molly's divorce had been rough on the kids. Seeing their parents miserable and splitting time between homes had taken its toll.

"Hi, Finn. How are you?" Molly's voice was full of hope that he'd give her just a little something nice.

"Fine," he clipped.

The smile on her face fell when he refused to look at her but she recovered fast, focusing on her kids. "Let's go grab my stuff from the office and then we can go home and play before dinner."

I waved. "See you tomorrow."

She nodded and gave me her biggest smile. "I can't wait. This is going to be wonderful, Poppy. I just know it."

"Thanks." I smiled good-bye to my best friend and ex-sister-in-law.

Molly looked back at Finn, waiting for him to acknowledge her, but he didn't. He kissed his children good-bye and then turned his back on his ex-wife, taking the stool Randall had vacated.

"Bye, Finn," Molly whispered, then led the kids back through the kitchen to the small office.

The minute we heard the back door close, Finn groaned and rubbed his hands over his face. "This fucking sucks."

"Sorry." I patted his arm and then went behind the counter to make his coffee.

The divorce was only four months old and both were struggling to adjust to the new normal of different houses, custody schedules and awkward encounters. The worst part of it all was that they still loved each other. Molly was doing everything she could to get just a fraction of Finn's forgiveness. Finn was doing everything he could to make her pay.

And as Molly's best friend and Finn's sister, I was caught in between, attempting to give them both equal love and support.

"Is everything set for tomorrow?" Finn propped his elbows on the counter and watched me make his latte.

"Yes. I need to do a couple of things for the breakfast menu, but then I'm all set."

"Want to grab dinner with me tonight? I can wait around for you to finish up."

My shoulders stiffened and I didn't turn away from the espresso drip. "Um, I actually have plans tonight."

"Plans? What plans?"

The surprise in his voice wasn't a shock. In the five years since Jamie had died, I'd rarely made plans that hadn't included him or Molly. I'd all but lost touch with the friends Jamie and I'd had from college. The only girlfriend I still talked to was Molly. And the closest I'd come to making a *new* friend lately had been my conversation earlier with Randall.

Finn was probably excited, thinking I was doing something social and branching out, which wasn't entirely untrue. But my brother wasn't going to like the plans I'd made.

"I'm going to a karate class," I blurted and started steaming his milk. I could feel his frown on my back, and sure enough, it was still there when I delivered his finished latte.

"Poppy, no. I thought we talked about giving up this list thing."

"We talked about it, but I don't remember agreeing with you."

Finn thought my desire to complete Jamie's birthday list was unhealthy.

I thought it was necessary.

Because maybe if I finished Jamie's list, I could find a way to let him go.

Finn huffed and dove right into our usual argument. "It could take you years to get through that list."

"So what if it does?"

"Finishing his list isn't going to bring him back. It's just your way of holding on to the past. You're never going to move on if you can't let him go. He's gone, Poppy."

"I know he's gone," I snapped, the threat of tears burning my throat. "I'm well aware that Jamie isn't coming back, but this is my choice. I want to finish his list and the least you can do is be supportive. Besides, you're one to talk about moving on."

"That's different," he countered.

"Is it?"

We went into a stare-down, my chest heaving as I refused to blink.

Finn broke first and slumped forward. "I'm sorry. I just want you to be happy."

I stepped to the counter and placed my hand on top of his. "I know, but please, try and understand why I need to do this."

He shook his head. "I don't get it. I don't know why you'd put yourself through all that. But you're my sister and I love you, so I'll try."

"Thank you." I squeezed his hand. "I want you to be happy too. Maybe instead of dinner with me, you should go to Molly's? You could try and talk after the kids go to bed."

He shook his head, a lock of his rust-colored hair falling out of place as he spoke to the countertop. "I love her. I always will, but I can't forgive what she did. I just . . . can't."

I wished he'd try harder. I hated to see my brother so heart-broken. Molly too. I'd jump at the chance to get Jamie back, no matter what mistakes he might have made.

"So, karate?" Finn asked, changing subjects. He might dis-approve of my choice to finish Jamie's list, but he'd rather talk about it than his failed marriage.

"Karate. I made an appointment to try a class tonight." It was probably a mistake, doing strenuous physical exercise the night before the grand opening, but I wanted to get it done before the restaurant opened and I got too busy—or chickened out.

"Then, I guess, tomorrow you'll get to cross two things off the list. Opening this restaurant and going to a karate class."

"Actually." I held up a finger, then went to the register for my purse. I pulled out my oversized bag and rifled around until my fingers hit Jamie's leather journal. "I'm going to cross off the restaurant one today."

I hadn't completed many items on Jamie's list, but every time I did, waterworks followed. The restaurant's opening to-morrow was going to be one of my proudest moments and I didn't want it flooded with tears.

"Would you do it with me?" I asked.

He smiled. "You know I'll always be here for whatever you need."

I knew.

Finn had held me together these last five years. Without him, I don't think I would have survived Jamie's death.

"Okay." I sucked in a shaky breath, then grabbed a pen from the jar by the register. Flipping to the thirtieth-birthday page, I carefully checked the little box in the upper right corner.

Jamie had given each birthday a page in the journal. He'd wanted some space to make notes about his experience or tape in pictures. He'd never get to fill in these pages, and even though I was doing his list, I couldn't bring myself to do it either. So after I finished one of his items, I simply checked the box and ignored the lines that would always remain empty.

As expected, the moment I closed the journal, a sob escaped. Before the first tear fell, Finn had rounded the corner and pulled me into his arms.

I miss you, Jamie. I missed him so much it hurt. It wasn't fair that he couldn't do his own list. It wasn't fair that his life had been cut short because I'd asked him to run a stupid errand. It wasn't fair that the person responsible for his death was still living free.

It wasn't fair.

The flood of emotion consumed me and I let it all go into my brother's navy shirt.

"Please, Poppy," Finn whispered into my hair. "Please think about stopping this list thing. I hate that it makes you cry."

I sniffled and wiped my eyes, fighting with all my strength to stop crying. "I have to," I hiccupped. "I have to do this. Even if it takes me years."

Finn didn't reply; he just squeezed me tighter.

We hugged each other for a few minutes until I got myself together and stepped back. Not wanting to see the empathy in his eyes, I looked around the restaurant. The restaurant I'd only been able to buy because of Jamie's life insurance money.

"Do you think he'd have liked it?"

Finn threw his arm over my shoulders. "He'd have loved it. And he'd be so proud of you."

"This was the one item on his list that wasn't just for him."

"I think you're wrong about that. I think this *was* for him. Making your dreams come true was Jamie's greatest joy."

I smiled. Finn was right. Jamie would have been so excited about this place. Yes, it was my dream, but it would have been his too.

Wiping my eyes one last time, I put the journal away. "I'd better get my stuff done so I can get to that class."

"Call me afterward if you need to. I'll just be home. Alone."

"Like I said, you could always go eat dinner with your family." He shot me a glare and I held up my hands. "Just an idea."

Finn kissed my cheek and took another long drink of his coffee. "I'm going to go."

"But you're coming by tomorrow?"

"I wouldn't miss it for the world. Proud of you, sis."

I was proud of me too. "Thanks."

We walked together to the door, then I locked it behind him before rushing back to the kitchen. I dove into my cooking, making a tray of quiches that would sit overnight in the refrigerator and bake fresh in the morning. When my watch dinged the minute after I'd slid the tray into the fridge, I took a deep breath.

Karate.

I was going to karate tonight. I had no desire to try martial arts, but I would. For Jamie.

So I hurried to the bathroom, trading my jeans and white top for black leggings and a maroon sports tank. I tied my long red hair into a ponytail that hung past my sports bra before stepping into my charcoal tennis shoes and heading out the back.

It didn't take me long to drive my green sedan to the karate school. Bozeman was the fastest-growing town in Montana and it had changed a lot since I'd moved here for college, but it still didn't take more than twenty minutes to get from one end to the other—especially in June, when college was out for the summer.

By the time I parked in the lot, my stomach was in a knot. With shaking hands, I got out of my car and went inside the gray brick building.

"Hi!" A blond teenager greeted me from behind the reception counter. She couldn't have been more than sixteen and she had a black belt tied around her white uniform.

"Hi," I breathed.

"Are you here to try a class?"

I nodded and found my voice. "Yes, I called earlier this week. I can't remember who I talked to but he told me I could just come over tonight and give it a shot."

"Awesome! Let me get you a waiver. One sec." She disappeared into the office behind the reception counter.

I took the free moment to look around. Trophies filled the shelves behind the counter. Framed certificates written in both English and Japanese hung on the walls in neat columns. Pictures of happy students were scattered around the rest of the lobby.

Past the reception area was a wide platform filled with parents sitting on folding chairs. Proud moms and dads were facing a long glass window that overlooked a classroom of kids. Beyond the glass, little ones in white uniforms and yellow belts were practicing punches and kicks—some more coordinated than others but all quite adorable.

"Here you go." The blond teenager returned with a small stack of papers and a pen.

"Thanks." I got to work, filling out my name and signing

the necessary waivers, then handed them back. "Do I need to, um, change?" I glanced down at my gym clothes, feeling out of place next to all the white uniforms.

"You're fine for tonight. You can just wear that, and if you decide to sign up for more classes, we can get you a gi." She tugged on the lapel of her uniform. "Let me give you a quick tour."

I took a deep breath, smiling at some of the parents as they turned and noticed me. Then I met the girl on the other side of the reception counter and followed her through an archway to a waiting room. She walked straight past the open area and directly through the door marked *Ladies*.

"You can use any of the hooks and hangers. We don't wear shoes in the dojo, so you can leave those in a cubby with your keys. There aren't any lockers, as you can see," she laughed, "but no one will steal anything from you. Not here."

"Okay." I toed off my shoes and put them in a free cubby with my car keys.

Damn it. I should have painted my toenails. The red I'd chosen weeks ago was now chipped and dull.

"I'm Olivia, by the way." She leaned closer to whisper. "When we're in here, you can just call me Olivia, but when we're in the waiting area or dojo, you should always call me Olivia Sensei."

"Got it. Thanks."

"It'll just be a few more minutes until the kids' class is done." Olivia led me back out to a waiting area. "You can just hang out here and then we'll get started."

"Okay. Thank you again."

She smiled and disappeared back to the reception area.

I stood quietly in the waiting room, trying to blend into

the white walls as I peeked into the dojo.

The class was over and the kids were all lining up to bow to their teachers. *Senseis*. One little boy was wiggling his toes on the blue mats covering the floor. Two little girls were whispering and giggling. An instructor called for attention and the kids' backs all snapped straight. Then they bent at the waist, bowing to the senseis and a row of mirrors spanning the back of the room.

The room erupted in laughter and cheers as the kids were dismissed from their line and funneled out the door. Most passed me without a glance as they went to find their parents or change in the locker rooms.

My nerves spiked as the kids cleared the exercise room, knowing it was almost time for me to go in there. Other adult students were coming in and out of the locker rooms, and I was now even more aware that I would be the only person tonight not wearing white.

I hated being new. Some people enjoyed the rush of the first day of school or a new job, but not me. I didn't like the nervous energy in my fingers. And I really didn't want to make a fool of myself tonight.

Just don't fall on your face.

That was one of two goals for tonight: survive, and stay upright.

I smiled at another female student as she emerged from the locker room. She waved but joined a group of men huddled on the opposite wall.

Not wanting to eavesdrop on the adults, I studied the children as they buzzed around until a commotion sounded in the lobby.

Determined not to show fear to whoever came my way,

I forced the corners of my mouth up. They fell when a man stepped into the waiting area.

A man I hadn't seen in five years, one month and three days appeared in the room.

The cop who'd told me my husband had been murdered.

The Birthday List is available now!

acknowledgements

Thank you, dear reader! With all of the books to choose from these days, I am so grateful you chose *Tinsel*.

I'd like to give special thanks to my incredible team for all the work they do on each of my books. My editing and proofreading team: Elizabeth, Elaine, Julie, Karen and Kaitlyn. My cover designer: Sarah. My formatter: Stacey. I am honored to work with such talented and smart women.

To my publicist Dani, thanks for all you do! And to the team at Brower Literary, thank you for promoting my books all across the world.

Thank you to each and every blogger who takes the time to read and post about my stories. I owe my career to book bloggers, and I can't thank you all enough for the endless support. Perry Street, you never cease to amaze me with your kind words. They always find me when I need them most. Thank you to all of my author friends for being so supportive and always being there to answer questions or bounce ideas around. A special thanks to Natasha Madison for being an all-around beautiful friend.

To my family, thank you for celebrating each of my successes. Thank you for holding my hand through each of my failures. Your unconditional love gives me wings.

also available from
DEVNEY PERRY

Jamison Valley Series
The Coppersmith Farmhouse
The Clover Chapel
The Lucky Heart
The Outpost
The Bitterroot Inn

Maysen Jar Series
The Birthday List
Letters to Molly

Lark Cove Series
Tattered
Timid
Tragic
Tinsel

about the author

Devney is a *USA Today* bestselling author who lives in Washington with her husband and two sons. Born and raised in Montana, she loves writing books set in her treasured home state. After working in the technology industry for nearly a decade, she abandoned conference calls and project schedules to enjoy a slower pace at home with her family. Writing one book, let alone many, was not something she ever expected to do. But now that she's discovered her true passion for writing romance, she has no plans to ever stop.

on't miss out on Devney's latest book news. Subscribe to her newsletter!
www.devneyperry.com

Devney loves hearing from her readers.
Connect with her on social media!

www.devneyperry.com

Facebook: www.facebook.com/devneyperrybooks

Instagram: www.instagram.com/devneyperry

Twitter: twitter.com/devneyperry

BookBub: www.bookbub.com/authors/devney-perry